GAELAN'S DESTINY

GAELAN'S DESTINY

THADDEUS MCGRATH

@ 2020 Thaddeus McGrath

All rights reserved. This book or any portion thereof may not be reproduced or used in any manner whatsoever without the express written permission of the publisher except for the use of brief quotations in a book review.

TABLE OF CONTENTS

Introduction: Sacrifice 7
Chapter 1: Chance Encounters 11
Chapter 2: Night Terrors 45
Chapter 3: Memory Lane 49
Chapter 4: Perspective 81
Chapter 5: Intertwined 87
Chapter 6: Group Therapy 119
Chapter 7: Espresso 145
Chapter 8: iT 149
Chapter 9: Old Flame 177
Chapter 10: Small Victories 203
Chapter 11: Revised Schedule 219
Chapter 12: Age of Enlightenment 221
Chapter 13: The Heist 241
Chapter 14: Prophet 267
Chapter 15: Down Time 287
Chapter 16: Adoptions 309
Chapter 17: Alive 333
Chapter 18: Consequences 359
Chapter 19: Shattered 387

INTRODUCTION
SACRIFICE

The late fall evening in the German Black Forest was cold and dry. The moon, two nights shy of full, cast a glow over the tall trees. Sophie Bertrand stood with five women, wondering what she was doing there. The light of the fire glimmered against her olive skin, black hair and bright hazel eyes. The dreams of voices calling her had started a month or so ago. Visions urged her to travel to a small town in Germany. There she met four beautiful women. *You are to be part of something greater than yourself. You are meant for more. You will become one of us, initiated into the incredible.* Another like her, Tilda, was also summoned. They hadn't understood their dreams fully until now. Efthalia, the leader of the women, walked towards a large dome of living branches and roots. She could hear the muffled moans and whines of the prisoners inside.

The captives didn't know one another. Their only common trait was the terror in their eyes, which bonded them without ever speaking a word. They were cold, scared and confused. They were bound and gagged, but not with rope or tape. They were locked up, but not in a room, a cell or even a house. Roots and branches gripped their limbs and entangled their jaws. Thicker branches from the same trees formed the dome that imprisoned them. Their fear, mixed with the cold night air, shook their bodies uncontrollably.

Branches receded to allow Efthalia entrance. She had long brown hair and bronzed skin, and appeared to be in her late thirties. Her face was partially obscured by the large hood of her black robe. Efthalia looked at the two captives and then up at the moon, whispering something in a language that neither woman had ever heard. Immediately, the branches holding one of the women, an attractive girl in her late-twenties, began to move. Slithering like snakes, they dragged her to the ground and out of the prison. She tried to scream through the tree branch in her mouth but the sound produced was nothing more than a muffled whimper. The prisoners locked eyes one last time, and the other, not quite twenty years old, tried frantically to free herself and help her fellow captive. Efthalia went to her and gently wiped the tears from her cheeks, speaking in German, "Don't worry, you'll have your time tomorrow." She then smiled and her beautiful face contorted into a sinewy grey mess, with black eyes and pointed teeth, momentarily, before receding to its human form. She then left and the large branches once again closed the natural prison, leaving the younger woman terrified, sobbing and alone.

Efthalia walked behind the helpless girl as she was dragged. Her five companions stood some 30 meters away, surrounding a stone altar next to a large fire. Three of them were also in their late thirties, while Sophie and Tilda were considerably younger. The fire seemed to make their shadows dance on the surrounding flora. The captive was dragged to the altar, where the branches lifted her off the ground and secured her face-up. Efthalia caressed her forehead, once again speaking in German, "You should be honored. You and your beauty will live on forever in us." The captive struggled to no avail, tears streaming down her cheeks.

Efthalia removed a large curved blade from her robe and muttered in the old language. She held the blade aloft, ready to strike. "NO!" Sophie yelled, drawing back in horror. Citlalli, who stood by her side, grabbed and restrained Sophie with an arm around her chest. She gripped her face with the other hand, clamping her mouth shut and forcing her towards the ritual.

"Quiet Sophie!" Citlalli hissed, "You need to watch." Then to Efthalia, "Continue."

Sophie watched wide-eyed as Efthalia brought the blade down to the captive's chest, just off center. She slowly penetrated the skin, tearing through the muscle and finally snapping through the bones. The captive, though gagged by a giant root, shrieked in pain with a sound so unnerving that her fellow hostage could hear it through her own panicked mews. The victim finally succumbed, rolling back her eyes and taking her last breath as Efthalia continued to snap through the front of her rib cage. Efthalia removed the blade and plunged her hand into the open cavity. She withdrew her bloodied hand, holding the victim's heart aloft, and speaking in the old language once more. Sophie shrank back in horror as Efthalia's face warped into the sinewy black-eyed creature. She was shoved to the side as Citlalli stepped forward, her face now wearing the same gruesome mask. The faces of the other two women also transfigured into hideous creatures. Only one woman, the other newcomer, remained unchanged, but her attention was fixed on the ritual, excited and eager.

Efthalia sank her pointed teeth into the heart, tearing a large chunk from it and swallowing. Blood smeared across her mouth and cheeks. She gasped in ecstasy as her face changed back to human form, but younger and softer than she had appeared before. She passed the heart, speaking in a form of Mycenaean Greek, "Eat and live Isis." Isis took the organ and consumed a large piece. Her face turned human once more, revealing short black hair and copper skin. She handed it to Citlalli, "Eat and live Citlalli." Once more, the heart was bit into and a warped face turned into a beautiful, younger version of the woman that had restrained Sophie, with long silken hair and fair skin. The heart was handed to the last woman with a contorted face, "Eat and live Akeelah." Akeelah tore into the heart and revealed a beautiful young African woman. She turned and offered it to the stunned Sophie. Her bottom lip quivered as she shook her head and took a step back.

"Fear not Akeelah, for she will partake in the ceremony on the third night." Efthalia looked to Sophie and gave her a reassuring smile and nod.

Akeelah's expression was that of disappointment. She turned to the last woman, young with pale-skin and blonde-hair. "Eat and live Tilda." The woman bit voraciously into the heart. Then she seemed to loose her breath as she looked up to the sky and screamed in pleasure and pain. When Tilda lowered her head back to the group, Sophie could see Tilda's human face, but now with black eyes and slightly malformed fangs grinning in guiltless pleasure. Her face contorted slightly and then returned to its human form. She looked directly at Sophie in disgust. All eyes were on her.

Efthalia put a hand on Sophie's shoulder, "It's alright Sophie. The first time is hard. But to embrace the true nature of power," Efthalia motioned to her colleagues, "to become one of us, you must feed off of the living. Worry not, for on the third night, the full moon, you will be part of us." She turned to the other witches who smiled approvingly. Sophie's pulse raced. She looked back to the prison dome, thinking of the young woman trapped inside. She walked towards the domed shelter, similar to the prison but for an opening at one side, the coven had erected, tears streaming down her face.

Efthalia looked to the group, "Tonight, the whore, tomorrow the virgin, then we complete the blood sacrifice on the full moon. We have waited far too long and now the eternal darkness approaches. Our numbers grow. Soon my sisters...soon." The others smiled and went to Tilda, congratulating and doting on her. Citlalli interrupted their chatter, "Sisters, the heart is but the beginning. There is more youth to harvest. Soon we will know who the seer is and soon we will be the goddesses we once were." The women grinned with wicked anticipation. More bones broke and the skin tore as five sets of hands ripped the organs from their victim's body. Their faces, twisted and inhuman once more, became muddied in blood as they gorged themselves, cackling and screaming like schoolgirls. Inside the prison, the younger woman contemplated her fate, tears drying on her cheeks in the cold night air.

CHAPTER I
CHANCE ENCOUNTERS

Two young couples walked through Wenceslas Square in the city of Prague. One of the girls, a blonde in her early twenties with a pixie-cut, looked to her boyfriend and spoke in Russian, "Yuri, are you sure about this?"

"Of course. They know the good places to go, not those stupid tourist traps." Yuri was tall and thin with high cheekbones, pale skin, and sandy brown hair.

They met the Czech couple—Matous and Jarka—in a restaurant. Jarka was captivating with long brown hair, and silky straight bands that fell like curtains over her eyes. Since he spoke Czech, Jarka and her boyfriend assured Yuri that he and his girlfriend would fit right in at the clubs they frequented, the ones where locals went, *not* the tourists. Matous led them through the swindlers and pimps in the square toward the river. As they approached the edge of the square, a grimy homeless figure limped towards them. He was tall and broad, with a full beard and disheveled hair; He reeked, almost of death.

"Just some spare change? You have to have something you can give? How about you two?" He looked to Yuri and his girlfriend Darya, "You have to have something to give me, eh?" He wheedled. Finally, Matous shoved him back and the man fell back to the ground. He glared up at them as they laughed and walked by, Darya adding to Yuri, "He smells and he's sooooo creepy."

Only when the couples turned down a side street, did the vagrant get to his feet and grin, limping in their direction.

Several minutes later, Jarka was speaking with the bouncer at the door of a trendy-looking riverside club. The club was dark and crowded. People danced and grinded on the enormous dance floor. Yuri bought shots of Slivovitz for everyone, and they headed out to join the gyrating crowd. Soon, some of Matous and Jarka's local friends—two men and a woman—found them on the dance floor. More rounds of drinks were downed, and soon the creepy homeless man was forgotten. After an hour or so, the drunk and sweaty group tumbled out of a side exit for fresh air. Matous offered, "We know another club not as crowded but just as good. Are you interested?"

Yuri made a mock bow and gestured with his hand for him to lead the way, "You are tonight's guide!" Two dark alley-turns later, Jarka stopped Matous for a kiss. The others giggled as the couple leaned against a wall in their passion. Yuri grabbed Darya and pulled her in for a kiss too, but she pulled away as the giggling suddenly stopped. Jarka motioned down the alley. The the outline of a figure was approaching, walking with a pronounced limp.

"I think we should go!" Darya yanked on Yuri's arm.

"She is afraid. She wants to leave." Yuri repeated in Czech.

"Nonsense! You shouldn't feel uneasy in our great city." Matous looked at one of his male companions and jerked his head toward the stranger. The friend curled his lips into an arrogant smile and strolled toward the homeless man. Heated words and then a muffled cry floated down the alley, like someone wanted to scream, but their breath was taken away before they could.

"There, now we can proceed." Matous smiled at his girlfriend and then at the Russian couple. Darya still tugged at Yuri's arm, but as she tried to pull him away, a firm grip came down on her shoulder. She felt herself being spun around to find Jarka pulling her in and kissing her. *What the hell are you doing?*" She yelled in Russian. Her shock redoubled when Jarka answered in fluent Russian, "Playing with my food." Jarka's nose had sunken into large V-shaped slits. Her cheekbones and jaw seemed about to rip through pale, wrinkled skin. Her eyes glowed red with a dark sliver where the pupil should be. Darya tried to scream but Jarka's hand grasped her throat. She looked wildly toward Yuri who was struggling against Matous's gagging arm. The other male and female smiled and licked their lips—they too had transformed.

"I've been waiting all night for this." Matous's jaw distended as his razor sharp fangs extended.

"Wait!" Jarka smiled at Matous, "Let him watch helplessly while she dies. His fear will make the blood so much sweeter."

Matous smiled, "I knew I turned you for a reason." Jarka opened her jaws and angled her head to tear out Darya's throat, when something struck her in the ribs forcefully and fell at her feet. The four vampires all looked to the ground to see their companion's head, face frozen in pain, staring back at them, skin beginning to bubble. They looked, as one, towards the homeless man, still limping toward them. There was something shiny in his hand. As he advanced, a full-sized katana slipped down from his sleeve. His beard was covered in blood.

"Am I interrupting?" the man spoke in fluent Russian. Darya tried to cry out for help but Jarka's hand still gripped her throat. Her eyes were wild with terror.

Gaelan Kelly leered at the vampires.

"Venántium pig!" The other female vampire charged him. In one swift move, Gaelan ducked and brought his blade across her midsection. As she tried to grasp at the wound, he stood up behind her and raised his sword high and then stabbed down along her spine, inside of her ribs. He pulled the katana straight back to him, slicing through her ribs and severing part of her spine. She shrieked in pain for a moment before his hand plunged into the open wound from behind. He tore out her heart and sank his teeth into it. More blood oozed into his dirty beard.

Gaelan's voice was deep and raspy, "The Venántium are the least of your worries!"

The remaining vampires threw Yuri and Darya to the ground and charged. Gaelan was able to behead the other male and slash Jarka before Matous slammed his forearm and knocked the katana free. With just days to go before the full moon, Gaelan didn't have to worry about the wolf getting out, but he also wasn't as strong as he could be. Matous brought his hand back and slashed at Gaelan, who painfully blocked the attack with both forearms. Gaelan brought his knee into Matous's gut and then into his face, where it met the vampire's fangs sinking into the flesh above his knee. Matous released his bite, but not before tearing through part of Gaelan's muscle. He threw Gaelan into the alley wall about seven feet above the ground. Gaelan came down hard as Matous spit, "You're not normal—Not human!"

Gaelan pushed himself to his feet in time to catch the pouncing Matous, shifting his weight and throwing the vampire against the wall while grunting, "Nice of you to have noticed!" Gaelan felt the searing pain of Jarka'a claws sinking into his back. She began to squeeze as one of his ribs snapped. He bellowed in pain and looked to the alley wall in front of him. He quickly jumped and placed both feet against the wall and kicked off with all of his might. They flew across the alley, and Jarka impacted the opposite wall, absorbing the force of Gaelan's body. As they fell to the ground, her grip released. They both sprang to their feet and Gaelan blocked her slash with his left arm and punched her across the jaw with his right, following through with his elbow. He retracted his arm and grabbed her face and neck, spinning her and pulling her backwards. He now held her off balance in a headlock, her body parallel to the ground with her face and chest up. He grimaced and she sank her teeth into his tricep, but he was able to grab his father's knife from the strap around his ankle. He brought it up and slammed it down into her chest, penetrating her heart. Her screech was ear-piercing for just a second and then he dropped her writhing body to the ground. He still needed to finish her, but saw Matous's impending attack and dove out of the way.

The male vampire landed next to Jarka's struggling figure, looking down at her before hissing at Gaelan, fangs bared and eyes afire. Gaelan was on the ground and breathing hard, and the vampire pressed his advantage and sprung. Matous hadn't noticed that Gaelan dove directly toward the spot where he had been disarmed.

Gaelan jumped up and met him head on with a katana in one hand and his father's silver blade in the other. With a one-handed upward slash from the katana, the blade cut Matous from groin to neck. He then quickly plunged his father's knife though the top of the vampire's skull. He dropped both weapons and thrust his hand into Matous's open chest. He pulled out the vampire's heart and ate it. He recovered his weapons and went to the beheaded vampire and did the same. Finally, he went to Jarka's twitching frame and cut her chest open to devour her heart. He stood and mumbled a prayer under his breath. The bodies of the monsters burned intensely for a moment, and then nothing remained.

Gaelan walked over to the couple. Yuri was gripping Darya tightly, trying to protect her from something he could not. She sobbed as they stared at his large frame, blood dripping from his beard.

"Please don't hurt us!" She cried, holding Yuri tight.

"Please, we won't say anything!" Yuri implored, looking into Gaelan's eyes.

Gaelan squatted down next to them, and looked over his shoulder to see the remnants of the vampires blowing away. He turned back to the young couple and spoke in fluent Russian once more, "What a bunch of assholes." His tone was jovial. Yuri stared, disbelieving, and Darya was still on the verge of hyperventilating. Gaelan continued, "Maybe next time you'll just give the beggar some money. I was trying to separate you from them back in the square. I guess it worked out for the better because it drew out the other three. Are you two okay?"

Darya's breathing slowed and Yuri was absolutely baffled, "You're not going to kill us?"

Gaelan chuckled, "No, just them. I don't have time to explain everything, but you speak Czech, right?" Yuri nodded as Gaelan went on, "I want you to go directly to the Church across the river and tell the priest that you encountered vampires," Yuri went to interrupt and Gealan held up his hand, "and *Venántium*. Make sure you say the word or they'll send you away as practical jokers. They'll bring you into a secluded area and ask you what happened. Tell them everything." Gaelan paused for a moment, "Well, not about my eating the hearts. That's—well, let's just call that a religious preference of mine that they don't necessarily condone. So as a favor, just leave it out. The rest is fair game. They'll explain everything and tell you ways to protect yourself and how you can help out those of us that hunt. Can you do that?" Both Yuri and Darya nodded, and then Darya finally whispered, "Thank you."

"You don't have to thank me. They're flesh-eating assholes that got what was coming to them. They prey on the innocent so I prey on them." Gaelan gave a half-smile, "But I'm guessing you won't be so cold toward beggars from now on." She shook her head vigorously with wide eyes in response. "Go on, get to the church. Don't stop for anyone."

The young couple continued to thank him effusively as they exited the alley and hurried for the church. Gaelan looked around and went over to a large puddle, scooping up some of the filthy water and cleaning his face. He re-sheathed his knife at his ankle and tucked his katana back up his sleeve. Then he made his way back to the square and to the hotel where he was staying.

The bellhop tried to intercept him but he held up his room key, "Mr. Svenson, room 314. My exposé on the local homeless is done and I need to wash up." The bellhop gawked, but let him pass. Gaelan took off the rags he had been wearing, and shaved off his beard. He was finally going to get a haircut in the morning. He stood in the shower as blood ran down the drain from his wounds. He then wrapped his torso tightly in bandages, wincing at his broken rib before collapsing into bed. Another hunt was successfully in the books.

Gaelan had been hunting secretly with Father Dennis Beaudreau's guidance for nearly two years, averaging about two hunts a month, and usually those too dangerous for other Benedicta Venántium—*Blessed Hunter*—teams. While the majority of jobs were lower-end 'shifters', Gaelan preferred to hunt vampires. They were a challenge—it wasn't unusual for Vampires to kill entire Venántium teams. The only thing he craved more was to hunt the werewolves—the ones he truly hated. He hadn't encountered any since he had killed five wolves in Canada eighteen months earlier, and the one that killed his parents and made him into a monster was still out there somewhere. It was because of that bite that he devoured the hearts of his prey, overcome by a craving. Over the months, he realized that with each kill—with each heart—he was becoming stronger. At the same time, he felt that it made him less human.

Gaelan grabbed a cellular phone and inserted the SIM card. He typed out the text to the Father Denny:

> *Another one bites the dust.*
> *Or should I say five.*
> *You were right.*
> *Vampires.*
> *Call me.*

Gaelan spent the next few days treating his wounds and drinking pear brandy. He knew Father Denny couldn't call without first escaping the suspicious eyes at the Vatican, but his silent phone was a painful reminder of how entirely alone he was. He had all the signs of full-on depression and he knew it. Here he was in a beautiful European city and he didn't even want to leave his hotel room. *What am I even doing anymore?*

Each full moon brought the hope of coming face to face to the beast that took his parents, but also forced him to hold the monster within him at bay. The monster that he hated, but that gave him the superhuman strength and ferocity to hunt other creatures. The monster that allowed his body to heal miraculously.

Except for the bites and slashes from the other freaks.

The wounds inflicted by the Vampires last night would take days to heal.

What am I even doing anymore? The question lingered.

It was three days before Father Denny was able break away and call Gaelan.

"FIVE?"

"Yup, five of them. Tough bastards too, but I don't think any were that old. At least not as old as *the Ripper* in New York."

"Still impressive kiddo."

"I know. I've been standing in front of the mirror having that same conversation with myself."

Father Denny chuckled at the other end, *"You're such an idiot. Don't let it go to your head."* Then Denny's voice dropped, *"How are you doing?"*

I'm alone. I'm fucking alone, and I'm tired, and I keep hoping the next hunt will kill me.

Gaelan spoke with a fake enthusiasm, "I'm just about done healing. I thought about taking in some sights."

"You can, but I was wondering if you wanted another assignment?"

"What'ya got?" A reason to move, at least.

"Four girls have disappeared in the town of Todtmoos, Germany." Father Denny hesitated.

"I'll get my ticket."

"I don't think it's werewolves kiddo. I think it's more vampires."

"Either way, I'm heading out on the next train."

"Okay. And Gaelan…"

Gaelan interrupted before Father Denny could finish his thought, "I know, I know. I'll be careful!"

"Alright smartass. But in all seriousness, be careful."

"I will. I'll talk to you soon."

"Take care kiddo."

It crept silently through the tree line, following the scent of human flesh. A cabin. It darted from the brush toward the sounds on the far side. It didn't have to go far—a woman came around the side of the cabin unaware of what awaited her. Gaelan's mother screamed in terror as it grabbed her and tore into her throat. Then another human, his father, screamed and charged. It grabbed him and lifted him off the ground…

Gaelan awoke in the train from Prague to Zurich, seat soaked in cold sweat. The nightmares plagued him regularly. Always the same—always hunting and killing his own parents at the cabin. If

Trey Marshall—the man now hunting him—hadn't seen and shot at the creature that tore into them, Gaelan would still be convinced that he slaughtered his own family.

In Zurich, Gaelan rented a car to drive into Germany and up to Todtmoos. The trip took the better part of a day. That night would be the night before the full moon, and Gaelan spent the day strumming his fingers on the steering wheel, forcing his breath and heart to slow as as the countryside flashed by the window. He could feel *it*. It was struggling to burst free, but he had no intentions of ever allowing that to happen again.

The town of Todtmoos was surrounded by rolling hills and had a population of only a couple of thousand. The incident was the talk of the town. It wasn't two minutes after Gaelan ordered a coffee at the sidewalk café on the central square that he heard the women at the next table whispering about the two local girls and two tourists who had disappeared three nights before. The bearded man eating alone just one table over inquired whether the waiter had heard that one was Scandinavian, Swedish he thought. *Terrible for the tourism industry, no? Yes, and the other was, what—African of some kind? French Algerian, the waiter replied.*

The two local girls, Gaelan gathered, were young, one nineteen and the other twenty-six. The older, Ilka Müller, had a reputation for catering to the baser desires of male tourists—a woman for hire. The younger girl, Marlene Schulte, worked at a local biergarten, and was apparently a saint who never hesitated to help a neighbor, or offer a smile. The authorities had combed the town and the Black Forest surrounding it as best as they could, but there were too few men in uniform for a full blown search.

The sun was already past its apex when Gaelan set out into the forest. In his hunts thus far, he had been either lucky or skillful, almost as if he was drawn toward the evil. But the Black Forest was expansive, covering more than 7500 square kilometers, and the girls were probably already dead. What a horrible and senseless way to die. He could almost feel their fear, in the moments before they died. The same fear his parents experienced. He shook his head.

He drove to the edge of the forest, further north than the police had searched. Whatever took the girls would not have stayed too close to civilization. He parked about 20 kilometers northwest of the town and set out on foot. He grabbed his katana, the *Wolf Blade*, and his father's Ka-bar knife, both coated in silver, and walked into the forest. The sun cast long shadows and the birds clamored in the trees before settling for the night. He walked for over an hour, following his direction purely on instinct. That's when he smelled it—*death*. Human death. And something otherworldly. He set off in a jog as the sun barely tickled the treetops.

He followed the scent for another thirty minutes. As the sun began to set and the remaining twilight cast haunting patches of shadows, he saw it. The body was covered in leaves, stuck to the crusting blood. He walked up to it cautiously, looking for signs of the thing that made the kill. Kneeling, he gently rolled it over to reveal the pale, lifeless face of a young woman. Her ribcage was torn open and the organs inside had been removed. It wasn't clean. Her death had been horrific. Rage filled him. Another life taken too early. Thoughts of everyone he couldn't save welled up to the surface—his parents, his fellow-hunters in China, every person that had died at the hands of something before he showed up. His hands were clenched as the urge to kill filled him. His body temperature soared and his pulse raced. It took all of his strength to fight back the change that threatened to overtake him. Hunting around the full moon was risky as he inched ever so closer to losing control. He took a breath, exhaling slowly. That's when he heard the twig snap.

When Gaelan looked up, the whites of his eyes were blood red. His body temperature immediately began to cool and his pulse slowed. The red in his eyes began to fade back to white and he started to smile, then recoiled, "NATALIA, NO!"

The shot hit him in the gut. His blades were thrown from his hands and the wind was knocked from him as he fell several feet backward.

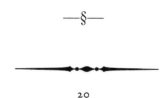

Natalia, one of Trey Marshall's companions, had come upon Gaelan standing over the body. She could see the open cavity—what was left of the woman's midsection. Gaelan looked up at her with eyes of red, already part werewolf. Before she even noticed him start to smile, she had quickly unholstered a pistol and fired at him, even as he screamed at her. She saw the blood leave his midsection. She began to fire several more rounds.

The pain was searing—like nothing he'd felt since the Middle East, back when he was a normal man. He didn't wait for the follow-on shots. He rolled onto his back, flipped his legs up and over and scurried behind a tree as more rounds flew toward him. She was a good shot. She stopped shooting and he knew she was closing in and trying to gain a better vantage. He heard her change the magazine in her pistol. He grabbed his stomach and clenched the wound. It was painful, but the bullets weren't silver. He could only assume that she had loaded a magazine of silver bullets to finish him off.

"NAT, PLEASE, HEAR ME OUT!" Gaelan was yelling in Polish, her native tongue, hoping that she would listen. "I DIDN'T DO IT!" He was gasping through the pain, "I CAME UPON THE BODY JUST BEFORE YOU FOUND ME. WHATEVER DID THAT IS STILL OUT HERE AND YOU'RE IN DANGER. YOU CAN KILL ME AFTERWARDS BUT JUST LET ME HELP YOU FIND WHATEVER DID THIS!" He struggled to his feet behind the tree, blood seeping through his fingers while he clutched at the wound. She didn't answer. He knew she was moving. He closed his eyes and listened, and smelled. Before she could come around the one side of the tree, he spun to the opposite side and caught her by surprise. She tried to swing the pistol toward him, but he swung his free hand down on top of her forearms and knocked it to the ground. Without hesitation, she punched the hand covering his wound. He recoiled in pain. When he looked up at her, the whites of his eyes were once again red.

Darkness was falling fast on the forest. Natalia pulled a silver coated knife from her boot, and slashed it down toward him. Gaelan blocked it, knocking the knife from her hand. She couldn't beat him in the open ground, but if she could find someplace confined, she could slash at him until he withdrew or she was able to make a killing blow. She dropped and rolled to the knife, picking it up and breaking into a run. The sun receded and the moon cast its light into the vast forest as she ran between towering trees.

Gaelan watched her run, his pulse racing, breath ragged. *She fucking shot me!* But through his rage, Gaelan could feel the beast's attention turn. Another scent was on the wind. Natalia was running toward danger. He grasped at his bullet wound and ran after her, "NAT GODDAMMIT, WAIT!" She ran harder. She was pulling away from him when he saw something strike her. She flew through the air and landed on her back, unconscious. He ran hard, forgetting about the gaping bullet wound in his midsection. When he came to her, branches and vines and had already begun to wrap around her. His rage took over and he punched and slashed at the crawling vegetation. Wood splintered and vines withered at his every blow. He bellowed in both pain and fury, trying to free his would-be killer. He never noticed the root that came up behind him and wrapped around his neck. He couldn't fight for both himself and for Natalia. He continued to try and free her as the root squeezed his neck tighter. He pulled forward and his vision began to fade. More limbs attacked him as he struggled to save Natalia. Finally, a giant branch struck his head and he everything went fuzzy. He saw the faces of several women as he went in and out of consciousness.

Gaelan struggled to see and hear. He felt himself being pulled and dragged for some distance. He was lifted upright and was being wrapped tightly by more roots and branches. Natalia suffered the same fate, still unconscious. They seemed to be in a dome of some sort, not constructed, but formed, of the very roots and branches from the towering forest. They were not alone. A young woman hung, bound and gagged inside their prison. As Natalia stirred, consciousness returning, roots wove their way between her jaw to gag her. Gaelan grunted from behind his gag, motioning with his eyes for Natalia to see the young woman. Did she understand? Natalia strained her eyes sidelong to see the woman, then back to Gaelan's still bleeding wound. *I'm not going to change Nat. I'm not going to let it happen.* Gaelan strained against his gag and tried to shake his head, as Natalia's eyes darted furtively from the moon to Gaelan and back.

"So you decided to venture into the woods at the wrong time." German proceeded the woman for whom the coiled limbs of their prison parted, melding into an arched entryway. "You almost disturbed the ritual," she smoothed her long brown hair, "which would not have made me very happy." Efthalia glared at Natalia and then turned to Gaelan. She looked at his wound, "A lover's spat?" She looked them both over, "Are you even German?" She walked over and curiously poked at his wound. He exhaled in pain. She licked one slender, olive finger and took a step back in shock. She looked up to the nearly full moon and back down to him. "Ha! I'm sorry we interrupted your hunt." Efthalia looked over to Natalia and back to him, "And to think I was about to spoil your prey." She caressed Gaelan's cheek, "Eat. Then come join us." She licked his neck seductively and turned to Natalia, "Dinner is served."

Efthalia turned her attention to the young hostage, now keening with terror. She chanted, low, throaty, as the keening rose to a muffled scream. The vines that held the unfortunate captive coiled, living, grotesque, pulling her from the wall, and dragging her after Efthalia's retreating form. Natalia, wild-eyed, struggled against her gag and twisted her body in a vein attempt to free herself from her bounds as the archway closed, muffling the woman's receding screams. Eventually, she stopped. Raising her eyes, now resigned, towards Gaelan.

It knew he was weakened. He gritted his teeth against the pain in his abdomen. He was too weak to bite through the tight gag, his concentration broken by the pain in his gut. *It* knew it could get out. The moonlight cascaded through their prison dome. He looked to Natalia, his eyes soft. *I'm sorry.* He closed his eyes.

Natalia watched him, fighting panic. Had he passed out from blood loss? Then she heard the first bone snap. Gaelan's body writhed and when he opened his eyes again, they were glowing red. Natalia stared as the bullet in Gaelan's gut was expelled, falling to the forest floor, still bloody. His neck twisted, bulging and sinewy. His head thrashed to and fro and snapped the roots that gagged him. His voice was inhuman, "When we're free," He winced and his voice turned to a growl, "run!" He snapped the branches that held his right and then left arms, then slashed at the roots around his legs with razor-like claws. His clothes tore as his body expanded and he tugged himself free. His change was almost complete when he looked back up at Natalia, their eyes locking one last time. Natalia closed her eyes, resigned to her fate. Then he charged.

The creature that had been Gaelan tackled her right through the side of the dome, branches and roots snapping and breaking in their path. They rolled and it landed on top of her, panting...drooling. He growled, then stood up and looked to the light. The coven stood around the stone altar lit by a large fire. Efthalia had a curved blade raised above her head. Three others circled the altar and another pair of women were off to the side, one struggling, the other restraining her. All motion stopped as their heads turned towards Gaelan and Natalia. It—Gaelan—stood almost eight feet tall, a hulking mass of muscle and fur. He looked up to the nearly full moon, sniffed the air and then looked back at the group with a throaty growl.

"Come, join us! Be with us!" Efthalia talked to Gaelan as if he were a child. He took a step. One woman was struggling, restrained by another. He could smell the fear from the being bound to the altar. He saw the welcoming look in Efthalia's eyes. He took in the scene with growing confusion.

"Look, by the chamber, the other one is still alive." Akeelah brought everyone's attention to Natalia, struggling to her feet. Gaelan looked back as well. His eyes locked with Natalia's. Then he slowly turned back towards the group, met Efthalia's gaze, and let out another slow, low, snarl. Efthalia's flawless brows knitted in confusion—her eyes, for a moment, blank. Then Gaelan charged. Instantly, the witch's countenance transformed into a mixture of anger, betrayal and fear. Her face shriveled and her eyes turned black as branches, thickets and roots lashed out at the charging figure, "It's *you*! You're the one!" As she spoke, the ground itself raised into a solid wall between the werewolf and the coven.

"FINISH THE RITUAL EFTHALIA!" Akeelah shrieked as Gaelan slashed and slammed furiously at the earthen wall she had risen.

"HE'S BREAKING THROUGH!"

"IMPOSSIBLE!" Citlalli threw Sophie to the ground and raised her hands to aid Akeelah. Instantly she winced in pain as she felt Gaelan's blows against the soil barrier resonate throughout her body. Just as Efthalia raised the blade to kill the young captive, she was struck and knocked back by a giant root. The flora that bound the young woman began to recede as Sophie rushed forward to rescue her.

"BITCH!" Tilda shrieked and joined Isis to regain control of the vegetation. Sophie had pulled the woman, unconscious, from the altar. She held one hand aloft, fighting back against Efthalia, Isis, and Tilda. Sophie's teeth were gritted, her brow furrowed in concentration. Her arm shook, then her nose began to bleed. She fell to her knees as the roots and branches turned toward her. She could no longer hold them.

"NOOOOOO!" Akeelah's shrieks broke Efthalia, Isis and Tilda's concentration and the wall of earth began to give way. Gaelan burst through and landed on Akeelah. He tore into her throat, nearly severing her head as he jerked his immense jaws back. Citlalli jumped back in terror as Gaelan threw the witch's body at Efthalia. The witches scattered as Gaelan pounced, landing in a crouch by Sophie and the unconscious hostage. He knocked Sophie to the ground next to the girl and brought his immense claw down on her chest. She looked into his eyes, terror overtaking her, as he brought his snout down to her. She began to whimper as he roared, teeth bared and salivating—then he closed his jaws. She had shut her eyes awaiting her fate. She gasped in pain as he pushed himself off of her chest and bounded toward the tree line.

When Sophie opened her eyes the creature was gone. She heard a scream not one hundred meters away. She grabbed the woman she had pulled from the altar and began to drag her, trying to figure a way to get her to safety. Movement caught her eye. Natalia sprang forward, stick raised in attack. Sophie tried to plead, in French, but Natalia merely saw another witch dragging the young woman.

A root lashed out, thwarting Natalia's advance. She didn't see Tilda emerge from the tree line, manipulating the vegetation against her. She recoiled, anticipating another blow, as the root lashed towards her again. Instead, Sophie raised her arms, and a wall of soil rose between Natalia and the living whip. Stern faced, Sophie swung her hand, and the dirt wall moved like a wave to knock Tilda over. She quickly clasped her hands together at her chest, commanding branches and roots to dig into Tilda's abdomen. Sophie screamed as she rapidly pulled her hands apart—in concert, the slithering vegetation tore Tilda into several pieces. Natalia stared, stunned, as the meaty clumps of what had been Tilda thudded to the grass. Sophie stared back, arms still raised, face stricken. Her eyes darted to the young woman, now unconscious at her side. Then she darted towards the tree line and into the darkness.

Gaelan was running on pure instinct. He swallowed the last shreds of Citalli's heart, raised his head, and sniffed the air. The excitement of the hunt welled inside him, unstoppable, as he sprang into the forest, dropping to all fours in pursuit of the scent. *Witches! Fear! Close!* He spotted his next victim, jaws snarling as he crouched to pounce.

He was ripped from the air mid-leap, his neck, wrists and ankles bound by coarse branches and scaled roots. Every time he broke or tore through one restraint, two more took its place. One witch had spotted him. Another heard her sister's call. Two figures, faces contorted and gray, raised their hands towards him. Efthalia hissed, spittle slick on her blackened lips, tightening the vine around his neck, "Last night we had the whore," She spoke in ancient Greek, "now we have to find the virgin, and finally that coward that believes herself an enchantress to finish the ritual." She closed her fists, causing the branches to tear into his skin. Gaelan struggled against the living vines, snapping what he could, and roaring in fury. Both witches winced in pain and exhaustion at his strength and will.

"IT'S HIM! I FEEL IT!" Isis shrieked in terror, "KILL HIM! KILL THE SHEEP IN WOLF'S CLOTHING!" As the witches bared their talons, slashing at the air in a furious onslaught, branches tore into Gaelan, pulling flesh and fur in bloody clumps. He struggled, snarling, even as the pain and blood loss pushed him towards unconsciousness. He tore at another vine, feeling his muscles weakening.

"AAAARRRRGGGHHHH!" Isis shrilled as the curved sacrificial blade tore through the front of her chest, Natalia thrusting with all her might.

"INSOLENT BITCH!" Efthalia rounded, commanding a vine to wrap around Natalia's throat as she pulled the blade free. At Efthalia's command, the vine lifted Natalia off of the ground by the neck. Natalia dropped the dagger and clawed at the creeping limb as it squeezed the very life from her. Before she lost consciousness, she heard a thunderous boom and dropped to the ground, free. Efthalia lay stunned, pinned momentarily by an enormous tree trunk. The werewolf snarled as he freed his second arm, splintering the tree that held him. A cross-section of trunk, still attached to the twisted branch around the monster's wrist, shattered free. With a thrust of Gaelan's powerful arm, the trunk sailed, as if it were a ball and chain, towards the stunned Efthalia. It struck—again, and again, and again, until what remained of Efthalia was a bloodied, pulverized corpse. Gaelan tore himself free and bounded on top of her, ripping the front of her ribcage off and consuming her heart.

Natalia struggled to her feet, shrinking in horror as she watched Gaelan break himself free, rip through the Efthalia's ribcage, and tear into her heart. Then, blood still thick on his chin, he slowly turned and made eye contact with her. She took a step back as he snarled, his eyes glowing like hellfire. They both snapped their heads as Isis gagged and gasped for air. Gaelan lunged on top of her and slashed into her chest. Natalia seized the moment. She picked up the blade and ran back to the fire, glimmering in the distance. She found the young woman there, moaning but still unconscious. The days of dehydration had taken their toll. Natalia squatted down and pulled the woman's arm up. She slid her own arm in between the woman's legs and pulled her up and onto her shoulders. She stood and turned to leave when she heard the growl.

Gaelan had come into the clearing by the fire. Natalia turned to see his face. His eyes glistened and cut through her. His jaws were huge, and the fur around them was covered in the blood of the witches. He was on all fours but slowly stood up like a man. Natalia slowly squatted back down and lowered the young woman from her shoulders, holding her wrist and gently lowering her to the ground. Gaelan's eyes turned to the sacrificial victim and Natalia walked in between them, holding the blade horizontally along her forearm, "You want her, you go through me!" Her eyes were ablaze. She knew she couldn't stop him, but she would make him pay for the deed.

Gaelan slowly circled the pair and Natalia kept herself positioned between him and the girl. He stopped and watched, sniffing the air. The thing in front of him showed neither sign nor scent of fear. As Natalia stood her ground, the adrenaline of the fight began to wear off. Slowly, her knees became shaky and she had to concentrate to stay focused on his eyes, waiting for the attack. She realized that she was coming down from the adrenaline rush and figured there was only one thing to do—*she* attacked *him*. She let out a roar and rushed forward. Gaelan quickly batted the dagger from her hand and knocked her to the ground. He dropped to all fours and continued to stare into her defiant eyes. She shuffled backwards on her ass until she was once again by the young woman. Gaelan looked at the thing across from him. He still couldn't sense any sign of fear as the one protected the other. The face of the fearless one seemed so familiar to him. He began to circle them again, and continued to do so until Natalia, exhausted and drained of adrenaline, lost consciousness next to the young woman she was protecting.

Natalia awoke next to the young woman, the fire was smoldering just a couple of meters from them. Not more than two meters away, Gaelan Kelly was lying on the ground, naked. Natalia saw the dagger that had been swatted from her and silently pushed herself to her feet. She retrieved the dagger and crept over to Gaelan. She crouched down beside him and raised the silver coated blade. She stood over him, ready to strike, and looked at his face sleeping peacefully. She held the dagger aloft for several seconds before lowering it. She didn't know why, but she couldn't kill him like that. He had been right when she shot him. He didn't kill the woman she found him crouched over. He was there to kill the things that did it and he did so—*they* did so—together. She heard a moan and ran over to the young woman, who was barely conscious. Natalia spoke in German, "What's your name?" The woman was frightened and confused, not immediately recognizing Natalia from the prison the night before.

"Her name is Marlene, Marlene Schulte."

Natalia snapped her head back toward Gaelan. He had pushed himself upright and tried to cover himself, speaking in Polish, "She looks younger than the other girl I found. Plus, the witch who was talking to us last night had said something to the effect of 'last night the whore,' which, based on the town gossip, means that unfortunate girl was Ilka Müller."

Natalia looked at him for several seconds, not knowing what to do or say and then turned back to the young lady, "Marlene?"

The young woman nodded with tears in her eyes, then she continued in German, "I'm Natalia." Marlene looked over at Gaelan, still naked and covered in wounds. Natalia looked back to him and he at her. She finally turned back to Marlene, "That's Gaelan. We're here to help. You're going to be alright." Marlene shot up and embraced Natalia, weeping. Natalia held her tight and looked over to Gaelan, smiling back at her. Natalia laid Marlene back down and ran into the remnants of what had been the prison. She came out with large pieces of the clothing he had been wearing the night before, tying them together. She threw it at him without a word and went back over to Marlene. He tied it around his waste and stood up. Natalia was trying to help Marlene get to her feet when Gaelan walked over and scooped the young woman up effortlessly, "Come on, I got her." He spoke in Polish to Natalia.

They walked for about a hundred meters before Natalia spoke up in Polish, "We need to go that way!"

"I know." Gaelan answered in English. He walked on a little bit more and then motioned at the ground, "Would you please do me the favor?" At his feet was his katana that he had dropped when she shot him. He motioned about a meter away to his dad's knife. She recovered both and they turned in the proper direction. Not long after, Natalia spoke up again, also in English, "My vehicle is that way."

"That's great, but mine is that way and if you don't mind, I'd like to put on some clothes."

"We're going to my car!" Natalia was adamant.

"You go wherever you want Nat..."

"NATALIA!"

"Yeah, whatever. Anyway *Nat*, we're going to my car and I'm changing before we drop off Marlene here at the hospital. After that, you have my permission to kill me, okay? Until then, can you just be the slightest bit civil?" Gaelan's voice had enough of a condescending tone that Natalia was already beginning to regret not killing him with the dagger.

"Don't call me Nat!"

"Can we at least wait until she's in the car for you to bust my balls... *NAT*!"

"Keep calling me Nat and you won't make it as far as the car!" They walked on for several minutes in silence before Gaelan finally taunted her, "*Nat!*" He could feel her seething behind him.

They finally reached the car and Gaelan put Marlene on her feet while Natalia helped her. Natalia looked at the car and then to Gaelan, "Were the keys in your clothing?"

He walked several meters away and bent down to lift a rock at the base of a tree. The key was under there.

"I keep it by the vehicle just in case I..." Gaelan turned and Natalia was looking over his body, "Excuse me!" Gaelan pointed to his face, "My eyes are up here, thank you very much!"

Natalia, who simultaneously blushed and felt slightly bemused at his remark, bit her lips to fight back the slightest of grins.

"What was that?" Gaelan looked at her.

"What?" She looked around.

"That—that thing you did with your face? The 'almost smile' you just did? Are your face muscles gonna go into some type of rejection-spasms? Should I get some medication or something?" Gaelan taunted. Her face immediately went cold and she glared at him. "Never mind, that's better. For a minute there I thought something was wrong with you." He smirked as he opened the car for them. She continued to glower at him as he grabbed some bottled water for both of them. Marlene drank an entire bottle and Natalia then gave up most of hers. Gaelan went to the back of the car, took a spare set of clothes from the backpack in the trunk and changed behind the car. They set off driving toward the town and Marlene quickly fell asleep in the back of the vehicle.

They had been on the road about fifteen minutes when they saw a woman walking along its side. They slowed down as she turned, dirty and disheveled, looking for help. Sophie made eye contact with Gaelan and recognized him. She screamed and took off running. Gaelan remembered her face—a face he saw as he was dragged to the prison, then again when he had transformed. He sped ahead and whipped the vehicle in front of her. He jumped out of the car and charged toward her, Natalia was following close behind. Sophie was too terrified to do anything. She fell to the ground and began screaming. Gaelan approached her as she turned, still on the ground, to face him. She scurried back to a tree and screamed again. He stopped when he smelled the urine—she had wet herself in sheer terror. Gaelan didn't know why he hadn't killed her, but at that point, it didn't matter. He simply knew that what he had transformed into was so monstrous that the young woman in front him, fully capable of supernatural feats, was so terrified that she lost control of her bladder.

Natalia came up beside him and put a hand on his chest. Gaelan took the hint and stepped backward under her touch. Natalia went up to the young woman and dropped to her knees, speaking in French, "What's your name?"

The young woman whimpered, "Sophie. Please don't kill me!"

"Sophie, we're not going to hurt you." Before Natalia could finish, Sophie shot her eyes up to Gaelan in terror. He just looked down at her, not knowing what to make of her or what to think. "Sophie, listen to me," She turned back to Natalia, "we're not going to hurt you. I need you to answer some questions, okay?" Sophie nodded. "What was going on in the woods?"

Sophie's bottom lip quivered, "Initiation—it was an initiation ritual—into the coven. I was called here, to become one of them. They told me they were thousands of years old. That I would join them. Tilda and I." She looked back up at Gaelan, not trusting that he would stay restrained, then looked back to Natalia, "They kidnapped those girls!" Sophie began to sob, "I didn't know what they were going to do! The first night, they—they tore her apart. I tried to stop them but they just held me back! I should've done more!"

"It's okay Sophie, just calm down." Natalia tried to be soothing.

"IT'S NOT OKAY! THEY KILLED HER AND I COULDN'T—*DIDN'T* STOP THEM!"

Natalia took Sophie's face in her hands, "But you stopped them from killing *me*—from killing *Marlene*." Gaelan looked on, remembering how his mother calmed him down when they were camping, the night she was killed.

"Marlene? That's her name? Is she okay?" Sophie tried to calm down.

Natalia motioned to the back of the car, "She's asleep. We have to get her to the hospital. She's dehydrated and exhausted, but she's going to be okay. You saved her and you saved me."

Sophie's eyes softened and then she shot another terrified look at Gaelan.

"Don't worry about him," Natalia looked up at him, "I have him on a short leash." Gaelan rolled his eyes.

"Why didn't he..." Sophie directed her question to Gaelan, "Why didn't you kill me?"

Gaelan tried to think of a reason and couldn't, "Get in the car." He turned and walked back to the vehicle.

"Come on." Natalia helped Sophie to her feet and over to the car. Sophie got in and grasped Marlene, feeling comfort in the fact that she had saved her.

Natalia got in and looked at Gaelan, speaking in Polish, "What's your plan now, *genius*?" Gaelan rolled his eyes again and drove on.

About twenty minutes later, they were on the outskirts of Todtmoos. Gaelan stopped the car and turned to Sophie. She began to hyperventilate. He spoke in French, "Do you know how many nights the ritual was to last?"

She nodded, "Three."

"How many captives were there?"

"Two." Sophie quivered.

"The first night was the *whore*." He gestured quotation marks with his fingers, "Her name was Ilka and that—that was no way for a person to die." He glared at her. Natalia observed the exchange without interfering. "Last night was supposed to be *the virgin*. The head witch told me while I was, well, she said it to the *other side of me*. The final night was supposed to be one of their own. She mentioned the coward that calls herself an enchantress. *You* were the third night's sacrifice."

Sophie's eyes widened.

"Wake her." Gaelan gestured toward Marlene. Once Marlene was awake, he ordered, "Walk to the hospital and say you were abducted. Say you were taken to the nearby woods, but escaped after the other captive was killed. Tilda was part of the group that kidnapped you, but you can remember little else. It was dark and you couldn't see. You both ran in the night and didn't find your way back until morning. Stick to the story." Marlene and Sophie nodded and got out of the car.

Natalia helped Marlene out of the car and Gaelan got out to meet Sophie. He towered over her, imposing, "You saw what I am and you know what I can do." Gaelan held up a hand to prevent Sophie speaking, "You have a choice that I didn't. Forget about this and walk away. Live a normal life, as normal as you can. If you choose a path like the others," His glare made her tremble, "I'll know—and I'll be back for you."

After watching Sophie and Marlene leave, Natalia waited for Gaelan to settle in the drivers seat, then pulled the pistol from the small of her back and pointed it at his head.

"Drive!"

"Well no shit! I'm the one behind the wheel." He taunted. She had grabbed her weapon as she retrieved his blades.

"I'll kill you right here and now."

"No—no you won't." Before she could retort, he began, "First, we're too close to town and the shot will be heard. Second, you want answers. Third, you could've just let the witches kill me, and you didn't." Gaelan raised his eyebrows and looked at her sidelong.

Natalia held the gun tightly, pausing, "They would've come right back for her—for Marlene. The enemy of my enemy was my friend," She glared at him, "at—that—time!"

"Well, right now, the enemy of your enemy is *hungry*—at—*this*—time!" He taunted, "So I'm driving to the restaurant in the middle of town. I'm having a final meal, then I'll go wherever you like so you can kill me. I promise." He looked into her eyes, "And I don't make promises I can't or won't keep."

They pulled up to the little restaurant and Gaelan nodded to the pistol, "You may want to leave that in the car." Natalia eyed him suspiciously as he turned off the car and tossed her the keys. "I'd lock it." Natalia hid the gun in the glove compartment. Before she turned to follow Gaelan, she noticed several postcards and a stuffed animal in the back seat—a little wolf.

Gaelan was already seated in the back corner of the dining room when Natalia followed him inside.

"You hungry? I'm hungry."

"I don't want anything. Just get on with it so we can go." Natalia snapped.

The waitress came right over and greeted them cheerfully, even as she eyed their disheveled clothes. Gaelan's German was flawless, "Good morning. It was a long night of camping and hiking. Can we both have coffee, water, *lots* of water, and we'll both have an apple pancake. Oh, and some sausage as well." The waitress smiled and hurried off.

"I said I don't want anything!" Natalia snarled at him.

"Well tough shit cause I'm not eating my last meal by myself. So you can stare at it if you want, but it's coming no matter what." Gaelan's tone was provoking and Natalia glared at him. Gaelan switched to Polish. "You look at me with such disdain Nat, but you can't hate me any more than I already hate myself." He looked down, fidgeting with his napkin, "This thing that I am—this thing inside me—it's a constant reminder of the monster that killed my parents. I have become the very thing that I despise. I hate them," He looked back up at her with a rage in his eyes, "and I'm going to kill them and anything like them until I find one good enough to kill me and end this fucking nightmare!"

The waitress arrived with water and coffee. When she walked away, Natalia drank most of her water and then took her coffee cup with two hands. She raised it to her nose and breathed it in, then took a sip. She looked up to see Gaelan staring and then shot him a nasty look, "What did you mean that I want answers? How did you know?"

Gaelan half-smiled, "Well, it's not hard Nat."

"Stop calling me that!"

"Sure thing *Nat*. Anyway, you hunt things like me, so after what happened last night, you finally get to pick my brain. And because you want to know why things happened the way they happened. And finally, if you didn't want to talk, you would've shot me in the forest, or stabbed me with the dagger this morning." Natalia's eyes widened, but Gaelan was nonchalant, "It's okay, I wasn't gonna try to stop you. I was in and out of consciousness. When you came over, I figured you'd end it right there, but you didn't. So I figured you have some questions."

Natalia glared at him again. Across the table from her was a monster. A monster she had seen in his primal form the previous night and he was right, she did have questions, "Why are you here Gaelan?"

"Well, the story I heard was that my mother and father had a little too much to drink one night and one thing led to another..."

"STOP WITH THE GAMES GAELAN!" The few guests in the dining room turned to stare. Gaelan laughed out loud as if she just told a joke and everyone went about their business.

He dropped his voice to a hissing whisper, "Don't ask questions you already know the answer to—it's insulting."

"Dennis?"

"Yes Nat, Father Denny sent me, but you weren't supposed to be here. So here's my question: why are you here? Where are Trey and the others?" Gaelan's voice contained genuine concern, "Are they okay?"

"They're in Northern Germany. We were in Denmark for a shifter and Dennis sent us to Germany to aid in an exorcism."

"An exorcism?"

"Yes, all Venántium assist from time to time, unless of course they're Denny's little pet." She added contemptuously.

"Yeah, but why are *you* here?" Gaelan ignored the 'pet' comment.

"Because Trey had read about the disappearances and sent me ahead a couple of days ago to check it out. I'm sure since I didn't make contact yesterday, they're already on their way."

"Oh yippee. Maybe I'll even get to say hi." Before Natalia could say anything, he went on, "But how did you find me in the woods?"

Natalia was caught off guard by the question and the waitress arrived. They thanked her for the food and Natalia began when she left, "I didn't. I had been looking in the woods for two days for any trace of what was going on and I just—I ran into you." With everything that had happened, this was the first time that either one of them had given it any thought.

"How fortuitous for you, me and my stomach."

Natalia scowled at his flip tone. "Why didn't you kill me? Kill either of us?"

"Look at you. There's not enough meat to make it worth my while." Her scowl deepened, "Oh lighten up, I'm just kidding. Let me ask you something first: Why didn't *you* kill *me*?"

Natalia looked at him confused, "We already answered that."

"No, not this morning. That day in the bar on Long Island. When you, Trey and the others came to take me."

Natalia paused for a moment, "Dennis walked in with the shotgun."

"No, that's not it. You started to lower your weapon before that. You weren't going to shoot even with Trey yelling for you kill me."

"I..."

"Was it because you saw the poor kid laying in the hospital bed?"

Natalia's shocked look betrayed her, "You—you remember?"

"Yeah, it's hard to forget the face of the angel hovering over me. Of course now I know you just snuck in to check for bite marks." Gaelan watched as her face turned red. "I guess you haven't gone too soft. It didn't stop you from pulling the trigger yesterday."

"I hope it hurt." Her expression soured again.

"Oh it did." Gaelan tore into his pancake and spoke with his mouth full, "Mmmm, you should really try your pancake. It's heavenly."

"You didn't answer my question. Why didn't *you* kill *me*?"

Gaelan swallowed a mouthful of sausage, "The truth of it is, I can usually choke the wolf back. I just concentrate on the one thing that brings me peace I manage to keep it inside. But last night, I knew the—the fucking thing inside of me—I knew it was our only chance to get us out and save Marlene. I took a chance, just like I did in Canada."

Natalia's eyes narrowed, "Good thing this wasn't Canada. I don't know how Dennis can stomach working with you after what you did. Even if you didn't kill that girl I found you with, you still killed that woman in Canada."

"What are you talking about?" Gaelan's fork clinked hard against his plate. "I didn't kill any girl in Canada!"

Natalia leaned across the table, "You're a fucking liar Gaelan Kelly."

"Nat, I never killed a girl in Canada."

"You admitted it. The tour guide."

Gaelan let out a harsh laugh. "Ohhhhh, her. Yeah, I killed the tour guide, but I never killed a woman."

"Don't play stupid Gaelan, the tour guide was a woman!"

"No she wasn't" Gaelan's tone was cold.

"You just said *she*."

"Okay, I'll concede to the fact that the tour guide was female, but she was *not* a *woman*. That would imply she was *human*."

Realization began to dawn in Natalia's eyes.

"The tour guide, Evelyn. She was a fucking *werewolf*. One of them anyway." Gaelan took another bite of pancake.

Natalia was wide-eyed, "What do you mean *one* of them?"

"There were five. A pack. She was leading the tour group to an isolated location for the kill. Then they were going to trigger an avalanche to hide the bodies."

"They don't work in packs."

"Or maybe no one has ever lived to record that little tidbit of information. What Venántium team stands a chance against five werewolves?"

"You're telling me that you killed five werewolves in Canada?"

"Yeah, but I had to change to fight them."

Natalia mumbled to herself, "It wouldn't make a difference."

"What?"

"When you told us that you killed the tour guide, you said that 'no matter what you said, it wouldn't make a difference.'"

Gaelan smiled, "You have a good memory. I killed the tour guide and her entire pack of flea bitten assholes. They would've butchered the entire group, including Becca and her mom."

"Becca?"

"The little girl in the group. I promised her that I wasn't going to let anything happen to her and like I said," He raised his eyebrows, "I keep my promises. It's the reason I took a chance on turning, just like last night."

"The toy."

"What?"

"The toy in the back of the car. It's for her, isn't it?" Natalia inquired cautiously.

"Yeah, another promise that I would keep in touch. She likes wolves—I have no clue why she would anymore, but she still does." Gaelan laughed and shook his head.

"So you have no innocent blood—*human blood*—on your hands?"

Gaelan paused for a moment, then sat back in his chair. He looked down again, avoiding her gaze, "I never said that."

Natalia stared at him, his body tense with self-loathing and shame, "What did you do?" There was no accusation in her voice.

Gaelan didn't look up. "We had to take a building so another unit could advance down the street without fear of ambush." His voice was soft, "My best friend, Anfernee –he went first, kicked in the door to toss in a grenade. As soon as his foot hit the door, they fired. He was dead before I could get to him." Gaelan's breathing shallowed "I couldn't save him, and I just let the anger—the *rage*—I let it take control. I killed every enemy soldier in that building. I ran out of ammunition by the time I got to the last one. I threw my weapon at him before he could shoot me, and then pulled my knife." Gaelan's brow furrowed and his eyes were glassed, still avoiding her gaze, "I didn't just kill him. I hacked at him, and hacked and hacked. What was left wasn't even a body anymore. That's why I had my dad's silver knife that night. I never wanted to see mine again."

When Gaelan finally looked up, Natalia's face was soft with pity, "So I actually do have blood on my hands. What I did was disgusting—*inhuman*. I figure that this curse of mine is part of my punishment and, deep down, some part of me thinks I deserve it." His voice changed to anger as he talked through gritted teeth, "And that's the irony of it all."

"Irony?" Her voice a whisper.

"I somehow knew I wouldn't hurt you. Wouldn't kill you. But I didn't try to kill Marlene, or that witch, Sophie. Something in *it* knew that it should attack the other witches. I didn't kill the people in Canada, or Angel on my first night. No, the blood on my hands is from when I was *human*. So yeah, it's kind of ironic that all this time, this *fucking thing* inside me," His hands clenched, "is more human than I ever was." He dropped his head once more, self-loathing. He looked back up, shaking his head, "Sorry. The only time I've ever recounted that story was to my parents, the night they were killed." He turned away again.

Natalia didn't know what to say. This wasn't the flippant, wise-cracking monster they had been hunting. This was the broken boy she saw in a hospital bed—the young man that Father Denny had total faith in. She still had a duty to kill him; just because he hadn't killed yet didn't mean he never would. Choking back the words of sympathy that threatened to escape her lips, she picked up her fork and broke off a piece of pancake. "You're right, it's really good." Come to think of it, she hadn't eaten in a day.

Gaelan looked back to her with a half-hearted smile, "Told you so."

"You should finish yours. Don't let it go to waste." She looked down and continued to eat, stealing glances at him.

Gaelan finally took a few more bites before signaling for the check. He paid in cash and stuck the receipt in his pocket, "Let's get on with it." He forced a smile and they walked to the car. She handed him the keys and got in, taking the gun out of the glove compartment and putting it on her lap. He paid no attention to it as they drove for the better part of an hour. She guided him to the place where she had left her car.

"Pull over here." Her voice was cold again.

Gaelan took out the keys and gave them to her. She was caught off guard as he spoke, "My katana and my dad's knife are in the trunk. Please see to it that Father Denny gets them." He looked into her eyes and she stared back at him, the gun in her lap trained on him.

"What's your game Gaelan? You can't be this accepting."

"I am Nat. No game, no tricks. I made you a promise and I stand by it. We had breakfast, and now you get to kill me." Gaelan scanned the surrounding forest and then back to her, his face looked exhausted, "I'm tired Nat. I track these things and kill them, but I'm not convinced that we're even making a dent. What's the point? At least you have Trey and Angel and Kedar. I have no one. I talk to Father Denny every so often. Ten minutes at a time is all he can manage with the Vatican breathing down his neck. I got to see my aunt and uncle once, but even there, where I was supposed to be forgetting the bad shit, I ripped some poor kid out of a car for tickling his girlfriend. I was sure he was trying to eat her. Once again, it was *me*. I was the monster, not the thing inside me. The most enjoyable conversation I've had in the last two years was with a shifter on a Mexican beach right before I killed her." She saw in his eyes the same look of the broken kid in the hospital bed, "The only thing I have to live for is to kill the motherfucker that killed my parents, and I still haven't found it, and probably never will. Hell, the only werewolves I've found were the ones in Canada. So yeah, I'm tired. Tired and *alone*. I'm not running from death Nat—I *welcome* it." Gaelan turned away to once again view the Black Forest surrounding them.

"You still didn't answer my question." Natalia's voice was firm.

"Which one?"

"Why didn't you kill me last night? You said things like 'you knew it would be okay' and that 'you knew you wouldn't hurt me,' but how? *How* did you know? Why didn't you kill me Gaelan?" She was impatient.

"I told you that I keep it under control. That when the full moon comes, I concentrate on the one thing that brings me peace. It's what gives me the focus and self-control to keep it inside..."

"WHY DIDN'T YOU KILL ME GAELAN?" Natalia wanted a straight answer.

"It's *you*, Nat."

"WHAT THE HELL DOES THAT MEAN?"

"*You're* the one thing that brings me peace. *You're* the face of the angel floating over my hospital bed when I awoke. *You're* the one moment of peace I had when my world was shattered. You even stayed when I asked you to." Natalia inhaled audibly. "Yeah, I remember that too." Gaelan continued. "You didn't have to, but you nodded and held my hand until I went back to sleep. *You're* the thing that keeps it in check. So yeah, when I saw you hanging across from me, I knew *it* wouldn't hurt you. Even though you're the thing that keeps *it* locked up—and trust me, it's not a fan of that. I just knew it would be all right. I wouldn't let anything happen. It—I—didn't kill you because you're *you*, Nat."

Natalia stared, speechless. She lowered the gun.

"What are you doing?" Gaelan looked to the gun and back to her eyes.

"Just go."

"No."

"GO GAELAN!"

"I can't." He was adamant.

"WHY NOT?"

His voice was calm, "Because this is my car." He shrugged. Natalia closed her eyes in exasperation, pinched the bridge of her nose as if to ward off a headache, then dropped the keys and got out of the car.

Gaelan exited the car after her.

She turned and pointed the gun at him again, "Get back in the car Gaelan and drive away before I change my mind."

"Then change it Nat! You have a job to do and I made a promise."

"JUST GO DAMN IT!"

"NO!"

"What is wrong with you?" She sounded defeated.

"I want to know why you won't kill me."

"You saved my life last night. I owe you."

"And you saved mine, remember? We're even."

"No Gaelan, you didn't kill me after that. So that puts me in your debt. Now I'm letting you go, and *that* makes us even." She glared at him, "But make no mistake about it, the next time I see you, I *will* kill you!" She turned and walked to her car.

"What'll Trey say about this?"

She stopped and looked back, "I'm not going to tell him." She turned back to her car.

Gaelan paused for a moment, then grabbed the receipt out of his pocket and walked to her, "Give me a pen!"

She turned to him, exasperation clouding her face.

"A pen—give me a pen!"

"Here." Natalia found a pen in the console of her car and tossed it to Gaelan.

"WAIT!" He yelled as she slid into the car, scribbling furiously against the hood. She started the engine. "I made a promise to you before breakfast. You're not taking me up on it and that doesn't sit right with me. I always keep my promises, so I'm making it official. Sorry, but I don't know your last name." He handed her the receipt, folded over, "Besides, you dropped your cell phone in the car." He handed her the phone, stood up and now spoke in English, "I always keep my promises, Nat." He forced a smile.

"Call me *Nat* again and I'll hit you with the car. It won't kill you, but it'll hurt enough for me to feel good about myself." She scowled, her lips slightly turned up in self-satisfaction.

"There's that almost-smile again. You really need to learn how to do it for real."

Her face went stony. "I don't smile anymore Gaelan."

"Before either one of us leaves this world, I'm gonna see that smile of yours—that's a promise."

"Go now Gaelan, before I change my mind."

"Thank you."

"Don't thank me!" Her voice was all business, "Next time, I kill you."

"I'm not thanking you for letting me live Nat. I'm thanking you for listening to me." He smiled warmly, "And for being my angel."

Natalia drove a short distance away before pulling over, glancing through the rear view to make sure she was alone. She shook her head and fought back the urge to grin as she read.

Rain Check:

This receipt entitles Natalia to kill Gaelan Kelly at the time and place of her choosing. No expiration.

— Gaelan Kelly

CHAPTER 2
NIGHT TERRORS

Niu Dang walked around the orphanage doing her daily chores. Her name, literally *"Girl of the Party,"* marked her as an orphan. She wasn't unhappy per se, but recently moved into a home for teenage girls. She knew that her hopes of being adopted were lost.

Niu had befriended a fifteen-year-old girl in the new facility named Niu Guo, a *"Girl of the State."* They giggled about the unoriginality of whoever named them. "Anyway my name should be *Chēlún*!" 'Wheels'—Niu Guo was confined to a wheelchair. Like Chēlún, most of the girls at the home had some type of special need. Some had cleft pallets, some palsy, and some like Chēlún, had more serious physical needs. Niu Dang had no physical handicaps. It was her nighttime tendencies that kept her from being adopted. She had stayed with foster families twice before and, both times, was sent back. She would occasionally sleepwalk they said. That wasn't all that bad. It was the night terrors that the foster families couldn't handle.

Niu would wake, screaming and crying about vivid dreams. When Niu was seven, she went through a period of terrors, waking in the middle of the night, screaming and crying, and keening "Death on the rails—they will hit." Her foster-parents were annoyed at their broken sleep. Then, a week later, two high-speed trains collided, killing dozens of passengers. Though they continued to treat her kindly, Niu overheard them calling her creepy. They returned her to the orphanage a few days later.

It was the second family she stayed with, when she was ten, that sealed her fate as a "Girl of the Party" until she was an adult. A few weeks after arriving at their home, Niu woke screaming, gripping her foster-mother and insisting that she was going to die. "Beware the fire of many wheels, you are surrounded by flames." The foster parents were unnerved but assumed that Niu was reliving some old trauma. They wanted Niu to stay. Then, three months later, Niu's foster mother was driving home from a shopping trip when the driver of a gas tanker heading the opposite way had a heart attack and barreled across the median. The truck jack-knifed in front of her foster mom, engulfing her car in flames. Niu's foster father brought her back to the orphanage. The kind man cried when he dropped her off, explaining that her presence was a painful reminder of the death of his wife.

Niu didn't hold any animosity toward him or anyone else. She couldn't hold it against anyone that only remembered her night terrors—it was her defining trait. The only thing she did hate was going to sleep. Each night she would try to stay awake as long as possible only to succumb to the exhaustion. Every so often, Niu would awake having dreamt that something good was going to happen. That was the exception, not the norm. Her night terrors were vivid and she would awake screaming. She had kept the terrors to herself after her foster family's experiences, but she had seen other things and remembered the strange words that her dreams left her with. Sometimes they came true in a very short period of time, sometimes it took more than a year or two before they came to fruition. They usually differed from night to night, but it was when they began to repeat that she became anxious.

On this night, Niu awoke screaming in terror. She was sweating profusely and looking all around in fear. Chēlún scrambled into her wheelchair and went to Niu's side, but couldn't calm her down. She held Niu tight, trying to comfort her, but it was no use.

"It's okay—it's okay! It's just a bad dream."

But Niu couldn't be soothed. The dream happened on the same night each of the last three months—the night of the full moon. The dream, what she remembered of it, was the same each time. She and all of the girls are panicked, crying. She remembers seeing Chēlún on the floor. *He* circles her. She's unable to move, petrified with fear. *He* looks down and sees Chēlún on the floor, "Oh, I'll see to your friend personally." She remembers looking up and seeing inhuman eyes—the eyes of a monster. Just before she wakes each time, she remembers the snarl, the laugh, and the words, "You should be running." She had hoped that this was just a silly figment of her imagination, but the vivid dream was repetitive, just as the others were before they came true. And each time she awakes, the words echo in her mind.

"The monsters will come for me!"

Niu clenched Chēlún tightly, screaming and crying, knowing that as utterly impossible as her dream may have been, it would come to pass.

A continent away, an old man sat in a small, dimly lit room. He woke suddenly, not sure what time it was. He poured himself a drink of water from a copper pitcher into the lone cup. He rubbed his eyes and then stared at the wall, pondering the circumstances that led to his current predicament. His days blended together, identical now for years, maybe a decade. He had already read the various newspaper clippings that had been given to him. A small television in the top corner of the room showed news from all around the world. The languages varied, but the news was always the same: violence, war, famine, disease, death; Child molestation, serial killings, conflict between nations, suffering. The same gruesome lineup in print and TV, ever since his capture. The door opened and he turned.

A young, good-looking man walked in with a bowl of soup, some bread and fresh vegetables, "Dinner time. I hope you like it." He was very polite, "I made the bread myself from a new recipe I'm trying." The old man smiled and nodded. The young man looked down at the newspaper articles, "Did you see the article about the killer in Sweden? It's a shame what he did to those children." The old man did not respond.

"One day Medhir, you will realize that they are just trying to bring order to the chaos that the world has plummeted in to." The young man's tone was soft.

"And when your *masters* have what they want, what order will they bring? Does it bother you to be a lap dog to monsters, Gaius?" Medhir responded without turning his head.

Gaius laughed, "Monsters? I recently had tea with a wolf—a real wolf," He saw the old man shift at the talk of a werewolf, "outside of the Coliseum. But that's another story. I didn't come here to argue my friend; I came to inquire. Are there any new signs? We simply need to know how the eternal darkness rises. We need to know of the last seer. Have your dreams changed at all?"

"No. Always the same." Medhir bit into his bread, eager to camouflage his lie. He had been seeing an image, sporadically, for three months now. A younger girl and a monster circling her—the faces are blurred, merely shadows, never something he can remember. The same words whirl past the images each time: *The monsters will come for her*. Each time he sees the dream, he thinks about the news and how his captors—they prefer to be called his *hosts*—will impose their 'order' on this chaotic world. He looked up, "Does this mean you'll kill me now." His tone was nonchalant.

"No, of course not. The elders have told me that you will soon meet Efthalia. The signs of the previous seers have begun. She will come and you will both show us the next seer—the *final seer*. A prophet's mind and a witch's guidance. Then we will know how to let the darkness rise." Gaius smiled coldly, sadistically, thinking about a darker future, and then turned to walk out, "Enjoy the meal my friend. I would very much like to hear how you enjoyed the bread when I see you tomorrow. Until then," He glanced over his shoulder, "dream well."

CHAPTER 3
MEMORY LANE

Gaelan had texted Father Denny about the witches and told him that he was taking some time to himself. "I'm available if you need me, but I need to see my parents." Father Denny finally texted back a few days later that he understood.

Gaelan flew to New York. The conversation with Natalia had resurrected so many memories. He drove out to Long Island and tried to sleep in the rental car, parked by the cemetery, before finally ceding that he wasn't going to rest. He drove in shortly after it opened and parked the car, waiting several minutes before getting out. Then he took a deep breath and walked up to the gravestone.

It had been two long years since he buried them. In that time, he learned that the thing that attacked them was a werewolf. He had been bitten and he was now *cursed*. He realized that he was being tracked by Trey Marshall and his team, members of the secretive Benedicta Venántium. He learned that Father Denny, his high school mentor and friend, protected him, despite being a Venàntium once himself. Sent to Japan by Father Denny, Gaelan had studied with a martial arts and weapons instructor named Kenta Oonishi. It was there that he learned to choke back the monster inside him and use the increased strength, speed and agility it left him with. Father Denny had then sent him to China under an assumed identity, where he was trained as a *venator,* and learned about the creatures that hunt and prey on humanity.

His first hunt had ended in a bloody battle with underground creatures known as the cobalus, and he was able to fake his own death. Since then, with what little guidance Father Denny could provide from under the watchful eye of the Vatican, Gaelan had hunted on his own. He killed a fifteen-hundred-year old vampire in New York—far older than anyone believed a creature could be—and saved the life of the woman that broke his heart. He had killed five werewolves in Canada, and disproved the assumption that they were purely solo hunters, but none of them was the one who had victimized his family. He lived only for the day that he could find *it*—find the one that ripped everything from him.

Gaelan approached the grave slowly, two roses in one hand. Memories swirled. *Mom and Dad—why? Carly—you broke my heart. The camping trip was supposed to cheer me up. Anfernee—the war—have I always been a monster?* He closed his eyes, grimacing at the slavering face of the werewolf, of its glowing eyes, before him. He took a breath, loosened his grip that threatened to crush the rose stems, opened his eyes and squatted down in front of the headstone.

Jonathon and Cassandra Kelly
Loving Parents

"Hey guys. Sorry I haven't been around to see you. I'm sure you know how busy I've been." He placed the roses at the base of the headstone, "Nothing but the best for you guys—at least the best flowers from an all night grocery store." His half-hearted smile was quickly replaced with a grimace as he choked back his emotions. "I really miss you guys. I don't know what to do. Father Denny thinks that I'm meant for something more, but I don't wanna be here anymore. I just wanna see you guys again," He sighed, his voice cracked, "but I'm not sure that I'm even headin' your way when I go. Not after what I told you—what I did. And then I think about what happened to you and all I want is to find that motherfucker and tear it apart! I know it's wrong, but it's all I live for now—and I'm not even sure that I ever will. And this thing inside me—what it left me with—I don't know if I can keep it bottled in, or if I should even try anymore. I just wish you were here to help me. I could really use some advice."

Gaelan felt his eyes burn, "I met a girl. Well not really. She's hunting me. You'd like her. She shot me." He smiled to himself, "Her name is Natalia. The next time she sees me, she'll probably kill me. It's sad, but I'm okay with that. I just want it all to end." He looked down at the ground in shame, "I know that you wouldn't want me to talk like that, but it's the truth. I don't even know what I'm doin' or if it makes a difference. I've saved some lives, but does it really matter?" Gaelan shook his head, "I just wish I knew that all of this was for something—some reason. That this wasn't all a series of random violent acts. You guys used to say it. Father Denny says it—everything happens for a reason, right? What the hell is all of this for?" After several seconds, he stood and composed himself. "Just put in a good word for me, okay?" He kissed his fingertips, then gently laid his hand on the headstone as a tear rolled down his cheek. "I love you guys." He turned and walked away.

Less than an hour later, he drove by the front of Reverend Washington High School, and coasted into the parking lot of a bar. Reverend Washington was where he had met Father Denny, before his life was turned upside down. The bar wasn't open yet, but there was motion inside. Gaelan walked up and pounded on the front entrance.

"WE'RE CLOSED!" He pounded again and stood back as someone walked to the heavy oak door and turned the lock. "I SAID WE'RE CLO..." Tom Murphy, the bar owner and Father Denny's longtime friend, came up short, "Holy shit!"

"Hey Sir, I was in the neighborhood." Gaelan smiled.

"Holy shit," Murphy repeated, glancing over his shoulder into the bar. "Come in. Come in! Have a seat!" Tom grabbed two glasses and came around the bar with a bottle, "Here." He looked over his shoulder, again.

"You okay Sir?" Gaelan knew that the man was not at ease.

"Well, it's just, ya know..." Tom couldn't find the words and shrugged.

"First time you're drinking with a werewolf?" Gaelan smiled.

Murphy laughed tautly. "Yeah. I'd say it is."

He poured them both a drink.

Gaelan smiled and raised his glass, "Then this calls for a toast. To the one of us that can lick his own balls!"

Tom bellowed in laughter, "That's lookin' on the bright side!"

"Yeah, I could use more of it nowadays." Gaelan took a sip and savored it, "Bourbon?"

"Of course." Tom grinned, "*Real patriots drink bourbon.*"

Gaelan grinned back. That was the exact phrase he had told Carly Perrino to repeat to gain entrance into *Murphy's Law*. "Well I figured that would get her in the door."

"Oh it did. And boy did she have a story. She saw his face you know, the vampire, and said that you came in just before he tore into her. She said that you fought it and killed it, and then went after her, but you choked it back." Tom took another sip and seemed to relax, "What the hell happened?"

"That thing was strong—stronger than anything I faced before. The only way I had a chance was to let it out a bit. Guess I was lucky it was the full moon. It wasn't enough though. Carly shot the thing just before it took off my head. Just pissed it off, but it distracted him enough for me to tear his face off." Gaelan paused and looked at his drink, "I was so worked up and on the cusp of changing that I jumped on top of her. But I managed to choke it back."

"Well, it all scared the shit out of her."

"I know. That's why I sent her to you. Father Denny told me that you know about the Benedicta Venántium and I figured she'd at least have someone who can relate."

"Yeah, well, it was a good call cause she needed it."

"How's she doin'?"

"Good question from someone whose heart she broke."

"She told you about that too?" Gaelan seemed surprised.

Tom smiled, "You don't talk about surviving a werewolf and vampire fight without some of the past coming out."

"After she kept calling and talking about the nightmares and insomnia, I knew she needed someone to talk to." Gaelan felt his own isolation, "Someone to let her know that she's not alone."

"That's pretty damn decent of ya. She'd probably like to see you. I can give her a call and let her know to come by after work…"

"No!" Gaelan immediately shot back, then eased his tone, "Don't do that. I don't wan...need to see her."

"She feels guilty ya know."

Gaelan looked down at his glass and turned it about, fidgeting, "I never should've blamed her. I was angry." He looked up, "I'm still angry, but not at her. What happened between us crushed me, but she didn't send that fucking thing..." Gaelan caught himself, "Sorry about the language."

"Yeah, my virgin ears are ringin.'"

Gaelan forced a smile.

"The point is, she didn't kill my parents and she deserves a good life."

"Yeah, well, the good life part is rough right now."

"How so?"

"She's on desk duty for post-traumatic stress. She only takes the day shifts and locks herself in her apartment with defenses against everything creepy crawly out there. She said she tried to talk to a couple of people close to her—tried to open up to them—and they just told her she needs some *down time*. She comes here to sleep in my guest room half the time because she can't get any rest on her own. Says she likes knowing that I get it, and that I'll back her up without question if shit goes down. She tells me about every report that finds its way across her desk—wants to know if I think there's something more sinister at work. One of those things about being a cop," Tom poured himself another and topped off Gaelan's glass, "you get to see the shit that the world offers everyday, non-stop." Tom cocked his head and his tone softened, "She asks about you too, wondering if I hear anything. You should really see her."

"I can't thank you enough for being there for her. And I can't thank you enough for helping out Father Denny and me that morning."

"You know not to thank me Gaelan. I've known Denny a long time and I know what we did was right. Don't ask me how, I just know. Speaking of which, Denny gets me the occasional secret message. Yeah, I know about his Vatican job and the watchful eye, but after talking to you now—You're gonna change the whole balance of things. You're gonna change the world Gaelan."

"I wish I could believe that myself." Gaelan took a sip of his drink.

Tom smiled, "You sure I can't call Carly and get her here?"

Gaelan swallowed the last of the bourbon, turned the glass upside down then stood up, "I'm sure." He thought on it for a moment, "It's for the better. Thanks for everything Sir"

"Tom! I called my father *Sir.*"

"I'll make sure to check in more often, Tom." Gaelan gave Tom Murphy a hug and turned to walk out.

"Gaelan?" Tom looked torn. "I can't—I won't lie to her if she asks if I've heard any news about you. What do you want me to say?"

Gaelan paused for just a second then smiled, "Tell her I've been out killin' vampires like it's cool."

Tom smiled back and nodded, "I can do that. You take care, *venator.*"

Gaelan left the bar and drove to the house he grew up in. He thought that the sight of it might be painful, but he was relieved to see that it had been vastly renovated by its new owners and didn't much resemble the house he left. Next stop: the coffee shop where he and Carly had their first date. By the time he cruised passed its yellow awning he was done cruising memory lane. After two years of killing monsters, he was ready for one of the hunts to end his life. His only drive in life was to kill as many creatures as possible in the meantime. It was only his promise to Father Denny that kept him from committing suicide. He tapped Denny a note:

> *Mom and Dad are good.*
> *Ready to hunt.*
> *Send me a job.*

It occurred to him as soon as he hit send: there *was* one more place to visit before his next assignment rolled in. The drive from Long Island took nearly five hours, and the windy road through the mountains took another forty-five minutes until he finally pulled into the parking lot where the cabin rentals were. Shenandoah National Park. Ten minutes to walk to the more isolated cabins that his parents' had preferred. Two years later, and scraps of yellow tape still clung to the trees. Apparently, no one liked to rent the cabin where two people were killed by a *'bear'*.

He could almost hear them, Mom and Dad, laughing as they returned from a hike. There was the campfire, where he had broken down telling them about Anfernee and what he had done to the enemy soldiers. He didn't approach the fire ring where they sat that night. Instead, he arced around the clearing and stopped at the exact spot where he had come out of the woods to find that *fucking thing* holding his father by the throat, his mother already dead. He clenched his hands and felt his breathing shallow as the rage built inside him. *I will fucking find you.*

A twig snapped.

Gaelan spun around to see a Park Ranger coming out of the tree line just a few meters behind him. He steadied himself, unclenching his fists. "Evening Sir, how are ya?"

"Just fine, and yourself?" The Ranger stood still.

"Great thanks. Just taking a look at the cabin."

"You know this place is no longer being rented, right?" The ranger was still.

"It's too bad, it looks like a great little spot." Gaelan glanced at the cabin for the final time. "You have a great night." He turned to walk back down the path to his car.

"GAELAN KELLY?"

Gaelan stopped and slowly turned to see the Ranger with a pistol drawn down on him.

"You're Gaelan Kelly, aren't you?"

"I'm not sure what you're talking about. Who are you?" Gaelan's tone was caustic. *Was this even a man?* The sun was still above the horizon and Gaelan wasn't sensing or smelling anything supernatural.

"Don't you worry about who I am. You're Gaelan Kelly!"

Gaelan began to suspect that he was a collaborator—someone working with the creatures, "Maybe I am, maybe I'm not. What's it matter?"

"Put your hands on your head and get down on your knees! NOW!"

Gaelan complied, surveying the area as he dropped to his knees, "What now?"

"Now we make a phone call." The ranger pointed his pistol at Gaelan with one hand and fumbled to retrieve his cell phone from his pocket.

The ranger lowered his eyes to the screen, intent on making the call. Gaelan seized the moment, rolling forward and grabbing both a hand-sized stone and thick branch. Gaelan's momentum brought him upright, closing the distance between them and throwing the stone. The stone hit the ranger's chest as Gaelan slashed the branch across the ranger's hands and knocked the gun away, before throwing his weight and strength into the ranger, tackling him to the ground. Gaelan landed on his chest, his knees pinning the man's upper arms while grabbing his throat, "Now I'll ask the questions, and if I don't get an answer, or don't like the answer I get, I start breaking fingers. Then I move on to bigger bones." Gaelan paused glowering. "Who sent you?"

"No one!" The ranger was gasping for air.

Gaelan bent the man's index finger backwards, "Who—sent—you?"

"NO ONE! I COME HERE EVERYNIGHT!" The man yelled through the pain.

"WHY?" Gaelan loosened his grip on the man's throat despite his rage.

"Because I figured you might be back." The Ranger panted.

Gaelan stood and picked up the discarded gun, "Sit down. Now!" The man lifted himself up painfully and sat down on a nearby rock. Gaelan sat across from the ranger with the gun trained on him, "Who do you work for?"

The man's eyes were confused, his answer almost disbelieving. "The National Park Service."

Gaelan dropped the magazine from the gun, but kept the weapon trained on the man, one round in the chamber. *Silver bullets.* "Pretty fancy for a federal employee, and pretty coincidental seeing as we both seem to know who and *what* I am." Gaelan reinserted the magazine and pointed it at the man's knee, "So I'll ask you again. Who are you working for?"

"I'm a park ranger asshole, and if you're gonna shoot me, then shoot me."

Gaelan cocked the trigger, "Then why the silver bullets? Why check for me? How did you know about this place?"

"Because I caught a glimpse of what you were going to—what you *have* become."

Gaelan lowered the weapon slightly, "How do you know?"

The ranger didn't answer.

"Trey?"

The ranger glared, silent.

Gaelan lowered the pistol, "You were with Trey Marshall the night I—*we* were attacked." The ranger remained silent, "Have there been any other attacks?" Gaelan softened his tone, "Please! Have there been any others?"

"None here." The ranger spoke cautiously, "Nothing since you. We occasionally hear about a wild animal attack in other national parks and it makes me wonder. Mostly about what you've been up to."

"Trey told you to watch out for me, didn't he? He figured I might come back here at some point."

"You or the one that attacked you. I come here every night and wait. I should've taken the damn shot."

"Yeah, you should've. If it makes you feel any better, some people don't hesitate." Gaelan absentmindedly rubbed his stomach where Natalia shot him, "Funny thing is, I came here hoping to find it—find *him*—by sheer luck. At least one of us got lucky." Gaelan looked at the ranger, who wriggled uncomfortably where he sat, "What's your name?" The ranger continued to glare at him. "Really, you can't even tell me your name? How about I just call you Ranger Rick?"

"Edwards. Ranger Nick Edwards."

"Nick—you don't mind if I call you Nick, do you?" Edwards glared, silent once more. "What did you see that night? Please, I just wanna know."

After a moment, Ranger Edwards began to speak.

"It was massive, and ran like a man, but faster—*much faster*. It was like nothing I'd ever seen before. I only caught a glimpse of it. Trey was shooting at it when I came into the clearing, but I saw it," He sighed, "and I've slept with the lights on ever since."

Gaelan nodded his head, "You and me both."

Gaelan stood up and raised the gun. The ranger's breathing shallowed. Then Gaelan let the weapon flip in his hand and extended his arm to the Ranger, handing the pistol back to Edwards with the muzzle pointed toward his own chest, "Here, this is yours."

The ranger extended his own hand, cautiously at first, then grabbed the gun and backed away, yelling, "GET DOWN NOW!"

"Nope. We already went through that. You said you didn't want to hesitate again, so don't." Gaelan shrugged, then turned to walk back towards his car.

"WHAT THE HELL ARE YOU DOING? STOP!"

Gaelan turned and looked back to Edwards, whose hands were shaking with the weapon in it, "Please, do it. Do me the favor."

Finally, Edwards lowered the gun "What the hell is wrong with you?"

"I'm tired Nick. I'm just—plain—tired."

The ranger lowered the pistol, his brow furrowed in confusion.

Gaelan shook his head and turned back toward his car, "Jesus, I can't get anyone to fuckin' kill me! What the hell is wrong with people nowadays?" Edwards holstered his pistol once Gaelan was out of sight, checked his phone for cracks, then scrolled for Trey Marshall's number.

"SONAFABITCH!"

Trey Marshall and his team were hunting a shifter way out of phone range—he hadn't gotten Edward's message for a day and a half.

"What's wrong?" Angelo Silva spoke first.

"Kelly—Gaelan fucking Kelly!"

"Did he kill again?" Kedar asked, nonchalant. Natalia almost snapped that Gaelan had never killed a human, but stopped herself. No one knew that she had seen or spoken to him.

"No. That was Nick Edwards."

"Who?" Natalia cocked an eyebrow.

"Nick Edwards. He's the forest ranger we stayed with when Kelly was attac...*bitten*. He scouts out the spot where it happened and keeps an ear to the ground for suspicious animal attacks around the full moon."

"So?" She was impatient.

"So he spotted Kelly a day ago when we were after that fucking shifter! He saw him right at the camp where he was bitten. We need to book tickets to the U.S."

Natalia could feel her teammates' excitement at the prospect of the hunt, but couldn't shake the sense of dread that had settled over her. She had told Gaelan she was going to kill him the next time she saw him, but to be honest, she was in no rush to do either. Or maybe it was knowing the truth while her team didn't that made her uneasy, or Trey's obsession with Gaelan? "Do we even know where he is? And what about our next assignment? The Vatican already has us going to Austria."

"Fuck the Vatican and fuck Denny. He knows Gaelan killed that woman and he's still protecting him somehow."

"Even if he is," Natalia's tone was cold, "it's still a needle in a haystack."

"IT'S THE BEST LEAD WE'VE HAD IN OVER A YEAR!"

The entire team was silent for several seconds. Trey was about to speak when Natalia cut him off, "So if he was at the scene of his parents' death, then where does he go from there? Back to New York?" Natalia forced her voice to be calm—this meant too much to Trey for her to mess up.

"Edwards said in the message that he called his name and Kelly took off, so we have to assume that he wouldn't go to the places that we'd expect, like his school or to that banker that worked with his dad—Rosen. He might not even be in the States anymore." Trey sounded exasperated.

"We'll figure it out brother." Angel interjected, patting Trey on the shoulder.

"Maybe there's one more thing we can try." Natalia looked to Trey, "When we were in Canada, the group of survivors..."

"Yeah, what about them?"

"Do we have the notes on them?" Natalia looked to Kedar.

"Yes."

"There was a little girl there, and her mother, do you remember?"

"Vaguely, but what's that have to do with..."

Natalia cut Trey off, "I remember her talking about someone they met. Someone who promised to visit." Natalia had never lied to her team before—now she had to, to test her theory without mentioning her time with Gaelan, or the stuffed animal wolf she spotted in his back seat.

"So?" Trey groused.

"Seriously Natalia, what's that have to do with anything?" Angel chimed in while Kedar looked on with a raised eyebrow.

"I never said anything and it bothered me when we finally saw Kelly in the airport. I think she may have been talking about him. It makes me wonder if maybe he has some type of infatuation or obsession with the child." Natalia wasn't sure if they were buying it.

"Why are you just telling us this now?" Trey was dumbfounded.

"Maybe I didn't think it was plausible. Maybe I thought it might be too much of a jump to connect it. Maybe I just had a run in with a witch and I'M A LITTLE ON EDGE."

Trey's demeanor immediately softened. He was shocked by her tone and embarrassed by his own, "Sorry—I didn't mean to..."

"I'm just trying to say that if he *is* in the States, then maybe it's worth a shot."

After a brief silence, Trey turned to Kedar, "Do you have the names?"

"Jennifer and Rebecca Guerin. They live in Michigan."

"What's the next assignment?" Trey looked to Angel.

"Bodies in Austria. Organs were missing. Sound familiar?" Angel looked to Natalia who shook her head in disgust.

"Shit." Trey was pondering when Natalia broke in again.

"Why don't Angel and Kedar scout out Austria while we get tickets to the U.S.? We'll meet up in three days. The little girl will probably be more willing to talk to me, but I can't go alone—if we do find him or get a lead, we'll need more than one person."

Trey stared at Natalia in disbelief. She had never been so forward before. But she had a point about the girl, and no matter how slim the chances, he wanted—*needed* to follow though. Anything to kill a werewolf. "You guys good with that?"

"Yeah, no problem." Angel looked to Kedar and nodded to Trey.

"Alright then, let's get moving." Trey began to put his things together and Natalia went to gather hers. Now it was time to do the fact checking she needed with Trey there to hear it.

Aunt Sarah broke down in tears when she saw Gaelan at her doorstep. Seated in her sunny kitchen, he told her about his visit to his parents' grave and the campsite where the *"bear"* had killed her sister and brother-in-law. Uncle Bob rushed in an hour later—Sarah had called and told him to come home early. He was still in his coveralls with "Director of Maintenance, Regional Transit Authority of Columbus" over the left breast. Extricating from his uncle's bear hug, Gaelan happily accepted a beer. *"Director of Maintenance?* Congrats on the promotion!" Gaelan smiled and took a swig.

"Thanks buddy. About a year ago now, that bastard Marcus finally retired, and…"

"Oh shush Bob. You're staying with us again Gaelan, I insist!" Aunt Sarah cut in.

"I can't this time. There's something I have to do."

"Something more important? All we get are the occasional post-cards and now you're just stopping in?"

"It's something I've been putting off for a while."

"What is it? Can we help?" Bob interjected.

"Not unless you want to visit a friend's family for me."

"Sure! What friend?" Bob chuckled.

"My buddy—my best friend—who I lost overseas." Gaelan saw his uncle and aunt's crestfallen faces, "It's okay, seriously. It's just that I've been running all over the world and haven't ever stopped by. It's time. But I couldn't be back home and not stop by to see my favorite aunt and uncle first."

Sarah smiled, "We're you're only aunt and uncle."

"Which means you can never drop on the list." Gaelan grinned.

Gaelan checked his phone as he drove away from his Aunt and Uncle's house. He had made sure to say *goodbye* as Sarah cried and clung to him—*No use pretending this couldn't be the last time.* Still no message from Denny. He drove into the night, stopping once for gas and a quick nap under a parking lot light. When the familiar nightmare of killing his parents woke him in a cold bath of sweat, he drove on, crossing the North Carolina line, and pulling into the Dawkins' driveway mid-morning.

"Oh—my—word!" Mrs. Dawkins came out of the front door to meet Gaelan, and enveloped him in a pillowy hug. Mr. Dawkins' arms soon wrapped them both—he seemed to be praying under his breath. It was a full minute or two before they broke the embrace

"How have you been sweetie?" Mrs. Dawkins had tears in her eyes.

"I'm okay. Best as I can be." Gaelan lied.

"Well, you'll be better inside with some fresh sweet tea and breakfast, and we ain't gonna take *no* for an answer." Mr. Dawkins' look was simultaneously soft and stern.

Gaelan wasn't hungry, but wouldn't think of arguing, "I never could resist Carolina sweet tea."

Once inside, Mrs. Dawkins and Gaelan sat at the kitchen table where Mr. Dawkins brought him a tall glass of sweet tea and cooked eggs, ham and grits.

"We love your postcards honey. What has you travelling all over the world?" She set the overflowing plate in front of Gaelan, and took his hand.

"Soul-searching I guess. Trying to find my place in the world. I mostly do aid work for those in need. Sometimes it's disaster relief, sometimes its just spur of the moment. All in all, it's worthwhile, but sometimes I wonder what little difference it makes."

"Oh sweetie, it makes all the difference, especially to those people you're helpin'."

"I guess."

"So tell me all about where you've been."

Gaelan talked about Japan, China and Europe. He mainly talked about the sites and the food, not wanting to accidentally slip up and mention anything he had really been doing. They ate and had a good laugh or two, until Gaelan finally said, "I just wish I wasn't alone in my travels."

"You been thinkin' about him, haven't you, and what you went through?"

"Yeah. I think about him a lot." Gaelan stared at his iced tea. "Baby," Mrs. Dawkins massaged his forearm, "You can't bring him back and you can't change the past. It's what you do from here that defines you."

"That's where your wrong. I think what I did just after Anfernee was killed is what defines me."

Mr. Dawkins put a hand on Gaelan's shoulder, "Son, I want you to listen to me and listen to me good. This is gonna be hard to hear, but," He waited for Gaelan to meet his eye, "your parents' deaths don't have anything to do with what happened after our boy died."

Gaelan's breathing was shallow, "You don't know what…"

Mr. Dawkins cut him off, "Son, did Anfernee ever tell you I was in the army?"

Gaelan nodded, "Infantry."

"Well, I was in a couple of places that weren't all too friendly. It don't take no rocket scientist to listen to your citation and realize what happened."

Gaelan was wide-eyed, his mouth open and his glassed over, "You know?"

"Not everything, but it's easy to figure out. People in that position sometimes can't hold back. What they do, they do outta love and loss, as messed up as that may sound. Whatever you did—it doesn't make you anything less for it. You're a *good person* Gaelan Kelly. You are."

"You don't know that." Gaelan shook his head.

"Son, your parents didn't die to fulfill some universal justice. It may seem that way, but it's not. You can't blame yourself for what happened—for what happened to our boy or what happened to them. Life just has a funny way of throwing a shit-sandwich at you and seeing just how much you can swallow. You gotta start livin' for yourself, not tryin' to make up for some perceived sins of the past."

"It should've been me that kicked in the door. I should've taken the hits. I should've gone down." I single tear trickled down Gaelan's cheek.

"But it wasn't." Mrs. Dawkins interjected, "That still doesn't make it your fault. And that don't make what happened to your parents some kind of karma. You gotta realize that baby. You don't need to accept it right now, but some day you're gonna realize that things happen for a reason, but not the reasons you might think."

"I really wish I could believe that, but there are things in this world that make me doubt it." Gaelan looked down at his plate. Evil was real. People died. His sins were revisited upon him, and upon those he loved.

"It's okay to doubt son." Mr. Dawkins' tone reminded Gaelan of his own father, "It's just not okay to blame yourself. You say you're helpin' people, then keep on helpin'. Keep your head clear and keep pressin' ahead. If you're only lookin' where you've been, you'll never see where you're goin' or what you need to do to get there." Gaelan silently nodded, but was still full of doubt.

Gaelan listened to more of the Dawkins' small talk, and cleaned his plate, enjoying the warmth of their home despite the emptiness he felt.

"You sure we can't get you to stay baby?" Mrs Dawkins was half pleading.

"I'm sure. I gotta get to the airport. I fly back overseas tomorrow."

He said his goodbyes and drove off, not knowing where to.

Still ready to hunt.
Would also like to talk.
Could use a friend right now.
Please call me.

There was no response from Denny. As he drove, he thought about Anfernee, lifeless in his arms. He thought about his parents—how they were ripped from him. He thought about putting the gun to his temple the morning after he first transformed. He drove for a while before pulling over at a desolate part of the highway. He got out and sat on the ground, leaning against the front bumper of his car. The night air was crisp and the moon was less than a quarter full, waning toward the new. He took out a bottle of bourbon and took a long swig, paused for a moment, then pulled out his cell.

There was a knock at the door. Becca Guerin, doing her homework on the living room sofa, looked at her mother.

"Get over here sweetie." Jennifer crossed the room and looked through the peephole, "Who is it?"

She didn't immediately recognize the man and woman standing outside her door.

"Ms. Guerin, I'm with National Geographic. We met in Canada about a year and a half ago. I was wondering if we could ask you some follow-up questions."

"Just a minute!" She looked at Becca, "Get in there and hide. You know what to do."

"Mommy..."

"Don't argue, just do it!" Her voice was a harsh whisper and Becca ran to the coat closet, clutching her stuffed animal. Jennifer Guerin displayed the cross around her neck prominently and cautiously opened the door, "Um, this seems kinda late for an interview." She eyed them suspiciously.

"It's just a couple of questions regarding animal attack survivors and how they cope. Can we come in?" He looked down and saw the line of salt along the base of the door.

"Sure, come on in." She took a step back and kept her distance. Then she nodded at the counter, "I poured you some water. Please, have some."

Trey looked at Natalia and then at the goblets—silver with ornate religious symbols etched into them. He picked them up, handed one to Natalia and said, "I'm not real thirsty right now."

Jennifer Guerin immediately reached her hands behind her back and pulled out a .45 caliber pistol and a sharpened iron stake, "I insist!" Her hand was steady.

Trey looked at Natalia and nodded, "Na zdrowie!" He took a huge mouthful of water, opened his mouth to show Jennifer and then gulped it down. Natalia was less animated, but followed suit. He finished swallowing and smiled at Jennifer, "I prefer my holy water with ice." He looked to Natalia, "Do you think we can get Malaria from old holy water? That would just be a kick in the ass, wouldn't it?"

Jennifer Guerin slowly lowered her weapon, "Who are you?"

"Well, there's salt along the door frame and some etchings along the foundation of your house. The UV light over the door is a nice touch and then you handed us these silver goblets, very pretty by the way, with holy water, all before pulling the pistol on us. I'm assuming the bullets are silver, holy water dipped and blessed in multiple religions? Same with the stake?" Trey noticed the subtle look of astonishment on her face, "Either you are the most superstitious woman that we have ever met, or you have a pretty good idea of who we are?"

"You're those...*hunters*."

"We prefer *venators*." Natalia scanned the entryway and living room.

"Yeah, that's it. Father Gutiérrez told me about you." Jennifer tucked the pistol behind her back and into her pants.

"First and foremost Ms. Guerin, never invite somebody in. The blessings you have etched into your foundation are to prevent the entry of unwanted evil—*unwanted*. The second you invite something into your house, it's no longer *unwanted*. Always play it off with something like 'the door's open', or 'what's stopping you?'" Trey cocked his head, "And why all these precautions anyway? It was a bear that attacked your group in Canada, right?"

"And you told us that you were with National Geographic, just like you said when you knocked." Jennifer eyed Natalia, who was now exploring the living room, "Excuse me..." Before Jennifer could speak, Trey interjected.

"Fair point, but I'm sure the good Father told you why we are so discrete?"

"Yeah. Something about general knowledge of these things would lead to more loss of life than tracking them in secret."

"That's the general idea." Trey was trying to keep Jennifer talking while Natalia looked around. "That's a nice piece. Where did you get it?"

Jennifer was focused on Natalia's examination of the living room, "The local supplier is a rabbi...Rabbi Frohman."

"Quality equipment. We'll have to remember that if we're ever..."

"Can I help you?" Jennifer took a step in Natalia's direction.

"Yes, you can. We thought you had a daughter." Natalia was monotone.

Jennifer was caught off guard, "I—she's at a relative's house." Jennifer pulled the pistol back out and moved her finger over the trigger. Trey noticed.

"Miss Guerin, we don't mean anything by that. It's just that we think there is, well, a thing that may have shown an interest in your daughter."

"A *thing*?"

"Yes, a person we know to be, well, not a person. We think he may have some sort of interest in your daughter. We also believe he's responsible for the disappearance of your tour guide back in Canada." Trey watched as Jennifer's brow furrowed in anger, "We were wondering if we could talk with her—with both of you?"

"I think you both should leave. Now!" Jennifer began tapping the pistol against her leg.

"It's okay," Natalia raised her voice louder, "WE'RE REALLY CLOSE TO CORNERING GAELAN AND KILLING HIM."

"NOOOOO!" Rebecca burst out of the closet and ran to her mother, "MOMMY, DON'T LET THEM HURT GAELAN!"

"You know Gaelan Kelly?" Trey was taken back.

Jennifer Guerin was kneeling and holding Becca close, "Shhhhh, baby, it's OK." She looked up, "The real question is, do *you* know Gaelan Kelly?"

"We know he's a bloodthirsty killer." Trey half growled.

"Then I guess you really don't know him at all." Jennifer stood, handed Trey her pistol and walked toward her kitchen, "You sound American, and she -" She nodded toward Natalia, "sounds Eastern European. Whiskey or vodka?"

"I'm Canadian!" Trey retorted, confused.

Natalia shrugged and followed Becca and Jennifer into the next room "Vodka. Please."

Jennifer took out a bottle of vodka, cut up a lime, and filled four glasses with ice. She poured fruit juice into one and gave it to Becca. She put the others on the table in front of Trey, along with the lime slices and the bottle. No one said a word as she poured the vodka and dropped a slice of lime in each glass. She raised her glass to her guests, "What was it you said? Nasdra..." She paused.

"Na zdrowie." Trey nodded and drank.

"Na zdrowie." Natalia drank.

"Nozdrovia!" Jennifer took a drink.

"Good enough." Trey fidgeted with his glass.

"What's it mean anyway?" Jennifer took a sip.

"It's a way of saying *cheers* in Polish." Natalia's tone was still icy.

Jennifer nodded, "I like it."

"You were saying that we don't know Gaelan Kelly." Trey's gaze bordering on rage. "What makes you say that?"

"Because he's a superhero, that's why!" Becca's glare was equally intense. Chuckling, despite himself at Becca's response, Trey pulled out a chair and joined the women at the small kitchen table.

Natalia's tone softened as she turned to Becca, "Becca, right?" Becca nodded and Natalia looked to Jennifer, "May I?"

"Oh please, be my guest."

Natalia ignored the sarcasm in Jennifer's voice, "Becca, that's a nice stuffed animal." Natalia motioned to the fuzzy object in Becca's lap "Is that a wolf?"

"Yup!"

"You like wolves?"

"Most."

"There are some wolves you don't like?"

Becca looked at her mother and her mother nodded, "The wolf monsters. I don't like them. I sleep with my lights on because of them."

"So do I sweetie," Trey interjected, "which is why we need to find Gaelan. He's a wolf monster sweetie—a werewolf."

Becca pursed her lips and glared at Trey, ready to defend her friend again.

"Gaelan is no more a werewolf than you or I." Jennifer calmly reached over and massaged her daughter's back, as if to sooth her.

"Ma'am—Miss Guerin—I hate to burst your bubble, but I can absolutely guarantee you that he's a werewolf."

Jennifer took another sip of vodka and winced, "Damn, I don't usually drink it straight!" Her tone was friendly, "So you've watched him kill people? Tear someone apart?" She raised her eyebrows.

Trey looked to Natalia and back to Jennifer, "I'm not sure how to tell you this, but he admitted that he killed your tour guide. The young woman that went missing that night."

Natalia watched Jennifer and Becca's bodies tense.

"That bitch deserved it." Becca's words dripped with ice.

"REBECCA MARIE GUERIN!"

"What mommy? I'm not deaf. I heard what Gaelan said when he covered my ears!"

"That doesn't mean you get to repeat it, now apologize to our guests!"

"But they want to hurt Gaelan!"

"Apologize young lady—Now!"

Becca looked at Natalia and Trey and muttered, "Sorry."

Trey's mouth hung open. "What the Hell?"

"It means that our tour guide was exactly what Becca called her, or rather repeated what Gaelan called her."

"And that means she deserved to die?" Trey was appalled.

"If you only knew how literal Becca is being." Jennifer sipped and winced again.

He looked at Becca and then back to Jennifer, "Since when does someone who acts like a jerk deserve to *die*?"

"We never said it was because she was a jerk. Though she was that. We said," Jennifer looked toward her daughter, "and don't you dare repeat it again little missy. We said that she was a *bitch*."

"What is wrong with you?" Trey was aghast.

"*Bitch*." Natalia paused, resting a hand on Trey's forearm, knowing that she had to guide him back to the conversation.

Jennifer raised her eyebrows, acknowledging that Natalia understood.

"Bitch. Like a female dog. You're saying that she was…" Natalia looked to Trey, and watched the realization light his face.

"SHE WAS A WEREWOLF?" Trey sputtered.

"Yeah, she was a werewolf, in the truest sense of the word. And she and her pack wanted nothing more than to tear us apart." Jennifer continued to rub Becca's back.

"Pack?"

"Yes, *pack*. Five of them."

"They don't hunt in packs." Trey shook his head.

"Oh really?" Jennifer took another sip.

"Ma'am, my team and I have killed nine wolves, and never once have they hunted in packs."

"Well maybe you need to get out a little more." Jennifer smirked.

"Look, there's no recorded evidence of them hunting in packs, so you're saying that you saw something that no hunter in over two thousand years has seen."

"Or lived to tell about it." Natalia interjected, making the same point Gaelan made to her.

"What?"

"What she said." Jennifer motioned to Natalia. "Who else has a chance against a pack of werewolves other than, you know, *Gaelan*?"

"Jesus f'ing..." Trey pushed his chair back with a screech. "Jennifer, can you please just tell us, plain and simple, what happened?"

"He saved us. Plain and simple." Becca chimed in with a look of contempt that matched her mother's.

Jennifer snorted in an attempt to stifle a laugh at Trey's bewilderment. Natalia took another sip of vodka to hide her own smile.

"Be nice sweetie." Jennifer half-rebuked her daughter and turned back to Trey, "The bit..." She caught herself and looked at Becca, "I mean the female dog lady, was our tour guide and brought us to an area where her non-existent-until-now-pack–" Trey rolled his eyes, "disabled our car and wounded one of the hikers. We all thought it was a bear. That's what she told us. And we followed her, not realizing that she was leading us into a trap. Another hiker was wounded when he tried to peel off from the group. Just enough to still be mobile—just like the first guy. We saw the outline of the thing that did it and out of nowhere, this incredible, and good-looking," She raised her eyebrows to Natalia and then continued, "man, Gaelan, dives on the thing and starts beating it and stabbing at it. Then a second one shows up and he fights enough to force them both back. He joins us and follows the female dog, Evelyn—that's what she went by—and it turns out that he can see in the dark. Of course, we found out why later on."

Trey interrupted, "Wait, what? He can see in the dark? And it was the full moon but he hadn't changed?"

"Yes and yes." Jennifer snapped at Trey. "Anyway it turns out he was watching the two things, the werewolves, keeping their distance and herding us in the direction we're going. Evelyn had told us there was a ranger tower where we could call for help and Gaelan figured that he could defend it. Then he sees *two more* werewolves waiting for us, and he starts pushing us to hurry. We get into the valley and there's no tower, but for some reason the wolves aren't attacking. Gaelan was the one who put two and two together. Evelyn says that she's going to turn him and make…" Jennifer started to tear up, and the hand rubbing Becca's back picked up speed "I'm sorry. She said she'd make Becca's death quick and the rest of us were the feast. Well that BITCH didn't realize that Gaelan was already, you know, *gifted*, and he drove a silver blade right through her goddamned heart," She wiped her eyes and glared at Trey, "and then he handed me the knife. I didn't know what for. He turned to Becca," She choked back a sob, "and said that he had to do something horrible to keep his promise." She paused to compose herself.

"What promise?" Trey asked, his tone almost respectful.

Becca spoke so that her mother didn't have to, "He promised me that he wouldn't let anything happen to me or anyone else. He doesn't make promises that he doesn't keep."

"What horrible thing did he do sweetheart?" Natalia's voice was soft. The hair on the back of her neck was standing up, knowing what Gaelan himself had already conveyed to her.

Jennifer composed herself, "He turned into something that we absolutely could not believe. Something horrible, but something incredible. He changed right in front of all of us as we watched, totally dumbfounded. This incredible person had changed into the very thing that was hunting us, so he could *fight them*. He killed two more in front of us. The last two ran off. He hunted them down the next day, but that's beside the point. The point is that he handed me a silver blade to kill him after he fought those things. After he was weak. Becca here ran to him. It was still him in there, even though he was *different*." She looked at Trey and Natalia, trying to get them to understand, "I thought that he was going kill her and I charged at him with the knife." Jennifer laughed, "As torn up as he was, he grabbed me and lifted me off the ground. But he didn't hurt me. He just looked down at Becca while I screamed and pleaded with him. I thought he was going to kill her, but with God as my judge, you can ask anyone there, he hugged her instead. He put his hand on her back, and pressed her against him. Then he let me go and he collapsed. I could've killed him, but I didn't. I couldn't. We stayed with him all night nursing his wounds and covering him up. This one right here," She caressed her daughter's face, "she wouldn't leave his side." Jennifer looked to Trey with a firm yet caring gaze, "So yeah, Gaelan is no more a werewolf than you or I."

"But you just said you watched him change!" Trey was confused.

"Mommy he doesn't understand." Becca was almost pitying.

"What don't I understand?"

"I tell Becca every night. There are the wolf monsters, the *werewolves*. And then there's Gaelan. He could've—should've torn us to pieces, but he didn't. Sure, he may occasionally look like them, but no matter what he thinks or what anyone else thinks, we know that he's the furthest thing from a werewolf there is. And that's the story Mr. Marshall, *plain and simple*, just like you asked." Jennifer finished her drink and took a deep breath, "All I can ask is that if and when you find him, you realize that. He won't ever hurt you because he's not what you think he is. I'd stake my life on it."

Trey looked at her, not knowing what to think, "Thank you Miss Guerin."

"Please, call me Jennifer." She insisted.

"Thank you Jennifer. We'll be going now," Trey stood up, "but one last thing. Becca, did Gaelan send you that toy?"

Becca nodded and hugged it tightly.

"It arrived yesterday. After all, he made a promise to keep in touch and like Becca said, he won't make promises that he can't or won't keep."

Trey nodded his head and he walked to the door with Natalia in trail.

"Thank you Jennifer."

"Mr. Marshall?"

"Trey." He insisted this time.

"Okay, Trey. It was Gaelan who sent us to Father Gutiérrez. He was the one who told us about the hunters and told me to take care of them. You and any other hunter like you are always welcome in my house. Stay safe."

Trey nodded and smiled. He turned to leave.

"Mr. Marshall?"

Trey turned around to the soft voice that beckoned him, "Yes Becca, what is it?"

"Don't hurt him. Please don't hurt Gaelan. Please!" Becca had tears in her eyes.

Trey was speechless. He smiled weakly and half-nodded, then walked out with Natalia in trail.

Trey gripped the steering wheel tightly, "Is everyone around here batshit crazy, or did I miss something?"

"They say he didn't attack them." Natalia repeated. Gaelan hadn't fed her a bunch of lies. She was relieved—surprised at how relieved she actually was—but what the hell was she suppose to think now?

"My ass. If that story is true, then he probably collapsed from the exhaustion. But seriously, for as long as we've been doing this, have you ever heard of them hunting in packs? And who knows what lies he fed to them." Trey was disgusted, "And that poor little girl thinks he's some kind of hero. Holy shit, this guy is incorrigible."

"So what do you want to do?" Natalia probed.

"You were right. He does have a thing for this family, but I don't think he's heading this way anytime soon. I say we ask a local contact to keep an eye out."

"Alright, I'll take care of it." Natalia kept her tone neutral.

"Thanks." Trey drove to the hotel and they walked to their rooms, "We have an early flight tomorrow. Hopefully Angel and Kedar had more luck than we did."

Natalia nodded her head as she went to her hotel room. She washed up and got into bed. She had started to nod off when the phone rang.

"Hello?"

A voice answered in Polish, *"Don't hang up, please."*

"Who is this?" Natalia sat up.

"It's..." He tried to think of something clever but couldn't. He answered in English *"It's Gaelan."*

"How did you get this number?" Natalia was surprised and angered.

"In Germany. You dropped your phone in the car. I dialed my number before I gave it back to you, so I'd have it. Sorry."

"Are you really sorry or is this some type of sick obsession?"

"I'm truly sorry. Father Denny hasn't answered my calls in days and I just needed to hear a familiar voice."

"I'm not familiar Gaelan. I don't know what kind of game you're playing…"

"I know, that's why I'm calling. I'm gonna have to break that promise to you."

"What promise?" She was caught off guard, wondering what he was talking about.

"That promise to see you smile before one of us dies. It's not gonna happen." He sounded defeated.

Natalia's tone turned curious, less indignant, "Why, what's happened? Did you hurt someone?"

"No. NO! Nothing like that. I'm just done. Done with all of it. I already explained it to you and I can't even get one of your friends to shoot me. I've finally decided that I can do it myself."

It took a moment for Natalia to realize that he was talking about the park ranger. Then she realized she could hear the slurring in his speech. "Have you been drinking?"

"No. Yeah. Yes, okay? Yes. I've been drinking."

"Oh that's a good way for a manic depressive to act." Natalia rebuked him.

"I'm not a manic depressive!"

"Jesus Gaelan, I had one conversation with you and you are the walking definition of a manic depressive!"

"Well, what do you care? We're not familiar, right?" He unsheathed his sword and laid it in front of him. His father's knife was already lying on the ground in front of him.

"It doesn't mean I want you to kill yourself."

"Wha… I don't get you! You shoot me, then you don't stab me, then you won't kill me when I want you to, but tell me that you're going to when you

see me next, and then tell me you don't want me to kill myself. Have YOU been drinking?"

"No! Yes, but just a little. That's not the point! I just don't know why you are so determined to do it now?"

"What do you care?"

"I figured you needed a reason to call me." She tried to keep him talking.

"Well, as stalker-creepy as that sounds, I actually just called to tell you where I am."

"Why would you do that?"

"Same reason as Germany. I want you to come and get the sword and the knife, but I changed my mind. Give the sword to Father Denny, but give the knife to Trey. He found it after my parents were killed and he seemed to like it. At least he can put it to some good use." Gaelan took a deep breath. He was accepting what he was about to do, *"And tell Father Denny it wasn't his fault. I just couldn't do this anymore."*

Natalia leaned into her phone, as if she could reach out to him, "Why now Gaelan? Tell me."

"I went to visit Anfernee's parents..."

"Anfernee. Your friend from the military? From the battle?"

"Yeah, that's him. It was tough. Before that, I went to my parents' grave. I told you Nat, there's no one. I can't reach out to Father Denny anymore. I'm sick and tired of all the death that surrounds us—surrounds me. I just want to be done with it all, so please find a way to come get the sword and knife. And tell Trey and the guys that I'm sorry. Or don't. It really doesn't matter."

She realized he was actually serious and for some reason, felt helpless about it, "Don't."

"What?"

"Don't. Please. Don't do it."

"Nat, no offense, but you're confusin' the ever-livin' shit outta me."

"I told you not to call me Nat!"

"Don't change the subject—Nat!"

She could picture his smug expression, but at least she still had him talking, "Why would you do this? Why would you just give up?"

"I didn't call you to talk me out of it. I called because I wanted you to come get the sword and knife, that's all."

"No, you called because," She changed her voice to try to sound like him, "you wanted to hear a familiar voice."

"I don't sound like that! And yes, maybe I wanted to hear a familiar voice before I take my life. I just figured I'd call someone that would be happy that I'm doing it. Jesus, what is wrong with you?"

"What's wrong with me? What the hell is wrong with you? Why would I be happy? You're the one about to quit on life and break not one, but two, promises you made me, Mr. I-don't-make-promises-I-don't-keep!" She tried to imitate his voice again.

"I just wanted to talk to someone before…"

"Then talk! But don't be a liar and back out on what you promised."

"What do you mean by TWO promises?"

She had him thinking about something else now, "Yes, two. The first was the smile. I didn't even remember that one, and I'm not sure that's ever going to happen so don't hold your breath. But the second was that I get to kill you."

"What?"

"The paper. The IOU."

"Fuck." He realized she was right.

"It's a written contract Gaelan. That's a promise." There was silence at the other end. Natalia wanted to make sure he was listening, "You did promise me Gaelan, and you don't make promises you can't or won't keep."

"What's it matter to you anyway?"

"Maybe the man I met in Germany wasn't the same man I thought we've been hunting all this time. Maybe the man I met didn't strike me as a quitter. Maybe I still feel I owe you something for saving my life. Or maybe I'm just like you, and I'm sick and tired of the death that surrounds us and I don't need you to add your corpse to the pile."

"Why not?" His tone was serious.

She was taken back by the question, "I don't…"

"Why not Nat? Why would you want me to live?"

"Because I do! Because I'm your *angel*, right? What kind of angel wants to see their person dead?"

Gaelan took a breath, *"I'm sorry Nat, I won't call you anymore."*

"I didn't say tha...WAIT!" She tried to keep him talking.

"What?"

"Promise me."

"What?"

"Promise me you won't do it!" Her voice changed, "Please!" She could hear him breathing heavily. She could only imagine he was debating what to do, "Gaelan?"

"I promise."

"What?"

"I promise I won't kill myself tonight."

"Or any other night! Promise me."

"I promise I won't kill myself at all. Okay? FOR CHRIST'S SAKE, I JUST WANTED SOMEONE TO COME GET MY SHIT, THAT'S ALL! What do you want me to do?"

"I want you to live. To hunt, to fight, and to live! Do what you set out to do and find the one that took your family. Don't quit. That's what I'd expect of them, not you. If you're going to die, at least go out fighting. Protecting. Go out helping us. Just like you said, let one of these hunts finally kill you."

"Why does it matter to you?"

She thought about it, "You can ask me that another time. Just remember that you promised!"

—§—

Gaelan looked at the device in his hand and shook his head. He looked up at the quarter moon and took another drink. He resheathed his katana and his father's knife. He closed his eyes and saw Anfernee, the men he killed in combat, his parents, and the monster that made him. He clenched his fists and then pictured Natalia. His breathing slowed and he calmed himself before fading off to sleep.

The next morning he awoke to a buzzing sound. He was still in the deserted field. The empty bottle of bourbon sat next to him, not far from the katana and ka-bar. His phone—the buzzing was his phone:

Did you keep your promise?

It was from Natalia.

Yes.

He stood up and began to throw his gear in the car when the phone buzzed again:

Good.
Now go see a certain little girl in Michigan.
She and her mom would really like to see you.
Don't ask about it.
Text after your next hunt.

He wasn't sure what to make of it. He didn't know if he should be hurt or impressed that she had checked up on his story.

He drove north. When he finally arrived at the Guerin house, Jennifer and Becca hugged him so tight that he thought they would crack a rib. He stayed for dinner and a good night's rest, telling them about all of the hunts he had been on over the last eighteen months. They teased him about Natalia when he told them about their adventures in the German woods, and they all laughed and cried deep into the night. Before going to bed that night, he sent one last message:

In Michigan now.
Thank you!

Natalia didn't receive the message until after she landed in Austria. She fought back the urge to smile.

CHAPTER 4
PERSPECTIVE

Gaelan waited until Becca was outside to talk to Jennifer. He didn't know any other way to say it, so he just let it out, "The night before last, I was going to kill myself."

"WHAT?" Jennifer was taken completely by surprise.

"I was ready to do it. It wasn't the first time I thought about it, but it was the closest I had come since the first time I realized what I was."

"Why would you want to do that? What's going on?"

"We never really talked about it, but when I was bitten and became, you know..."

"You can say it Gaelan, it's not like it's a secret." Jennifer tried to put him at ease.

"When I became a werewolf, the thing that attacked me killed my parents right in front of me."

"Oh my God Gaelan, I'm sorry. I never kn..."

"It's okay, not many people do. Before that, I lost my best friend overseas when we were in the military. I lost people in China when we were hunting these horrible underground monsters. I'm constantly surrounded by death and I don't want to do it anymore. I just want it to be over." He shook his head in defeat.

"Gaelan honey, you have been through more than any person should ever have to experience, but you can't..."

Gaelan interrupted her before she could finish, "I visited my parents' grave for the first time since they were taken. Then I saw my buddy's folks. I don't think you understand—I couldn't save my best friend, I couldn't save my parents, I can't save all the people that are torn apart by things that shouldn't even exist. Things like *me!*"

"Not to be blunt sweetie, but that's a goddamned cop out!" Gaelan was caught off guard by Jennifer's tone. "People die everyday! Lots of people every—single—day. It's a fact of life. It sucks! We can't even sleep with the lights off anymore. But you can fight. You're able to make a difference. The crazy thing is, you have something inside you that you hate, but those of us that have witnessed it, see it for what it truly is—a gift." She saw Gaelan's grimace but pressed on. "Not to mention you seem to have forgotten that *you,* lucky bastard that you are, can live forever" She raised a hand to silence Gaelan's protests. "I remember what that bitch Evelyn said to you about immortality. And yet you want to take your own life? Life may have dealt you a shitty hand, trust me, I get it. But it's how you play it that defines you. There are plenty of assholes out there who would trade places with you in a heartbeat, and for selfish reasons too. I understand that more than you know. But you, whether or not *you* know it, whether or not *they* know it, are there for people that *need* you. You don't get to stop Gaelan. And if you need proof of it then," Jennifer turned toward the window, "BECCA!"

Jennifer's daughter came running in from outside, "What is it mommy?"

"I think Gaelan needs a hug."

"Oh." Becca giggled and threw herself onto him.

Gaelan smiled at Jennifer over Becca's ginger hair, feeling her every heartbeat, the rise and fall of her back with every breath, while tears formed in his own eyes.

Hours later, Gaelan was cleaning the dishes when his phone buzzed.

Sorry kiddo, everything okay?

Jennifer came up behind him, "Go on. I'm guessing you need to take that."

"No. It's okay..."

"Go!" She smiled at him and took over at the sink.

He walked to the side and wrote:

Everything is good now.
I'll be okay.
What about you?

There was a brief pause and Father Denny wrote back:

Things okay.
Not great.
We'll talk in person soon.
Have a job for you.
Actually need your help bad.

—§—

Send it

—§—

Slovenia.
Missing persons.
One team missing as well.
Fear the worst.
Need your help.
Sorry

—§—

Don't be.
I'll fly out ASAP.
Talk to you soon

—§—

Thanks kiddo!
Be safe.

Gaelan walked back into the kitchen with a worn look on his face.

"You have to leave, don't you?" Jennifer was drying her hands when she saw Gaelan. He nodded. She walked to him and touched the side of his face, "It's funny, back in Canada, I tried to convince you to stay with us. But now, I wouldn't let you stay if you wanted to. I couldn't. Not when there are people out there that need your help." She caressed his cheek with her thumb, then suddenly pulled his face to hers and kissed him. He dropped his arms partway, not knowing what to do, then embraced her and reciprocated her passion. They lost track of the amount of time and finally released one another. She looked up at him, breathing heavily, "Okay, I had to do that just once. Now go do what you need to and, if you get the chance, go find that little chippy that was here asking about you and start hunting with *her*." Her smile was meaningful.

Gaelan's face turned red, "Wha...what are you talking about? I don't even..."

"Oh please, even I wouldn't kick her outta bed. Now you need to say goodbye to someone."

Gaelan closed his eyes and reluctantly nodded.

"You're leaving again, aren't you?" Becca looked up from the laundry she was folding as Gaelan and her mother walked in.

"Yeah munchkin. I have to."

"I know. I just wish it wasn't so soon." She hugged him tight, "You're gonna help people, right?"

"That's right."

"Good. We'll be here when you come back to visit."

Gaelan knelt, smiling, "Do me a favor—don't grow up too fast, okay?"

"Too late." Becca grinned back, stretching onto her tippy toes. He gave her a kiss on the forehead and stood to do the same to Jennifer.

They walked him to his car and Jennifer tried to sound confident as tears trickled down her cheeks, "This is what you're meant to do, now go get 'em." He nodded and drove away. Gaelan spent half of the ride to the airport thinking about the emotional roller coaster of the past few months. He tried to clear his head and think about the hunt ahead and the missing team. He arrived at the airport and bought a ticket to Slovenia, thinking about where to begin.

CHAPTER 5
INTERTWINED

Gaelan arrived in the Slovenian capital of Ljubljana a day later. According to Father Denny, a local priest had reported that the bodies that were discovered looked like victims of animal attacks, mostly in pieces, and unidentified. With so little to go on, Gaelan decided to take the reporter cover again and went to the last hotel the missing team had stayed at.

From the outside, the hotel was a bland and modern structure that didn't stand out in any way. Inside, the lobby's contemporary decor was inviting—comfortable, Gaelan thought, but no culture. He casually strolled to the concierge desk and spoke in fluent Slovene, "Good afternoon Sir, I was wondering if I might inquire about a friend of mine that I was supposed to meet here."

The concierge was polite and inviting, "Certainly. What's the name?"

"László Kovács." The team leader's Hungarian cover.

"I'm sorry Sir, it appears you missed him. He checked out two days ago."

"Checked out? Are you certain?"

"Yes Sir. It has the checkout time and says he paid in cash." The concierge looked up, "I'm very sorry." It didn't make sense that a team that vanished had neatly checked out of their hotel. He decided to head to the police station and inquire about the three missing persons.

At the station, Gaelan deliberately made his Slovene sound broken, claiming that he was a freelance reporter looking into the disappearances, but to no avail. The team was missing, the police were silent on three bodies that had been discovered, and he wasn't sure about his next move. Faced with dead ends, he decided to take a look at the spot where the bodies had been found. He headed to the east side of the city, about a kilometer shy of where the Ljubljanica River flows into the Sava. It was there that the river flows around a tiny island of trees and grass with a sandy area on west side. It was also there that the bodies had been found.

Gaelan looked all over the island then crossed over to the south side of the river. He strolled up and down the paralleling highway and railroad tracks, looking for an obvious kill site or nesting area. *Nothing.* There was a large forested area to the south, but it didn't make any sense. In New York, the vampire had wanted the bodies to be found. The unidentified and torn corpses here were meant to remain hidden—why would they kill and feed in the forest, then dump the bodies elsewhere? He made it about half- a-kilometer, backtracking up the river when he came to an overpass bridge. The dozen or so homeless men living underneath were none too happy to see him, glaring stonily from across the river.

Twenty minutes later, Gaelan approached the bridge for the second time, this time on the side of the river where the homeless men crouched. As he ducked past the first station, a number of the men started to yell, waving homemade clubs, broken bottles, and at least one shiv, ominously. But this was no display of anger. The men were terrified. Gaelan squatted down, refusing to back away, "I want to talk about the bodies that were found." The men's breath quickened. Gaelan sat, attempting to appear unthreatening. "I want to find out who did it and I want to stop them. I could use a little information." The group continued to eye him suspiciously. Gaelan could barely make out their whispers " *... not a cop... doesn't care about us... kill him first.*" He called back out, "I'm not a cop. I asked, but the cops didn't want to help. I'm employed by an organization that takes things like this pretty seriously. You have no reason to believe me, but I'm here to help."

"YOU CAN'T HELP! GO AWAY!" It was hard to tell from which of the disheveled, bearded, dirty men the yell erupted from.

"That may be, but I'm going to try. If I can't ask questions, I guess I might as well sit here and wait for something to happen." Gaelan reached into the grocery bag and brought out a bottle of plum brandy. He popped the top and took a drink, "Mmmmmm, this slivovka is tasty." He took another sip.

One man ventured forward, brushing past his comrades admonitions to stay still.

"The bodies washed up on the bank about a half-kilometer up." His eyes darted from Gaelan's face to the bottle in his hand.

Gaelan nodded, "That much I know. I was just there, but there's nothing." He took another drink. He saw the man's eyes move to the bottle, "The river?" Gaelan motioned towards the water, "Has anyone seen anything?"

"Aleks did. Didn't you?"

"QUIET!" Another man, apparently Aleks, snarled.

"I just want to talk." Gaelan tossed the bottle to the first man, who grabbed it from the air and greedily twisted the top off. Aleks grabbed the bottle from his buddy and took a swig. The first man howled in protest, signaling a fight, when Gaelan reached into the bag and took out another bottle, "Settle down. That's not how you look out for each other." Gaelan took a drink, and motioned for the men to share.

Aleks spoke, "We don't like outsiders in these parts. What if we decided to take your stuff and float you down the river?"

Gaelan closed his eyes and slowly cranked his head side to side, cracking the bones in his neck, "You're more than welcome to try." No one moved forward and several men put their weapons out of sight, "No takers?" He looked around the group, "Okay, then let's keep talking."

"No one here wants to talk." Aleks was adamant.

"I'm not trying to frighten you, but I need more information or else I think there are going to be more bodies."

"No there won't." Aleks took a drink and stared down Gaelan.

"What makes you so sure?"

"The parts stopped floating three days ago."

"The parts?"

"What they found, those were the big pieces." Aleks took another drink and stared intently at the ground as if lost in thought. No one seemed to want to ask him for the bottle still gripped in his hand. Gaelan tossed the second bottle to one of the other men.

"Aleks? ALEKS?" Gaelan raised his voice to snap Aleks back to the conversation. The man no longer looked confrontational. As he lifted the bottle to his lips once more, his face was full of fear.

"What did you see?"

"The parts—body parts, floating down the river."

"Do you know where they came from?" Aleks just stared. "Aleks, do you know?"

Aleks answered, shaken, "Up the river. I moved down here with others to get away."

"Why did you feel the need to move?"

Another one of the men spoke up, "Why do you think the police don't care about the bodies?" Gaelan looked at the man quizzically. "No one reported those people missing. No one reported *any of us* missing. We're the forgotten. No one cares."

Gaelan dropped his head, realizing that he was among those that society turned a blind eye to. He looked up, "Why are you so sure it's stopped?"

"You say you work for some interested organization? The reporters we talked to before went up river and then everything stopped. I don't know if they found what they were looking for, or if it found them. I don't really care either."

"Reporters? Four of them?" Gaelan immediately thought of the other Venántium team.

"Yeah. They said they had talked to other people around the city and they thought that the bodies were people that had disappeared from some of the homeless shelters."

"That's why you're all here and not at a shelter?" Gaelan looked around. He observed the collective nods. "Can you show me where you think the bodies were coming from?"

"No one is going with you mister" An elderly man with chipped teeth piped up.

"No one is going, but I can tell you." Gaelan nodded and Aleks continued, "Go north, where the main highway crosses the river. That's where I used to stay. Just to the west, along the south bank, there's a stream that empties into the river. That's where I saw them coming from."

"Thank you." Gaelan looked around, "Stay in a group and watch out for each other." The men watched as he went up to the top of the road. He left the grocery bag behind. The original homeless man went over and opened the bag. Inside was another bottle of brandy and a couple of dozen cans of pasta in meat sauce with a can opener.

Gaelan backtracked down the river to his car and drove to the bridge that Aleks described, then walked westward about two hundred meters along the bank. He came to the stream, which he assumed the Venántium team had found as well. He grabbed his backpack, then started the trek along the stream once more. The sunlight began to dwindle. Any later and he would have missed the drainage pipe, about a meter in diameter, half submerged in the stream. Gaelan didn't fancy crawling down the pipe, so he squatted next to it and shone a flashlight inside. The smell of decay and death hit him immediately. The pipe stretched back further than the light could go. He decided to stay above ground and follow the path where the drainage pipe led. About a half kilometer up the bank, he came to an abandoned processing plant just as daylight was starting to fade.

A large metal door barely hung onto its hinges, open just wide enough to walk in without touching. Gaelan drew his katana from his pack and entered, taking care to be as silent as possible. His eyes were adjusting to the pitch-blackness. He walked into the heart of the structure, noting tall ceilings, cement walls, exposed steel girders and rod iron bars. He followed the sound of trickling water to the beginning of the drainage pipe. The smell of death was overwhelming. Gaelan dropped to a knee and rummaged through his pack. He slowly stood with his sword in one hand and a portable ultraviolet light in the other. The light worked to repel most creatures but also had another use. He raised it over his head and turned it on. The dust in the air, white flecks of paint on the walls all glowed eerie blue-white, but the floor where he stood was an inky, sticky black. It was too saturated with blood and fluids for this to be just another kill sight—*this was a butchering facility.*

Satisfied that the interior was deserted, he swept the grounds. Several sets of relatively fresh tire tracks led to the northbound lane on the main road. Soon after, he too was driving north. The vampire in New York had kept a room in a nice hotel—Gaelan had found the key after he killed the creature. Not much, but at least it was a place to start.

Half an hour later, he was settling in the lobby bar of an upscale hotel close to the center of town, observing his fellow patrons for anything out of the ordinary.

"It's horrible about those killings, eh?"

Gaelan was caught off guard by the bartender's question. Was his cover blown?

"You mean the bodies from a few days ago? Yeah, horrible."

The bartender looked at him wide-eyed, "No! You haven't heard? There were more bodies found up north, in Tržič."

"Tržič?" Gaelan paused.

"Yeah, horrible business." The bartender turned to another customer as Gaelan's mind raced. The homeless men were wrong. The killers hadn't stopped, they just migrated north. Was that why the Venators had checked out and disappeared? He took down his drink in one shot, dropped some cash on the bar and walked to his car. An hour later he was in Tržič.

Here too, body parts had washed up on the bank of the river. Gaelan left his backpack in the car and started to trace its path just before midnight. A disadvantage for sure, but the last thing he needed was to be caught with a katana and a knife so close to the crime scene. When the sun began to rise, he was exhausted and no closer to finding the creatures responsible for the killings. He checked into a local hotel and got a few hours of sleep before setting out again in the mid-morning.

Like he did in Ljubljana, he tracked down groups of homeless living underneath the bridges along the river. But unlike the men in Ljubljana, these people wouldn't talk, despite the brandy and food he offered. Their fear was palpable. He dropped the brandy and food, leaving frustrated. No features stood out on the tourist map he had purchased at the hotel. He either had to get really lucky or find someone that was talking—then he remembered what Aleks had said. *Dammit, why didn't I think of this sooner?* Gaelan backtracked to the bridge. One dingy man snarled from the shadows. "I didn't know you wanted it back! It's gone!" The grocery bag, now empty, was gripped in his dirty hand.

Gaelan held up his hands, "It's okay. That's not what I'm here for."

The man eyed Gaelan suspiciously, "Then what?"

"Homeless shelters in and around the city. Where are they?"

"There are four—three churches and a private shelter."

"The private shelter, where is it?"

"In the heart of the city, just south of the main shopping mall, by the entrance/exit ramp for the highway. There are signs."

"Okay. You have an extra jacket and pair of pants I can buy off you?"

"WHAT?"

Gaelan took out a handful of cash and handed it to the man, "That should be enough to get you some new clothes and a couple of good meals."

The man, now wide-eyed, took the money and gave Gaelan his pick of the clothing from a weathered bag. Gaelan took a ripped up jacket and the worst looking pair of pants he could find. He also grabbed a set of gloves, with many of the fingertips torn or missing. He traded another man some money for his torn boots and was on his way.

Gaelan figured whatever was responsible for the killings might be using the homeless shelters to pick victims that wouldn't be missed. The creature or creatures wouldn't be using the church shelters, so that left the private shelter. He picked up a cheap electric hair clipper at a hardware store, then shaved his head to match the stubble on his face. No longer suspiciously well groomed, he drove to an isolated spot by the river and parked. He stripped down naked and glanced around. There was no one to observe him as he dropped down in the semi-dry dirt by the water's edge. He grimaced, "Mom, you'd be horrified."

He put on the rags he bought from the homeless men and threw his own clothing, katana and bag in the trunk, then hid the key. He made his way back toward the shelter and took up residence across the street, watching it and making sure that he was seen. He acted twitchy, glancing suspiciously at the structure and pacing. It finally worked. Somewhere late day, a middle-aged woman came out of the shelter with a cup of coffee and walked across the street. She was shorter, pretty and plump, with dark hair.

"Coffee?" She asked.

Gaelan just eyed the woman, then the coffee, then back to her face, mimicking the suspicious glances the homeless men had greeted him with.

"It won't bite. The sun's not going to be up much longer and it's supposed to be a chilly night."

Gaelan cautiously took the paper cup.

"Are you from around here?"

He took a sip and shook his head, then took another sip.

"Do you have a place to sleep?" She looked him up and down, and seemed to note his lack of belongings.

He shook his head again.

"Why don't you come inside, have something warm to eat and decide for yourself if you want to stay. The soup kitchen is always open and we have beds." She smiled warmly.

Gaelan reluctantly nodded and followed her inside, maintaining his grudging façade. She led him to a table and walked away. He looked around and saw about a dozen other individuals around the room, some eating alone, some talking in groups and pairs.

"So, what brings you here?"

Gaelan snapped his head back around to see the woman had brought him some soup and a roll. Gaelan took a big bite out of the roll as if he was famished, and took a couple of spoonfuls of soup.

It was a salty broth with a little meat and vegetables, and lots of potatoes. She continued to smile while he looked down at the bowl. Finally, he spoke in fluent Slovene, "Came from the south. It's not safe there."

"Not safe. Is somebody after you?"

He shook his head vehemently, "No. It's just not safe. They found dead people on the river. I walked for a few days. Someone took all my stuff when I was sleeping two nights ago. I have nothing."

"Oh my. Don't worry about those things now. It's just like I said, we have soup and a warm bed. You can stay as long as you like and we have boxes of donated clothing in the back that you can pick from. This place is a sanctuary."

Gaelan grumbled a half-hearted, "Thank you."

"Do you have anybody you can call?" She inquired.

"No."

"Who cuts your hair?"

Gaelan took in more of the soup, acting as if he hadn't eaten in days, "Found a razor." He took a big bite of bread and talked with his mouth full, "Needed to get rid of the lice."

"Ahhhh, clever. I wish we had more thoughtful ones like you. It would make the sheet cleaning less arduous." She smiled and finally left him alone.

Gaelan finished the soup and sat, looking down most of the time, then glancing up suddenly, looking around and then back down. He hoped he was coming off as the kind of loner the killers were looking for. *God he was tired.* He spent the better part of the night walking the river. He yawned and made his way into the back to investigate the sleeping arrangements. Small, individual rooms, each with a cot and a lamp. Some of the rooms were already occupied.

"It's so everyone has their own privacy. We want to make it feel like a home, not a warehouse full of cots." The woman handed him a small cup of hot cocoa, "Here, it's to get a little sugar in you, and it has vitamins that you've probably been lacking."

Gaelan nodded and grumbled a thank you, then drank. Exhaustion flooded his body making his arms and legs feel like lead. He hadn't felt this tired since he lost his parents. He sat down on the bed and realized the room was spinning.

Gaelan awoke with the ground shaking underneath him. He sat up and put his left hand down, only to snatch it away—*a body*! He lowered it back down cautiously, and felt the person next to him, still breathing. Another person lay to his left. His head was still spinning and with no light, he couldn't see. *I can't see anything*! The drugs must be still affecting his ability to see in the dark. He closed his eyes and forced his breaths to steady. When he opened his eyes, he could see the eleven people lying around him. Even with the new moon so close, the wolf inside him was metabolizing whatever they gave him more rapidly than the other people.

The ground beneath him shook violently once more. *A truck. I'm in a fucking truck*! From the feel of the road, or lack thereof, they were driving somewhere rural. He had no clue how long he had been unconscious. He carefully crawled over the other 'passengers' and felt for their pulses: drugged, but alive. From what he could tell, there were three homeless men, one man and two women of Middle-Eastern descent, and two men and three women of Asian origin. Migrants, probably low-income workers who, like the homeless, wouldn't be missed.

Eventually he felt the truck slow, then stop. He laid back down in his original spot and closed his eyes as the door scraped open. There was tinkering outside, and then the back door rolled up into the roof of the carriage. He was the third from the door, and the third to be pulled from the truck by two Slovene-speaking men. The men grabbed Gaelan under his armpits and by his ankles, walked several steps and then dropped him, unceremoniously, on the hard ground.

Both men sounded nervous, "Hurry! I don't like to be here when the car arrives."

"Shut up and just get this done so we can get out of here! It won't be long."

"Do you think they wake up before it happens?"

"I don't care. Either way, you've seen what's left in the morning. Just keep going."

Both men turned back to the truck to remove another occupant. Neither heard Gaelan spring to his feet and approach them from behind. He wrapped his arm around the neck of the nearest man, making a 'V' with his forearm and upper arm around the man's neck, flexing against the carotid artery as he pushed the man's head forward with his free hand. The man barely grabbed at the arm around his neck before blacking out. Gaelan dropped him, and the other man turned to see what was going on, "What are you doi…" Gaelan hit the remaining man in the throat with the meaty part of his hand, between his thumb and index finger, then spun the gasping man around, grabbed the back of his head and slammed it off of the bed of the truck. The man fell to the ground, unconscious. Gaelan turned back to the first man, now twitching as the blood rushed back to his head. Gaelan straddled him, grabbing the top of the top of the man's head and lifting it off of the ground. The man opened his eyes just in time to see the heel of Gaelan's hand coming down to strike the bridge of his nose. The nose broke with a crunch and the man's head snapped backward into the ground, knocking him unconscious. Gaelan patted them both down and found a pistol on one of them, and a knife and the truck keys on the other. At least he now had some weapons.

Gaelan hoisted the two unconscious passengers back into the bed of the truck from which they were pulled. He couldn't get everyone to safety and finish the hunt, and he sure as hell didn't need anyone getting in the way while he looked for whatever was coming to dinner. He thought about trying to tie up the two collaborators, but there was no time for that. He left them where they lay and looked around.

A string of lights hanging from the wooden beams above cast a dim glow. He could hear water flowing. A giant wooden water wheel stood in disrepair. It was a mill of some sort, apparently long abandoned. The walls from the ground to the beams were made of heavy stone, slowly being overwhelmed by moss and mildew. Old windows were boarded over with cracked and partially rotted wood. The crossbeams of the ceiling were large and seemed sturdy, but their cobwebbed coated A-frames had seen better days. Invading vines crept through large holes in the roof. The mill should have smelled dank and dirty, but instead it reeked of death, just like the abandoned processing plant. This was an active kill site.

Gaelan moved toward the wall, away from the van. The large barn doors where the truck had entered stood partially open, just beyond the reach of the dusty lights. It was already dark outside. He deliberated his next move—*take the truck to safety or continue the hunt and prevent future deaths*? His thoughts were cut short when a woman walked in before he could decide. She was young and beautiful and walked slowly, sauntering across the floor without care or fear. Gaelan shrank into the shadows as she made her way into the mill. He raised the gun and balanced it on his left forearm. His left hand grasped the knife, blade forward. *Something isn't right about her.* She saw the truck and moved closer, as if curious. Then she spotted the unconscious men and her face twisted into a mask of confusion, then fear. *Who the hell was she? Was she just in the wrong place at the wrong time?*

Thwak! Before Gaelan had the chance to register anything else, the woman fell backwards, grasping an arrow sticking out of her chest. She screamed and sat up, both hands in the air. The ground in front of her rose up, seemingly liquefied, blocking another arrow and a volley of bullets that followed. *WITCH!* The mill started to rumble as roots burst through the floor, creeping and twisting as if they had a mind of their own.

"WATCH OUT!" A voice bellowed in English.

Gaelan could see the woman's face beginning to turn ashen gray and sinewy, her eyes already pitch black. Before he could squeeze the trigger, her earthen shield blocked his view. The roots were now slithering in his direction, like snakes turning back and forth. She hid while the vines sought her prey for her, feeling for him and whoever shot the arrow.

"SHIT! IT'S GOT M…" The stranger's voice choked into a gurgle.

Gaelan darted forward, bounding over the wriggling roots and toward the wall of dirt, now about four feet high and growing. He dove headfirst up and over, squeezing the trigger as he started his descent. His bullets found their mark, and Gaelan twisted his body mid-leap to land on top of the witch's crumpled form. The earthen wall began to collapse around them as the witch hissed and snarled in pain and anger, grabbing at his gun and throat. Gaelan made her pay for leaving his left hand unguarded. He sank the blade deep between her ribs and into her heart. She screamed in agony as he withdrew it and thrust it into her temple, twisting it. The screaming stopped and the creeping roots began to dry and wither. The wall that had protected her was now just a pile of soft dirt surrounding him and his kill. He was about to tear into her chest and eat her heart, but resisted when he heard the coughing and gagging from the front of the mill.

Gaelan stood and turned toward the truck. *What the fuck?* His arms went limp, his mouth slacked—Natalia was staring back at him. Kedar was right next to her drawing down at Gaelan's chest.

Gaelan was confused, "You were the other team?"

"Who the hell got to that bit…" Trey stopped mid sentence as he stepped around his colleagues, quickly raising his pistol. His throat was red from the strangling vines. Angel was right behind Trey, weapon in hand as well.

"DROP THE FUCKING GUN!"

Gaelan looked at each one of them, before shifting his gaze back to Natalia. The venators were glancing from Gaelan to the witch's corpse.

Trey bellowed again, "I SAID DROP THE FUCKING GUN!"

Gaelan dropped the gun as ordered, then dropped the knife without being told, "You're the other team?"

"There's nowhere to run now asshole." Trey grinned like a kid on Christmas morning, practically bubbling with excitement.

Gaelan looked down to the witch, glanced back to the truck and then looked back to Trey, "This doesn't make sense. It doesn't add up. *You're* the other team?"

"Goddamn, look at you? Have you been living on the streets?" Angel wrinkled his nose in disgust.

"It doesn't matter," Trey taunted. "This is the end of the line dumbass."

"What are you doing here?" Natalia interjected before Trey could shoot, "Did you kill that thing?" Gaelan was still looking down to the witch, "GAELAN!" He snapped his head back to Natalia, "What—are—you—doing—here?"

"Hunting, same as you. But why didn't he tell me you were the other team?"

"Why didn't *who* tell you?" She asked.

"Denny! Who the hell else would he be talking about?" Trey smiled, "I guess he finally wanted us to catch you. Even the old man has finally come to his senses."

Gaelan shifted his glances to each of them, "You were in Slovenia this whole time?"

"We ask the questions asshole!" Trey snapped back.

Gaelan pressed, "Have you been in Slovenia this whole time?"

They silently looked at him until Kedar finally spoke up, "No." "No?"

"No, we've been in Austria. What do you mean by 'the other team'?" Kedar seemed to be the only one who understood Gaelan's confusion.

"Austria?" Gaelan's look of confusion turned to dread, "We've gotta get outta here, right now!"

"You're not going anywhere, asshole!" Trey became agitated but held his trigger finger, shifting the pistol in his hand.

"Gaelan, what's wrong?" Natalia's voice seemed to echo his concern without understanding what had caused it.

Gaelan stuck his hand into his pocket.

"WHOA! FREEZE! DON'T FUCKING MOVE!" They all barked at his movement, but no one fired. Gaelan slowly pulled out a set of keys from his pocket and tossed them to Kedar.

"There's a truck back there, full of homeless and migrants. They were brought here by people—collaborators—and we have to get them outta here right now."

Trey snarled back, "*We* aren't going anyway, you fucking moron! This is the last place *you'll* ever see."

"Fine Trey, I don't give a rat's ass! Just fucking shoot me, be done with it, and you and those people get the hell outta here!"

"*You* killed the witch?" Angel couldn't believe it.

"If you weren't the team in Slovenia, then they're still missing! And there's no way that that truck back there was meant for just a witch. Just kill me and get the fuck outta here."

Trey still didn't shoot, "What are you playing at? You think you have everyone fooled, don't you? Like you're some sort of do-good-er, but *you're not*. You're just a filthy piece of shit that I'm finally going to put down!" Doubt colored Trey's bluster.

"I'm not playing Trey. There's no time. Just fucking shoot me and go!" He looked over to Natalia, "Please, just shoot me and get the team and the truck to safety."

"How do we know that you weren't here with the witch, or what's even in that truck?" Trey centered his pistol again.

Gaelan kept looking at Natalia, "Nat, just do it. *Please.*"

"No." She lowered her weapon, "We can't kill him."

"Natalia, what the hell are you doing?" Angel and Kedar's expressions matched Trey's look of disbelief, both at her actions and the fact that he called her *Nat*.

Before anyone spoke again, Gaelan caught a whiff of something—something not right. He lifted his head slightly, sniffing the air. That smell—*New York*! He snapped his head up, looking to the ceiling.

"What are you…" Angel never finished as he too looked up.

Multiple sets of eyes were glowing from the rafters.

"WATCH OUT!" Gaelan yelled.

Seven vampires fell on top of the group. Gaelan jumped to meet one of the attackers. Trey managed to fire and hit another of the creatures. It screeched and hissed but the attack never stopped. One fell directly on Kedar's back, knocking the crossbow away and slamming his head into the ground several times before placing him in a chokehold. One creature fell beside Angel, smacking the pistol from his hand and swinging an uppercut into his jaw so hard that the hunter was unconscious before he hit the ground. Natalia rolled out of the way and came up pointing her pistol at her would-be attacker. Before she could take aim, another creature slammed the gun from her grip. She swung her arm around and backhanded the thing with the heel of her hand, turning its head. It turned back to her with a look of anger and returned the favor. The blow knocked her silly and it grabbed her by throat, simultaneously spinning her and locking her arm behind her back. The creature Trey hit lay hissing and screeching as the blessed bullets seared into its flesh. Another descended next to it, catching Trey's arm with a snarl. Trey winced as the vampire twisted his arm and squeezed down on his wrist. The pistol fell from his numbed hand while the creature grabbed him by the shirt, pulling him in close and baring razor sharp teeth. Instead of ripping his throat out, the vampire lifted Trey off the ground and slammed him down on his back, knocking the breath from his lungs and dazing him.

Gaelan dodged the initial onslaught, but in a blink of an eye, the final vampire was lunging at him with fury in its eyes. Gaelan grabbed the creature's outstretched wrists and thrust his foot forward and into its gut. He released its wrists, locked his fingers together and pounded downward, knocking the creature face first to the floor. Before he could press his advantage, a kick landed behind his right knee, dropping him. He turned, now on one knee, and blocked the follow-on kick from a second vampire. With his attention diverted, the prostrate vampire lunged from a crouch and landed on Gaelan's back, slamming his head several times into the ground. Gaelan felt each of the monsters take one of his wrists and twist, lifting his arms up behind his back. The hard soles of their shoes pressed painfully into his calves, where they stepped to hold him in a kneeling position. He grunted as blows rained on his chest and gut, struggling to catch his breath as he surveyed the room. The Venántium were restrained, but none were being bled.

Trey was dragged by the throat towards the vampire he had shot. Recovering from the burn of the holy-water soaked bullet, the wounded creature stood and lifted Trey off of the ground. It's snarling face morphed into its grotesque true form, eyes glowing like embers, then back to its human visage.

The vampire holding Kedar complained loudly, "They killed Laurentia. First Efthalia disappears, now this. They must know!" The snarls of a dialect unknown to the venators echoed off of the mill's stone walls. Gaelan however, understood every word.

"They don't know a thing. The witches are arrogant and careless." The one restraining Angel snapped back, tightening his grip as Angel came back to consciousness. The creature that had dragged Trey to its wounded comrade paced the room, glancing down at the decaying body of the witch.

Trey struggled to look at each of his team. When his eyes fell on Gaelan, his glare relayed the sentiment—*this is all your fault.*

"We'll know what they know long before sun up. We'll peel their skin and hang their corpses like trophies, but before that, they'll talk." The creature that was pacing the room the group spoke. "Bring the woman to me. They'll listen to her screams and talk to end her suffering. Then their horror will truly begin."

Gaelan could tell that the creature circling the group was the leader. He surveyed how the rest of Trey's team was doing. They were all hurt and dazed. He finally locked eyes with Natalia, who returned his gaze just before the lead vampire took her. He felt helpless in the shadow of the new moon. He watched as she defiantly grabbed and punched at his wrists without fear or hesitation. Gaelan could see she held an inner hatred for the things. The head vampire dragged her several feet away as the other creatures turned and positioned their captives to face him. The creature held up his hand, which became wrinkled and distorted. His fingernails grew into large, razor-sharp sickles. He turned his finger backwards and gently caressed Natalia's cheek. She tried to pull her head away and outwardly spit at his very touch. The vampire turned his nail around as he continued his finger down the side of her jawline. The nail began to cut the side of her neck. She gritted her teeth and took deep breaths so as not to let him have any satisfaction. The blood dripped down her neck and the rest of the creatures became excited, tightening their grips on their captives.

"I KILLED EFTHALIA!" Gaelan screamed out in plain English.

At once, all of the creatures turned to him. The head vampire stopped digging into Natalia's neck and glared, "English it is then." He moved the nail to the other side of Natalia's neck and dug it into her flesh, but held it steady, "Now, what did you say?" Natalia looked into Gaelan's eyes, trying to shake her head.

"I said I killed Efthalia. I found her and some other witches in the woods and caught them by surprise. She had a lot to say before I killed her."

The vampire raised an eyebrow, "And what was that?"

"Let them go and you can tear me apart. What's the worst that happens? You give them a head start? It'll make the hunt more interesting. You can see how long I last before you go after them, but at least give them a head start."

The vampire smiled and moved his hand to the back of Natalia's head, gripping her hair like a vice, "I have a better idea. You tell me everything, and I make her death painless. You don't, and I carve her to pieces. Then we have our fun with you. Maybe you'll last longer than the other hunters that followed us here. Their screams were delicious. I almost didn't want to finish peeling the flesh from their bodies. But we did need to eat." His smile was so sinister that even Gaelan was unnerved, "Now, tell us about Efthalia." Gaelan finally knew the fate of the other team and shifted his gaze from the vampire to Natalia. "Nothing? Very well. Perhaps this will loosen your tongue."

Trey began yelling to her, "NATALIA! NATALIA, LOOK AT ME! DON'T THINK ABOUT IT AND LOOK AT ME!" Angel and Kedar began yelling for her. But Natalia's eye's were fixed on Gaelan's. Her face softened as the vampire's nail began to dig into her neck. She looked at him and remembered a promise he made. She looked at him and—*she smiled*. The vampire continued, "Such a pretty face. Once I peel it off, you can wear it and watch while I eat. Then you'll tell us everything."

Gaelan was hyperventilating as the vampire's nail dug deeper into her neck. He broke her gaze hung his head. He seemed to go slack, then he screamed in rage and pulled his arms, still held aloft behind his back, inward and down. The surprised vampires couldn't hold onto his wrists. He used the momentum to swing his arms down and around, past his lower legs. He grabbed each of the ankles that were standing on his calves and sprang to his feet. The two vampires restraining him were thrown horizontally into the air on either side of him.

Gaelan wasted no time—he screamed in rage and thrust himself forward. In midair, his advance was halted when the head vampire pulled his talon from Natalia's neck and caught him by his throat. Gaelan gripped the creature's forearm tightly trying to release some of the pressure on his own jugular. "Impressive," it snickered, "but in the end, *too little, too late.*" The vampire loosened its grip ever so slightly just as Gaelan's vision began to blur, "Ah, ah, ah—I want you to see this. Besides, you need to tell us about Efthalia." Gaelan blinked, barely breathing, trying to focus on Natalia's face. The new moon had weakened him, and he was going to watch her die. Like Anfernee. Like his parents. For the first time ever, he yearned for the monster inside of him—he wished he could become the wolf.

The vampire pulled Natalia by her hair to her feet, and distended its jaw. Its face contorted as a row of razor sharp teeth and two prominent fangs glistened in the dim light. Before it could reach her throat, the vampire stopped and grimaced, slowly turning back to Gaelan. He hissed to the other vampires, half angry, half frightened, "Kill him!" Gaelan's grip on its arm was intensifying. The creature felt its grip loosening, the neck seeming to swell beneath its claws.

Gaelan forced his words through the grip on his throat, "Too little..."

"KILL HIM!" The vampire screeched and dropped Natalia to the ground as Gaelan's fingers contorted and dug into its flesh.

Gaelan's voice was a deep, throaty growl, "Too late!"

Gaelan opened his eyes to reveal an otherworldly glow of yellow and red. He thrust his leg forward and the creature flew back, hitting the stone wall hard enough to crack it. Natalia stared up at him as he transformed. His change was quick and fluid. By the time he turned back to the other vampires, the change was complete.

He bounded toward Kedar and Angel and their vampire captors, grabbing the vampire's faces in a downward motion and slamming them to the ground with his claws. Kedar and Angel were sent sprawling on the ground as the werewolf leaned all of its weight forwards, and the vampires' skulls cracked with a sickening, wet crunch.

Gaelan straightened and turned. The vampire behind him released Trey and hurled itself toward Gaelan's monstrous form. Gaelan caught the vampire midair, roaring in pain as its claws tore into his flesh. In one motion, he slammed the creature into the ground then turned and tossed the body into the two vampires that had restrained him only moments before.

Trey scrambled to find his gun as he pulled a magazine from his ankle strap. Angel was still dazed but managed to dive onto one of the writhing vampires with a crushed skull, grabbing it in a chokehold. Kedar pulled a knife from his boot and plunged it into the creature's heart. He then tossed the knife to Angel, who thrust himself on top of the other wounded creature, stabbing it in the heart and twisting the blade.

Gaelan was now fighting off four vampires that swarmed around him, darting in to claw at him, then back out of reach. Finally catching one of the creatures, Gaelan threw it to the ground, and dug his claws through the things back, gripping its spine. Another lunged in to attack, but was thrown backwards by Gaelan's powerful kick, and quickly dispatched by Angel and Kedar. Gaelan lifted the vampire in his grip, then sank his teeth into its midsection. His massive jaws jerked to and fro as the vampire shrieked in agony. With a single, powerful motion, he pulled the vampire's spine in opposite directions between his claws and teeth. The vampire was torn in two, shrieks subsiding in a sickening wet tearing. The werewolf tossed the lower half to the ground and tore the heart out of the upper, consuming it in a single gulp.

Several shots rang out as Gaelan spun to see two vampires fall to the ground, hissing. Natalia lowered her weapon and charged, drawing a metal stake and sinking it into the heart of one monster. Gaelan pounced on the other and clawed at its chest furiously until he had exposed its heart. He tore it out, deaf to the vampire's screams, and swallowed it whole.

Only one vampire now remained—the creature that was going to peel Natalia's face. Its movement caught everyone's attention, but Gaelan was the first to react. The vampire caught him mid pounce and threw him into the wall. This vampire was stronger than the others and Gaelan stood up, dazed. It attacked. Charging low, slashing across Gaelan's mid-section and coming up to its full height behind him, it jumped onto Gaelan's back and sank its teeth into his left shoulder. Gaelan roared, threw his right claw over his left shoulder and grabbed the vampire by the head. He threw his body weight forward and slung the vampire up and over his own body, slamming the creature into the ground. He raised both his claws and thrust them down and into the vampire's ribs. He squeezed until he felt several of them crack, and then lifted the creature into the air and threw it into the wall. The creature recovered but was slowed by the injuries. It charged Gaelan and tried to duck low and slash. This time Gaelan was prepared. He dropped low to match the movement, caught the vampire's wrist, then shifted his weight to swing the creature up and over his frame and into the ground.

The vampire rose to it feet, only to be slashed across the torso by Gaelan's claw, which then came back across its throat, drawing blood on both swipes. The vampire tried to defend itself, but Gaelan grabbed the creature by the top of the head with his right claw, and its throat with his left, pulling the thing's face to his own while opening his monstrous jaws. The vampire screeched in horror as Gaelan bit down on its face. Gaelan shook his head back and forth violently even as his teeth tore through the cheeks and into the creature's skull. Soon, the screaming turned to a horrific gurgle, then silence—Gaelan had bit the creature's face clean off. He dropped the body to the ground, straddled it, and clawed furiously to expose and devour the heart.

The sound of a pistol slide locking into position echoed through the mill. Gaelan stood and turned, blood still dripping from his jaws and snout. Trey's pistol, now loaded with silver, pointed at his chest. Before he could squeeze, Natalia jumped in front of him with her hands raised high, "TREY NO!"

"NATALIA, GET THE FUCK OUT OF THE WAY!" Trey bellowed at her as the werewolf approached her from behind.

"NATALIA, WATCH OUT!" Angel screamed. The monster was right behind her, crouching down as if to pounce.

"NATALIA!" Kedar joined the chorus, "NOOOOOOO!"

They watched in horror as the werewolf came up behind her, raised its massive left claw and brought it to bear upon her. Instead of slashing at her, it forcefully grabbed her right shoulder. She spun her head to see the claw and then felt the force of its arm. The werewolf pushed her to the side and out of the way, baring its teeth at Trey.

"TREY, DON'T! DON'T YOU DO IT!" Natalia's voice was imploring.

The werewolf roared and opened its claws, holding its ground.

Why was Natalia still alive? The hunters paused momentarily, stunned. Natalia jumped in between them again, this time facing the werewolf.

"NO! YOU DON'T GET TO DO THIS!" She shoved at his midsection, but it was like hitting a tree.

"NATALIA, WHAT ARE DOING? GET OUT OF THE WAY!"

The monster glared over her head at Trey. She pounded her fists on its chest, "YOU DON'T GET TO DO THIS HERE! DO YOU HEAR ME? YOU DON'T GET TO DO THIS!"

Angel ran forward and grabbed Natalia, dragging her back. The werewolf looked down at the motion then snapped its head back to Trey.

"TREY DON'T! PLEASE! DON'T!" Natalia's voice began to crack as she broke free from Angel's grip and ran in between Trey and Gaelan once more.

Trey paused, looking from Natalia to the wolf in disbelief. *What the fuck?*

The wolf roared. Natalia gazed up at it's slavering jowls, eyes pleading. Then, to Trey's utter disbelief, Angel stepped forward to stand in front of Natalia, facing Trey. *What the fuck is going on?* Trey adjusted to aim over Angel's shoulder, but before he could squeeze the trigger, he felt the hand come down over his grip. Kedar's hand covered the pistol, thumb behind the trigger, then gently pushed down, feeling Trey lower it.

What the fuck? Angel turned and nodded to Natalia. She turned and shoved at Gaelan, "GO!" She shoved at him again, "GET OUT OF HERE! I KNOW YOU CAN HEAR ME! GET OUT OF HERE!" She shoved him again "YOU DON'T GET TO DO THIS TONIGHT! DO YOU HEAR ME? NOT TONIGHT!"

The werewolf now looked down to her, cocking its head to one side like a confused Labrador. The three men stared on in disbelief. Natalia shoved at the monster furiously with absolutely no fear. It looked down at her without malice. "GO!" Natalia's voice softened, "Please—go." The wolf finally took a step backward, looked up, and locked eyes with Trey. It gave a defiant roar before looking back down to Natalia.

"Go!"

With that, it bounded toward the side of the mill and jumped through one of the boarded windows, splintering the planks and disappearing into the night.

The venators stood motionless, staring at the window. Kedar finally spoke, "We need to check these bodies before they burn."

"You protected him." Trey continued to stare at the window, but everyone knew he was talking to Natalia. She didn't answer. He turned to her, agitated, "You protected him!"

"Not now!"

"FUCK YOU! FUCK YOU NATALIA! YOU PROTECTED HIM!"

"Not now Trey!" She hissed.

"This wasn't the first time, was it? The witch he talked about—you were with him in Germany and didn't say anything. You've been protecting him all along." Trey was breathing heavily, "ANSWER ME GODDAMMIT!"

"YES, OKAY? Is that what you want to hear? He saved my life just like he saved our lives just now." Natalia's glare met his own.

"HE'S A FUCKING WEREWOLF!"

"YOU HEARD JENNIFER GUERIN!" She calmed herself, "He's no more a werewolf than any of us."

"ARE YOU FUCKING KIDDING ME?" Trey's rage was palpable, "YOU'RE JUST AS FUCKING BLIND AS SHE IS!" Trey mumbled at first, "You chose him over us." Then he raised his voice again, "YOU CHOSE HIM, A FUCKING WEREWOLF!"

Natalia retaliated, "I DIDN'T CHOOSE ANYONE!"

Trey paused for a moment, still visibly angry, "Well, you can *not choose* anyone somewhere else. After we get back, you can find a new team to work with." Trey glared at her, "This way you can make sure nobody else shoots yours and Denny's little pet."

Natalia deflated, as if punched in the gut. Angel and Kedar froze in disbelief. Their team had been together for almost ten years. Finally, Angel spoke. "We need to get out of here. Natalia, why don't you ride with Kedar in the moving truck. Trey and I will take the car. Let's head right to the church."

Kedar nodded and moved toward the truck, but stopped when he realized that Trey and Natalia were still glaring, motionless. Finally, Natalia walked directly at Trey. Without breaking her stride, she shoved the money and hotel room key that she had found on the vampire into his chest and pushed him back, "I didn't do it for *him,* you stupid bastard!" No one mentioned the tears in her eyes as she marched toward the truck. Kedar gave one last nod to Angel and followed her. Angel grabbed Trey, "Go get the car started." Trey slowly walked outside the main doors of the mill and Angel recited a prayer out loud. The vampire corpses and the body of the witch burst into flames. Before they left, all that remained of confrontation were several spots of fine dust and the splinters of the boards that Gaelan had burst through into the night.

Gaelan woke naked at the side of the river. The sun wasn't yet above the horizon, barely lifting the veil of darkness. He pushed himself to his hands and knees and winced. His body was covered in slashes and bruises. When he reached his hand over his left shoulder, his fingertips came back covered in blood. The bite was still fresh. He inhaled, taking in the smells of the river—stronger to the south, in the direction it flowed. His senses seemed heightened, despite the new moon. He lowered himself into the river and the cold of the water seemed to reverberate through every cell in his body. He began drifting, then swimming with the current. About 30 minutes later, the northern outskirts of Tržič slid into view. Gaelan swam on, diving below the water whenever a bridge crossed the river, surfacing to search the banks for his car.

The drive back to town was quiet in both vehicles, until the occupants of the truck started to wake. By the time they arrived at the church, the banging and yelling had reached a fever-pitch. The four venators gathered behind the truck. The only one who spoke any Slovene, Natalia, stood close to the priest who joined them. Trey stayed to the back, his anger still evident.

The priest quickly calmed the terrified survivors, explaining that they were drugged as part of a human trafficking plot, and recued by a team from Amnesty International.

"Cover story?" Angel asked. He stood with Kedar, forming a barrier between the feuding venators. Natalia nodded and translated as best she could. The priest lead the group into the sanctuary and assisted with the interviews. Each victim recounted a bowl of soup and a cup of hot chocolate at the shelter, then *nothing*. No memory from that point on, until waking in the truck.

Trey turned and walked to the door without speaking. Angel stopped him, "Where are you going?"

"To find that shelter."

"We're all exhausted and not thinking straight. Why don't we..."

"I'm thinking just fine!" Trey snarled, "I'll go on my own." Angel rolled his eyes to Kedar, who shrugged in return, then both followed Trey. Kedar caught Natalia's eye and motioned towards the door.

The silence in the car was deafening. No one wanted to bring up the events of just hours before. The sun was coming up when they finally found the shelter, tucked away from the main mall, near the entrance to the highway. They kept their distance for several minutes and observed people going in and out. They all looked to be vagrants.

Satisfied that no immediate danger lurked, the team made their way inside. Three men sat at a long wax-cloth covered table; another on a faded chair. A woman with long gray hair stood from her perch on end of the table, chattering and motioning with her hands.

"Slow. Slow. I Slovene not good!"

Natalia was able to piece together the woman's words, 'Boss people gone' and 'No food.' She looked to Angel and Kedar, "Apparently the people in charge left and there is nothing left."

Kedar pushed open a door to a back room, "More people in here! Drugged!" He reemerged, "Who knows how long this has been going on or how many people they were planning on feeding to these creatures." He shook his head in disgust.

Trey made no sign of giving direction, so Angel piped up "Well, this is a dead end. Let's call the priest and have him send some volunteers over here. We can go take a look at the hotel those things were staying in."

"You all go ahead." Trey's voice was sullen, "I'm gonna look around here some more."

"Trey, what is wrong with you?" Kedar shook his head. "You wanted to come here on your own, now you want to stay by yourself. Why are you in such a rush to get rid of us?"

Trey paused, "I didn't want you to come because I wasn't going to come to the shelter. I wanted to try and get Kelly's trail and I didn't want anyone jumping in front of me this time."

Natalia rolled her eyes and looked away.

"Trey, brother, let it go for now. They'll be another time and another..." Trey interrupted before Angel could complete his thought.

"*Another time and place?* It's been over a year since we saw him, and before that, it was another year. God only knows when I'll ever see him again. Next time, no one's getting in my way!" Trey stormed out of the shelter.

"Trey!" Angel went after him. Kedar squeezed Natalia's shoulder before heading out the door.

Natalia followed, dejected, expecting to have to catch up as Trey would be storming toward the car. Instead, she almost ran into their backs, frozen at the doorstep, jaws slack. She looked around them to see what caused their halt. Sitting on the hood of their car, arms folded in wait, was Gaelan Kelly.

Breaking from his revere, Trey walked forward, reaching into his jacket. Gaelan pursed his lips and cocked his head in disappointment. *This isn't the time and place!*

Trey stopped, his hand still curled around his weapon.

"You didn't find anyone working in there, did you?" Gaelan started before anyone could speak.

"You have some balls on you, boy! I'll give you that." Trey snapped.

"What did the two guys I kicked the shit out of tell you?" Gaelan didn't bother to look at Trey, but could see from the look on the others' faces that they didn't know what he was talking about, "GODDAMNIT!" Gaelan spat in disappointment, "They probably woke up when we got jumped, and headed right back here to warn the others."

"What the hell do you think you're doing?"

"I'm following up on the hunt and..."

"YOU'RE NOT A FUCKING VENATOR!" Trey yelled, then continued through gritted teeth, "You're a goddamned werewolf piece of shit!"

"Oh yeah, Trey? Well," Gaelan retorted as if he were on a school playground, "*your face is ugly*!"

Natalia turned her face away, hiding a hint of a smile. Angel chuckled, "You better shoot him now Trey, cause I'm starting to like him." Trey shot Angel a caustic look, "I'm just saying—it was funny."

"Trey..." Gaelan began but Trey cut him off.
"Don't talk to me like we're friends asshole! We're gonna get in the car, drive someplace quiet and I'm gonna put a silver bullet in you. Then this hunt will finally be over."

"Okay. *Backseat middle*, I call it!" Gaelan turned and opened the backdoor of the car, jumping in and closing the door behind him. He tilted his head to look out the window to see that everyone, including Trey, was staring at him in disbelief, "WE GOIN' OR WHAT?" Gaelan shouted out and shrugged his shoulders.

"GET THE FUCK OUT OF THE CAR!"

Gaelan complied and held his arms out in confusion, "What is wrong with you? First we're gonna take a drive and shoot me, now I'm not allowed in the car!"

Trey hissed back, "What are you playing at? You told me to shoot you last night, now you're jumping in the back of the car. What are you planning?"

"I'm not planning anything. Let's drive someplace where you can shoot me, but we do need to talk on the way. So seriously, are we goin' or what?"

"We can talk right here."

"*Holy Mother of God* Trey, you're confusin' the shit outta me!"

"Maybe I will just shoot you here, you arrogant little prick!"

"Well, since we're on the subject, why didn't you shoot me last night?" Gaelan raised his eyebrows.

"I didn't have a clean shot." Trey glanced over his shoulder at Natalia, who glared a hole through his back.

"I'm not talking about that! When I first came out to see the witch—by the way, that was an awesome shot!" Gaelan gestured to Kedar, who tipped his head at the compliment, "I'm talking about right then! You should have put a bullet in me, right there, but you didn't. Then you said you were gonna kill me, and I told you to do it and get outta there, but you didn't. Why?" Trey stared, silent. "Why Trey? Answer the quest…"

Trey bellowed, "BECAUSE OF HER!" He lowered his voice, "Because of Denny! Because of Jennifer Guerin! You have everyone fooled into thinking that you're something more than just a fucking monster."

Gaelan nodded, "And I'm guessing from the looks of things, I screwed up the chemistry on the team?" Gaelan didn't wait for a response. "And you probably know by now that we met in Germany?"

"I put two and two together when she saved your ass last night."

"Did she tell you that she put one in my gut when she saw me? Without hesitation?" Trey's face betrayed his surprise. Gaelan looked to Natalia, "It still hurts a little."

"Good." She said coldly.

Gaelan looked back to Trey, "So stop holding anything against her or anyone else. You still had the chance to shoot me and you didn't. And to be honest, until last night I would have welcomed the bullet."

"What do you mean 'until last night?'" Angel chimed in.

"Doesn't it bother you?" Gaelan waved his hand at the shelter, "All of this?"

"It's troubling. Very troubling." The group turned to Kedar. "He was right last night. Those people weren't just for a witch. Those vampires were there to meet her. And this shelter isn't the work of a misguided group of human lapdogs. This is a complicated operation that required a great deal of resources and coordination."

"EXACTLY!" Gaelan exclaimed. "And not just here. Similar killings started in Ljubljana. There's a *network*." Gaelan turned to Kedar and pretended to wipe a tear from his eye, "You had me at *it's troubling*."

Angel laughed out loud until Trey's look cut him short. "What? He's funny!"

"But in all seriousness, Kedar's right." Gaelan intervened, "And have you ever encountered two different types of creatures working together?" The silence was all the answer he needed, "Yeah, me either."

"Oh, in all your *experience*?" Trey's sarcasm was thick.

Gaelan rolled his eyes, ignoring the slight, "The funny thing is, those same vampires were supposed to meet one of the witches that Nat and I killed in Germany."

"Natalia!" She snapped.

"Can I finish a sentence, *please*? Jesus! They said first Efthalia disappeared, then, whatever the hell the name of the one we killed last night was. They *need* a witch for something and they think we know why."

"Wait." Angel interrupted, "You understood them?"

Gaelan nodded and Natalia added, "Just like you understood the witches in Germany."

"Yeah, an unexplained side effect of my little condition. But the point is that there's something bigger at work here and we are, albeit coincidentally, a step ahead for once. Of course, I was hoping to get some answers from the people that tried to serve me for dinner, but they're gone."

"I guess they didn't realize this dinner bites back?" Angel raised his eyebrows.

Gaelan smiled and shrugged, "Anyway, let's talk about that on the way."

Trey rounded on Gaelan, "On the way where?"

"Wherever you decide. You wanna drive somewhere secluded and put a bullet in me, I'm not gonna stop you. Otherwise, we're all takin' a trip."

Trey was about to speak when he was jostled by Natalia's shoulder slamming into his back.

"Just shut your fucking mouth for once and get in the car." She stalked by Gaelan and narrowed her eyes at the sword and backpack on the ground next to him, "Throw that shit in the trunk." Gaelan did as she said and then got into the back of the vehicle while she took the driver's seat. After Natalia's comment, Angel and Kedar didn't even bother talking to Trey. They glanced at each other uncertainly and climbed into the back of the car with Gaelan.

Gaelan looked to each of them, mumbling, "I'm kinda hopin' for the bullet option."

"I may join you." Angel said with wide-eyes, and Kedar nodded in agreement. Natalia's sideways glance silenced them. Trey seethed for another minute, before he conceded defeat and folded himself into the passenger seat.

Natalia shifted the rearview mirror to see Gaelan's face, "So where are we going?"

"To get some wine." Gaelan grinned, "I know this great little place in France!"

CHAPTER 6
GROUP THERAPY

"Tell me again how a Venántium team interfered with the rendezvous?" Gaius asked.

"He...he..." The woman fumbled for words, "He came in disguise, as one of the homeless. I drugged him like the others, but he must have had an antidote." Her voice trailed off as she stared beyond the handsome man to the imposing figures behind him. They looked through her and the group of humans she huddled with, indifferent.

"And what of you two? You say he took you by surprise?"

"Yes," One of the truck drivers muttered, "we weren't looking and he knocked us out. By the time we woke up,"

The other driver took over, "We could hear that the vamp..." He glanced up at the figures in the background, "I mean the *masters*, had arrived and were dealing with the intruders."

"Apparently not. It would seem that a Venántium team managed to eliminate *seven* individuals who should have had no trouble dealing with their kind. And you can tell us *nothing* about them?"

"No sir! When we saw that the group of masters had the hunters, we ran out the back. They never told us to stay." The driver's voice trailed off.

Gaius turned to look over his shoulder. The large figure in the middle looked to him and gave one small nod. He looked back to the group and eyed all of them.

"My lords?" The woman from the shelter spoke, addressing the figures behind Gaius in a terrified whisper, "We serve loyally. We act without question. What's going to happen to us?"

Gaius looked to her, "You're going back to the shelters."

Everyone in the group mumbled in relief and some even grabbed one another's hands to rejoice.

"Thank you my lords. Thank you!"

Father Denny asked the airport taxi to drop him off at the edge of his long, winding driveway. As he walked around the bend, a figure came into view, just beyond the house, practicing with a sword. *Gaelan*! His message had asked Father Denny to *meet him for wine*, and that it *couldn't wait*. Denny put Father Francesco Librizzi in charge of Venántium operations and taken some personal time, explaining that he needed to clear his head. He smiled and hurried his pace, then froze. Three figures were walking along the tree line to the opposite side of the house, staring intently at Gaelan. Denny crept closer, then dropped his bag and dashed forward when he recognized Trey Marshall and his team.

"GAELAN, RUUUUUN!" Trey, Angel and Kedar turned, wide-eyed.

Trey started, "Denny, wait!" and held up his hands. Father Denny never broke stride. He hit Trey with his shoulder, full on in the midsection, and took him to the ground.

"GET OUTTA HERE GAELAN!" He yelled. But instead of running for the tree line, Gaelan came towards Denny and Trey, the latter of which lay struggling in the priest's chokehold. "Gaelan, what are you doing?"

Gaelan was standing in between Kedar and Angel, choking back a grin, "I'm watching you choke the shit outta Trey. Can you stay just like this while I go get a camera?"

"Fuck—you—Kelly!" Trey managed to gurgle through Father Denny's grasp.

"Seriously Father, you can let him go. It's alright."

Father Denny loosened his grip and pushed Trey off of him, "Alright? It's all right? WHAT THE HELL?"

Father Denny jumped to his feet, "We needed a place to talk things over and I needed you here. It's important."

Gaelan tried to help Trey to his feet. "DON'T TOUCH ME ASSHOLE!" Trey rolled onto his hands and knees, and Angel and Kedar helped him instead.

Father Denny looked up to the house and saw that Natalia was on the front porch watching the exchange with her arms crossed.

"So much for this place being our little secret!" Father Denny was angry, "Why the hell are they here? Only you and I knew about this place, now it's a clubhouse? What were you thinking?"

Gaelan's face tightened, "Good to see you too. Happy you're okay."

"Don't try to turn this on me! These people have been trying to kill you and you bring them to the only safe place we have. What…"

Gaelan lost it, "WE? WE? WHEN THE FUCK HAS THERE BEEN A WE?" Father Denny flinched as if slapped. "The last time *we* were here, you thought *I* had killed someone. *We* came up with grand plans to start fightin' back and since then, *I've* gone all over the world doin' whatever *you* ask. It takes days for you to respond when I contact you, and now I ask you here cause I—*we*—have something really fuckin' important to talk about and you think I'm throwin' a house party. THANKS FOR THE FUCKIN' CREDIT!" Gaelan turned and walked toward the house yelling over his shoulder, "THERE'S A KEG IN THE BACK AND STRIPPERS IN THE HOUSE!" He stormed past Natalia without a look and slammed the front door. His voice echoed from inside the house, "ANYONE ELSE AROUND HERE WANNA KILL ME OR FUCKING JUMP MY SHIT?"

In the silence that followed, all eyes turned from the front door to Father Denny.

Angel broke the silence, "Well, that went better than the last time we were all together."

Father Denny ignored Angel and addressed Trey, "What the hell are you doing here? Last time I saw you, you told me you were going to *kill* him."

Trey stretched his neck and rubbed his throat, "I'm starting to think that I should have killed him and saved myself all this fun."

Natalia joined them on the driveway. "He's right though. You need to know what's going on."

"Just what the fuck *is* going on?" Angel and Kedar raised their eyebrows to hear the priest curse.

"First and foremost, none of you," Natalia looked at each of them in turn, resting a final glare on Trey, "know Gaelan Kelly."

"Natalia, right?" Father Denny's tone was sarcastic, "I watched him grow up. I knew he had the ability to beat that thing in him. I knew he would be able to hunt like no one else. So what makes you think you I don't know him?"

She nodded. "That's nice. Did you also know that he's been trying to get himself killed? That he wanted us to kill him? That he wanted *me* to kill him?"

"When he first changed. Yes. We talked about it."

Natalia nodded dismissively, "Except that I talked him out of killing himself not two weeks ago." Natalia stared hard at the priest.

"Bullshit! He's come to grips with the thing inside him!"

Natalia interrupted, "It's not the wolf!" She lowered her voice, "It's what he did before. You know about his war experiences?"

"Yes."

"And you know what he did?"

"I read the citation for his medal. He never wanted to talk about it." Father Denny's voice trailed off.

"He told me *everything*."

"When?"

"In Germany. We were having breakfast…"

"BREAKFAST?" All four men exclaimed at once.

Just then, Gaelan came out on the front porch and everyone turned to him.

"GAELAN, WAIT INSIDE. WE'RE TALKING!" Father Denny yelled, pointing at the front door.

Gaelan stared at him wide-eyed for a second, then replied with equal volume, "SURE! WHY NOT? I'LL BE PLAYING WITH MY LEGOS WHILE THE GROWN-UPS FUCKING TALK!" He turned and stormed back inside, slamming the door behind him.

Natalia ignored the interruption and snapped at the men, "Not like that you pigs! We had just finished killing the witches and drove the girl we rescued to the hospital. Then I turned my gun on him and he drove to breakfast, saying he wanted a last meal. I let him have it since I couldn't really shoot him in the middle of town. He told me everything. He told me what's haunting him. He told me that he thinks he's the monster and the werewolf is more human than he is! And then told me that he *wanted* me to kill him."

"Why would he tell you?" Father Denny was hurt.

"Because when he finally wanted to open up, you weren't there."

"What?"

"*You weren't there,* Father. You weren't there for him to actually talk to. He told me that he's alone, that there's no one for him. You send him on hunts and that's it. He's tried to reach out. And when I talked him out of killing himself, you hadn't talked to him in days. I wasn't his first choice, *you* were! But I was stupid enough, or *lucky* enough, to pick up the phone. He called to ask me to get his sword after he was dead and give it to you, Father. You were the one he wanted to talk to, and you—weren't—there. So *none of you,*" she rounded on her teammates, "truly knows Gaelan Kelly."

"Hey, I'm starting to like him!" Angel tried to defend himself, "And he threw me into a tree when we first met!" Natalia rolled her eyes.

"I thought he was okay." Father Denny was visibly shaken, "I thought we were making a difference."

"Maybe you are, but that doesn't matter. The burden he carries is enough to break anyone. And after everything that's happened, he brought us here, to talk to *you.* Not anyone else. He still needs *you*—and I don't need to tell you this little reunion didn't go the way he wanted."

—§—

No one said a word as Father Denny walked to the house.

"What are you doin' kiddo?"

Gaelan looked up at him and went back to packing, "What's it look like?"

"Gaelan, stop." Gaelan slid his sword in and rolled up the top of the pack, "Gaelan, please—stop!"

"WHY? WHAT THE FUCK DO I HAVE TO STAY FOR?" He glared at Father Denny, then calmed himself, "There's nothing for me here. They can tell you what we found and you can send me instructions. I'll be—oh hell, what the fuck do you care where I'll be."

He stood up and threw the pack over his shoulder. "Get outta the way Father!"

"No." Father Denny had tears in his eyes, standing between Gaelan and the door.

"I'm going." Gaelan slowed his breathing, trying to sound calm, "Nothing has changed. Just tell me where to meet them."

"Everything has changed Gaelan! Everything!" Tears streamed down the priest's rugged face. "I pushed you away!"

"No." Gaelan's tone was softer, but dismissive, "I wouldn't be here without you. Got it. But I need to go!"

"SHUT UP! YOU WOULDN'T BE HERE WITHOUT HER!" Father Denny motioned toward the driveway, "I wasn't there for you! I wasn't there and she was—and it's my fault!"

"It's nobody's fault, I just need a couple of days." Gaelan struggled to remain calm.

"It's *my* fault! I pushed you away—*deliberately*!"

Gaelan was shattered, "Why? Why would you..."

Father Denny cut him off, "Did you find the team that disappeared?" Gaelan's eyes closed in remorse as he slowly nodded his head.

"That's why kiddo. That's the seventeenth team that's gone—the ninth in the last three months. And I've lost more than fifty individual venators since I took over. A hundred and twenty people. *Gone.* I've been sending you to the hunts we talked about.

The ones I know are dangerous, and the more I know, the more I push you away!" Father Denny sobbed, "Because I was prepping myself for the day you don't send a message back." He fell to his knees and wept.

"Father!" Gaelan dropped his pack, fell to his knees and put a hand on Father Denny's shoulder, "I get it. A lot of us did it back when I was a Marine, and I do it now." Father Denny looked up at Gaelan, still sobbing "Whenever you tell me people have disappeared or have turned up dead, I try to think of them as numbers because it's easier."

"BUT YOU'RE NOT A NUMBER! YOU'RE MY KIDDO!" Father Denny grabbed onto Gaelan, and Gaelan hugged him tightly back, "You're not a damned number and I'm so sorry!" He could barely breathe, "I sent over a hundred and twenty people to their deaths. They're dead because of me! BECAUSE OF ME!"

"Stop it! It's not because of you Father, it's because of what we fight!"

"But I sent them! Their blood is on my hands!"

Gaelan pulled back, grabbed Father Denny by his shoulders and squeezed, "I'll tell you what you told me—*cut that shit out right now*! You hear me?" Gaelan scolded, "You have more experience in the field than all of us put together. You know that people die out here! All—the—time! It's not your fault. People—*venators*—we're gonna die, whether you give the command or not. We're fighting a war that we're not supposed to win, but we're going to goddammit, you understand me?" He used his sleeve to wipe Father Denny's face.

"Watch your language." Father Denny smiled weakly.

"Really, that's what you're concerned about?" Gaelan paused when Father Denny cocked his head, then continued, "Okay, okay! I'm sorry. Let's not go there right now."

"Okay." Father Denny sniffed and composed himself, "I'm so sorry I didn't get back to you when you needed me."

"Don't worry about it."

"What do you mean *don't worry about it*? You were going to kill yourself. Don't shrug it off kiddo. You promised me you wouldn't and..."

"Whoa!" Gaelan held his hands up, "First off, that promise was made before I found out I was a werewolf, so I hate to tell you, but that's voided right there. Second, I'm still here, so no promise broken. I visited some people, and it made things worse for a while, but I got through it. It's over."

"You got through it by talking to her." Father Denny motioned his head toward the outside of the house again, "Because I wasn't there for you."

"Either way, I got through it!"

"You don't just get through it kiddo. What's going on?"

Gaelan paused for a moment, "Father, you know the guilt I feel about losing my parents—losing my friend overseas. It's not going to go away. What I did when I was—*human*. That will always haunt me. It's been killin' me even more now that I realize this thing inside me seems to have more restraint than I ever did. I've been hunting all over the world, most of the time getting someplace too late to do anything but witness the carnage, and all I can do is hope that it's *him*. It's been almost three years since *he* killed my parents and there's no sign of *him* anywhere. We've only hunted down werewolves the one time in Canada, and *he* wasn't one of them. I visited my buddy's parents and I guess it all came to the surface. I just wanted it to end."

"And now?" Father Denny sounded concerned, "Feelings like that don't just go away."

"You're right, but I'm okay right now. I have a new focus and we'll explain it to you. I'm sorry about yelling. I wouldn't have gotten so upset but hell, you're the only family—not my aunt or anyone else—the only *real* family I have left."

Father Denny hugged him tight again, "I'm sorry kiddo. I'm gonna be here more and we're gonna meet more. This time, *I* promise."

—§—

"YOU TURNED? THREE NIGHTS AGO?"

Gaelan and the Venators were recounting their hunts to Father Denny.

"Yeah. It surprised everyone, especially me!"

Kedar asked, "How long have you been able to change outside of the full moon?" Everyone turned to Gaelan. Even Trey.

"Siiiiiince," Gaelan looked at his watch and began rapidly counting with his fingers for several seconds, "three nights ago." Angel and Father Denny smiled while Natalia rolled her eyes.

"And you controlled it?" Father Denny sounded cautious.

"It's weird, but when I transformed in Germany..."

"YOU TRANSFORMED IN GERMANY?"

"Are you gonna raise your voice every time I tell you something?" Gaelan snapped, then continued, "I *had* to. It was our only hope, and somehow I knew I could keep it focused." He shot a glance at Natalia. She turned away quickly, but not before Trey and Father Denny noticed her face soften momentarily, "But the other night was different. I felt naked without it. I felt like I timed the hunt wrong and I was going to sit there and watch everyone die." He looked toward Natalia again and back to Father Denny, "And for the first time, I *wanted* it!" Gaelan's face was troubled, "I found myself asking for it. Begging for it to help me. I wanted to change. And I did."

"And you controlled it." Angel jumped in.

"It's weird. It was *me*, just me in my most primal state. I wanted to rip the vampires to pieces, but not you guys. And I let it all go. In Canada, I took a chance. In Germany, I felt confident I could focus it. But the other night, I wanted it and, well, yeah, I controlled it."

Gaelan looked around at the faces staring at him. Trey barely concealed his disgust. Angel and Kedar had mouths agape in astonishment. Father Denny smiled ear-to-ear. Natalia wore her normal look of indifference, though Gaelan could've sworn he saw the slightest hint of a smile. Gaelan continued, "The question is what were the vampires doing meeting up with a witch? And those vampires were well organized. That head vampire wasn't just any old bloodsucking asshole, he was *strong*, older than the rest of them."

"A vampire's a vampire!" Trey was dismissive.

Gaelan rolled his eyes to Father Denny, who chimed in, "We're learning that's not the case. Some of them are older and stronger than others."

"The oldest known creature was the 334-year-old vampire, yes? It bragged to the team that killed it?" Angel asked.

"Yeah, that's what the Venántium records say, but does every creature you kill mention how old it is?" They looked at him in silence, "Well, the vampire I killed in New York said no one had touched him in over fifteen hundred years."

"OH BULLSHIT!" Trey exclaimed.

"That's what he said before I killed him, and he was strong. He almost tore my head off. I held the wolf back that time and I wonder how I would've fared against him even if I *had* turned" Trey glared as Gaelan continued "And then the hiking guide in Canada," Gaelan sighed deeply realizing that this wouldn't help the conversation, "the one I admitted to killing. *She* said she could give me immortality. She was a werewolf and said she was immortal. I don't think that they live for a couple of hundred years. I think they live until someone or something kills them. And I think the the older ones have an edge."

"The vampire really said it was fifteen hundred years old?" Kedar probed.

"Yeah, and that's not even the craziest part about him. We're pretty sure he was Jack the Ripper." He leaned back with a smile and his hands behind his head in a cocky pose, "I killed *Jack the Ripper.*"

"Do not fool with us please." Kedar's indignation was cut short when he saw the same confident look on Father Denny's face. "You're not fooling with us?" Gaelan shook his head. Kedar looked to Trey, "That really is amazing."

"It's all hearsay! What proof is there? We're taking this asshole's word for it? Why isn't any of this in the centuries of Venántium history?"

Before Gaelan could respond, Natalia broke her silence, "FOR CHRIST'S SAKE TREY, WAKE UP! You said it yourself—he's a *goddamned werewolf!* Who else has a chance of beating these things and living to tell the tale? You saw what he did to those vampires.

I saw what he did to a coven of witches. A whole fucking *coven* of witches! Do you think we—you—any normal Venator stands a chance against that? He can do things we can't, and gather information we could never live to collect! But after all," She stood and pointed at Gaelan, staring at Trey, "he's a GODDAMNED WERE-WOLF, RIGHT? You're more interested in killing him than saving lives. Get the fuck over it!" Natalia stormed to the door, grabbed the packed bag she had stashed next to it, and walked out. As everyone looked to Trey, Gaelan stood up, picked up his own backpack and walked out behind her.

"Well?" Angel said.

"Well what?" Trey was defensive.

"She's doing what you told her, brother." Kedar raised an eyebrow at Trey.

Trey rolled his eyes and went to get up, but Father Denny stopped him, "She won't go too far. Gaelan followed her and he's more than any one person can take, trust me." He turned to Angel and Kedar. "Would you give us the room please?"

Angel nodded and he and Kedar walked to the kitchenette.

"What?" Trey's tone was defensive.

"What did you tell her?"

Trey had his arms folded, "I told her that she chose a werewolf over us. I told her that she could find another team." He turned back expecting to be scolded, but Father Denny just looked at him with a pitying smile.

"*What?*"

"I told you a while back why I left my team, *our* team. Because I couldn't watch you go down a path consumed with hate."

Trey snapped back, defensively, "YEAH DENNY, I KNOW!"

"Did you ever consider that maybe, just maybe, someone else who thinks the world of you is leaving for the same reason?"

"She chose a *werewolf!*"

"No, she chose to not let *you* kill Gaelan. There's a world of difference old friend. It's the same decision I made, and you know that I hate those fucking things just as much as you do."

Trey hung his head, "Shit."

GAELAN'S DESTINY

"The question is, what are you going to do about it?"

—§—

"So, you goin' my way?" Gaelan caught up to Natalia.

"Go back Gaelan." Natalia didn't even turn to look at him. They were halfway down the long driveway that led out to the road.

"Yeah, that's not gonna happen. I'm like a walking case of herpes. You can't get rid of me."

Natalia turned, "You're disgusting! Besides, I'll lose you eventually."

"Not when I can sniff you out!" She turned and looked at him with renewed disgust. "Okay, that didn't come out right." He tapped his nose, "Werewolf, remember?"

"I know what you meant. It's still disgusting. And all the sniffing won't help you when I lead you to a crowded area and scream that you're trying to assault me." She shot him a triumphant glance.

"You would do it too, wouldn't you?"

"Just wait and find out. Or save yourself the trouble and go back to the house." She turned off the driveway and onto the road.

"Wait. Wait!" He put a hand on her arm which she yanked it away instantly. "Jesus Nat!"

"NATALIA! MY NAME IS NATALIA!"

"Yeah, that's great. I'm just trying to thank you for the other night."

"I didn't stop him for *you* Gaelan! I don't care what happens to you! Just go away!"

Gaelan nodded, "Okay. That's not what I was talking about, but okay. I just wanted to thank you for keeping your promise."

"What?" She threw out her arms, confused and frustrated.

"You smiled, remember?"

Their eyes locked for a moment. "I don't remember anything."

"Yeah, okay." He smiled, "You keep telling yourself that."

"Gaelan, there is no *us*! There is nothing! This obsession with me…"

"Oh you think I'm obsessed now, huh?"

"Well, aren't you?"

"*No*! I just saw those things about to kill the person who shot me in the gut and I was like *oh hell no, she's mine!*" She rolled her eyes, but Gaelan saw her face soften as she looked away. "Anyway, thank you for letting me see that smile, even if it was just once." He turned to walk back to the house.

She let him take a couple of steps, sighed, and then called out after him, "Are you really going to let a girl walk on a dark road at night by herself?"

Gaelan turned around as if looking for someone who wasn't there, eventually alighting on Natalia's puzzled face, "Oh, you mean *you*! I thought you said a *girl*, and not some scary-amazon-warrior-ruthless-assassin." She pursed her lips and cocked her head. He smiled and walked back to her, "So where we goin'?"

"We'll know when we get there."

"NATALIA!" They both spun around. "NATALIA!" Trey yelled again as he ran around the edge of the driveway and sprinted towards them, "Don't leave!" He was out of breath, "Please!" He motioned to Gaelan, "Can you give us a minute?"

Gaelan nodded and went to leave only to be brought up short.

"NO!" Natalia spat. "He's not going anywhere. Whatever you want to say to me, you can say it in front of him."

Trey looked at Gaelan and then back at Natalia, "I'm an idiot! A selfish asshole that is too –" He reluctantly used Denny's words, "blinded by hate to see what's really going on." He hung his head, "I know what you meant when you said you didn't do it for *him*, and I owe you. Thank you for not letting me kill an innocent man." He looked to Gaelan, who's stood, slack-jawed, "Shut up asshole."

"I didn't…" Gaelan started, but went silent when Natalia raised her hand.

Trey continued. "When you jumped in between us—I mean, I *hate* them Natalia. I hate everything about them and want them gone. All I saw was one of *them*, not him. He's still an asshole, but you were right and I was wrong. I was wrong for blindly wanting to kill the little prick, and I was wrong for telling you to leave. I'm sorry. Please don't go!" Trey got down on his knees, "I was so wrong! Please, I'm begging you to keep the family together—to *forgive* me."

"Get up, *idiot*." Natalia choked with emotion.

Trey stood up, "Please don't leave!" His voice was equally shaky.

She leaned in and hugged him, "Okay." She buried her face in his shoulder and her body shook, "Okay."

"I especially don't want you to leave with ass-munch over there."

Gaelan shrugged, "Still standing right here, hearing everything you say."

"That's the point." Trey hugged Natalia tighter even as Gaelan saw her smack him reprovingly on the back.

Gaelan shifted, uncomfortable. "Hey, you guys tell Father Denny that I had to take care of something in town, but I'll be back later, maybe tomorrow."

Trey straightened, his tone instantly authoritative. "No! Get back to the house. We have more to talk about."

Natalia picked her head up off Trey's shoulder and looked at Gaelan, her eyes bloodshot. "Please." Trey added. Gaelan stood, refusing to acknowledge the gesture.

Trey's conciliatory tone vanished. "You want a fucking *pretty please*? Cause I'm sure as shit not getting down on my knees again."

Gaelan stared at Trey for several seconds before seeing Natalia cock her head and raise her eyebrows. Gaelan sighed and turned back to the house, then called over his shoulder, "You gonna make it without losing your breath this time?"

"Little prick." Trey grumbled and followed with Natalia, who once again hid the hint of a smile.

"So we know the vampires want a witch for something. We know that these things are older than we ever thought. We know that the creatures seem to have a well-organized support network. So where's that leave us?" Father Denny looked around.

"Well, we would have been able to question someone, but ass-licker over there let two collaborators get away." Trey motioned to Gaelan.

"Oh, I'm sorry. I was actually undercover until Dickeye McGee over there decided to come busting in." Gaelan retorted.

"It was my hunt!"

"No—it was *my* hunt!"

"Would both of you just SHUT THE HELL UP!" Father Denny finally interjected. "It doesn't matter. The question is where do we go from here?"

Angel spoke up, "Gaelan said there were homeless people missing in another city. Maybe we focus our attention on finding these shelters?"

"Good idea, but there are too many cities and ten times as many shelters for us to cover without spreading our resources too thin." Father Denny looked around for other ideas.

"Kedar, you worked for terrorist groups, right?" Everyone turned to Kedar at Gaelan's question.

"We did not call ourselves terrorists."

"Po-tay-to, po-tah-to. I don't care about the semantics."

"Is this gonna be a problem?" Trey stood up to defend Kedar.

Gaelan raised his hands in mock surrender "Look, Kedar and I both fought in a war that will mean absolutely nothing years from now, and in the grand scheme of things, it was pretty fucking trivial compared to what we're doing now. There's no offense intended. Just follow my train of thought for a minute." Gaelan turned back to Kedar, "You trained somewhere, right?"

"Yes."

"And you had weapons and equipment?"

"Of course."

"What's this have to do with anything?" Trey was impatient.

Angel's eyes lit up, "Where did you get the money?"

"EXACTLY!" Gaelan chimed back in, "Where did the money come from?"

"*Follow the money*. I like it!" Father Denny's eyes lit up, "But how?"

Natalia spoke up, "I will call some people I know. They may be able to help me track down the origin of the funding for both of the shelters."

"If that doesn't pan out we need to look at privately established shelters in major urban areas around the world and see if we can find a financial link." Father Denny continued.

"That's a shit ton of work." Trey sighed.

"It just so happens that I have the manpower we need." Father Denny sounded eager.

"Yes, but you must tell everyone to be careful." Kedar had genuine concern in his voice, "If they know we are searching, they will either go deep underground, or try to tie up loose ends, then come after us with a vengeance. Either way, they won't take it lightly."

Trey asked, "Who is this mythical *they* you keep talking about?"

Gaelan started slowly, "Think about it Trey. If we're right, *they* are creatures that have had thousands of years to perfect the art of concealing their existence, and amassing an absurd amount of wealth to help them do it."

"Okay smart guy, if *they* are actually organized, rich and powerful why haven't *they* just eliminated the Venántium already?"

"I think I have the answer to that one." Father Denny interjected, "What's the only other institution that spans millennia and has unfathomable wealth?"

Angel let out a laugh of disbelief, "The Catholic Church."

"Yup. When you couple the Church's wealth, power and reach with its partnership with the other major religions, the result is staggering. We've probably been at a stalemate all this time. Call it fate or divine intervention, or maybe just blind luck, that all this time we, and all of the hunters, have been backed by the only organization that could rival the wealth and power that the enemy have amassed."

Gaelan added, "That, or *they* haven't decided to make their move yet. If they're immortal like the wolf in Canada said, they have time on their side."

The room went quiet for a moment.

"They probably have spies within." Kedar was matter-of-fact.

"That's a certainty. It's one of the reasons he brought you here. I told Gaelan that I trust you Trey—with my *life*."

"Don't try and butter me up now."

"Oh, you're still a dick Trey, just a very trustworthy dick." Gaelan interrupted with a smirk.

"Yeah, well the jury's still out on you, asshole." Trey snapped back.

"Would you two quit it?" Father Denny raised his hands in exasperation, "Right now we're the only ones that know about this. I will try and keep it that way, but at some point, this information is going to have to come out. We can't fight a war by ourselves, but we can at least figure out what we need to do."

"Okay, but how?" Angel asked the obvious.

"I can head back to Slovenia to find the other shelters, maybe backtrack to other disappearance sights. It's a shot in the dark, but maybe it'll lead somewhere."

"No!" Trey responded.

Gaelan looked to Trey, defiance in his eyes, "What do you mean *no*?"

Trey took a deep breath, closed his eyes and rubbed his temples. He grimaced, straightened, opened his eyes, and sighed, "I know I'm going to regret this, but I talked it over with Denny." Trey looked at Natalia, "And Natalia, I am serious about the fact that I was wrong. So serious that," Trey paused, swallowed hard, and clenched his fists, "I'd like you to stay with our team—*for now*."

"Well when you say it that way, how can I resist?" Gaelan's sarcasm was biting.

"Look dipshit, it's taking a lot for me to ask, okay?" Trey clenched and unclenched his fists.

Before Gaelan could respond, he heard a cough and turned to see Natalia glaring at him, eyes wide. He rolled his eyes at her and turned back to Trey, but before he could answer, Father Denny spoke up, "Look kiddo, you've been trying to get yourself killed. It's like you said, I can't be there for you as much as I need to. You told Natalia that you're all alone out there. Well now you don't have to be."

Gaelan stared at the floor for a moment. He looked up at Father Denny, then around to Angel, Kedar, Trey and finally Natalia, her face tense with anticipation. He exhaled with a puff and walked to Trey, extending his hand, "I'd be honored."

Trey took his hand. "There are conditions."

Gaelan wanted to say something facetious, but he bit his tongue.

Trey continued, "First, it's *my* team, so you follow *my* lead and *my* commands while you're with us, got it?"

"Got it."

"Second, lose the pig-sticker ninja sword."

"Not gonna happen." Gaelan glanced to Father Denny.

"Trey, that sword comes in handy." Father Denny backed Gaelan.

"How? When we get attacked by a flesh eating salad?"

"Why don't you ask the dozens of shifters and vampires I've killed with it, or the colony of cobalus I cut my way through, or maybe those last two werewolves in Canada that I gutted?"

There was a moment of tense silence before Trey spoke again.

"Fine, keep it. But there's one more thing."

"Yeah, sure thing *boss*, what else?" Gaelan was flip.

Trey spat, "You keep that *fucking thing* inside you. Don't let me see it. Do you understand me?"

Trey's hatred for werewolves was matched only by Gaelan's—the one thing they truly had in common.

"I understand."

"Okay then, it's settled. You get to tag along for now."

Gaelan grinned maniacally and pumped Trey's hand forcefully up and down. "Golly gee Mr. Marshall! We're gonna be one big happy family!"

"I'm so regretting this already." Trey disentangled his hand from Gaelan's.

Angel laughed, "Okay, but now what?"

Trey nodded to Gaelan, "It's like *junior* here said. Back to Slovenia to see if we can find any leads."

Trey and his team packed up and readied the car.

Gaelan turned to Father Denny, "Well, I guess I better bring a jacket and gloves when I go to Hell, huh?"

Father Denny chuckled, "I told you kiddo, The Lord works in mysterious ways."

Gaelan tensed and turned away.

Father Denny raised his hands in defeat, "Sorry kiddo, another time."

"Yeah, another time." Gaelan gave Father Denny a half-hearted smile, "I guess this is it then?

"For now. At least now I can get messages to you directly through Trey." The two embraced, "I know you've been trying to get yourself killed. Well now you can't. Now you have to take care of them—of *your team*—got it?"

Gaelan nodded into Denny's shoulder, then broke away.

"Now go on. You get to be a pain in *their* ass now." Father Denny affectionately pushed Gaelan out the door.

"Okay, but stock up on the wine. You're getting low and I still have a key. I actually have friends now, so don't go makin' me look bad when I bring them back here."

Father Denny grinned and made a fist, "Get outta here you little shit!"

Gaelan looked back over his shoulder, "You be careful too, okay?"

"I will kiddo."

Gaelan walked to the car with the team in wait.

"Let me guess, back seat middle?" Angel grinned.

"It's like you're in my head!" Gaelan threw his stuff in the trunk.

"Bullshit! You sit up front with me."

"Whatever you say, *Captain Fun-Sponge*."

Angel and Natalia slid into the back of the car on either side of Kedar. Gaelan leaned back from the passenger seat and smiled at Natalia. She rolled her eyes and turned away. Father Denny waved from the porch as the car pulled away.

"So, *Jack the Ripper*?" It was five miles of awkward silence until Kedar spoke up.

"Yeah," Gaelan turned and nodded with a grin, "We're pretty damn positive. He had my ex-girlfriend and…"

"Your ex-girlfriend?" Angel wiggled his eyebrows.

Natalia narrowed her eyes, and Gaelan laughed awkwardly, "Well shit, I guess I better start at the beginning. I'm not keeping any secrets, so here goes…" He began his story.

It crept out of the tree line darted toward the cabin. The woman coming around the side of the cabin was caught off guard. She screamed in terror as the thing grabbed her and tore into her throat. The other human screamed and charged. The beast grabbed him and lifted him off the ground…

"*NOOO!*" Gaelan woke, disoriented, eyes wild, head thrashing from side to side.

"Everything okay Gaelan?" Angel spoke up. Three sets of eyes stared at Gaelan from the backseat. Trey glanced furtively at him, then back to the road.

"Yeah, Everything's fine." Gaelan muttered. In the hour-long conversation about his life, he hadn't mentioned the nightmares.

"Trey?"

Trey looked to him and back to the road again.

"What?"

"When my parents were—When we were attacked. You saw *it*, right?"

"Yeah." Trey said dismissively, then looked to Gaelan, "Why?"

"I remember it like it was yesterday. That fucking *thing* attacked my parents and I went after it. But in my nightmare. In my nightmare it's *me*. *I'm* killing them." Gaelan shook his head and looked out of the window.

Trey depressed the gas pedal, and the sound of the wheels on the road got louder.

"Look, I want nothing more than to hit you in the face with a cast-iron pan, but I'll tell you this honestly. I saw the werewolf that attacked you and your parents. It was big and fast. Bigger and faster than I have ever seen. And it wasn't *you*."

Gaelan kept his eyes on the scenery blurring past the window. "That means a lot."

"Just stop jerking around and mumbling in your sleep." Trey strummed the steering wheel, "It's creeping everyone out."

"Tell me again why we didn't fly?" The long drive was getting to Gaelan.

"Because the Vatican keeps cars on standby." Trey seemed relieved at the change of topic. "This way we can travel without having to rent vehicles. Denny insisted on it back when he was hunting; said it kept our movements from being tracked and made us less predictable. He's right too. He compared it to the horse-riders of old." Trey laughed, "I think maybe he *was* one of the horse riders of old." Gaelan chuckled in response.

Trey went on "For falling backwards into a mentor, you sure hit the lottery, junior."

They stopped at a gas station along the way.

"Stretch your legs. We got a ways to go." Trey pulled the car up to the pump and everyone got out, groaning at their cramped joints.

"Nat, can I ask you something?" Gaelan walked over cautiously.

"It's Natalia. Do you understand me? Na—Tahl—ya! Can you say that?"

"Nope. Too long. It's *Nat* for your own safety."

"What are you talking about?"

"My dad was a pilot and that's the rule for a callsign."

"A what?"

"A callsign—your code name. You got Trey, Angel and Kedar. They're all two syllables or less, but Natalia is three, and that's just dangerous." She stared, brows creased, as he rambled on. *Was he dense? Stubborn? Crazy?* "Because let's just say you have three vampires coming up behind you. I say 'Natalia, watch out!' but by the time I hit the 'ya', it's too late. It's dinnertime. But I say 'Nat, watch out!' you're already spinning and BAM! You're cuttin' heads off like it's cool. See, I'm savin' your life—*Nat*."

Definitely crazy! "I'm fondly remembering shooting you now."

"*Ouch*, that cuts deep. But we digress. Seriously, I wanted to ask you something."

"Holy shit Gaelan, what is it?"

"When I was in the military, and again at the Venántium compound in China, we would all ask each other how we got there. You know, the reason why we joined. But I'm an outsider to this team, and you guys know each other—and your stories. All of you know my story. I don't know anything about any of you, other than the fact that you used to want to kill me. And Trey *still* does." He joked. Natalia fought back the beginning of a grin. Gaelan saw it, "There's that muscle twitch in your face again. You gonna be alright?"

"Shut up and get in the car." She shook her head, still trying to hide her smile.

"I'm goin'!" He smiled and then looked to Trey, "You want me to drive for a while?"

"You want a non-anesthesia hemorrhoid surgery with a butter knife?" Trey retorted.

"Jesus! A simple *no* would've sufficed. That's an image I don't need to think about, but I'm guessing you do, *often*, because, you know, that came to you really quick. How long have you had this fascination with sphincters, and mine in particular?"

"GET IN THE FUCKING CAR!"

Gaelan grinned ear-to-ear at the ability to get under Trey's skin.

They drove for about five minutes before the silence was broken.

"Hey Gaelan, did you know I was a paramedic in Madrid before I became a venator?" Angel had overheard Gaelan and Natalia's little talk.

Gaelan turned, "No shit?"

"Yeah. I liked that kind of thing, but I didn't have the patience for med school. So I drove ambulances. It was good work. Some days were great—saving lives, and seeing the look in that person's eyes, or their families'. And then some days were shitty. Really, really shitty. But the ironic part is that it was my day off that turned out to be the shittiest." He paused in deep thought, then continued, "I was walking home from the wine shop with a friend when we heard moaning. It was more of a pathetic whimper. It got louder as we came to a little stone bridge that crossed a creek about ten feet below. I called down, 'anyone there?' and someone yelled back, 'Please! I fell and I need help!'" Gaelan knew where this was going.

"Miguel had a bad feeling, but I just wanted to help. The water was much colder than I thought it would be. It came up to my knees." Angel began breathing deeply through his nostrils, his body tensing at the memory. "Where are you? I asked. There was a moan and splashing in response. Someone was choking or drowning. I called out as I waded toward the victim. Can you stand? Are you hurt? I could feel that something was wrong as soon as I put my arms around him to help him stand. His back—*it's* back—felt misaligned, abnormal. Then, just like that," Angel snapped his fingers, "it spun. Its eyes were like black mirrors. Its face was shriveled, but taut. The mouth opened wider than it should've been able to. Teeth like razors. Its claws sank into my chest." Angel pulled his shirt up to reveal four scars on his right breast and a fifth scar to the lower left, leading off in a different direction, "It couldn't hold me. I fell back into the water. But then Miguel hit it from behind. He never went for help. I don't think he saw what it was until it turned on him. I came up with a rock, somehow, and hit it in the head as hard as I could. When I grabbed Miguel, I could see a large section of his jugular was gone. He looked into my eyes. As dark as it was, I could see his eyes, and he mine. His look went from fear to acceptance. And then he was gone." Angel's fists were clenched. Angel shook his head, "Anyway, my rock hadn't killed it. It was about to kill me as I sat there crying, when I heard the *thunk* of an arrow hitting its mark, and then the shifter was screeching. It turned to run and then another arrow hit it. All of a sudden, this crazy ex-Israeli Special Forces bastard was on it's back, stabbing it like the fury of Hell itself. He had jumped from the bridge to finish it off. They'd been hunting it, tracking local disappearances for days. They were just a few minutes too late for my friend." Angel shook his head, "I guess we got that in common, huh?"

Gaelan nodded, "I'm sorry about Miguel."

"Thanks." Angel smiled weakly and turned to the window. Natalia put her hand on his knee. Angel took her hand and squeezed it without turning his head.

Gaelan looked over to Trey and saw that Trey was looking back at him, then turned his attention back to the road, shaking his head a little. Gaelan shrugged it off. He still didn't know much about Natalia but at least felt a little connection to her. Now he knew something about Angelo Silva as well. No one felt like talking after that. They crossed the Italian/Slovenian border and less than an hour later, they were in the city of Ljubljana. "Alright, let's try and figure out where this shelter is." Trey finally broke the silence as they entered the city limits.

"Take the next exit and drive for about two miles down the main road." Gaelan was looking ahead and felt the cold glare Trey shot him.

"I thought you didn't know where it was."

"I don't, but I know where to find out. Trust me. *Please*." Gaelan looked to Trey and then at the others in the back, looking for support. Trey sighed with skepticism but followed the directions. Before long, Gaelan recognized the bridge, "Okay, pull over and wait a minute."

Trey had no sooner stopped the car and Gaelan jumped out and ran under the bridge.

"This isn't right." Trey spoke aloud.

"It is odd." Kedar agreed.

"Give the kid a chance. Seriously, if he wanted us dead, he would've done it before driving across Italy, *twice*." Angel was the voice of reason.

After a few minutes, Gaelan came back up and jumped in the car, "Okay, I know where it is now."

Everyone looked at him in disbelief and Kedar asked, "How?"

"I talked to my peeps under the bridge."

"I'm not even going to ask. Just tell me where to go." Trey started the car.

Less than ten minutes later, they arrived outside of the building that housed the homeless shelter. There were boards over the windows and Gaelan could read the sign in Slovene, CLOSED. Trey cautiously approached the front door, then paused, turned around and looked at Gaelan, motioning with his head. *How about you go first.* Gaelan shrugged his shoulders at them, wide-eyed. Natalia shot him another of her scolding looks. Gaelan looked around at the expectant faces, then rolled his eyes, hung his head and walked forward in disbelief. As he passed Natalia, he pointed with two fingers from her eyes to him, "It's like a laser beam burning into me!" Then he walked past Trey.

"Hey, you're the hardest to kill, right?" Trey hissed.

"Whatever... *chicken shit*!" Gaelan gripped the door handle, ready to force it open.

Trey's retort was cut short when the door swung wide. Gaelan and Trey exchanged a glance before he took a step towards the door, stopped, and raised his face to sniff the air.

"What is it?" Angel whispered uneasily.

Gaelan drew his sword, "Death."

Gaelan could see in darkness, but Trey drew a flashlight and Kedar, Natalia and Angel all popped UV lanterns. Gaelan led them to the back where he stopped and lowered his sword. Trey came up behind him first, "What's the matt... Holy God!"

"I've seen some sick shit, but this..." Angel didn't know how to finish the sentence. Naked bodies were nailed to the walls. Some were headless, some disemboweled, others with their ribcages splayed as if dissected.

"Well, I'm not gonna lose any sleep over this." Gaelan's tone was dismissive.

"What's wrong with you?" Natalia retorted.

Gaelan motioned to a woman's body. "She's the one that drugged me." He pointed with his sword to another one, "That was one of the drivers," He looked around, "and that's the other. Curious how their heads are all still attached."

"Someone wanted you to see them." Kedar continued to look around.

"Yeah, but why?"

Natalia answered, "Because they want you to know that this trail ends here."

"Yeah, and if we stick around, we'll take the blame and get a lot of attention we don't want." Angel started for the door.

"I guess we managed to piss some people off after all." Trey actually sounded pleased as they got back in the car.

"Yeah," Gaelan raised his eyebrows, "Now we just gotta figure out just *who* we pissed off."

CHAPTER 7
ESPRESSO

Gaius sat at an outdoor café across from the Roman Coliseum sipping an espresso and watching the carefree people walk by, enjoying the brisk night air. A ruggedly dressed, aggressive looking man rounded the corner and walked directly up to the table, sitting down with a scowl.

"May I get you an espresso Lucos?" Gaius spoke in Latin.

"Do I look like I want an espresso?" Lucos glared across the table.

"No, I think not. My apologies."

"Why did your—*masters*—call me here Gaius, and why the entourage?" Lucos motioned to a neighboring table. He could smell the vampires even before he sat.

"I'm sorry my friend, but there have been *developments*."

"What sort of developments?" Lucos was dismissive.

"Several enchantresses and immortals are missing and assumed dead."

"Why should I care if a handful of witches and vampires are dead…and call them what they are?"

"You should care because one of the witches was to bond with the seer and reveal the final prophet. Her replacement disappeared as well. I needn't remind you that the time approaches. The final prophet will tell the masters how to open the gate. If the Hunters have discovered the prophecy, they will do everything they can to find the gate before we do."

"Then your so-called *masters* can step up their timeline and tear them all to pieces."

"If they reveal the existence of your kind or theirs, there will be a war with man, and the masters' weakness will be exposed as long as the sun shines."

"That's right. *Their* weakness, not mine." Lucos looked over at the table of vampires accompanying Gaius, then back to his host, "And I know what happens if our existence is revealed. It would get rather—*messy.*"

"Then you know it is better for all parties to continue unexposed. Once the Eternal Darkness is upon us, the masters will have no vulnerabilities. Loyalists will ascend, the Hunters will be eradicated, and humanity will be enslaved. The time of man will come to an end. But first they need to find out where the gate is, and how to open it."

Lucos stared condescendingly at Gaius, "Spoken like the true loyalist, eh? And one that believes in a fairytale prophecy. I don't have to tell you what that prophecy did to me and my kind, do I?" Gaius shook his head as Lucos continued, "And now I'm supposed to feel bad that your little mystics aren't working out? What say I get you a fortune cookie and we see what that reveals?"

Gaius cautiously changed the topic, "What have you found out about the unsanctioned wolf?"

Lucos averted his gaze and shifted, "Only what we were told. He disappeared in China and hasn't been seen since."

"The masters want to know the progress you've made." Gaius pressed.

"The masters can kiss my hairy ass at dawn. If they want to know about him so bad, let them look into it."

The vampires at the neighboring table, two impeccably dressed men and a woman, all stood up. One of the men walked over with a scathing whisper, "Watch your tongue, *animal!*"

Lucos slowly turned his head and locked eyes with the man, "Speak to me again *boy,* and I'll gut you like the insignificant pig you are and piss on your carcass as it dissolves." He turned back to Gaius, "Tell your watchdog to curb his tongue Gaius, lest he find out how I truly feel about his kind."

"They know how you feel about them, and about the prophecy." Gaius treaded lightly.

Lucos leaned across the table and hissed, "No. They truly have *no* idea."

Gaius spoke in a soft tone, "I'm sorry to have offended you. The masters simply wanted me to keep you informed, and find out if you knew anymore about the unsanctioned wolf. Please accept my apology."

Lucos looked him up and down and settled back in his chair, sighing, "Accepted."

Gaius fidgeted his chair.

"Something else bothering you, Gaius?"

"This is awkward my friend." Gaius averted his gaze, but heard Lucos' groan of displeasure. "The masters would like you to send some of your wolves when we find another willing and capable enchantress." Before Lucos could interrupt, Gaius corrected himself, "*Witch*! A willing and capable *witch*. Are you willing to send your people? Once more, I don't want to offend."

Lucos nodded solemnly, choking back the words he wished to say, "Name the time and place. Tell your masters I will send my best. This is my promise."

"Thank you my friend."

Lucos waved him off dismissively, "It's no trouble. Good night Gaius." Lucos looked at the vampires, "Oh, and remember to feed your watchdogs and take them for a walk." He smirked and strode away.

Gaius and the vampires settled into the leather seats of their black SUV.

One of the vampires leered, "Why do the masters allow him such leeway? So much disrespect? And you, *lackey*, allow it."

"Because they have seen what he can do." Gaius shifted his gaze out the window, "What he and his kind are capable of. I don't mean to offend you, but make no mistake about it, you were there as a *show* of force. Had the masters intended for force to be used," Gaius turned back to the vampire, "they would have sent more of you. Many, many more."

CHAPTER 8
IT

It had been weeks since Slovenia with no new leads. It mattered little as Father Denny had more pressing cases for the team to deal with. Trey, Angel, Kedar, Natalia and Gaelan walked down a narrow street in one of Buenos Aires' ubiquitous shantytowns. An old friend of Father Denny's had reached out for assistance. According to the priest, a young boy's body had been found badly charred, and three men and two women had been arrested for his abduction and murder. A seven-year-old girl was found with them, and the police figured that they saved her from a similar fate at the hand of a cult.

The girl had been taken to a local church orphanage for care. For the first few days, everything was fine. She was healing, but clearly traumatized, repeatedly telling the Mother Superior that she "couldn't stop it", that "it was too much" and "it hurt" when she tried to fight. *The poor girl must have been assaulted by her abductors.*

Then the incidents started. Children were being attacked and beaten by an unseen assailant. The antiquated security cameras were reviewed, but every tape was warped and fuzzy for the duration of the attack, twitching back into focus on an image of the injured child. Then, just a few nights before the team's arrival, Mother Rosetta was found bloodied and unconscious at the bottom of the long staircase in the main hall. She could have tripped, but upon review, the security footage showed the same anomaly as the attacks on the children. Once again, there were no clear answers and they couldn't interview the Mother Superior as she was still unconscious.

Father Manuel met the team at the entrance to the orphanage and led them through the halls to the main office. Another priest, a nun teaching at the orphanage, and the bishop stood to greet them.

"Thank you so much for coming." The bishop spoke in Spanish, while Angel translated highlights for the rest of the team. "We would not have asked if we did not suspect something that requires your attention."

"It's our pleasure and duty to help your Excellency."

The bishop shifted uneasily.

"You were told of the girl?"

"Yes, abduction victim. The attacks occurred after she arrived, correct?"

"Yes. We believe that she is—possessed." The Bishop seemed uneasy.

Angel glanced towards Gaelan, who nodded his understanding and turned to the others

"Possession" he whispered.

Trey visibly tensed; Kedar and Natalia both closed their eyes and sighed.

Angel continued, "What proof do you have? This is a catholic orphanage, correct?"

"It is." Father Manuel answered.

"And she stepped onto holy ground without alerting you?"

"She showed signs of distress, but we believed it was because of the trauma she had endured." The Bishop continued, "Nothing stood out as peculiar until the chapel."

"The chapel?" Angel was intrigued.

"It's easier if we show you." Father Manuel turned on the monitor.

"We were told there was no video evidence?"

"Please." The bishop intoned.

The other's gathered around the screen. The bishop and the nun stepped backward next to the other priest, as if unwilling to be close to the images. Gaelan could hear their whispered prayers, accompanied by the faint click of rosary beads.

The video was grainy, and black and white; there was no sound. A line of children filed into the main chapel. Father Manuel whispered that they were gathering to pray for the recovery of Mother Superior after her fall. Then, towards the end of the line of children, the image began to twist and distort. Just as quickly, just before Angel could ask what they were looking for, the picture waivered back to normal. A young girl stood, clearly agitated, at the chapel doors, unwilling to enter. Two sisters bend to comfort her, but to no avail. The picture twisted out of focus again as the nuns turned to lead the girl away from the door. When it refocused, only an empty hallway remained.

"So you think she's distorting the picture somehow?" Angel asked.

Father Manuel didn't answer, but rewound the tape, pausing where the nuns and girl turned to leave. "Here." He advanced the tape frame by frame. The liquid, blurred quality of the girl's face could have been an issue with the recording equipment. But then the girl glanced up at the camera. Her eyes, which darted away too quickly to see at normal speed, were swollen, distorted, and milky white; unearthly. The nun's Hail Mary intensified behind the group, her breathing shallow. After a pause, Angel spoke.

"She seems distressed, but not in any pain. So how is it that she can walk everywhere on consecrated ground? Has this place been desecrated?"

"It has not, and that's why you're here my young friend." The last priest spoke up, "I'm Father Hector." He extended his hand to Angel.

"Father Hector is our exorcist." The bishop seemed uneasy uttering those words.

"I asked Father Dennis to send you." Father Hector glanced around at the entire team with a warm expression.

"That's fine Father, but why us? We were in Europe. Wasn't there a closer team?"

"I deferred to Dennis's expertise. I asked for the best team he had."

"For an exorcism?" Angel was incredulous.

Father Hector's face grew grim, "For *this* exorcism. I believe we are dealing with a falleN onE."

Angel fell silent, his quickening breath matching the nun's frantic rosary.

Natalia sensed the shift in Angel, and tapped Gaelan on the leg.

"falleN onE?" Gaelan watched their faces fall, "What am I missing?"

"What you're missing, young man, is the fact that we are dealing with something so vile that it unnerves even the stoutest of hearts." Father Hector answered in English.

"Apparently my English is almost as good as your Spanish." He smiled at Gaelan and added, "Come, we have much to talk about."

Father Hector passed out cups of coffee in his cramped room, then pulled a bottle of Fernet out from under his bed, and added it to his steaming cup. "For the nerves."

Gaelan accepted the proffered bottle and thanked the priest. He was about to unscrew the top when Trey snatched it out of his hands with a scathing look. Gaelan raised his hands in defeat, expecting Trey to hand the bottle back to the priest. Instead, Trey stalked to the opposite corner, then stared directly at Gaelan with a triumphant smirk as he poured liquor into his own coffee.

"Dick." Gaelan mouthed silently at Trey.

Father Hector began, "Once they brought the evidence to me, I began testing Eliana. Just a normal conversation with a lovely young girl—at first. But out of nowhere, she would blurt out the most hideous things. Once we were talking about flowers, walking in the gardens, when she turned to me and told me, calm as anything, that the smell of the dead boy was the greatest bouquet of all. Her smile..." Father Hector trailed off and took a big drink of his spiked coffee, "Believe me, I have seen a lot, but that smile chilled me to my very soul. Then the poor child broke down sobbing, complaining that she didn't feel good." He paused, seemed to steel himself, and continued. "I had placed a crucifix under her mattress, wondering if she would react. She didn't, but when I went to retrieve it the next morning, the head of the Lord was missing. There was no burning or scarring on her hands. The next day, I pretended to bump into her while holding a cup of holy water. I expected it to blister her skin. Instead, it simply evaporated and left no mark. She looked me straight in the eye, told me that she liked to be dirty enough to warrant a shower, then urinated in her pants." Father Hector crossed himself. "Almost instantly, her eyes rolled back and her voice turned deep and raspy. She said 'stop toying with me priest,' and began to speak in tongues. The air in the hallway seemed to heat up and I felt as if I was being physically pushed away from her. Luckily, Father Manuel knew what was going on. He and three of the sisters restrained her and locked her in a room, then I contacted Father Dennis immediately. This is something more than just a demon. Much more powerful. Attempts to feed her or get her to drink are useless. iT wants to make sure that she's weak for the rite." Father Hector took another sip.

"Have you ever encountered one before Father? A falleN onE?" Natalia asked.

"Once. I was called to a village when I was a missionary in the Philippines. A falleN onE had possessed a man. He had taken part in a séance in an attempt to speak to a dead relative. iTs name was rahaB. The man, or rather iT, was killing people, and making a shrine from their skins. iT called other things to iT, mostly shifters and witches. It took several teams of venators to track them down, and some were lost in the fighting to subdue iT. Once captured, I attempted to exorcise iT. A normal demon will fight, but holds no real power. Its only purpose is torment. They are normally vanquished by a competent exorcist, but the longer a person is held, the harder it is to pull the thing from them. The falleN—they are incredibly strong from the outset. The will of the victim is taken almost completely; fighting iT is far too painful. That's why Eliana said she couldn't stop 'iT.' That she wasn't strong enough. She wasn't talking about her captors, she was talking about the falleN onE."

"But how was she opened up to iT?" Natalia sounded concerned.

"I confronted iT as the others intervened, commanding iT to say iTs name. iT laughed at me, but in the name of God, I compelled iT. iT said one word—molocH."

"Should that mean something?" Trey asked.

"iT is known for the sacrifice of children. The ones taken into custody must have killed the poor young boy to bring iT forth. Somehow Eliana was open to possession, perhaps through forced ritual and dark prayers; perhaps she was deceived into drinking human blood, or maybe just tricked into playing a game of Ouija."

"Why didn't she just run away? I mean, why did iT stick around here to be caught?" Suddenly five sets of incredulous eyes were upon Gaelan. "What?"

"This is your first exorcism?" Father Hector seemed downcast.

"Yeah. What's wrong?"

"John," Kedar called Gaelan by his father's name, "demons cannot come into our realm on their own. They cause problems and may even kill through possessed ones. But during an exorcism, the exorcist and those assisting him are opened to demonic attack.

Unlike normal demons, a falleN onE *can* cross into this world. Possession is bad enough: iT can wreak havoc, destruction and death, murdering for pleasure. But if iT gets out, for one night, iT will create unimaginable destruction. The light of the sun will ultimately vanquish iT, but until then, iT is said to be unstoppable."

Gaelan was frustrated, "I don't remember reading about this."

Father Hector looked at Gaelan, "At the compound, you are taught about things—creatures—that you can fight. But to have knowledge of a entity that was once an *angel*, that could lay waste to the very land. That is something else entirely."

"But you haven't answered my question. Why didn't iT just run away and try to get out?"

Natalia finally spoke up, "The only way that iT can come through to this realm is during the exorcism. If the exorcist doesn't vanquish iT, iT will eventually tear through the one that is possesses. There are several instances recorded where Venántium were called to assist in an exorcism, only to be lost in some horrible 'natural disaster' that laid waste to the entire area."

"Okay, so how do we stop it? 'Cause there has to be a way, right?" Grim looks were Gaelan's only reply.

"If the situation becomes dire, one of the venators will compel iT, through a certain prayer, to possess his or herself. iT becomes trapped within the venator, who is burned alive. The venator dies and iT is vanquished."

Gaelan turned to Father Hector, "The falleN onE, in the Philippines, how did it end?"

"rahaB was already too strong. One of the venators, a young woman from Norway, could see that iT was about to tear through; she said the prayer and compelled iT to possess her. She screamed in pain until she was overcome by iT. iT used her body to kill three venators, two of her own teammates, before she was doused with holy oil and lit afire. That was the only time I encountered a falleN onE...until now. It's also the only time I ever lost anyone." Father Hector poured Fernet into his empty coffee cup and drank it straight.

Gaelan was still trying to process it all, "So then why conduct the ritual at all?"

"Because otherwise iT will graduate from pushing people down stairs to skinning them. And iT could find a priest to torture into conducting the rite to free iT." Father Hector downed the Fernet left in his cup, "I'm going to get some fresh air. I'm sure you have much to talk about." He poured some more liquor into his cup and then handed the bottle to Gaelan on his way out.

"Denny's little pet doesn't have to do them?" Gaelan looked at Natalia somberly.

"I'm sorry I said that. You never knew about the rite. It wasn't fair of me." She was sincere.

"Everyone prepare yourselves for tonight." Trey shook his head in frustration.

"We're starting it at night?" Gaelan was confused, "I thought you said the sun will stop iT?"

"Yeah, but iT can hold out, dug in like a tick, until sunset. Then iT'll tear out. We start in the middle of the night so if iT does get out, we have less time until sun up." Trey walked out.

"You okay?" Angel looked to Gaelan.

"Here I thought I knew all about monsters." Gaelan shook his head and looked out the window, "Now I know why everyone hates exorcisms."

"Yeah, it's not our favorite." Angel smiled and shifted his gaze to Natalia, walking up beside Gaelan.

Natalia slipped her arm under Gaelan's and led him out of the room, "Come on. We'll need our strength tonight and Father Manuel recommended a restaurant just down the street." As they walked, Kedar squeezed his shoulder and Angel rubbed his head.

"Not that I mind, but you're all being a little too nice to me, ya know, for having wanted to kill me so recently." Gaelan looked around at them.

"Once we start the rite," Natalia continued to lead him down the hallway, "we are one team. Everyone's first exorcism is a challenge. I guess Father Denny figured it was time you were exposed to it." Gaelan looked down at Natalia, feeling her arm wrapped around his. She looked up at him, but didn't return his smile. Instead, she released his arm and walked ahead, "Come. We're all going to need our strength and I'm hungry."

"You heard the lady." Angel walked faster to catch her.

Gaelan fell in step with Kedar, "You seem off. What's bothering you?"

"I have seen a demon jump to the body of a venator during a right." Kedar didn't make eye contact, "For several seconds, the possessed are unaware and unable to do anything. The demon has complete control. When the possessed try to fight back, the pain begins."

"Then what?"

"It's like the exorcist described. The possessed can be forced to hurt their very friends. But I have also seen a venator have the strength to hold it in. To not let it jump again."

"What happened then?"

"His teammates held him down while the priest finished the rite and cast the demon back to Hell."

"Damn."

"The rest of us have all seen firsthand what a *demon* can do, and this is no ordinary demon.

"Do you think we can beat iT?"

Kedar was silent for a moment before he strode to catch up to Natalia and Angel, "I do."

It was just after midnight when Father Hector blessed each of the venators. Gaelan went through the motions, allowing years of ritual and habit to take over, rather than argue about a worthless gesture. The priest addressed them, "I alone will speak and perform the ritual. At no time will you acknowledge iTs presence. I will pray over Eliana and attempt to vanquish the unclean."

"There's no attempting Father. There's just doing." Trey growled.

Father Hector was about to admonish Trey for interrupting, but thought better of it, smiled, and nodded, "Whatever happens, continue what prayers your faith dictates, be they Hebrew, Islamic, Hindu, Buddhist. I will conduct the Catholic ritual. We will all be open to attack. iT may leave Eliana for short instances in an attempt to possess you. The attacks will be brutal and iT will attempt to use your body against those around you. But iT will always return to Eliana. She is iTs gateway to our world. No matter what happens, your job is to continue to pray and keep her restraints intact. We cannot and will not fail." Father Hector surveyed each of them, "One way or another, Eliana's ordeal ends tonight." They all nodded in consent. "Prepare yourselves."

They followed the priest up the flight of stairs that Mother Rosetta had been pushed down. The rest of the children, and most of the staff, were spending the night in local churches due to 'construction' happening overnight. Four nuns waited for them by the door at the end of the hallway. Father Hector stopped to pray with them, then seemed to steal himself as he reached for the doorknob.

One of the sisters murmured as they stepped inside, "God be with you."

The room was a cream color; curtains obscured the lone window. Squares on the wall hinted at framed pictures that had been removed along with most of the furniture. To one side, a small table held a crucifix, several bottles of holy water, and a small book bound in black leather. Buckets of holy oil and butane torches reminded the venators of the worst-case scenario Father Hector had described. Lanterns in each corner illuminated the bed, and the girl, bound to the bedframe by her wrists and ankles.

She looked terrified. Gaelan wondered if she knew that they were there to help, or if she just thought that she had been rescued from one hell, only to suffer through this one. Natalia and Trey filed around to the far side of the bed, Natalia closest to her head. Angel and Kedar took their spots on the opposite side. Gaelan knelt at the foot of the bed and grasped the rails underneath. Father Hector took his place to the right of Gaelan.

"Father, I don't understand, what did I do?" Eliana had tears in her eyes. Gaelan fought the urge to speak.

Eliana looked around, wild eyed, at the people kneeling by her bed, "Why won't they let me go? I don't want you to hurt me like the others did!" She looked pleadingly at Father Hector, her voice a pitiful whine, "I'll be good, I promise I won't tell anyone about this and I'll just run away. Please let me go."

Father Hector ignored her pleas and opened the black leather book.

"Lord have mercy."

The venators repeated in unison, heads bowed, "Lord have mercy."

"Christ have mercy."

"Christ have mercy."

"Please Father, Please!" Eliana sobbed.

"Lord have mercy."

"Lord have mercy."

"Almighty Father and Creator, Blessed Son and Savior, Holy Spirit and Bringer of Light, One Trinity, One God, have mercy on us."

"Have mercy on us."

"Please Father! I'll be good!"

Was this a mistake? Gaelan couldn't help but wonder.

Father Hector continued, "Hear our prayers, Lord God, Lamb of God..."

"I'll let you touch me—" Eliana's sobbing flowed into a voice far older than her own, " ⌜anywhere⌟ ."

"Hear us and give us strength." Father Hector's voice became louder and more determined.

" ⌜You'd like that, wouldn't you? A little body like this? Or maybe I should've inhabited the little boy instead. Maybe you would've liked that better?⌟ " Eliana's laugh was hollow, almost metallic. The room took on a sudden chill.

"Give us the strength, Oh Lord, to bring the darkness into the light. We implore the angels and saints to pray for us. Holy Mary, Mother of God,"

" ⌜WHORE!⌟ " Eliana's voice was completely inhuman.

"Pray for us!"

"Pray for us!" Gaelan joined the others.

"Saint Michael, prince of angels and protector of Heaven,"

" ⌜SLAVE!⌟ "

"Pray for us!"

"Pray for us!" Gaelan could hear the focus in the others' voices, and worked to remain as steadfast as they were.

"Saint Gabriel and Saint Raphael, archangels of light,"

" ⌜LACKEYS! Those who would rather serve than rule.⌟ "

"Pray for us!" Father Hector was unfazed.

"Pray for us!"

" ⌜Do not think for one moment that they don't hate you as much as we do. You are the favored when we are the deserving. They will rejoice when the rivers run red with your blood and earth is stained with your bile!⌟ "

"Saint Peter, Saint Paul, Saint Andrew..."

" 「Pray to them all priest! They cannot help you or this world!」 " iT began to cackle and then roared, lunging against the bindings toward Father Hector. The room went from cold to hot and the book in his hand crumbled to ash. Father Hector continued down the list of saints, naming them effortlessly. He didn't need the book to perform the rite.

" 「Hurry priest. Begin it so I can tear through this flesh and lay waste to your land. This is but the beginning. The keys to the gates are almost upon us!」 "

Father Hector paused and stared at iT. *Was he unable to continue?* Gaelan raised his eyes. Eliana's face was pale with dark lips and black veins clearly visible through the skin. Her skin and hair were clammy, and she was sweating profusely, covering her body in a veil of fluid. iTs eyes turned towards Gaelan. They were milky white, but he could faintly see where the pupils should have been. He snapped his eyes toward the floor, cursing himself for failing to keep his head down in prayer. Out of the corner of his eye, he could see the others were still staring at Father Hector in concern.

" 「This little cunt is mine. I will rip her apart or stay inside her like a festering disease. You've already lost!」 " Raspy and cackling, iT suddenly bellowed, " 「BEGIN IT PRIEST!」 "

Father Hector, still motionless and silent, continued to stare at iT as the room began to chill once more. iT went to speak again, but Father Hector cut iT off with a thunderous resolve, "ALMIGHTY FATHER, JESUS OUR SAVIOR, You gave your disciples the power to cast out the evil; to bring light to the shadows; to send the wicked back to the pit!"

" 「IT HAS BEGUN! I will rupture this flesh and feed on your souls.」 "

"I call on you oh Lord, as a humble servant and a shield of Heaven, to give me the power to cast out the unclean!"

" 「The beginning of the end is upon you!」 "

"And in your Holy Name I say," Father Hector locked eyes with iT, "LEAVE THIS INNOCENT, LEAVE THIS PLACE, LEAVE THIS WORLD!"

Eliana's body convulsed as iT fought to maintain a hold on her. Gaelan clenched his hands tightly around the bedframe as the iT began to resist. The room was so cold that everyone's breath was clearly visible.

"Grant your most unworthy servant the strength, courage and faith to vanquish the unholy. In Your Holy Name I command the unclean, LEAVE THIS INNOCENT, LEAVE THIS PLACE, LEAVE THIS WORLD!"

Eliana's body convulsed and then she looked up, " ⌜Fool priest, The Eternal Darkness approaches and we will be set free!⌟ "

"I say to yoU," Father Hector paused a moment before using iTs name, "molocH, I CAST yoU OUT! Depart, liar and seducer of the innocent!"

" ⌜YOU DARE USE MY NAME!⌟ "

"Leave in the name of our Lord and Savior Jesus Christ, whose love and glory yoU fear. yoU are powerless before Him, a prisoner of the darkness where yoU dwell. His eternal light has banished yoU to the pit where yoU are to remain for eternity."

Eliana's back arched almost to a breaking point, and it seemed as if her restraints were the only things holding her to the bed. She screeched an unearthly sound of pain and then fell back to the bed. She looked up and roared. Gaelan felt himself slamming into the wall. He looked up to see the others recovering from the same assault. iT was fighting back. The bed shook, then peeled away from the very floor, levitating as if suspended by Eliana's small body. The room itself began to shake and the walls cracked, dust fell from the ceiling. Father Hector stood resolute. Gaelan scrambled to regain his footing as the others tried to bring the bed down. He grabbed the bed and slammed it to the ground. At this point, even Trey was happy to have Gaelan's strength there.

The struggle between the priest and iT was physically manifest. iT would muster some awful force and attempt to break through Eliana's form. Father Hector would pray as if gathering some unseen power, then command iT to leave, the sinew in his neck standing as he strained. Gaelan held fast to the bed so as not to be thrown back again, even through the repeated blows of iTs retaliation.

Minutes melted into hours. Gaelan refused to pray to any Higher Power as he felt it was useless, but his thoughts turned to those who never let him down. *Dad, Mom, I hope you can hear me. Actually, I know you can hear me! I need some help here—This little girl needs some help!* His concentration was broken when Eliana screamed in pain. *Eliana*, not the thing inside her. Everyone's blood ran cold when they saw the cause of her pain. From under her skin, it looked as if nails were trying to claw their way out.

For the first time, Father Hector advanced from the spot where he stood. He pressed a crucifix against her chest and poured holy water over her body, bellowing, "I COMMAND yoU, FOULEST ENTITY, RELINQUISH yoUr HOLD ON THIS INNOCENT CHILD!"

Eliana's body seemed to relax for just a second, then convulsed as iT screeched,

" ⌜ This is but the beginning priest. We will be set free and burn our way back to the gates of heaven! I am but the harbinger of things to come! ⌟ "

"I cast yoU out, filthy servant of darkness, and render yoU powerless on Earth. In the name of God our Father, be gone and return to the Hell from where yoU came. For it is He who commands yoU, He who holds yoU powerless, and He who condemns…"

Before Father Hector could finish, Eliana's body went limp. Immediately, Angel stood and screeched an unearthly howl, his eyes milky white. He grabbed Kedar and threw him back and into the wall. Then he clenched his fists and yelled in pain. A second later, he fell to his knees and looked up, his eyes once again his own—Eliana's body convulsed and she screamed again. The claws began trying to scratch through her again and once more, Father Hector charged forward with the crucifix and holy water, "I COMMAND yoU, FOULEST ENTITY, RELINQUISH yoUr HOLD ON THIS INNOCENT CHILD!"

Eliana's body went limp and then Natalia stood, diving on Trey, biting into his arm and scratching at his face. Trey yelled, "FIGHT IT NATALIA! FIGHT IT!" She screamed in pain and fell to the floor. Gaelan wanted to rush to her, but knew he had to stay where he was. Natalia looked up in horror to see the scratch marks on Trey's face bleeding. He shook it off and scurried back to the bed. Father Hector hadn't waited for iT to come back to Eliana, he pressed the crucifix to her chest and poured the holy water, "I COMMAND yoU, FOULEST ENTITY, RELINQUISH yoUr HOLD ON THIS INNOCENT CHILD!"

iT roared in pain as iT re-entered her body. Her body went limp and Kedar stood, grabbing the priest by his collar and throwing him backward. Kedar's hand sizzled as it touched the priest and iT roared. Kedar fell to his knees and looked at his hand. The blistering began to heal immediately as iT left his body. Father Hector charged forward as Eliana raised her head and looked at him, eyes milky white.

" ⌜She is weakening priest! She will break and then you will feel my pain a thousand times over!⌟ "

"I COMMAND yoU, FOULEST ENTITY, RELINQUISH yoUr HOLD ON THIS INNOCENT CHILD!"

Gaelan knelt unyielding at the foot of the bed, struggling to maintain his focus. Then he felt it—a million burning needles stabbing at his skin. He gritted his teeth and the pain passed. iT roared in agony and anger. Needles, again, and again he fought through the pain. iT roared once more as Father Hector continued the rite. Eliana's head raised and looked towards Gaelan at the end of the bed.

" ⌜YOU ARE NOT ONE OF THEM!⌟ "

Gaelan fought to keep his concentration, averting iTs gaze. He felt the onslaught on his body, the burning and pain, and fought through it again.

" ⌜YOU ARE NOT ONE OF THEM!⌟ " Father Hector continued to pray and the others began to tense as they knew who iT was talking to and what iT was talking about, " ⌜You are not one of them! You are a half-breed!⌟ "

Gaelan strained to block out everything but his own thoughts. *Breathe! Remember your training in Japan. Mom and Dad. My Team. Natalia—my angel! Breathe! Can't let them down. Can't let them down. Can't let them down!* Gaelan repeated it in his head as he heard iT address him.

" ⌜Now half-breed, destroy them and set me free!⌟ "

iT didn't seem able to possess him. He continued to concentrate, shutting his eyes and focusing on Nat's face.

" ⌜DESTROY THEM NOW!⌟ "

Gaelan glanced up at the milky white eyes staring at him. The others in the room seemed to notice his expression of disdain. Trey caught Gaelan's eye and gave a subtle shake of his head. Gaelan dropped his head once more, trying to ignore the voice. The searing pain that revisited him lasted only seconds. iT screeched in rage and began speaking in a language only Gaelan understood.

" ⌜FILTHY HALF-BREED TRAITOR!⌟ "

Gaelan kept his eyes shut as the bed shook violently.

" ⌜I WILL NOT ALLOW YOU TO STOP THE ETERNAL DARKNESS!⌟ "

Father Hector commanded iT to leave Eliana's body again. Her bonds strained under her violent convulsions.

" ⌜I WILL END THE PROPHECY TONIGHT!⌟ "

iT hissed in rage, then Eliana screamed as the claws tore at her skin. Blood oozed from her tortured flesh.

"JESUS, iT's BREAKING THROUGH!" Angel cried out and stood to press down on Eliana's shoulders.

Father Hector pressed the crucifix to Eliana's chest and poured holy water over her slight frame. iT screeched and foam poured out of Eliana's mouth. Angel yelled out, "I'LL COMPEL iT! DON'T HESITATE!"

"NO!" Everyone, even Father Hector shouted. They still had a chance to beat iT.

" ⌜I WILL TEAR YOU APART SHEEP IN WOLF'S CLOTHING!⌟ " Eliana shrieked in the dead language.

"WE DON'T HAVE TIME!" Angel yelled and began, "IN THE NAME OF GOD OUR ..."

At that, Gaelan stood up and looked directly at it, cutting Angel off, "WHAT DID YOU SAY?"

"Do not engage iT directly!"

"molocH, WHAT DID yoU CALL ME?" Gaelan bellowed at iT, ignoring the priest's warning.

" ⌜You understand Enochian?⌟ " iT seemed puzzled and stopped clawing.

Gaelan then spoke in iTs language, "I don't care what this filth is that we're speaking," He switched back to English, "What—did—you—call me?"

"DO NOT SPEAK TO iT! LEAVE HERE NOW!" Father Hector bellowed.

" ⌜You dare to use my name?⌟ " iT now spoke in English.

"I have others for you too. What did you call me?"

" ⌜I will rip you open and feast on your innards?⌟ "

"REMOVE HIM!" Father Hector yelled.

"GAELAN, GET OUT!" Trey roared.

Father Hector looked from Trey to Gaelan to Eliana, then shouted, "I COMMAND yoU, FOULEST ENTITY, RELINQUISH yoUr HOLD ON THIS INNOCENT CHILD!" Eliana's body convulsed but iT's eyes remained on Gaelan.

" ⌜I WILL HAVE YOUR BODY AND SOUL!⌟ "

"THEN COME AND GET ME YOU PISSANT PIECE OF SHIT!" Gaelan waved his fingertips toward himself. He felt the stabbing sensation again and gritted through the pain as Eliana's body momentarily relaxed before convulsing once more. iT roared in anger and Gaelan taunted, "Oh that's right, we both figured out yoU can't!"

"GET OUT!" Father Hector screamed.

Gaelan pointed at Father Hector, "FINISH THE GOD-DAMNED RITE!"

" ⌜If I can't have you,⌟ " iT looked around the room, " ⌜I'LL HAVE THEM!⌟ "

Eliana's body relaxed once again, then Natalia's eyes turned milky white. She stood and grabbed Trey, throwing him backward and shattering the glass in the room's lone window. Natalia fell to her knees as Eliana's body convulsed, then immediately went limp again. Trey lifted himself to his feet, his hand grasping a shard of glass. When he looked directly at Gaelan, his eyes were milky white. He brought the glass up to his throat, a sickly grin on his lips.

"NOOOOOO!" Natalia screamed. Angel and Kedar yelled with her.

Before Trey could cut his own throat, Gaelan yelled out, "I COMPEL yoU IN THE NAME OF GOD ALMIGHTY TO LEAVE THIS VESSEL AND TAKE MINE IN ITS STEAD!" He spun to the others, "DO IT!"

Gaelan's body convulsed as Trey fell to his knees, confused. He looked up and saw Gaelan shaking unnaturally, hearing Natalia's "Dear God!" She instinctively jumped on the bed and began removing Eliana's restraints. Angel grabbed the holy oil as Gaelan rose to his full height and opened his milky white eyes. With a flick of his hand Angel was slammed into the opposite wall.

" ⌜With this body, I don't need to tear my way through!⌋ " iT sneered. Gaelan advanced toward Father Hector. Trey rushed to the side of the bed and grabbed the holy oil, but Kedar grabbed him and stopped him, "WAIT!" Kedar turned and positioned himself directly in front of Gaelan, "You're stronger than iT is! You can hold iT!" Gaelan's hand grabbed Kedar by the throat and lifted him high. Kedar gurgled, "I—know—you—can."

" ⌜He is...⌋ " iT stopped speaking and Gaelan's grasp opened, dropping Kedar to the floor. Gaelan's eyes shut and he angrily whispered in his own voice, "You wanted in." his whisper became deeper and throaty, "Now you can stay in!" His eyes opened and the whites were blood red with yellow pupils. He fell to his knees and sank his growing fingernails into the wood floor.

"FATHER, FINISH THE RITE!" Kedar yelled.

Angel got to his feet and ran over, "You can do this! Hold iT in!"

Trey ran over and unbound Eliana's ankles. Natalia rushed the child out of the room and ordered the priest and nuns to get her to the chapel.

Father Hector was praying as fast as he could, "Leave in the name of our Lord and Savior Jesus Christ, whose love and glory yoU fear. yoU are powerless before Him, a prisoner of the darkness where yoU dwell—"

Gaelan's eyes began to turn milky white at the fringes, " 「He is... 」 "

Trey ran to him, "You got this junior! You can do it! HOLD iT!"

Gaelan's eyes turned red once more and his voice went raspy, "My mind. My body!" His entire body burned with intense pain, but he steadied himself.

The skin of Gaelan's forehead sizzled where Father Hector laid the crucifix, "I cast yoU out, filthy servant of darkness, and render yoU powerless on earth. In the name of God our Father, be gone and return to the Hell from where you came. For it is He who commands yoU, He who holds yoU powerless and He who condemns yoU!"

In his head, Gaelan could hear the voice, " 「*WE WILL RISE! YOU CANNOT STOP US! WE WILL HAVE OUR ETERNAL DARKNESS! WE WILL BURN YOUR WORLD TO ASH! FEEL THE FLAMES!* 」 "

Gaelan snarled aloud as pain seared through his body, "IS THAT ALL YOU HAVE?"

Natalia ran back into the room, slid to her knees in front of him and held his cheeks in her hands. She wasn't sure if she was talking to Gaelan, a werewolf or a demon, but she implored him, "You hold iT in! I know you can!"

Father Hector prayed, "And it is in His Holy Name that I command yoU, foulest entity, relinquish yoUr hold on this innocent!"

Gaelan looked back into Natalia's eyes with his inhuman werewolf eyes, and with his fanged teeth, he smiled at her. In his mind iT screeched, " 「*YOUR WORLD WILL BUUUUUUUUUURN!* 」 " He closed his eyes and growled, "But not tonight. *Now go to Hell!*"

Father Hector roared, "TREMBLE BEFORE THE MIGHT OF THE LORD AND IN HIS HOLY NAME, I CAST yoU OOOOOOOOOOOUT!"

Gaelan's back arched and he screamed in pain. The floor under his hands exploded into splinters and he fell back. His body suddenly relaxed and steam billowed from it. Father Hector pressed forward to Gaelan and thrust the crucifix into his chest, "We must be sure!" He threw holy water on his body.

Gaelan snatched the bottle from the priest's hand and looked up, his eyes now fully human. He took several gulps of the holy water and poured the rest over his own head, "We're gonna need more of this," He could barely catch his breath, "cause holy shit I'm thirsty."

A moment of stunned silence descended before Angel and Kedar let out a relieved laugh. Natalia turned her face to hide her snicker. Gaelan poked Natalia to look at him, then pushed the corners of his mouth into a smile with his thumb and forefinger. She covered her grin and looked down again, giggling. Even Trey grinned in relief.

Gaelan pushed himself to his feet, "Father, I just wanted to say..."

Father Hector was not smiling. He took several steps back from Gaelan.

"Father, is everything okay?" Trey inquired.

"The deed is done. I must go!"

"Father, what's..."

"I HAVE TO GO!" Father Hector darted from the room, down the stairs and out of the orphanage.

The rest of them stood in silence, staring at the door. Gaelan finally spoke up, half-joking, half-serious. "Was it something I said?"

"No, it was something Trey said." Angel looked to Trey.

"Me?"

"Yeah." Angel sighed, "I thought he might have missed it, but he didn't."

"WHAT?" Trey was wide-eyed, wondering what he had done.

"You called him *Gaelan*."

Trey immediately realized the gravity of the situation, then lashed out, "IF YOU WOULD'VE KEPT YOUR GODDAMNED HEAD DOWN AND MOUTH SHUT, I WOULDN'T HAVE SLIPPED!"

Gaelan thought about arguing, but just dropped his head, "You're right."

"I KNOW I'M RIGHT! And what the fuck were you thinking commanding iT into your body? That could've been the stupidest idea *ever*!"

Gaelan took a couple of breaths and finally spoke, "I need some fresh air. I'll talk to you guys later." He walked out without answering.

The others looked at Trey. When Gaelan was gone, he snapped defensively, "WHAT?"

"I was going to take iT into my body," Angel muttered to Trey, "and he cut me off and got iT talking."

"Yeah, but we were all yelling to cut you off, you know that." Trey was softer toned but defensive.

"That's not all brother." Angel continued, then Kedar broke in.

"When iT had your body," Kedar explained, "you grabbed a piece of glass."

Trey looked down at a bleeding slice in his hand where he had held the shard. He looked up concerned, "Did I attack you guys?"

"No." Angel shook his head.

"Then what?"

Natalia looked at him, "You were going to cut your own throat and before any of us could do anything…"

Trey realized, "He pulled iT out of me and into himself."

She nodded.

"Well I guess I'm the asshole now, huh?" Trey muttered into the silent room.

Angel squeezed Trey's shoulder, "Let him get some air, and then we'll all talk later."

"Yeah. Sure. I gotta get in touch with Denny and let him know." Trey went to get his phone.

The next morning the Venators came out of their rooms to find Gaelan sitting on the curb holding a paper bag.

Kedar looked to Trey, "Were you able to contact Father Dennis?"

"No. The staff said that he had just received a call and was preoccupied." Trey sounded somber.

"I'm sure he's okay. We'd know if there was a something going on." Angel sounded more confident, "Besides, maybe he can explain the situation to Father Hector." He looked down at Gaelan, extending a hand to help him to his feet, "Long night?"

"Yeah, I just wanted to clear my head, you know, especially cause I had more than one voice in there last night." Gaelan smiled. "Do you really think Father Denny is okay?" Trey reluctantly nodded. Gaelan began, "I'm sorry abou…"

"Done deal." Trey cut him off, "We lived. We won. You had the last laugh on an entity that will now hold a grudge against you for all eternity. Cool?"

Gaelan half-heartedly nodded, "Yeah—I guess. When you put it that way, I'll have nightmares for the rest of my life and sleep with the blankets over my head, but okay."

"Hell, I do that anyway." Angel joked.

"Let's get this over with." Trey turned and led everyone back to the orphanage.

When they arrived, Father Manuel was waiting for them, "The archbishop would like a word."

"Archbishop?" Trey asked in disbelief.

"Yes. He's in my office." Father Manuel led them down the corridor to the main office.

Gaelan looked around to everyone, "Why do I feel like we're getting sent to see the principal?" Natalia slapped his arm.

The archbishop's robes were red and white. A scarlet zucchetto covered the top of his head. His back was turned to them when he spoke in a Spanish accent, "Close the door please."

They complied and stood in silence.

The archbishop sighed, then finally turned to them, "You should see your faces."

"Father Hector?" Trey was confused.

"I am Cardinal Hector Figueroa, archbishop of Buenos Aires."

Gaelan closed his eyes and dropped his head, "Shit!"

"Well that would be an understatement, wouldn't you agree?" The cardinal lifted an eyebrow.

Gaelan lifted his head and walked forward, "Hi, I don't think we've officially met." Gaelan extended his hand, "I'm *Gaelan Kelly.*"

Cardinal Figueroa paused for a moment, looking at Gaelan, and then at his hand before finally gripping it and shaking, "You're right, we hadn't *officially* met."

Trey interrupted, "Father Denny?"

"I talked to Dennis last night. We go way back. Even further back than he does with you. He's fine and I told him not to talk to you until I did. I may have given him a piece of my mind and if you know Dennis..."

"He gave you a piece of his back?" Trey inquired.

The cardinal smiled, "Yes. Yes he did."

"He has a tendency to do that." Trey half-smiled.

"I told him that I thought he was playing with fire," Cardinal Figueroa motioned to Gaelan, "and last night, I thought this pompous little ass was about to get us all killed."

Gaelan pounded his fist against his heart, "That's chokes me up Padre—gets me right here!"

"You weren't supposed to talk to iT, but since you did, what did iT say to you? You seemed to understand?"

Gaelan thought for a moment, then began, "When Angel was going to invoke the prayer, I knew I had to do something. iT couldn't get into me and realized what I was. iT told me," Gealan paused, "that I was a 'half-breed' and that iT would use Eliana's body to feed me like the dog I was." Gaelan looked down.

Cardinal Figueroa shook his head and smiled, "I thought you were going to get all of us killed, but then I watched you choke back an ancient evil that no human should have been able to. We were able to banish iT back to Hell and all walk away."

"No Cardinal, *you* were able to banish iT." Kedar interrupted, "We were just there to help."

Cardinal Figueroa grinned, "Regardless, the most important thing of all is that a beautiful little girl is alive and free because of *you.*" Cardinal Figueroa paused and stared at Gaelan, "And now, in my heart of hearts, I agree with Dennis, and I have to believe that God put you on this path for a reason, Gaelan Kelly."

"Padre, I really don't like to talk about that kind of stuff."

"Dennis told me you'd say that too." Cardinal Figueroa smiled and then put his right hand on the side Gaelan's face, "But it doesn't change what I believe." He traced the sign of the cross with his thumb along Gaelan's forehead, "So I bless you el nombre del Padre, y del Hijo and del Espiritu Santo," he brought his hand back, kissed it and then placed it back on Gaelan's cheek, "Amen." Then he lightly smacked Gaelan on the cheek, "Just like Dennis said, you truly are something special. Your secret is safe with me." Cardinal Figueroa turned to everyone else, "And just so you know, Mother Rosetta awoke early this morning. Eliana is sleeping by her side in the hospital. I cannot thank you enough for what you did here." He raised his hands and blessed the rest of them.

"Well, unless Father Denny calls with another assignment, I think we earned a day off." Angel raised his eyebrows.

Trey nodded.

They all shook the Cardinal's hand and Gaelan handed him the paper bag.

"What's this?" Cardinal Figueroa opened the bag and smiled. He removed a new bottle of Fernet.

"I may have finished that bottle you handed me after last night's ordeal. I didn't want to leave you hangin' Padre." Gaelan smiled and walked out behind the others.

"Go with God my friends!" Cardinal Figueroa murmured as he watched them leave.

They spent the day at a local bar. Kedar sipping on fresh squeezed fruit juice as the rest of the team drank bottle after bottle of Malbec.

"You know you were quite the *dupek* at that airport restaurant, don't you?" Natalia raised one eyebrow.

Everyone else looked to Gaelan curiously. 'Asshole' he mouthed. They all laughed as he retorted, "I had killed five werewolves and I was feeling really good about myself. And while I'll concede I was a colossal *dupek,* you gotta admit that it was really ballsy!"

"Tell us again about shooting him in Germany." Trey deadpanned.

A few minutes later there was finally a break in the team's laughter.

"I'm sorry about last nigh..."

"I told you that's over." Trey cut Gaelan off, "But you told us there are no secrets."

"That's right."

Trey glowered, "Then what the fuck did iT *really* say to you?"

Everyone seemed confused, except for Gaelan, "I wanted to wait until we were alone. I think Father Hector is good to go, but he kept the fact that he's the Archbishop a secret."

Kedar interjected, "Like we kept your name and abilities a secret from him?"

Gaelan's eyes widened, "Good point, but even so."

"Okay, so what did iT really say?" Angel pressed.

Gaelan swallowed hard, "iT really did call me a *filthy half-breed traitor*, but then iT called me the *sheep in wolf's clothing*." Blank expressions stared back at him.

"Oh, well that explains it." Trey chided, "That totally would've pushed me over the edge too."

Gaelan was crestfallen, "iT told me that iT would end the prophecy and that iT would not let me stop the eternal darkness. Then it called me a sheep in wolf's clothing."

Kedar inquired, "Do you mean wolf in sheep's clothing?"

"No. That's just it. I know it's weird, but when Nat and I killed those witches, I remember, even though I was changed, that the head witch called me the same thing—the *sheep in wolf's clothing*. It can't be a coincidence, and iT mentioned a prophecy."

"You know you sound completely insane right now, right?" Trey stared.

"Gaelan, there are no such thing as prophecies." Natalia spoke softly.

"You asked me what iT really said and I told you. That's all." Gaelan looked away.

"Well I, for one, am glad you didn't tell the archbishop." Angel's words were a bit slurred. He stood up unsteadily, "And it's not like I don't love you guys," He rubbed his hand through Gaelan's hair, "Even you JoJo…"

"JoJo?"

"Yeah, the dog-faced boy." Everyone laughed, and Angel brushed the imaginary dust from his shirt, "But I've got a date with those two over there." He pointed at two beautiful young women drinking at the bar.

"This oughta be good." Gaelan looked on in amusement.

"Watch and learn junior." Trey leaned back and crossed his arms. After a couple of minutes, the bartender brought over two bottles of wine. Angel held a bottle in each hand and wrapped his arms around the girls. They all smiled at the table as they walked by on their way out of the bar.

"Damn." Gaelan was impressed.

"He is our true Don Juan." Kedar smiled and drank his fruit smoothie.

Gaelan cocked his head and scrunched his brows, studying Kedar.

Kedar noticed, "What's wrong? Why are you looking at me like that?"

"Nothing, I'm just wondering how many times you're gonna shit tonight after all those smoothies." Natalia once again hid her face and even Trey laughed out loud as Kedar clanged his glass against Gaelan's and drank.

Trey then stood up, "Well boys and girl, I'm gonna go sleep this off. Good job—even you shit-stain."

Gaelan appreciated the compliment, "Thanks, and remember to pull that stick out of your ass before you go to sleep. It'll be lots more comfortable!" Trey raised his middle finger silently over his shoulder as he walked out of the bar.

Gaelan, Natalia and Kedar sat in silence for a minute. Kedar went to stand when Gaelan stopped him, "Kedar?"

Kedar settled back into his chair, "Yes?"

"How did you know?"

"Know what?"

"How did you know I could hold iT?"

"Natalia told us what your change was like. What you went through."

Gaelan looked over to Natalia, who shifted in her chair, "I'm sorry. I told them exactly what happened in Germany."

"It's fine."

Kedar spoke up, "Knowing what you hold inside of you, and then seeing how you controlled it—how you used it—that takes a special person. A special *soul*. I knew that you would feel the burning and the naked, exposed pain, and could still keep iT trapped."

"But I didn't even know. I did it so that you would burn me and not Angel."

"I know, and you saved Trey. We all saw it and I cannot tell you how much we appreciate it." Gaelan glanced at Natalia who half-smiled at him once more. He returned the gesture and looked back to Kedar, "But do you remember how I told you about the hunter that took the demon into his body?"

"Yeah, the one that held it in and trapped it."

"I could feel the thing ripping at my very being, my soul." Gaelan realized immediately that Kedar had been talking about himself, "But I knew that I could hold the thing inside of me. I knew I was strong enough and no matter what the pain, I would protect those around me and keep it inside." Kedar stood up and walked around to Gaelan, putting a hand on his shoulder, "And somehow I just knew that you had the strength to hold iT in." Kedar squeezed Gaelan's shoulder, "As-salamu alaykum, *my brother*."

Gaelan tapped his hand on top of Kedar's and responded, "Wa alaikum assalaam."

Kedar smiled and walked out.

Gaelan and Natalia sat in awkward silence for a minute. When they finally looked up simultaneously, a faint smile touched her lips. Then she looked away.

"I've already seen it, so don't try to hide it." Gaelan poked at her. She arranged her face into a passive mask once more. "Seriously though, I was fighting iT and when I saw you, I knew I'd be okay."

Natalia stood up and walked over to Gaelan, bent down and kissed him on the cheek, "You saved Angelo and Trey and Eliana. The least I could do was be your angel again." She walked by him, slowly dragging her arm over his chest and shoulder, "Good night, Gaelan."

"Night Nat." He sat in the bar alone and held up his hand for another glass of wine, feeling her lips on his cheek.

—§—

"I know what you're going to say and I had no idea that Hector was dealing with a falleN onE."

"Don't worry Denny, it's fine. We handled it and we're ready for another assignment, but that's not why I called you."

"You sound way too calm and level headed, which means something's bothering you. What's wrong?"

Trey sighed, "What do you know about prophecies?"

CHAPTER 9
OLD FLAME

"Perrino. PERRINO!" The Desk Sergeant shouted.

"Yeah Sarge, what's up?"

Carly had been looking through incident reports from the last few days. Just like she had everyday for the past year, since Gaelan Kelly had saved her from that *thing*.

"Take this nice lady's complaint. Her groceries were stolen from her on the subway." The Desk Sergeant cocked his head—this wasn't the first time old Mrs. Childs had been in to report a 'stolen' item.

"No problem, Sarge." Carly sighed. Mrs. Childs had probably left her bags on the train, and according to the sunset app on her desktop, the early winter sun would set at 5:42 PM. It was 4:47 when she hurriedly closed the interview, "I promise you ma'am, we'll do everything to get your groceries back." Another officer stood as she walked the tottering Mrs. Childs to the door, glancing nervously at the wall clock, "Carly, go! Mrs. Childs?" He extended his arm to the elderly woman.

Carly grabbed her purse and walked out, not even stopping to change out of her uniform. As usual, Chris McSorley waited for her on the precinct steps. "Hey Carls." His tone seemed almost shy.

"Hey Chris." She kissed him on the cheek, "You know you don't have to walk me."

"I was off shift too and I know you don't mind the company." Chris smiled. They walked for several blocks in companionable silence. Then Chris finally spoke up. "I know you're off the day after tomorrow. How would you like to grab some dinner? Maybe a movie?"

Carly's heart pounded. Chris was so sweet. She missed him. Missed their relationship. But she couldn't deny that he was no longer the only man in her heart. *Gaelan*. She stopped and took his hand, "I know it's been a while Chris. And you still know how much you mean to me, but..."

"Sorry, I didn't mean to..."

Carly felt a rush of resolve, "You know what? The day after tomorrow. I would love to go out. But let's go out during the day, okay? Maybe lunch and a stroll around." Carly was about to say Central Park. *No, not Central Park, that's where that thing was.* "How 'bout the Seaport. We can sit and talk and maybe..." She leaned in and kissed him.

He leaned his forehead against hers, "I miss you Carls. I don't care how long it takes, I'll be waiting."

She bit her lips and her eyes teared up before she kissed him on the cheek. She ran to her train, jumping in before the doors closed.

He shouted after her as she ran through the train doors, "THE DAY AFTER TOMORROW! I'LL BE THINKING ABOUT IT UNTIL THEN!"

She turned, smiled and blew him a kiss, then watched as the subway walls swallowed him and all semblance of civilization. She placed one hand on her gun and one on the rosary in her pocket. The crowd of commuters afforded her a modicum of comfort in the seemingly endless ride. She finally arrived at her stop and trotted up the steps, yearning to feel the last vestiges of sunlight cascading over the city.

Carly placed her hand, for a moment, on the religious symbols etched into her front door. Her landlord must have thought she was nuts, but he had just shrugged and accepted her deposit to replace the door at the end of her lease. Inside, she quickly secured five heavy locks behind her, then dialed her phone.

"Hey gorgeous, you home safe?" A deep, friendly voice asked.

"Yup!"

"You let me know if you need anything, okay?"

"Thanks Tom. Love ya!"

"Yeah, love you too sweetie. Stay safe!" The line went dead.

Carly hung up her phone and settled into the safety of her apartment. She left the house every morning as close to dawn as she could, hoping for a familiar face on her walk to the subway. She had been on desk duty since her attack—since she was taken by the vampire. She would sit at her desk, taking complaints and filing reports, until just before sunset. She had been placed on desk duty shortly after the night she was taken by *him*—the night her whole world changed. She knew her dad pulled favors to help her. That's why she'd been allowed to stay off of the street for so long, and why the Desk Sargent let her go early in the winter to make sure she made it home in daylight. She stocked her apartment with an arsenal of weaponry and holy water, and fell asleep each night with the lights on, and the hatred of the foul creatures that should not exist burning in her psyche.

Chris and Carly had grown apart in the months after Gaelan had confronted them. But following the incident with the vampire, he had been one of the first by her bedside to make sure she was okay, and had been checking up on her ever since. They had rekindled a bit of their romance, but Carly wanted to take it slow. Thoughts of Gaelan kept entering her mind, and she had only recently started to adjust to her "new normal."

She sat at her desk and listened to mundane complaint after complaint. Some were funny, some were just pathetic, and some were serious; the muggings, robberies, assaults. The funny thing was, she never got tagged to interview a female assault victim. Another favor her dad had called in. She mused about changing her major from criminal justice to trauma counseling. She hated the reality, knowing if she ever finished her online degree, she wasn't likely to find many vampire attack victims to help.

Carly was speed-walking to the subway the next afternoon when an uneasy feeling brought her up short. Her stomach clenched—one of those feelings Gaelan had taught her to trust. Movement down the alley, just out of sight of the police station, caught her eye. The sun was up, but the alley was mostly shaded. Carly reached her hand into her purse, feeling for the silver coated stake and her off duty weapon, full of blessed, silver bullets from Tom. She drew her pistol and moved cautiously into the alley towards the dumpster. She felt her adrenaline rise. *I don't want to be scared anymore!* She placed her back against the opposite side of the alley and sidestepped until she had a clear shot to the far side of the dumpster, "GET UP! GET UP AND OUT HERE NOW!" She moved further to the side and was now standing across from a person cowering, as if trying to hide in plain sight, "I said get up!" She lowered her voice.

A Latino girl in her late teens or early twenties, stood, trembling and staring at her, raising her hands at the sight of the gun. Her clothes were tattered rags and she was bleeding from one leg.

"Hablas inglés?" The girl shook her head. Carly didn't know much more Spanish than that. She quickly glanced around and saw a corner of the alley where the sun was shining through. She flicked her wrist and motioned with her weapon for the girl to step toward the sunlight. The girl's face was filthy, skin showing through only where tears had washed the grime away. She trembled and limped toward the sunlight, turning her back on Carly. Carly withdrew the stake from her bag and held it in her left hand, balancing her gun over her left forearm.

The girl stepped into the light and—*nothing*. She turned, still trembling, to face Carly and caught sight of the stake. Her eyes widened and she held up her fingers in front of her mouth like they were fangs, "LOS COMEDORES DE PERSONAS...VAMPIROS!"

Carly's blood ran cold. She looked down at the girl's bleeding leg: claw marks. Carly nodded and continued to point the gun at the girl, but lowered the stake and used her fingertips to pull at her pant leg. She hiked it enough to show the girl her calf...her scar, from an identical wound, inflicted by a vampire's claws. The girl didn't seem to care about the weapon anymore. She broke down and limped toward Carly, collapsing in her arms and weeping hysterically. Carly held her tight, "Shhhhhh. Okay. It's gonna be okay!" She pulled out her phone and hit the speed dial.

"*Hey sweetie, you home early today?*"

"Tom. I wouldn't ask if it wasn't important, but I need you!"

"*Where are you?*"

"Meet me at St. Peter's church and be careful."

"*Just stay put. I'm on my way.*"

"Why didn't we just order out?" Trey grumbled.

"Because he wanted to cook. And when's the last time you had a good, home-cooked meal?" Angel chided.

"We ate at a great restaurant in Argentina."

Kedar looked to Trey, "Yes, and that is the *last* time we ate at a restaurant. We usually just eat fast food, takeout and whatever we can find from street vendors."

"What's wrong with street vendors? It's the local flavor!" Trey shot back.

Angel shrugged, "Really Trey, when was the last time you sat down for a decent home-cooked meal?"

Trey seemed lost in thought for a moment. "It was with Laura, just before…"

Before Angel could walk back his question, Natalia took Trey's hand and turned his face to make eye contact, "Just give him this. He's really trying." Trey nodded, and his moment of melancholy passed. "Besides," She added, "when it's horrible, we won't ever have to do this again."

Gaelan opened the door to four dower faces. "Jesus guys, who's funeral are you goin' to?" He looked at them with a raised eyebrow.

"That smells pretty good!" Angel pushed his way in. The hotel was a step up from the places they usually stayed, with full kitchens and small dining rooms. Since the exorcism, they'd been to Ecuador to hunt a shifter, and Galveston, Texas, to track down a witch. Gaelan had popped for pricier rooms for some much needed R&R.

"So, what are you making?" Trey actually sounded friendly, and Gaelan looked at him sideways. "Look, I was told I had to come and eat whatever slop you're dealing, so I'm just wondering how long before I have to vomit." Trey was back to his normal caustic tone.

"Oh thank God. It is you! For a minute I thought you were something else." Gaelan grinned and went to the kitchen.

Everyone was already sitting at the table. There was red wine and sparkling mineral water, and the salad bowls were already full.

"Okay, here we go." Gaelan laid a huge tray of lasagna, fresh from the oven, in the center of the table. "Dig in!"

Angel cut several pieces and placed plates in front of Trey and Kedar and then himself.

Gaelan looked to Natalia, "You having any?"

Natalia was picking at the salad on her plate, "I don't eat meat. It's alright though, the salad is great."

Gaelan raised a finger, turned around and walked back to the kitchen, returning with a plate full of garlic bread and another lasagna tray that he laid down on the counter. He cut a piece and placed it in front of Natalia.

Before she could protest, he added, "Vegetable lasagna for the herbivore."

She looked at the dish in front of her and then looked up, "How did you..."

"C'mon. Yogurt parfaits and vegetable wraps. And then Germany—No one, and I mean no one, passes up German sausage." Everyone noticed the faintest of smiles that touched Natalia's lips.

"Yaaa, zatz vaat she said!" Angel tried his best to impersonate a German accent.

They all looked at him like he was crazy and then Kedar started to giggle uncontrollably. Everyone looked at him quizzically, then he said, "It's funny because the sausage is his penis. It's a German penis!" Kedar's laugh quickly spread around the table. Angel raised a glass of wine and everyone, even Trey, toasted.

Then, as everyone else was still lowering their glasses, Angel snatched a fork and skewered a mouthful off of his plate. "Holy shit that's good!"

Natalia took a bite of hers, closed her eyes and smiled.

"You're smiling. I see it!" Gaelan taunted her. She ignored him, kept her eyes shut and continued to savor the taste.

"It's excellent Gaelan. Thank you." Kedar swallowed and giggled again, "German sausage."

Trey was toying with his food. When he finally took a bite, he met Gaelan's gaze. "I guess we can keep you around a little while longer if your gonna play kitchen bitch like this."

Before Gaelan could retort, Natalia interjected, "Kitchen bitch? I guess a woman's place is in the kitchen? Shall I do everyone's laundry after dinner?" She glared.

"No! It's not sexist!" Trey tried to recover, "I don't mean bitch like..." He sighed, "Never mind!"

Natalia raised her eyebrow, "Mmmm hmmm!"

Gaelan sang, "You got in trouuuuuu-ble, you got in trouuuuuu-ble..." Angel and Kedar laughed along.

"And you're a biiiiiiig dick, and you're a biiiiiiig dick!" Trey sang back and shoved his mouth full of food.

"Where did you learn to cook?" Angel was talking with food in his mouth.

"My mom taught me most stuff. You'd be surprised how easy a lasagna is to throw together." Gaelan looked at the table, lost for a moment in the memory of his mom.

Natalia noticed, "Did she teach you the vegetable recipe as well?"

Gaelan raised his eyes and smiled, "No. That was my creation. When you make lasagna, you brown the meat and season it. I just switched out the beef with minced broccoli heads and swapped out the middle layer of noodles with a thin layer of eggplant that I pre-baked."

"It's delicious—truly. Thank you."

"You're welcome." He smiled.

Angel took a huge forkful off of her plate and ate it quickly.

"HEEEEEY!"

"Holy shit, the vegetarian one is just as good." Angel raved. Trey and Kedar looked at one another, then at Natalia's plate, and stabbed their forks simultaneously to steal bites while she poked at their hands playfully with her own fork.

Gaelan laughed and cut another chunk out of the tray for Natalia, "There's plenty."

This time she actually did smile at him, and Gaelan didn't taunt her. He just marveled at how beautiful she was.

Trey's phone trilled, interrupting their revelry. "Yeah? Yeah, still in Galveston." There was a long pause, "Okay, we'll make arrangements. You kidding? Okay, we're on our way." He hung up and looked around at all of them, "Throw a lid on this stuff and take it to go."

"What's up?" Angel sounded serious.

"That was Denny. He's chartering us a flight out of Scholes."

"Charter?" Natalia was surprised.

"Yeah, we're in a hurry."

"Where are we going?" Kedar was already standing.

Trey looked to Gaelan, "New York."

—§—

They landed in New York around 10PM. Denny thought there was a lead on the 'slaughter houses' and that time was of the essence. They took a cab directly to St. Peter's Church where a priest ushered them into the rectory.

"I can't believe you got here so quickly. The girl was brought here in hysterics. She was talking about vampires and said that there were many people that had already been killed, but more still alive."

"You called the Vatican?" Angel asked.

"No. Your local contact did." The priest called out, "MR. MURPHY!"

Gaelan gaped as Tom Murphy strode in, "Didn't think I was gonna see you again so soon." Tom gave Gaelan a hug, "And look at this. You're on a team now."

Gaelan released his embrace and smiled, "I kind of a adopted them. Trial run, but I think it's workin' out."

Trey cleared his throat.

"I'd introduce you, but you've already met."

"The owner of the establishment." Kedar was the first to recognize him.

"Yeah, where *we all* first met." A moment of awkward silence followed. Trey seemed about to speak, but Gaelan continued before he made a sound, "No time to make friends now, where's the girl you brought in?"

Tom shifted awkwardly. "Yeah, so here's the thing. *I* didn't bring her in." He led them into the next room.

Carly Perrino stood up from the sofa, where she had been sitting next to an older, chubby man with curly, thinning hair.

"Hi Gaelan." Carly said uncomfortably.

"Anyone you don't know in this town?" Trey spat.

"Carly, this is everyone. Everyone, this is Carly. My ex-girlfriend." Gaelan's aspect was flat. Natalia pursed her lips and raised an eyebrow, then walked over to introduce herself. Trey looked up and mouthed the words, 'Thank you God,' flashing a wolfish grin.

Angel squeezed Gaelan's shoulders and whispered, "Is this as *awkward* for you as it is *awesome* for us?"

Gaelan hissed back, "Remember when we first met and I threw you into a tree? Good times!"

"That hurts brother! That hurts." Angel turned to Kedar, who was chuckling audibly, "What?"

"It's funny, cause he threw you into a tree."

"Thanks Kedar. I was there."

Kedar laughed out loud, "I know, and so was the tree."

Introductions complete, Carly finally turned to Gaelan.

"Hey."

"Hi."

She smiled, "You look good. Ya know—a little less *regulation.*"

Gaelan ran his fingers through his shaggy hair and then rubbed his hand over the growth on his face, "Yeah, it saves money on razors and haircuts."

There was another awkward silence.

"Am I gonna stay invisible with all the young love and the fearless venators?" The Chubby man stood up, "If I wanted to feel like chopped liver, I'd just go down to Katz' deli!"

"Sorry." Tom broke in, "This is Saul. Rabbi Saul Feinstein."

"Another Irishman, huh?" Trey extended his hand.

"Saul is one of Denny's local contacts, like me, from back in the day." Tom explained.

Trey turned back to Carly, "Soooooo, how did you two meet?"

"There's time for that shit later." Gaelan wasn't about to let Trey extend the awkward reunion, "Why are we here?"

"This is Arianna. I found her in the alley by the police precinct."

"Was that a lucky coincidence?" Trey asked.

"I thought it might be a trap," Carly knew what Trey was thinking, "so I drew down on her and made her step in the sunlight. Then I saw her leg, and I knew. I showed her my scar and she collapsed on me."

"Your scar?" Natalia asked.

"Gaelan saved me from a vampire. That's when I learned about this shit. But it slashed my calf real bad."

Trey looked over to Gaelan and whispered, "Jack the Ripper?" Gaelan nodded.

Carly continued, "So I brought her here and called Tom. Father Ernest has been interpreting for us. As far as we can tell, she escaped from a place where vampires are holding people and using them," Carly swallowed hard, "as cattle. To feed."

Gaelan knelt down in front of Arianna, speaking in fluent Spanish, "Arianna?" She nodded, "You escaped the monsters? The vampires, right?" She nodded again. "Do you know where you were being held?" She nodded again. "Can you tell us?" This time she shook her head. "Can you *show* us?" Tears streamed down her cheeks as she froze in fear. Gaelan took her hands in his own, "Arianna, you saw the scar on Carly's leg, right?" She nodded. "I killed the one that did that to her. Now I want to go get the people that were with you and help them too. Can you help me do that?" She was hesitant. "Arianna, all you have to do is show us the building. I promise you that nothing will happen to you, and I keep my promises. Okay?"

She wiped the tears from her cheek and sniffled, then gave a reluctant nod, "How?"

"You'll drive with us, point out the building, and then we'll bring you right back he..."

"No!" She interrupted him, "How did you kill the one that hurt her?"

"I stuck a piece of metal through his heart, then I stuck that same piece of metal through his head, put my foot in his chest and pulled his worthless face clean off." Arianna seemed to sit a bit taller as she absorbed this information, and Gaelan asked, "What can you tell us about the building?"

"We were being held in the basement. It smelled of death. Those they took upstairs didn't come back." A sob escaped, "I was being taken upstairs. It was only one person taking me and I think he thought I was too small to do anything. I kicked him when we were on the stairs and ran. I found the exit as one of them," tears streamed down her face, "one of the *monsters*, dropped down and landed right behind me. The door was chained but I was small enough to squeeze out. She, the vampire, stuck her hand through and dug into my thigh." Arianna rubbed her leg, "But the sun burned her hand and she pulled back." She wiped the tears again. "We were brought to this country by coyotes. They told us we would have jobs in factories. Then we wound up in cages like dogs. I lost my brother and my cousin," she openly wept, "and there are more people everyday. Do you really think you can help them?"

"Yes, yes we can."

"We gotta work fast." Gaelan stood and turned to the team. "Before they close up shop, move on and erase all evidence, like in Slovenia."

"If they haven't already." Trey's tone was grim.

Gaelan shook his head, "I don't think so. I don't think they'd abandon an established factory in a city as big as this."

Trey could see the logic, "Then we need to get weapons."

Tom Murphy interrupted, "This isn't Saul's or my first rodeo." He hoisted a satchel onto the coffee table, "We got MP-5's, 9mm pistols and UV lanterns. They take the same ammo, and its all been blessed."

Angel spoke up, "9mm isn't going to give us a lot of stopping power."

Tom agreed, "Yeah, but if we do make it out onto the street, they're easy to conceal. And that's why we have cast iron stakes as well. Heart and head, right?"

"Why do you keep saying *we*?" Trey looked at him curiously.

Carly spoke up, "Because we're going with you."

Everyone looked at her and then to Gaelan.

"I speak for myself!" Carly snapped.

Gaelan shrugged, "You all settle this. I'm goin' in even if I do it alone!"

"Fine!" Trey conceded, "But I make the calls and you do everything you're told! Got it?"

They all agreed and began to prepare.

Carly approached Gaelan as the team drew weapons and ammo. She smiled at him, "I didn't know you could speak Spanish."

"There's a lot you don't know about me now."

"Maybe you can fill me after all of this?"

He half-smiled, "Maybe I will."

Natalia grimaced at the exchange as she loaded round after round into a magazine. Narrowing her eyes when Gaelan spoke to Carly, she wondered if that twinge she was feeling was anticipation of the mission, or jealousy. Angel stepped in front of her, giving her a curious look. She rolled her eyes in return and continued to load the ammunition.

"What do you want me to do?" Father Ernest addressed Trey.

"You have a church van, right Father?"

"Yes. It's out back." Father Ernest walked over to a key hook and tossed the keys to Trey.

"Thanks. You stay here. Prep for survivors and make arrangements, cover stories and passports. At some point, we'll get them to the Vatican or the compound."

Father Ernest nodded.

"I'll help Ernie." Before Rabbi Saul could turn, Trey tossed him the keys.

"You're driving!"

There was nothing unusual about the building. Located in lower Manhattan, its windows were darkened making it look dead.

"The entrance I ran out was there." Arianna pointed to the unlit alley, "And I remember the big building there. I passed those two bakeries when I was running down the street. People looked at me. Some tried to help but I just pushed them away and ran." Her lip trembled, "Are you really going to go in there?"

Gaelan turned around, "Yes. Yes we are. Rabbi Saul will take you back to the church and you can both wait there. If we don't come back, he'll get you to safety."

Gaelan looked at Trey and nodded. Trey spoke, "Remember, we make our way in, quiet as possible and get to the basement. Carly and Tom, you have lookout while we will get the cells open. God willing there's anyone left, we get them and we get out. Gaelan has lead. If we get separated, we get survivors to consecrated ground quickly. St. Peter's if you can, any church, synagogue and mosque along the way in a pinch. We've mapped them all. Then we rally in *Murphy's Law* tomorrow. Questions?"

Gaelan opened the door without waiting for an answer, heading directly for the door. Arianna stared after the team as they followed Gaelan down the alley. Then, just as Saul was shifting into drive, she jumped out of the car and ran in the same direction. "Hey!" Saul called after her. "I'm too old for this *mishegas*!" He shut off the car and ran after her and the others.

The door was chained shut.

"How do we..." Before Tom could finish, Gaelan grabbed the lock and chain in his left hand and yanked, snapping the chain.

"Never mind!" Tom whispered.

"Wait!" Arianna dashed towards them.

"What the hell are you doing here?" Angel asked, just as Saul came scurrying behind her.

"She ran after you."

"I can lead you right to them. It's the fastest way."

Angel looked at Gaelan, who shook his head doubtfully, but Arianna walked past them and opened the door.

Inside was a stairwell with cushioned walls—soundproofing. Arianna pointed down and put a finger to her lips. She crept down the stairs to the bottom entrance. As she was about to reach for the door, Gaelan grabbed her arm and pulled her back. He slowly cracked the door and the peered through: a plain hallway with more thick soundproofing, and dim, wall-mounted lighting glowing yellow. There was no movement. He closed his eyes to focus his hearing, but Arianna whispered, "This way!" and pointed. He opened the door and held his arm in front of her so she would stay behind. She motioned him to go right, down the hallway, and around the corner to the left. They crept forward, Tom, Carly and Kedar scanning behind them. Halfway down the hallway, on the left side, was a set of thick, steel, double doors.

Arianna nodded fearfully. Trey and the others pulled her to the rear and readied themselves. Gaelan gently turned the lever handle on each door—locked. He gripped tighter and began to apply more and more pressure, but it felt as if he was going break the handle. *Shit. It'll be too loud and I might jam it.* Carly sprang forward, pulled out a lock pick set and went to work. Everyone looked up and down the hallway nervously.

After about a minute, Carly stood up, looked at Gaelan and nodded, then backed away from the door. He slowly opened it—the smell of death was overwhelming. Inside, the lighting was a dim shade of red. A long corridor led to another large set of steel, double doors. Cell doors lined both sides of the narrow space. *Are we too late?*

He slowly advanced, cringing as the door clicked behind him, echoing down the passageway. A mixture of gasps, whimpering and sobbing filled the air.

"SURVIVORS!" He looked to Arianna, "SOBREVIVIENTES!"

Arianna ran up and whispered in Spanish, "We're here to get you out."

Two captives looked up in disbelief, then excitedly shook the others out of their terrified stupor. Men, women and children looked up at them through the bars. Hispanic, South East and East Asian—they appeared to be immigrants from around the globe.

"Is somebody there?" The urgent whisper came from a cell further down the hallway. Trey ran forward and peered inside. Two homeless-looking men huddled in a corner. A woman, probably a prostitute, cowered to the side, and a small group of teenagers crowded at the center of the cell. *I wonder how many of them were actually reported missing?*

"Are you here to help us?" A young black man stepped forward, speaking for the group.

"You're Goddamn right we are son!" He turned to Gaelan, "We gotta get these doors open. Now!"

Gaelan began speaking in several languages: Filipino, Korean, Chinese, Vietnamese, Indian, Arabic, Farsi, Spanish and Portuguese, "We're here to help."

Carly started to pick the first lock as the survivors crowded the cell bars and pleaded for them to hurry. Arianna extended her hands through the bars of the cell she had been kept in, grasping the hands of her fellow survivors—strangers that had become her family during their days or horror. Someone hissed, bringing activity to a sudden halt. Kedar's fist was held high, indicating the need for silence. Someone was at the lock on the other side of the door. Victims whimpered and cowered once more, while the venators pressed their backs against the wall and drew down on the doorway.

The door opened and three stocky men strode in, chatting in English. "...not gonna end up like Vinnie." The lead man, his eyes finally adjusting to the dim red lights, noticed the armed people pointing weapons as he and the second man came into the room, "WHAT THE FUCK?"

Kedar kicked the side of the second man's knee, dropping him to the floor and, before the third man could turn to run, he grabbed him and yanked him into the room, throwing him to the ground next to the second man. The first man stood with his hands up, "Don't fuckin' shoot!"

Carly sprang to her feet, ran forward and slammed the grip of her pistol into the bridge of the man's nose hard enough to break it and drop him to the ground, but not enough to knock him unconscious, "KEYS! GIMME THE FUCKIN' KEYS NOW!" She put her foot on his cheek, pressed his face into the floor and pushed the barrel of the gun into his temple.

"Okay! Okay! Here! Jesus, just take it!"

Carly snatched the keys and turned, tossing them to Angel who started trying them on cell doors.

Kedar pressed his weapon into the third man's face, "How many more collaborators?"

"None."

Kedar pressed harder and the man winced, "I swear! *They* don't like having us around. We just deliver the goods and work in shifts to bring them upstairs and then go back to the office."

"*What the fuck?*" Dread filled Trey's voice. The last cell, furthest down the narrow space, was inhabited by seven women in varying stages of pregnancy. They reached their arms through the bars and sobbed.

Natalia ran over, "We're here to get you out. Shhhhh..." She did what she could to comfort the hysterical women, while Trey and Gaelan made their way towards the double doors at the far end of the corridor.

Trey gripped the handle cautiously. The right hand door pushed open without resistance. "Holy Mother of God." His voice was half whisper, half whimper.

Gaelan peered over his shoulder. His breathing became shallow with panic and rage. A pile of mangled corpses: men, women, children, *babies*. Their blood was drained, their throats torn, their flesh bitten and ripped. Some were in pieces; some torn open where their organs had been devoured. The smell of decomposition filled the air. Two bodies appeared fresh—today's kills. The rest were in various stages of decomposition. The space appeared to be an old maintenance elevator shaft that the creatures were using as a gruesome garbage chute. Both Gaelan and Trey were so transfixed by the torn body of an infant that they didn't notice Natalia's approach.

"What's wrong?"

Gaelan spun around and grabbed her by the upper arms, "Don't!" She was about to knee his groin—*Don't grab me! –* when she saw the look of fear and sadness in his eyes. Trey had already shut the door, "Don't go in there sweetie." Trey's flat voice matched the look in Gaelan's eyes. Gaelan let his hands slip from her arms and he walked away without looking at her. By now, Angel and Carly had opened every cell but the one filled with pregnant women.

"None of the keys work." Angel was unnerved.

Gaelan walked over and grabbed the man with the broken nose, picked him up effortlessly and dragged him to the cell. "OPEN IT!" He snarled.

"I can't!"

Gaelan grasped the back of the man's collar and lifted him off the ground with one arm, slamming his face into the bars, again commanding, "OPEN IT!"

"He can't!" The third man spoke up, "We don't have the key to that cell. Only *they* do!"

With one arm, Gaelan heaved the man several yards into the opposite wall, where he fell unconscious, "Stand back!" He grasped the bars just above the lock, put his foot against the wall and pulled as hard as he could. Trey was about to say that it wasn't going to work when he heard the screeching noise of metal buckling. The metal distorted and shrieked as Gaelan's grunt became a pained growl. The metal distorted and simultaneously, the lock snapped and he fell backwards while the cell door flew open.

Gaelan got to his feet. His mouth was foaming and Trey and Natalia could see that the whites of his eyes were speckled with red.

Trey ran forward, grabbed his shoulders and stared into his eyes, "Breathe! Breathe and choke it back dammit. Breathe!" Gaelan shut his eyes. He began taking deep breaths and opened his eyes to look at Trey. His eyes were normal again.

Carly spoke up, "We gotta get these people outta here, now!"

"What about them?" Angel motioned his head toward the three men. Without hesitation, Trey grabbed them and threw them in one of the cells, shutting it, and replacing the lock.

The second man was on the floor of the cell, gripping his knee and talking through gritted teeth, "You're fuckin' crazy. *They'll* kill you for this. *They're* gonna kill all of you."

"Yeah, and what do you think they're going to do to *you*?" Trey snarled and walked away.

"Wait! Don't leave us! YOU CAN'T JUST LEAVE US!"

Natalia counted sixty-one survivors. Kedar cleared the corridor and they began emptying out of the cell room and making their way to the exit. Kedar peered around the corner to ensure the hallway was clear. The group was making their hurried way down the corridor when the stairwell door swung open, and four figures stepped out. Two men and two women, well dressed and good looking, walked toward him with a cold confidence. As they approached, the lead woman's face contorted, her eyes turned red and her smile revealed a mouth full of razor sharp fangs. Behind her, more vampires stepped into the dim corridor.

"Back! BACK!" Kedar commanded, just as Tom and Angel yelled out "STOP!" alerting the group to another posse of vampires approaching from the opposite direction. They were surrounded.

Kedar grabbed for a UV lantern as the female and her companions dashed toward him. Gaelan jetted forward, rolling and coming up in front of Kedar, slashing up and through her with his katana. While the female vampire let out a hiss of agony, Gaelan pulled the knife off his thigh and slammed it through the eye socket of the next closest vampire, impaling his head against the wall. He thrust his foot into the third creature, knocking her backward into her companion. Then he stabbed backward, thrusting the katana into the heart of the writhing creature on the wall. A swing forward and the female, still reeling from Gaelan's initial slash, met the same fate. He retracted it and spun, beheading her and the creature pinned to the wall in one motion. He pulled the knife free, and as the head landed heavily on the floor, he threw the blade into the skull of the fourth vampire. He rolled forward, thrusting his katana down into the heart of the third vampire he had kicked, and in one motion, stood and slashed up at the fourth vampire, cutting him clean through the rib cage and the heart, then exiting between his opposite neck and shoulder. As the top half of the severed creature began to fall, he grabbed the knife from its head and slammed it into the head of the third vampire on the ground. She screeched and gurgled as she died.

The execution took only seconds, but allowed Kedar the time to activate the UV lantern and throw one beyond Gaelan, creating a barrier against the creatures coming around the corner. Kedar, Natalia, Carly, Trey and several survivors stared wide-eyed and open-mouthed as Gaelan stood and turned back. Angel and Tom activated lanterns at the back of the procession.

Carly yelled out, "WE GOTTA MOVE!"

"These lanterns aren't going to last!" Kedar warned.

Gaelan looked at Trey, "I can hold them. Get everyone moving!"

Trey grabbed Gaelan by the shoulder and spoke chillingly calm, "I was wrong. I was wrong about the sword and I was wrong about choking *it* back." Trey continued, "Let *it* out. You let *it* out and make them pay." His voice grew colder, "You make them fucking pay."

"WHAT ARE WE WAITING FOR?" Carly urged the group into action.

Gaelan handed Trey his katana. He turned and handed his Kabar to Natalia. She took it and he gripped his hand tight around hers, for a moment meeting her eyes, before letting his hand slide away. He turned to Kedar, "Get them outta here." Kedar nodded.

"What the fuck are we waiting for?" Carly could feel her panic rising. Then, to her horror, Gaelan strode away from the group, down the hall, apparently unafraid while kicking the UV lantern past the stairwell door and toward the remaining vampires.

"GAELAN!" She shouted after him, but Trey and Natalia herded her into the stairwell, with the mass of survivors.

Gaelan slid on his feet, in a smooth sideways gate. He held his left hand up high and forward, his right clenched by his face. The first creature grinned ravenously and attacked as Gaelan moved past the cover of the lantern. Gaelan smacked his head down with his left hand and followed through with an elbow into the back of its neck. As the vampire hit the ground, Gaelan slammed his foot down on its head, crushing its skull. Two more charged. He caught one and spun, throwing it into the sidewall. The next one was fast, but Gaelan jumped, launching himself horizontal to wrap his legs around its neck, then stretching his body to its maximum length, and spinning to flip the vampire forward and onto its back as they both went to the ground. It bit into his leg and Gaelan yelled, coming down with an elbow to its forehead. When the creature opened its mouth, Gaelan broke its neck in a swift motion. He knew that wouldn't keep it down long, and several more vampires were advancing, diving and tearing at him faster than he could fight.

Several shots rang out and three vampires dropped, writhing. It was Trey, shooting with deadly accuracy. He used the UV lantern as a shield while two more charged. He calmly put blessed bullets in their heads, then advanced to thrust an iron stake quickly into the heart of the nearest one before falling back behind the halo of UV light. The last of the survivors had entered the stairwell as Trey's lantern began to flicker and fade. Tom followed the survivors up the stairs. Vampires leered and advanced, hissing and clicking in anticipation.

Trey was continuing to shoot even as he and Angel walked backwards to the stairwell. Before the vampires reached them, Gaelan's cries of pain and exertion transformed into an angry growl. The vampires stopped their advance on Trey and looked over their shoulders at the unearthly sound. One turned back to Trey, cocking its head as if confused.

"Good luck with that, asshole." Trey ran to the stairwell door being held open by Angel.

Angel had a wide-eyed look, "Is that what I think it is?"

"It's about to get real ugly in here." He squeezed past Angel, "Let's go!"

Kedar, Natalia and Carly were leading the group up the stairs when they heard shots, then screeches come from below. Survivors were crying and screaming in panic. Arianna and Saul were in the middle of the group, trying to help keep everyone calm and moving. Kedar got to the exit door and opened it. Natalia was right behind him when a vampire dropped down the stairwell from several stories above, advancing on her with teeth bared. Before she could react, shots rang out and the creature's head snapped to the side, thick dark blood spraying the wall. Natalia grabbed it by the throat and pushed it against the wall. Using Gaelan's knife, she stabbed its heart then flipped the blade up and slammed it through the base of its jaw, through the roof of its mouth and up into its brain. Three more dropped and more shots rang, hitting Natalia's attackers in the chest and head. Natalia advanced fearlessly, quickly thrusting the Ka-bar up through ribs, into hearts, and then swinging around and slamming the knife through temples and destroying the creatures' brains. She turned, expecting to see Kedar with his weapon raised, but found Carly covering her every move. Surprised, Natalia tipped her head in gratitude and Carly returned the gesture, neither saying a word.

Kedar was leading everyone into the alley when two more vampires dropped, advancing on the group of terrified captives. Kedar's aim was quick and true. The two recoiled in pain as blessed bullets riddled through their bodies. Another creature landed next to him. He spun to shoot it, but it grabbed his wrists and sank the claws of its other hand into his ribs, lifting him off the ground. Kedar braced for the pain to come, but the creature shrieked in anguish and its face began to sizzle and boil. It dropped Kedar, who immediately thrust his stake into the vampire's heart, then skull. He gripped his bloodied side and turned to see Rabbi Saul standing with a half empty bottle of holy water.

"What? It works better than Manischewitz!" Saul shrugged.

Kedar spun and put more bullets into the first two vampires that had dropped, then staked them as well.

As the group followed Kedar down the alley, several more vampires dropped to impede their path. This time they didn't attack, but held their ground, trying to herd them back inside. Trey, Angel, Kedar, Natalia, Tom and Carly charged to the front and pointed their weapons. Still the creatures didn't attack. Screams erupted from the rear as half a dozen more vampires dropped to surround them. The panicked survivors bunched together like a school of fish.

"Hold your ground and wait!" Trey commanded, forcing his voice to be calm.

"WAIT FOR WHAT?" Tom yelled.

As if on cue, a boarded window two stories up blew out and Gaelan, now fully transformed, crashed to the ground, three vampires falling with him, then slamming into the pavement with a sickening crunch under his weight. The ring of vampires hissed and charged at the werewolf with renewed fury.

The venators pushed to the back of the crowd as screams signaled an attack. The vampires however, seemed oblivious to their human cattle. Instead, they jumped on the walls of the ally and were crawling like insects toward the melee at the front, focused entirely on Gaelan.

This was the break they needed. Trey and Natalia charged forward while Kedar, Angel and Tom slowly covered the rear. They were on the offensive now. Trey crouched down and used Gaelan's katana to slash a vampire from behind, slicing just above its knees. To his surprise, the sword cut clean through its legs and the creature fell to the ground, screeching. He plunged a stake into its heart and then through its eye socket to finish it. Natalia moved as nimbly as a cat, watching Gaelan's every move. Each time he slashed or threw a vampire, Natalia was there to finish it off, stabbing and staking furiously. Whenever a vampire tried to blindside him, both Trey and Natalia were protecting his exposed back. Any creature that Gaelan, Trey or Natalia hadn't engaged, Kedar, Angel and Tom shot before it could advance.

Carly could not take her eyes off of the thing that Gaelan had become—an unstoppable, monstrous, killing machine. His body was torn and bleeding. The vampires inside the building had taken their toll on him. Chunks of skin were missing around his back and shoulders and yet he kept killing. She gaped as he picked up a vampire by its head, sank his teeth into its neck and tore its head clean off, then thrust a massive claw into its chest to devour the heart.

The remaining vampires turned to run, just to be driven and bloodily thrown back into the ally by the unstoppable beast, where Gaelan's teammates finished them with gunshots and stakes. Gaelan grabbed one vampire by the ankle and swung it in a high arc to club another. He threw the limp, bloodied creature in his grasp back into the alley and tore the other open to devour its heart.

The vampire Gaelan tossed landed not far from Carly. It was pulverized—battered and bloodied. She remembered the creature that attacked her—the monster that ruled her nightmares. She ran forward, pulling the stake, and dove on it. It tried to resist, but had no strength left. Carly plunged the stake between its eyes, pulled it and began furiously stabbing at the creature's heart. Before she could swing yet again, she was knocked away and rolled to the side. Gaelan had landed next to her. He snarled and placed his right claw on the creature's head and neck, which began to cave in under his weight. He grabbed the top of the creature's chest with his left claw and ripped it completely off, as if stripping sheets from a bed. He plunged his snout into the open cavity and swallowed the thing's heart. He brought his face up, dripping with thick, dark blood, and staring at Carly. Now down on all fours, he lurched toward her as she scurried backwards, still on the ground.

Gaelan examined the thing in front of him. Something inside him knew that she was not to kill, not food—but something about her was familiar. Police sirens whined in the distance. He took another step forward. She skootched further away, whimpering in terror. Before he could move closer, a figure jumped in between them. He growled and bared his teeth, but retracted when he saw it was *her*. Natalia didn't hesitate as she put her hands on either side of his massive head and spoke softly, "You have to go. You have to leave now!" He gave pause at her touch, and stood up.

"Go." Natalia implored, "Go! Now! You can't be seen. We'll meet you later. Hurry!"

The sirens were getting louder. Saul, Arianna and all of the survivors watched as a monster stood there in front of their rescuers. Gaelan glanced over at the survivors. The smell of their fear was thick in the air, but didn't interest him. Trey and Kedar came up behind Natalia. He paid them no bother as they no longer saw a monster, but a teammate. Natalia looked at him with soft eyes.

Gaelan cocked his head toward Carly, who was staring up at him in disbelief.

He sniffed the air for more of the things that attacked him. *Gone.* He looked back down at the angelic face.

"Go." She whispered.

He let loose a deafening roar, looked around once more and bounded upward. His claws dug into the brick and mortar of the slaughterhouse. He jumped up and across to the opposite building, and back again until he was on the roof where he disappeared from sight.

The sirens were getting louder. Trey mumbled a prayer and all of the vampire remains burst into flame and then turned into small piles of dust. Natalia turned and offered a hand to Carly, who grabbed it and got to her feet, "Are you okay?"

Carly began to recover from the shock of the encounter, while Natalia encouraged, "We need to leave, now, and you know this city."

Carly led everyone from the alley. Soon after, the children and pregnant women were in the van. "Get them to St. Peter's Rabbi, and tell Father Ernest to be ready for a bunch more survivors." Saul squeezed Carly's hand, and drove off. Carly turned and looked at everyone else, "Follow me as quick as you can." The venators hid their weapons under their clothes and helped usher everyone through the back alleys and side streets. Before long, police lights were illuminating the streets as Carly was maneuvering everyone toward the church. Less than an hour after the battle, they had everyone at St. Peters.

CHAPTER 10
SMALL VICTORIES

Gaelan woke to the pre-dawn light. His body was sore and he still had open wounds on his shoulder and back. *I have to get to St. Peters.* He could smell salt water nearby. He looked around, trying to get his bearings; trees, walking trails, a fountain. *Battery Park!* He skirted the edge of the park, using the greenery to conceal his naked form, then darted from alley to alley, trying to avoid the morning joggers and dog walkers.

He spied a clothing donation box at Trinity Church along the way, and decided to make a withdrawal. The clothing barely fit him, but did make him less conspicuous as he walked the remaining six blocks north to Saint Peter's. He opened the side door to the smaller chapel that branched off of the main sanctuary. Some survivors were sitting in the pews hugging each other, while others tended to those with medical needs. One of the survivors caught sight of him and gasped, and before he had a chance to make an exit, dozens of people surrounded him, reaching out to grasp his hands and touch his back, gushing in various languages. Arianna pushed her way through the mix, and without stopping, jumped into his arms, crying. His embrace lifted her off the ground and he squeezed her tight, holding her for several seconds.

"I kept my promise."

She wiped the tears from her eyes and nodded, "Yes. Yes you did. I don't understand. Are there more like you? Things that can fight *them*?"

His voice turned serious, "What I am. What I turned into. It's worse than any vampire. If you ever see something like that again, you *run*. Understand?"

She nodded.

He continued, "You can never tell anyone what you saw! You have to promise me! You can't tell anyone that you saw me, or saw what I turned into, or I won't be able to continue saving people like your friends. Okay?"

"Okay." She hugged him again.

"Aye yi yi!" Rabbi Saul made his way through the crowd, "You look like absolute hammered shit!"

Gaelan extended his hand, "Good to see you too!"

Saul looked Gaelan up and down and called for a first aid kit, "Look at you, all *fershlugina*. Let's get you patched up!"

"I'll be alright. Where's everyone else?"

"Oh, the hero doesn't need a Band-Aid, huh? Well, they're all at *Murphy's Law* for the rendezvous. So tell me, how is it that you expect to make it out onto Long Island bleeding through those rags of yours?" Saul raised an eyebrow, "Oh, so now he's speechless."

"Okay, okay! Just make it quick."

"Make it quick he says. I'm a rabbi, not a miracle worker!"

For the next forty-five minutes, Saul stitched and bandaged the bite and slash marks on Gaelan's body. "Ugh, you're a mess! But that should keep you in one piece for a while." Gaelan stood up and went to put his shirt on but Saul stopped him, "I don't think so. Arianna and the others got some fresh clothes for you from the donation box outside."

"Thanks—for *everything*." Gaelan's voice was tired.

"No, thank *you*. Ya know, I thought Denny was out of his everlovin' mind, but then last night, that was somethin'."

"About that…"

"I know, I know, I can't tell anyone. And everyone is keeping quiet to Father Earnest. The last thing Denny needs is that getting back to the Vatican. I'm smarter than you look." Saul winked.

Gaelan gave a half-hearted nod, then gave pause, "Wait. What?"

Saul continued, "What I'm tryin' to say is that you really are as special as Denny says. You're meant for somethin' big kid."

"Yeah, I keep hearing that."

"Well, someday you're gonna realize it. Until then, just keep doin' what you're doin." Saul smiled.

Gaelan wanted to smile back, but he thought about the room full of bodies. He thought about the baby they had seen. What good was he actually doing?

He shook his head and realized he needed to get to the others, "Hey Rabbi, I hate to ask you, but is there anyway I can get a ride to the Island?"

"Always with the take, take, take. What's with the young generation?" Saul turned, shaking his head.

Forty-five minutes of tearful goodbyes with Arianna and the other survivors, and Gaelan and Saul were on their way.

"I know this is gonna sound strange, but I need you to drive by the building again."

Saul was wide-eyed, "What are you, *meshuga*?"

"No, I have a hunch. I just need you to get within a few blocks."

Saul conceded and drove him to the building. It was about 15 minutes before Gaelan returned to Saul's parked car.

"Was it crawling with police?"

"No. Not a soul."

"But we heard the sirens. Someone must've…"

"Someone did." Gaelan looked at him seriously, "The place was empty. Deserted. The bodies were gone."

Saul thought for a moment, "What about the three we locked up?"

"Gone, but the cell was covered in blood and God knows what else. They didn't walk outta there, that's for sure."

"Damn. You know what that means?"

"Yeah. I was hoping my hunch was wrong, but yeah."

—§—

"I can't thank you enough Rabbi" Saul and Gaelan were pulling into the parking lot of *Murphy's Law*.

"Thank me? Do you know what traffic is gonna be like in the tunnel when I go back? I should just get a hotel room!"

"C'mon in. Everyone will be happy you did."

"Nah. You kids go ahead. I'm goin' back to help Ernie with the survivors. Their forged papers are comin' in and we're gonna get them to the Vatican or the compound in onezees and twozees." Saul gave a mischievous grin, "Besides, you and her got a lot to work out."

Gaelan shook his head, "Carly and I worked though everything we needed to alrea..."

"Not *her*! You can't see the forest through the trees, can you? I'm talkin' about that beautiful venator in there that knows how to handle a knife and has balls bigger than mine!"

"*Nat*? She doesn't...we don't...what are you talking about?" Gaelan was flustered.

"It doesn't take a brilliant, good-looking and incredibly witty rabbi like myself to see that there's somethin' there! You just make sure that it doesn't get away from you."

Gaelan shook his head, "Nat is...she's incredible, but you saw what I am. What I become."

"Yeah, I did. I shit my pants too. But she didn't hesitate to go running right up to you when you went all Chewbacca on steroids."

"She was calming me down. Nat doesn't care about me like that."

"You can keep believin' that, or you can take it from someone who knows a thing or two about nice Jewish girls."

"It's just I don't think that...wait, Nat's Jewish? How do you know?" Gaelan sounded surprised.

"Oh trust me, I know." Saul raised an eyebrow, "Is that a problem for a nice catholic boy like yourself?"

"No. No! It's not that. It's just—I truly don't know that much about her. I don't even know her last name."

Saul smiled, "Maybe you need to start asking questions like that, cause trust me, after what I saw last night, she'll start answering."

Gaelan shook his head, "Jesus, you sound just like Father Denny."

"I know, we're twin sisters. Now get your keister in there and tell everyone I said hi."

Gaelan nodded and then extended his hand, then changed his mind and pulled the rabbi into a tight embrace.

Saul hugged Gaelan back and joked, "Ugh, with the huggin' and the emotions. Get in there before you make me cry!"

"Thanks for everything." Gaelan stepped out of the car. "Take care of all of them for us."

"With my life, kid. With my life!" Saul smiled, "I'll see ya around."

The door to the bar was unlocked. Tom, Carly, Angel, Kedar and Natalia stood when he walked in. Carly ran to hug him.

"Hey." He grinned and winced.

"Sorry!" She let go at the sound of his pain and smiled.

"It's okay, I'll live."

Natalia looked away.

"You look like ass, so I'm not gonna hug ya." Tom was smiling big and gripped Gaelan's hand like a vice, "That was a helluva show!" Gaelan shrugged it off and looked at his teammates.

Angel walked over and extended a fist, which Gaelan tapped. Angel shook his head, "I don't know if we're that lucky, that good, or both, and I don't care."

"Me either." Gaelan answered, exhausted.

Kedar smiled, "Good to have you back, *brother.*"

Gaelan extended his fist to Kedar, "Good to be back." He saw the bloody tear in Kedar's shirt, "Your ribs!"

Kedar tried to do his best Gaelan impression, "It's okay, I'll live."

Gaelan laughed, then went silent. Natalia came up behind Kedar, giving a half nod of acknowledgement from over his shoulder. He said nothing as he strode toward her. She looked at him curiously before he enveloped her in a tight embrace.

Natalia stood for a moment, unsure of what to do, then she grabbed onto him and held him tight. He pressed his face against the top of her head, glad to see her, to smell her, to feel her. Angel looked at Kedar with a raised eyebrow and a grin. Kedar smiled back. This time it was Carly who looked away with the pangs of jealousy.

"I'm glad you're back." Natalia said cool and emotionless, as they finally stepped apart.

"Me too."

Angel turned to Natalia with a provocative grin, then raised his hands up signaling, *I didn't say a thing,* at her glare.

"Where's Trey?" Gaelan looked around.

Tom spoke up, "He said he was tired. He took a bottle of bourbon to the back to relax."

"Is he okay?" Gaelan asked.

"Yeah, he wasn't hurt. He's fine." Angel answered.

"But is he *okay*?"

"Why wouldn't he be?"

Gaelan looked at each one of them, ending with Natalia, then began to walk to the back, "Because he saw what I saw, and I'm *not* okay."

Gaelan entered the back room where Trey was sitting by himself in a chair next to a curtained window, staring blankly at nothing. He had a glass of bourbon next to him. The bottle was already a third empty.

"Mind if I join you?"

Trey looked up and paused to think, "Sure. Whatever." He went back to staring at the curtains.

Gaelan picked up the glass and drained it, grimacing at the burn. Then he took the bottle from Trey and took a swig before handing it back, "What, you afraid to drink from the same bottle as werewolf?"

Trey dropped his grimace, snatched the bottle from Gaelan and took a swig. He handed it back to Gaelan and looked at the window once more. Gaelan walked to the window, turned around and sat, leaning with his back against the sill.

"What?" Trey finally met his eyes.

Gaelan took another sip and handed the bottle across, "You still thinking about it?"

Trey took the bottle, "I can't get it out of my head." He took a drink and looked at the window again.

"Me either. I'm guessing that you've seen some ugly shit, and I have too, but..." Gaelan couldn't finish his sentence.

Trey leaned forward and handed him the bottle, "To small victories."

"Is it really a victory?" Gaelan took the bottle.

"It was for sixty-one people, and seven unborn lives."

Gaelan nodded, "Yeah." His voice showed more resolve, "Yeah! Your Goddamned right!" He took a drink.

"I usually am." Trey's grin didn't last. "If there are places like that all over the world, then we have to figure out where they are and shut them down."

"Have you called Father Denny to check in?"

"I was waiting to make sure you got back."

Gaelan pretended to wipe a tear from his eye, "Aw, you really do care."

"No. I just didn't want to tell the nice old priest that his dog ran away." Trey smirked.

Gaelan shook his head as he smiled, "Ya know, Rabbi Saul taught me this great word—*schmuck*!" He stood up made for the door.

"Hey asshole?" Trey called.

Gaelan turned around, "Yeah?"

"Nice job last night."

"Thanks." Gaelan nodded, then smiled, "You weren't so bad for a man of your age either." He turned to walk out.

"Hey dipshit?"

Gaelan stopped and turned, half-exasperated, "Yeah?"

"Nothing. I just wanted to see how many names you'd answer to. I have dozens more." Trey grinned.

Gaelan shook his head with a smile and walked out muttering, "Fuckin' *schmuck*."

GAELAN'S DESTINY

—§—

The crisscrossed wires, state-of-the-art computers, and fiber optic cables seemed out of place in the room with its marvelous vaulted ceilings and ancient, frescoed walls. Father Denny rubbed his eyes with one hand and sighed. He had lost his share of friends during his many years as a venator, but now the Vatican teams, *his teams*, were disappearing at an unprecedented rate. The Council had taken notice, and Cardinal Klug seemed to relish the perceived failure of Denny's leadership. *Bastard doesn't consider the human beings behind those numbers.* And an even more disturbing thought: were the Venántium being actively hunted? By whom? Why now? How? *And this damned prophecy nonsense!* None of the major religions had recognized a prophet since Muhammad, or acknowledged an actual prophecy. Nothing referred to a "sheep in wolf's clothing." Demons lie, that was no surprise. But why would it lie to Gaelan about this?

Nhu Hoàng walked in with a cup of tea and a phone. She had begun working with Father Denny shortly after fighting the cobalus in China. Gaelan saved her life, her sister's life and most of their team. It had taken months for her to recover fully, and now she tried to help Father Denny as much as she could.

"You look like you could use a cup of tea Father." She smiled.

"Thank you Nhu." He took the cup and watched as her face fell, "What's wrong?"

"Phone call for you." She placed the phone in Denny's hand. Nhu turned to leave, eyes downcast. Most calls meant mission updates, but included casualty reports. She also knew that when calls came in, that meant there was at least someone left to call.

Denny sat in silence. "Hello?" Not the call he expected—not at all! To his delight, Trey reported that everyone was alive and well. As well as could be, considering what they had found.

"*Find us more places like this. No, find us every single goddamned one of them!*" Trey demanded.

Denny sat in silence after the call, burdened by what they found. He was going to have to take it to the Council at some point. Questions would be raised about what he knew, when he knew it, and how this team had survived seemingly impossible circumstances. Denny's head was spinning. He had to figure this out before Gaelan's existence was exposed. He took a couple of deep breaths and blessed himself. *Find the pattern.*

Father Denny stared at the screen. The shelters in Slovenia were in small, regional cities; intentionally inconspicuous. *But New York? What would make New York attractive enough to take on the risks of operating in such a high profile location?*

Father Denny smacked his forehead, and crossed himself. *Ports!* New York and New Jersey are both major port cities. He started listing major port cities around the world. Denny began thinking of it like an airline model. The smaller cities would be more difficult to hide a population of supernatural creatures, so they just needed, Denny was disgusted by the thought, feeding facilities. It was apparent from the account in New York that more creatures could go unnoticed in major urban areas. That was where they needed large facilities and lots of people to filter through. Denny spent hours looking into different cities and researching homeless shelters. He began amassing a list of places that might be used as slaughterhouses like the ones in Slovenia.

He deduced that there would be numerous sites in major cities all over the world that were unidentifiable and used for such horrific means. He had to focus on the small cities in order to make some kind of connection. That would hopefully allow them to track their way backwards and identify places in the larger cities. The quicker his list of shelters could be investigated, the sooner they could find a link and possibly bring down the entire network. Sending people into a haven where vampires and possibly other creatures amass to feed amounted to nothing short of suicide. Fortunately, Denny knew just the people for the job.

Gaelan gathered everyone together around the bar at *Murphy's Law*. "Everyone see the news coverage of what we did last night? Catch the chatter on the police band?"

"No!" Angel sat up. Kedar and Tom turned in unison to face Gaelan.

"I didn't hear anything." Carly squinted.

"Exactly."

"But the police responded. We saw them there." Tom puzzled.

"Oh they responded alright. But who made the call?"

Trey was the first to put the pieces together, "Motherfuckers. What do you think..."

Gaelan cut him off. "I went back this morning. Everything's gone except a bloody mess in one cell that used to be our three friends."

Carly shrilled "You're saying the police are working for the vampires?"

Gaelan tread lightly, "At least the ones who took their call. And I'm guessing it's not just the NYPD. The homeless wouldn't talk to the police in Slovenia."

"They don't know who to trust." Natalia chimed in, face grave.

Gaelan looked to Carly, "Just be careful, okay?"

"I will."

Not long after, the group was saying their goodbyes.

"I hope this trip to the Law was better than the last." Tom grinned, looking around the team that had first met there to kill Gaelan, and now worked with him. He walked over hugged Gaelan for a long moment, "Don't be a stranger." He turned and saluted the group, then disappeared into the back room. Gaelan stood back as the venators gathered their things. Trey was about to snipe at Gaelan to get his ass moving when Angel grabbed him by the arm. Angel turned back to Gaelan, "Take your time. We'll be outside." Gaelan caught Natalia's eye as she turned to follow the others.

"I like them." Carly walked up behind him.

Gaelan turned to face her, "I..."

She interrupted him, "I..."

They paused for several seconds. "You go."

"Okay." Carly smiled, "I wanted to say thank you. Thank you for coming and for what you did. And I also wanted to tell you that

I'm sorry. I know that I wasn't there for you when you needed me and..."

"Carly stop." He interrupted and she stared at him, "Don't thank me—*ever.* I will always be here if you need me, that's not even a question. And don't apologize. We were growing apart and I was too blind to see it—or accept it."

"No, I should've been honest and I especially should've been there for you after you came home. I know I threw the PTSD in your face in the interrogation..."

"Was that before or after I told you to go fuck yourself?"

Carly snickered, "Yeah, we both said some stuff we shouldn't have. Of course now I know a tiny bit of what you're dealing with, thanks to the asshole that attacked me, so I feel like," Her eyes filled, "I pushed you away. *They* took you camping and they were *killed* because of me!"

"Stop!" Gaelan pulled her in and hugged her tight, "Stop. I never should've said that. It's not your fault. It's not anyone's fault. The only one I blame is the fucking thing that made me what I am."

Carly stepped back and sniffled, "It—it looked like you did? Last night?"

Gaelan nodded, "I'm sorry about that. I—*it*—*me*—I wouldn't have hurt you. I know I scared you, but I recognized you and, well, I'm sorry."

"It's okay." She paused to think, "Do you remember when you jumped on top of me, that night?"

Gaelan seemed ashamed, "Yeah, I do. Again, I'm sor..."

"Let me finish." Carly's voice was soft, "You told me that I never wanted to see what you become. Remember?"

"Yeah." Gaelan mumbled.

"You were wrong. Last night I saw what you become." She laid her hand on the side of his face, "You were beautiful."

He closed his eyes and leaned into her hand, "I'm a monster."

"No. The thing that attacked you was a monster. But last night, I watched you. You took what happened to you and turned it into something else." She caressed his cheek with her thumb, "Something wonderful. You remember that."

He took her hand in his, "Thank you." He opened his eyes and stared into hers.

Carly's eyes welled once more, "Even with everything that happened, you know I never stopped loving you, right?" He nodded. "You and I will never—it'll never be that way again, will it?"

Gaelan pressed his lips together and shook his head, then he pulled her in to hug her, adding, "You know I'll always love you, right?"

"I know." She began to cry, "I'm so sorry."

He hugged her tight, "Stop. No more apologizing. Okay?"

"Okay." She looked up at him, "So this is goodbye?"

"No, not goodbye." He kissed her forehead, "This is just some time until my next visit."

"That sounds much better."

Gaelan walked to the door and Carly said, "I like her. Natalia. I like her a lot." Gaelan rolled his eyes and smiled. He went to walk out and Carly tried to imitate his younger awkward voice, "Ask her to get some coffee sometime." And she giggled.

He shook his head, laughing, and left.

She was left standing there, feeling both better and saddened, then she remembered the day and time. She took out her phone and called.

"Hey Chris. About that, I can't make it today. No, it's not that, I was thinking, how about going out tonight instead? Yeah, that's right, I said *tonight*. It's time to start living again. Okay. I'll see you tonight." She hung up the phone and turned to see Tom standing there with a big grin on his face. She looked at him, wiping the tears from her face, and smiled, "Oh shut up!"

—§—

Gaelan got into the backseat, Natalia between him and Angel. Kedar was driving and Trey rode shotgun. Everyone was staring at him.

"What? I didn't fart or anything!"

Angel spoke up, "We took a vote while we were waiting. We know we said we would work together for the time being, but we've decided we want you to be a permanent member of the team."

Trey seemed defeated, "Yup, three to one in favor." Natalia slapped him in the back of the head, "Ow! Damn! Okay, it was unanimous!"

Gaelan looked around with a big smile, then his face changed, "I don't know. I'm getting a lot of offers and my agent said this is a good year for free agency so I oooomph…"

Natalia elbowed him in the ribs, "Okay. I'm honored! Touched. Really, I am. Just stop hittin' everyone!"

"Seriously!" Trey emphatically rubbed the back of his head.

Gaelan felt Natalia lay something on his thigh: his father's knife in its sheath. As he took the blade, she wrapped her hand around his and squeezed it, holding it for several seconds, before slowly dragging her hand away from his.

"She is a good person. Strong. I like her." Natalia looked forward. "We have a lot in common."

"Oh yeah, like what?"

"Like," She turned and looked up to him with a smirk, "both of us have shot you."

"That's harsh!"

"No fuckin' fair. I haven't shot you!" Trey chimed in.

"Yeah you did!" Gaelan corrected him, "When I transformed in the school chapel. You shot me in the leg."

"That doesn't count!"

"A shot's a shot. Not my fault your aim sucks."

"I haven't shot you." Angel made a pistol out of his hand and pointed it at Gaelan over Natalia's head.

"You tried. Then I threw you into a tree."

The car erupted with laughter.

"Can I change my vote?" Angel chided.

"Re-count!" Trey exclaimed.

"No backzees!" Gaelan retorted.

"I haven't shot you yet." Kedar craned his neck.

"And that means a lot to me."

"Like I said my brother, *yet*." Kedar grinned.

"Okay, that was the most disconcerting part of this conversation. You see what you started?" Natalia shrugged and stifled another smile.

As the car slid into traffic Gaelan lowered his voice to a whisper, "Can I ask you something?" She nodded, "What's your last name?"

Natalia closed her eyes, no longer willing to fight the exhaustion of the previous night, "Sokolsky." She let the weight of her body ease into his and rested her head on his shoulder. For a moment, the rest of the world and the horrors of the slaughterhouse drifted away.

Kedar broke his brief respite of peace and asked, "Where do you want to go?"

There was a long pause before Gaelan finally spoke, "We need to see a family friend."

Seth Rosen started shouting as soon as Trey and Natalia walked into his office, "I haven't seen or heard from him, and I wouldn't tell you if I!" Then he saw the familiar face walk in behind them, "Gaelan?"

"Hey Sir." Gaelan smiled awkwardly at his father's old friend.

"Wha? I don't? What's going on?"

"We need your help." Trey was very courteous.

"Help? HELP?" Seth was wild eyed, looking from Gaelan, to the people that had tried to strong arm him, and back to Gaelan. "Gaelan, what's going on?"

"Well, it turns out that we were all approaching the same problem from different angles. We've kinda decided that it's better to work together."

"Gaelan, you once told me that you were helping people and ticked off some big organizations. That these people," Seth waved his hand toward Trey and the others, "were looking for you. Now you're all the *best of friends*? You don't call, and when you do you're cryptic. Now you show up with the people I thought you were running from and I'm supposed to think everything is fine?"

"You're right Sir. It's not fair and I haven't told you much. I will tell you most of the truth."

"Most?"

Gaelan nodded gravely. "We're all going after an organization that is heavy into human trafficking, slavery and murder."

"Murder?" Rosen's voice trailed off into a hazy whisper of disbelief.

"Killing large numbers of people indiscriminately."

"How are you mixed up in all of this?"

"I told you that after my parents died, I wanted to help people. This is it. I've found my calling and I'm not gonna stop until I've seen this through. I've seen way too much death in my life. Now I can do something about it."

"Okay. But I want the whole truth with what's going on."

"We'll tell you what you need to know, and that's all."

"Why?"

Trey was less courteous, "Because he wants you to be able to sleep at night."

"You've met Trey and Natalia. That's Angel and Kedar." Gaelan continued, "We've been following a human trafficking ring and finally found what we could only call a..." Kedar thought of some subtle words and spoke up, *"Processing facility."*

"Yeah, a processing facility, when we were overseas. It wasn't pretty. But then we found one here in the city," Gaelan swallowed hard, "and it was even worse."

Natalia chimed in, "We need you to try and find the link between them. The first two were homeless shelters in Slovenia, and the third is a faceless building in New York. At a glance, they have nothing in common, but maybe you'll be able to find something beyond just who owns them and how they were bought or leased. Some kind of common thread."

Rosen nodded slowly, "I can do that. It may take a little time."

Trey interjected, "Take more than a little. Be cautious and don't do anything that can be traced back to you or this office in any way. Cover your tracks and cover them deep."

"I'll try." Rosen sounded unsure.

"Don't just try Sir." Gaelan looked at him earnestly, "These people will not hesitate to kill you. They will kill you and anyone you know to stay a secret. I wouldn't ask if I could think of anything or anyone else."

"Gaelan, stop. I told you that I would be there to help you out when you needed it. I meant it. Your dad was always there for me and if helping you out means I also get to help others in need, well, then, bonus." Rosen forced a smile.

"Seriously, you need to be very careful." Angel felt a need to press the point home.

"I will. But how do I contact you?"

Gaelan scribbled the number to one of his disposable cell phones on a piece of paper,

"Call or text me and let me know if or when you've found something."

"I will."

CHAPTER 11
REVISED SCHEDULE

Medhir Ramachandran sat and meditated. He opened his eyes as the door creaked open.

"Hello my friend."

"Gooday, Gaius." After years of confinement, Medhir saw no more need to be unpleasant.

"Any new dreams?"

"No."

Gaius flicked an imaginary piece of lint from his cuff in annoyance. "Well no matter. It seems that we will finally be able to have that meeting we talked about."

"I finally get to meet Efthalia." Medhir raised his eyebrow. His dreams had shown him a women screaming and being attacked by *something*. But it had been months.

"No, I'm afraid not. Efthalia won't be coming."

"No?"

"No." Gaius was rather abrupt.

Medhir saw a rare opportunity to get under Gaius' skin. "But I thought I was going to meet with Efthalia." He pressed, "Is there no longer going to be a ritual?"

"Rest assured my friend, there will be a ritual."

"But you said Efthalia isn't coming. I'm confused." Medhir felt a twinge of delight at Gaius' discomfort.

"*Efthalia* was not able to make it."

"But why so long? She was supposed to be here months ago. I can't say that I was eager for the meeting, but I was intrigued. What happened to her?" His dream was beginning to make sense. The eyes and faces of the women had contorted to something unnatural, similar to the vampire faces he had seen.

"There were complications."

"What kind of complications? Is she alright?" Medhir feigned concern.

Gaius' tone was polite but weary, "You will not be meeting her. That is all you need to know."

"Surely. My apologies. So, who is it that I will be meeting now?"

Gaius sighed, "Her name is Genevieve. That's all you need to know." He realized how curt he was, then he called over his shoulder as he walked through the door, "Dream well my friend."

Medhir resumed his meditative position, but his mind was racing with the images he hadn't shared: The witches and vampires he'd seen screaming in pain, a pointed weapon of some indeterminate type, young Asian girl's face with the eye's of something unnatural hovering over her. He cleared his mind. *May my thoughts always be mine, and mine alone.*

CHAPTER 12
AGE OF ENLIGHTENMENT

Panic and fear filled the air. The small group of people didn't know where they were or why they were there. Some had gone to a homeless shelter, some were migrants looking for work. All of them were now following one man that had been abducted with them, and a small group of armed individuals that seemed to be leading them down a brick-walled corridor.

"ON YOUR RIGHT!" Gaelan yelled and threw his knife in a backhanded motion into the skull of one of two vampires that came from the shadows. It screeched in pain as two of the others shot it, and it's still hidden companion, with their shotguns. UV lights sizzled the skin. Angel lunged forward to stake both creatures, and retrieved Gaelan's knife.

Kedar was still reeling from the drugs he had been given at the shelter. His head was blurry, yet he firmly gripped the pistol and stake that Angel had handed him. Gaelan hadn't been thrilled about letting anyone else play bait, but Trey had convinced him, saying if the GPS tracker they were using was discovered, Gaelan could still track them down by scent. They had investigated eight homeless shelters in the past few months. Three turned out to be feeding sites. This time they were in Bulgaria.

The group was several meters from the exit door when it swung open. Four figures stepped through, covered head to toe in some kind of armor. Their faces were totally obscured by hardened black masks. The UV light Trey trained on them had no effect. A shotgun blast snapped one's head back and sent sparks flying, landing the creature on the floor. A moment later, it stood up and shook its head, faceplate cracked, but secure. It shrieked angrily, about to attack, when a fifth vampire entered the hallway. The humans collectively gasped: the final vampire was at least six foot eight inches, probably taller, and had to weigh three hundred pounds. Soon, all eyes were on Gaelan: survivors in sheer terror, venators in expectation, and vampire faces obscured behind their masks.

"What the fuck is everyone lookin' at me for?" He was still breathing heavy from the fighting. Natalia gave him a wide-eyed look and Trey turned his arms out as if to ask, *what are you waiting for?*

"OH THAT IS SOME BULLSHIT!" Gaelan reluctantly walked forward, shaking his head, "You know what you are?" He looked from Trey to Angel to Natalia, "Y'all are some racist muthafuckers." His voice trailed into a disgruntled mumble, "Makin' me go first. That is total horseshit!"

The vampire with the cracked face shield strolled forward. They sized each other up and Gaelan swung his katana around, slashing at the vampire from the abdomen up to the chest. The blade damaged the Kevlar, but sparked at the metal coating underneath it. Gaelan could see metallic mesh at the armor's joints. The creature looked down at the damage Gaelan had inflicted, looked up slowly, then spun its arm around to backhand him. *I swear this asshole's smiling in there!* Gaelan blocked the blow, dropped and spun his leg, sweeping the vampire's feet out from under it. *Clear a path to get everyone out. Then figure out how to fight these fuckers.*

Gaelan popped to his feet and charged. The other vampires readied themselves but Gaelan ran to the side, pushing off the floor and seemingly running two steps along the wall before swinging his leg around to kick the closest vampire. The creature's head snapped and it landed in a crumpled pile. Gaelan used the momentum to punch into the next closest vampire's chest and knocked it backwards against the opposite wall. He spun as the fourth vampire grabbed him, driving his arms up and in between the creature's own arms, grabbing the vampire's head and pulling it into his thrusting knee. Gaelan thought he felt the armored facemask crack at the blow.

All that remained was the enormous figure in the doorway. Gaelan charged at the thing's midsection, but the creature interlocked its fists and swung just as Gaelan hit its abdomen. The blow pummeled Gaelan to the ground, knocking his sword from him. Before he could recover, the giant vampire lifted him up and over its head and threw him down into the ground. As Gaelan gasped his breath back, trying to shake the stars from his eyes, the vampire reached down and picked him up by the throat. Gaelan punched blindly forward, but his fist was caught by the thing's massive hand and thrown back into his own face. Gaelan could hear Trey yelling, "SHIT!" over the ringing in his ears. The other vampires were beginning to recover. The giant holding him snarled from behind the mask and spun, throwing Gaelan's limp body through the brick wall and sending bits of brick and mortar flying through a cloud of dust.

The enormous vampire turned towards the cowering humans, then slowly cracked its neck to one side and the other, echoing down the hallway. The other vampires were on their feet and advancing. Trey and Natalia fired several slugs to no effect. The vampires were about to reach their victims when the wall erupted again.

Gaelan ran straight through the damaged wall, hit the enormous vampire from the side, and slammed it through the opposite wall without breaking stride. The other creatures spun towards the explosion. The giant came flying through the gaping hole, shattering more brick along the way, and landing on its back. Gaelan followed, diving onto its chest and pummeling the creature beneath him. The faceplate cracked under the torrent of blows, then split in two. The vampire, face gnarled and fangs bared, looked up to see the human face with inhuman eyes and equally large fangs. It had just a moment to register its dire predicament, then tried to scream before Gaelan slammed his open palm down on its face, plunging his partially transformed index and ring fingers through the sunken red eyes. Gaelan thrust his thumb into the roof of the screaming creature's mouth, anchored himself with his other hand against the thing's lower jaw, and pulled. In a flash, the top part of the vampire's face was ripped free. The mandible and whipping tongue were all that remained below a slick of blood, bone and brain matter. The giant's body thrashed as Gaelan stood and dropped what was left of the creature's face. When he turned to the remaining vampires, his eyes glowed yellow and red. One by one, they stepped backward toward the surviving humans.

Natalia was the first to act, charging forward and leaping with her knees tight to her chest, then thrusting her feet forward into the space between a creature's shoulder blades, launching it directly towards Gaelan. The humans were not the only ones to snap back to action. As Natalia fell to the floor with a thud, another vampire grabbed her by the face, lifting her from the ground. Natalia saw her tormentor's head snap to the side at Trey's shotgun blast, but its grip never slackened. It turned toward Trey, still gripping Natalia tight. That's when a massive force slammed the vampire sideways. Blackish blood sprayed in an arc as it crumpled and released Natalia. It looked to see its remaining comrades were on the floor beneath a set of armored legs. Gaelan stood with the top half of the vampire Natalia had kicked to him in one awesome claw—the weapon that he had battered Natalia's assailant with. He dropped the torn creature, still thrashing.

"Hey asshole," Trey pointed a shotgun at the twisted face showing though its shattered faceplate. It's head became a bloody crater.

The fight was over in minutes. Angel finished off the two surviving vampires with shotgun blasts to their now exposed heads. Gaelan grabbed one as it dropped, and pulled the front and back of the creature's bloodied neck to pry it open like a shucked oyster. He plunged his claw down the cavity and pulled out the heart. The giant, tongue still frantically thrashing, met the same fate. One by one, he devoured the vampires' hearts.

His teammates backed away, looking on with fascination and disgust. Finally, Gaelan, still mostly human, looked up from all fours, frantically switching his eyes from venator to venator. When his inhuman eyes met Natalia's, his face covered in blood and fangs bared, she smiled. Gaelan closed his eyes and let her warmth wash over his mind. He steadied his breath, and choked the wolf back, dropping from the balls of his feet to his knees.

Angel had run back to get Kedar and the survivors. Trey walked past Gaelan, "You gonna sit there all day?" Then added over his shoulder, "And clean that shit off your face so we don't have to explain it to anymore survivors."

Gaelan popped to his feet and started frantically wiping at his face. Natalia brought up her arm and cleaned the rest of his face with the back of her sleeve, then gave a satisfied half nod. Gaelan mumbled the prayer and the bodies were incinerated.

The people were escorted to local safe houses on hallowed ground. Once they were safely away, the team got in their own vehicle and everyone was uncomfortably quiet.

"Why the hearts?" Trey broke the exhausted silence that had descended on the car. Everyone turned to Gaelan, sitting in the backseat.

"I—I think that's what *it* craves. Instead of hunting humans, it hunts other monsters. Instead of eating people, it eats their hearts. That, and an occasional deer, or goat, or, well, around the full moon, *it* gets really hungry." Gaelan continued, a little more serious, "I'm getting stronger. You can all see it. I think that's why it wants the hearts. I can feel it. When I eat their hearts, I feel myself getting stronger."

"Well then let's get you many more of them." Kedar said with a woozy smile.

"How are you feeling?" Natalia asked.

"Still a little fuzzy, but good enough to go question the ones that drugged me!"

They knew that most collaborators didn't know much, but with a little luck, they might know the location of another feeding facility.

"Everyone realizes that *they* are aware of what we're doing, right?" Angel paused, "Their armor, the UV protection, and the fact that they came in to block the exit. They were waiting for us. It's going to get harder, and next time I wouldn't doubt we are shooting at bulletproof mega-soldiers. And sooner or later, they're going to realize what our strength is." He motioned toward Gaelan, "And they're gonna have silver bullets to even things out."

The gravity of Angel's words sank in before the awkward silence was broken again.

"Hey dumbass," Trey turned from the driver's seat and looked at Gaelan, "Why didn't you fully change?"

"I was trying to keep it under control, but when that big bastard threw me through the wall, it started to come out on its own, like a defense mechanism."

"So why not just let it out?" Trey looked at Gaelan like he was an idiot.

"You told me to keep it inside." Gaelan looked at him confused.

"Yeah, then I told you in New York to let it out."

"I thought that was a one-time thing!" Gaelan and Trey kept trading glances like the other was crazy.

"No." Trey sounded exasperated, "It's just what you are. Like your little friend Jennifer Guerin said, you're no more of a werewolf than we are. I get it now. I trust you. We all trust you." Trey paused as if the others were supposed to join in, but they were too stunned to contribute. "Just use it when you need it, *dumbass!*" Trey shook his head in mock-bewilderment, turned forward and kept driving.

After a bit more awkward silence, Gaelan began, "Trey?"

"Yeah?" Trey sounded dismissive.

"Do you think we could clarify little things like my being allowed to fully change before, you know, I GET THROWN THROUGH A FUCKING WALL!"

Trey chuckled, "You're the only dumbass that didn't know. And by the way, that looked like it hurt."

Kedar laughed aloud.

Gaelan looked at him, "Dude?"

"It's funny because of karma. You threw Angel into a tree, and now you got thrown through a wall." Kedar laughed harder, and Angel joined in.

"Jesus, would you guys just let that one go?" Gaelan rolled his eyes.

Angel looked over to Gaelan, still smiling at the thought of him getting thrown through a wall, "Racists?"

Everyone looked to Gaelan again, and Trey added, "Yeah, what's up with that one?"

"Yeah. Racists! Y'all are a bunch of anti-" Gaelan thought for a moment, "lupites."

"Ha!" Trey snorted. Even Natalia smiled at the joke.

"That's pretty good. You just think of that?" Angel asked.

"No." Gaelan answered, "It kinda came to me when I was getting THROWN THROUGH A BRICK WALL!"

Everyone laughed again as they headed toward the homeless shelter where Kedar had been drugged. Gaelan looked down at Natalia sitting next to him, "Thanks, for back there." She looked up at him and then playfully nudged him with her shoulder. He smiled and closed his eyes, feeling his body heal.

It was less than an hour before they were back at the homeless shelter. No vagrants wandered the block anymore. The lights inside were out.

"Wait!" Gaelan whispered urgently as they started to exit the car.

"Somebody's dead, right?"

Gaelan nodded at Trey's question, "Pull back and wait for me to scout it out."

Natalia's whisper was indignant, "No one goes anywhere alone!"

"That was before I played human wrecking ball for that walking, armor-plated tank back there. If there are anymore like him inside, I'll fall back and we can either follow them to their nest or find a better moment to attack."

Trey started the car, "Okay. You got ten minutes to meet us. We'll be under the overpass a half-mile back." Gaelan nodded, grabbed his sword, watched the vehicle back off and went sniffing around.

"We shouldn't have left him alone." Natalia sounded as worried as she was angry.

"I don't like it either, but this is what? The sixth place we've taken down? He's gotten us out of more than a few jams, and if he thinks he can scout it by himself, I trust him." Trey looked around at his team's astonished faces, "Yes. I meant it when I said I trust him. Okay? I trust the little peckerwood. I trust his judgment. I trust him to watch my ass and more importantly, I trust him to watch your asses!"

"I know he's definitely watching Natalia's ass." Angel smirked.

"Hayooooh! Ow!" Natalia slapped Trey and Angel on the backs of their heads.

"Natalia is right." Kedar spoke up, sounding slightly less groggy, "I think the two of you are just a pair of," They all looked at him as struggled to find the word, "anti-lupites!" He smiled and put his head back again.

Trey and Angel began laughing and Natalia tried to fight back a half-smile, then remembered that Gaelan was still out there. She turned toward the window and was going to ask how long it had been when she saw a large, odd shape moving toward the car from the shadows.

"Movement!" She whispered and grabbed her shotgun.

As the rest of them grabbed their weapons and turned, they could begin to make out Gaelan, running toward them, with something over his shoulders. They jumped out of the car to meet him.

"We gotta move quick! Pop the trunk!" Trey reached in and opened the trunk, then turned back to see what was so urgent. "I brought you guys a present!" Gaelan dropped the body of a young man, good looking, well dressed and unconscious, into the trunk. His face was battered and bruised, but he appeared otherwise unharmed. "Seriously though, we need to get some chains and locks and get somewhere secluded—*quick!*"

Trey was the first to speak, "YOU BROUGHT A FUCKING VAMPIRE?"

"I don't know about you guys," Gaelan shrugged, "but I'm sick of getting piecemeal information from useless lackeys. And by the way, the lackeys in question at this site were ground meat by the time I got there. So I figured we might get some answers from someone who actually knows something."

Angel put his hands on Gaelan's shoulders, "I don't know if you're crazy or genius, but I love both!"

"You're sure he's a vampire?" Trey asked.

"Oh, I'm sure. And I'm equally sure that his two friends won't be joining us."

Natalia looked up with a fondness in her eyes, "You shouldn't have gone alone."

"I'm sorry. Really. But we seriously need to get moving before he wakes up."

Trey put his hand on the trunk lid.

"Wait!" Gaelan leaned into the trunk and punched the vampire several times in the face, "Okay. I don't know how long he'll be out, so let's get moving!"

"Wakey, wakey." Trey poked at the vampire chained to a weight-bearing pillar in an old farmhouse that they had found. They had wrapped so many chains around the creature that it resembled some sort of ironclad mummy. "C'mon sweetheart, open your eyes." Trey looked back over his shoulder at Gaelan, "You sure you didn't just beat some poor bastard to death?"

Gaelan shrugged his shoulders, "His friends were all fanged out, and a human's face would be way more messed up with the way I hit him."

Natalia walked up next to Trey and pulled out a switchblade.

"What are you…" but before Trey could finish, she sliced into her hand, and squeezed her fist to let the blood begin to pool. She snapped her wrist and spattered blood across the unconscious figure's face. Following several quiet seconds, the vampire sprang to life, face contorting as it lunged forward against the chains.

"Told ya!" Gaelan grinned at everyone's startle.

The vampire's face returned to human form and he seethed, pulling at his chains several times before calming down and surveying his captors, "Well, this is a first." He spoke in Latin before asking in each language, "Bulgarian? Russian? Slovenian?" He looked to Angel, "Español?"

Angel answered, "English."

"Ahhhhh, English. You're way out of your territory." His accent was a mix of the Queen's English and a hint of Australian, "To what do I owe the honor?"

"The places where you take people to kill and feed—we want the locations." Trey's tone was ice.

"Oh darling," The creature mocked, "do you think they tell little ol' me every location? I was merely told that trouble was brewing here and loose ends had to be, well, let's just say that there are no more loose ends." He smiled and let his fangs extend before letting his face sour to a cold, killer glare at Trey. Before anyone could say anything else, Natalia advanced and punched him across the temple. The creature spit on the floor and smiled at her, "If I wanted a kiss, I would've called your mother." Natalia flinched as if she was the one who had been slapped, then let fly several more punches and a roundhouse kick across the thing's face, avoiding his jaws. The vampire spat, then let out a heavy sigh, "Sorry about the mother comment love. Apparently it's a sore spot. Hope she wasn't someone I ate. Now run along little girl, you're boring me. In fact, you're all boring me and if you run now, I may lose your scent before sunriiii... aarrrRRRGGGGHHHHH!"

Natalia was breathing heavy from the ineffective onslaught she had unleashed. She was caught off guard when the creature screeched and writhed in pain, its face glowing and its skin beginning to blister and sizzle. As quickly as it started, it stopped and the creature's face slowly began to heal. Everyone looked back toward Gaelan.

"Sorry." He was pretending to play with one of the UV lights he took off of a shotgun, "Darn thing has the trickiest switch." His tone was nonchalant. He looked to Natalia and winked, then tossed the light to her. He saw the affection in her eyes before she turned back to the vampire. She allowed herself a half grin and dripped with sinister intent. She clicked the UV light on, pointing it toward the ground before slowly tracking it up his body and letting it hit the exposed skin just above his collar. The vampire thrashed in pain so hard that the pillar shuddered, and dust fell from the ceiling.

"How's my kiss now?"

"I'm going to peel the flesh from yourrrraaaAARRRGGGHH-HH!" He was cutoff by another burst from the UV light.

Trey walked up beside her, "We can talk, or I can let her see if your head outlasts the battery charge. Your decision."

The creature closed its eyes and steadied its breathing while its face healed. "You'll have to forgive me. Where are my manners? Of course we can talk. The problem is that I don't know of any other factories."

"Factories?" Natalia spat.

"Yes love, that's what we call them. Our food goes in. We keep them in cages until feeding time and then we dine. A meat factory, just like you have for cattle, no?"

"They're *people*, not cattle." Trey's tone hardened.

"Oh darling, you're all just cattle to us. You can be toyed with, sexually exploited, used. But really, in the end, you're all just a meal waiting to be served." The creature's matter of fact tone simultaneously made Trey's blood boil and run cold. "It's nothing personal darling, just the food chain and the circle-of-life kind of stuff, you know?" Natalia raised the light again but before she turned it on, the vampire added, "I have used a few of the factories in different cities. I may remember where one or two of them are. I could show you." He raised an eyebrow.

"Sure, we'll just walk you right in on a leash." Trey said.

Before the vampire could respond, Angel asked, "How do you find out where the factories are?"

"We make a call. Tell them our location and it's checked against our phone signal, then we're told where the factory is at the time."

"And if you don't want to use it?" Trey interjected.

"Call of the wild, darling. Thrill of the hunt. People disappear all the time. Sometimes we even leave the leftovers to be found, just to raise the smell of fear in the city." Gaelan thought of the first vampire he faced in New York.

"Why do it at all? Why kill and feed on people? Why not animals?" Kedar didn't sound as disgusted as curious.

The vampire gave a condescending little chuckle, "After all this time trying to hunt us, all those centuries of anecdotes passed down, and you still know nothing about us."

Natalia hit him with a quick burst from the UV light, "Answer the question!"

"I've been polite, so you should really stop doing that?" His calm tone and demeanor was out of place. Trey looked to Gaelan, who gave him a silent nod of acknowledgement, then walked around to the side. The vampire sighed, "Life begets life children, as best as we can understand it. You are all as good for our health as you are tasty."

They all stared, Gaelan finally speaking, "So you *are* immortal?"

"Am I speaking German?" The vampire sighed again, mumbling in German, "How is it that any of you were able to surprise me?"

"How old are you then?" Gaelan raised an eyebrow.

"Twenty-four." The vampire smiled patronizingly, "I've been twenty-four for quite some time now."

"How long?" Angel wondered.

"A *long* time." He sneered again and everyone could once again see that he made his fangs visible.

Gaelan was curious now, "So what happens to vampires that don't feed on humans."

The vampire laughed, "I wouldn't know. There's not a soul that's turned down the chance at living forever to help out a race that we've evolved beyond. A race that does to each other what we do to them, or worse. Bloodthirsty. Selfish. Treacherous. You all know about the dark years with the plague." They were hanging on his every word. In all of the years of hunting and all of the handed-down knowledge, they hadn't come close to learning this much, "How we," his tone became melodramatically ghoulish, "*the creatures of the night,* made our play at humanity."

"Yes, and the combined religions led the Venántium and pushed back your kind." Kedar stated.

The vampire laughed aloud, "That's what you *believe*, you naïve little calves. You didn't push anything back. You were thrust in the middle of an all out war."

"War?" Gaelan continued to ease his way from the creature's direct line of sight. The vampire seemed to notice that his captors were no longer collected in front of him.

"Yes, *war*. When the Catholic Church, in all of its wisdom, decided to let the nobles know about the existence of our kind, it began an arms race like the world had never seen. The greedy and cunning began seeking our kind out and helping them—nothing like betting on the winning side, don't you agree? In return, a few were *turned*."

"Turned?" Gaelan asked.

The vampire turned to Gaelan again, "Are you just here to repeat the words I say, or would you like to hear what happened?"

Gaelan was almost starting to like the bloodthirsty asshole, "I'm all ears."

"Those newly turned nobles then took it upon themselves to turn others, thinking, I'm sure, they could rule forever, and more effectively than we did from the shadows. The army of the *new* grew while the old guard, the true bloods, were distracted by another conflict."

"The Venántium?" Trey asked.

The vampire chuckled at the question, "No darling. To acknowledge you as an adversary is for a nest of snakes to acknowledge a mouse as a threat."

"Said the vampire in chains." Trey retorted.

"Touché. But no. The conflict was a war between species. We, and the enchantresses, were fighting the werewolves. By the time that war had ended, the army of new vampires was rampaging across Europe. They refused to acknowledge the elders or know their place. Your wretched little Venántium would kill them during the day, but your kind was helpless in the dark of night. So no darlings, it wasn't your efforts that destroyed the threat. It was ours."

"How is a human *turned*?" Kedar finally asked, "Is it the bite?"

"No. Those who are bitten gain the ability to absorb immortality through the taste of blood and flesh, but it leaves one with far less power than a true blood, and the ability to look human for only short periods of time."

"Shifters!" Angel spat.

"Yes, that is what you call them."

"Why make them and not full vampires?"

"Some of our followers are loyal enough to be rewarded, but not trustworthy enough to become full-bloods. Even a shifter is immortal, and that's enough for most. Besides, a shifter gives *you* something to hunt. A shiny distraction from everything going on under your noses."

"And full-blooded vampires?" Trey asked.

"To be fully turned, the bitten must consume the blood of a vampire."

"So a vile full of vampire blood can be used to make more of you?"

"No darling. Therein lies the rub. The blood must be consumed directly from the vampire at the time of the bite. It's as if the blood of the master is run through the body of the *turned* all at once. It ensures that we can decide who becomes one of us. We are very selective."

"You can't just make little fanged babies?" Gaelan sneered.

"No." The thing sighed, "There are sacrifices to living forever. We are unable to procreate."

"Hmmm, so powerful and yet shooting blanks." Trey poked fun and asked out loud to no one in particular, "You think they make a pill for that? Vampiagra?"

Gaelan snickered, mainly because he could see that it angered the vampire.

"Why stop it? Why stop the spread of your kind?" Angel asked.

"Because there is an order and a reason for things. The newly created ranks were unaware of what needed to be done and why there was even a," The vampire raised an eyebrow, "*falling out*, with the werewolves. They were unaware of our greater destiny. Every vampire that didn't bend a knee was destroyed. Even some of those that did swear allegiance were destroyed. We let the church believe they played a much bigger part than they did in our 'population decline'. Now they keep our secret as much as we do."

"How do we know you're not just making all this bullshit up?" Trey was dubious.

"Because darling, I was there."

"So how long have you been twenty-four? *Really*?" Gaelan wanted the others to hear it for themselves.

"Thirteen-hundred and forty-seven years. But who's counting?" The vampire smiled and seemed to be stretching his head from side to side.

"Why keep it? Why keep the secret if humanity is no real threat?" Angel wondered.

"Unfortunately, humanity *has* become a threat. With our weakness known and little trinkets like," He motioned toward Natalia, "you're little night light there, we have become just the slightest bit more vulnerable. Of course, your age of enlightenment was also your path to ignorance. Who would actually believe in vampires? No, humanity has turned a complete blind eye to us. Until your threat is mitigated, it's better to stay in the shadows."

"And no government has ever become aware of your presence?" Natalia asked.

"You know, you have such a lovely voice when you're talking and not burning me. And yes, governments have gotten more information than they should have, on occasion."

"*They have*? Are they making their own monsters?" Trey was astounded.

"Do you honestly believe we'd let that all happen again? The information about our existence is usually discredited before it ever becomes a threat. Witnesses are served up on a platter, metaphorically or not." He licked his lips menacingly.

"You said usually." Trey questioned.

"No one foresaw an Irish-Catholic president for as much of a threat as he became."

"Kennedy?" Gaelan interjected.

"Again with the single word sentences? Yes, he had become aware of our existence sometime before his political run. Maybe it was the Pope himself that talked to him, or perhaps he witnessed something during the war. In any event, he began setting up teams of investigators and, what with the spread of communism and all, looking into the possibility of weaponizing our abilities. He had to be dealt with."

Gaelan was still in disbelief, "Vampires killed Kennedy?"

The vampire raised his eyebrows at Gaealan to confirm it, "We have had loyalists throughout every government and government agency, law enforcement and the like, for centuries now."

Natalia met Gaelan's eye, "New York."

Gaelan turned back to the vampire, "Why the war?"

"I just told you!" The vampire seemed offended and looked to Trey, "Really darling, you need to get smarter individuals." Trey shrugged in partial agreement.

"No, why the war with the werewolves?"

"Ohhhhh, well then, that's another story for another time." Natalia raised the flashlight, but kept it turned off. "But suffice it to say, there was a piece of information about our flea-bitten friends that didn't sit well with us."

Before Gaelan could press the subject, Trey asked, "What did you mean by mitigating your weakness?" While he talked, he stepped next to Natalia, their shoulders touching, and he ever so slightly tugged at the back of her pants. Without hesitation, she began to casually move backward, slowly.

"Oh, a little of this and a little of that." The vampire taunted. "You can't be talking about those stupid armored suits." Trey was taunting.

"No, but however did you get through Bjørn?"

"Lots of firepower, but that's not important. I want to know what you know about," Trey paused to make sure he could see the look on the creature's face, "*prophecies.*"

The vampire narrowed its eyes at Trey, "I'm not sure what you mean darling. Fairytales?"

Trey could tell the creature was lying, "I guess you don't really know that much, next to a demon I mean."

"A demon?" The vampire was intrigued.

Angel interjected, knowing what Trey was trying to do. "Ohhhh, not just any demon. One of the falleN that told us *all* about the impending eternal darkness. But we figured you've been so forthcoming, you might want to elaborate on what he was talking about. You've been so talkative and all."

The vampire leered at each one of them frantically.

"Is it because you figured you'd get loose and kill us all before sunrise? Yeaaaah, that's not gonna happen, *darling.*" Trey continued. "Where are these prophecies coming from?"

The vampire looked around nervously and finally spoke, "That's how you survived tonight. That's how you surprised me. One of you is the…"

"Reason why you and the werewolves had a little falling out?" Angel said, taking another step back.

"THE SHEEP IN WOLF'S CLOTHING!" The vampire bellowed at Angel, snarled, flexed and lurched, shaking the pillar. There was a distinct metallic whine, then a series of snaps as weak links in the chains gave way. The creature threw its arms up, breaking the chains off, its face contorting and fangs bared. Before it could spring forward, Natalia shone the UV light into its face, sizzling the skin. Hissing through the pain, "I'm going to finally rip off that arm and beat y..uugggghhhhh!"

Gaelan had lunged forward from the side and thrust a kick into the creature's ribs, sending it crashing into the wall. The vampire spun in time to see Gaelan's fist coming down, and feel the blow drive its head into the ground. Gaelan grunted, "I guess that makes me the *sheep.*" Before the vampire could even attempt to get up, Gaelan grabbed both of its wrists and pulled them up and behind its back, locking both if its arms. He thrust his boot into its spine several times, cracking the vertebrae, then grabbed the immobilized vampire in a tight chokehold.

The vampire gurgled, "You—will—fail!"

"FAIL AT WHAT? WHAT IS THE PROPHECY?" Gaelan yelled at the vampire as he shook it, "WHERE ARE THE PROPHECIES COMING FROM?"

"You may as well kill me!" The vampire struggled against Gaelan, who thrashed the monster's spine with his knee to prevent it from healing.

"No, I'm not gonna kill you." Gaelan spun the creature around, "That's her pleasure!"

The vampire hissed as it found Natalia standing ready. She thrust a stake down into its heart, and Gaelan released the creature. It sat upright, unable to stand, gasping, trying to remove the stake. It shrieked out in pain as Natalia hit it with the UV light again, sizzling its face. She held Gaelan's katana, blade down and, with a single backhanded motion, swung and took the vampire's head clean off. She mumbled the incantation and the body burst into a bright fire and then settled into nothingness.

They stood in silence, trying to comprehend everything that they had just learned. Gaelan turned and stared at Trey, who finally asked, "What?"

Gaelan exclaimed elatedly, "I told you there was a prophecy!"

"Alright Nostradamus, take it easy!"

Gaelan smiled, "But seriously, after all this time, we don't know jack shit about what's really going on."

Angel walked up, "Well, we know a little bit of jack now. Just not all the shit."

Kedar spoke up, "We didn't find out where the other slaughterhouses are." Gaelan smiled and tossed Kedar something. He caught it and examined the cell phone in his hand, "The vampire's?"

"Yup. I took it off of him when I rolled him up. Maybe we can see where he's been and see if there are any records. And maybe there'll be an address or two that was texted."

Kedar smiled in return, "There are times, brother, when I believe I could kiss you."

"You're gonna have to buy me some fancy-ass Perrier for that!" Gaelan smiled.

"Alright lovebirds, let's get the hell outta here. Kedar, see what you can get from that thing." Trey led Angel and Kedar to the door.

Kedar excitedly called out, "It's not even password protected!"

Gaelan walked over to Natalia. She was still holding his sword and he bragged, "It's got a nice balance, right?"

"I actually liked it more than I thought." She handed it to him, but didn't let go. Their hands met, "Thank you—for that."

He wanted to ask her why she hated vampires so much, but didn't want to risk ruining the moment. He looked into her eyes as their hands continued to touch. Her smile was genuine. His eyes went wide, and she continued to smile while raising a finger to his lips, then bringing it to hers, "*shhhh*." She squeezed his other hand hard along the tsuka, then released it and walked toward the exit. He stood there, in a moment of childlike bliss, before she called back, "Come on, *darling*!" in an uncanny imitation of the vampire's accent.

"Oh c'mon! That is totally not cool! That's just creepy!" Gaelan shook his head in repulsion, "Seriously though, I'm telling everyone you smiled—twice in one day!"

She spoke up in return, "They'll never believe you, *love*!"

"Ugh! That is just plain wrong! I think I need a shower." Gaelan could swear that before she walked out, he actually heard her giggle.

CHAPTER 13
THE HEIST

"It doesn't matter! We're taking a night off!" Trey's voice was a mix of compassion and firmness.

"We have more addresses! Leads we can investigate! We can backtrack to some of the addresses that didn't pan out. We have to keep going!" Gaelan's voice was equally charged. Natalia, Kedar and Angel watched the exchange in silence.

"Look at them!" Trey motioned to the rest of the team, "Look at *me*! We're not like you. We can't just keep going. Hell Gaelan, *you* can't even keep this up!"

"I can! I *can*!"

"BUT WE CAN'T!" Trey was more forceful, "The last two addresses were abandoned, and when we do find them, they're gonna be ready!"

Gaelan looked at the team. Kedar and Angel were clearly hoping for some rest, while Natalia seemed eager to keep hunting, but even she was clearly spent. He looked back to Trey, "You remember that room. You saw what they're doing." Gaelan's eyes were bloodshot from fatigue and raw emotion.

Trey put his hands on Gaelan's shoulders, "I did. I did and I haven't slept right since. I hate them and want them dead as much as you, but we're no good if we can't fight, and right now I'm telling you, *we—can't—fight.*" Gaelan knew it took a lot for Trey to say that.

He dropped his head, knowing Trey was right. Trey squeezed his shoulders, "I know. Trust me, I know. We'll hit the road in a day or two, after some solid sleep and some decent food." Trey could see Gaelan's eyes soften, "Who knows? Maybe we can get you to make some of that lasagna again." He smiled and watched as Gaelan closed his eyes, nodding silently. "Okay then, let's get some food, grab a hotel and a shower, and then get some real sleep."

They had been to seven different addresses that they had pulled from the vampire's phone. The vampires at the first site had full body armor again, but the team had armor piercing ammunition to crack the vampire defenses. The next two sites were abandoned 'factories', and the others were just nightclubs and restaurants. There were a handful of other addresses they could drive to in under a day, but Trey was right. They had been going non-stop since New York. Between Father Denny's list and the vampire's phone, they barely had time to catch their breath.

Dinner was quiet with everyone too hungry and tired to speak for much of the meal. The wine they shared seemed to effect them more than usual. Angel smiled, "Boys and girls, I'm going to sleep in a real bed with real sheets and wake up without pain in my back for the first time in weeks."

Everyone stood and followed his lead. Natalia fell back and, as Trey, Kedar and Angel walked out, she turned and grabbed Gaelan's hands. She impulsively kissed him on the cheek and whispered softly in his ear, "You're right. We should be out there fighting." She pulled back and stared into his eyes. Gaelan could see her eyes were bloodshot and had bags underneath them. He thought it made her that much more beautiful. Beautiful, but tired. He sighed and spoke softly, "No. We both know that Trey was right. We'll hit them twice as hard tomorrow." He leaned in and kissed her on the forehead, withdrawing slowly.

Their rooms were in the same hallway and they simultaneously opened their doors. They turned to look at each other one last time. Before she walked in, Natalia smiled at Gaelan. He gave her a smile back and a slight head cock, but said nothing. She touched her finger to her lips as if to tell him not to ruin it. He pretended to zip his lips shut, grinned and watched her giggle silently before walking into her room. Gaelan sighed deeply and went into his own room. He flopped onto his bed, and fell dead asleep almost instantly, Natalia's smile his last thought before he lost consciousness.

His buzzing phone startled him awake.

I HAVE TO TALK TO YOU!

—Seth Rosen

Gaelan sat up and texted back.

CALL ME!

The phone rang thirty seconds later, "Yeah? Hello?"

"Gaelan, it's Seth Rosen. I did what you asked me to do and things are getting weird. What have you gotten yourself in to?"

"Mr. Rosen." Gaelan tried to rub the sleep out of his eyes "What's goin' on?"

"Gaelan, I was doing research into the addresses you gave me. Every time I got to scratching more than the surface, I hit some type of firewall."

"You didn't do it from your office right? Tell me you didn't!" Gaelan was wide awake now.

"No, I didn't. At first I thought you were being a little paranoid, but I knew that your new so-called friends were kind of dubious characters and I figured I'd use internet café's and different places to do research."

"Not all in the same area, right?"

"I tried not to. I used places in New York and out on the Island. Then I took some vacation time once I got the uneasy feeling. I travelled to some different states, and at one point, I went overseas and logged in from there."

"That's good, but you don't have some identifiable login for what you're doing, do you?"

"No, some of the stuff was just searches into companies and people. I also had a friend of mine at the SEC give me an anonymous login years ago when I was looking into an insider trading deal. I used that everywhere I went."

"Just be careful."

"That's just it Gaelan! What the hell is going on? There were times when I was digging and the entire internet café went dark because of a power surge. That in and of itself wasn't suspicious, but when it happens four times in four different places, that's too much of a coincidence for me. Tell me what exactly is going on?"

"Okay, first off, where are you now?"

"Jersey."

"Good. When we're done talking, destroy your current phone, get another burner and text me that number."

"Will do."

"Second, I don't want you doing anymore research. I shouldn't have asked you…"

"That's just it Gaelan. I'm not doing anymore research because I found it!"

"Found what?"

"I found your common thread!"

Gaelan's heart began to race, "Are you fucking kidding me? Shit! Sorry."

"It's fine, and yes, I found it."

"What is it?"

"Well, I looked at all the addresses you sent and each private shelter was established by a separate entity. Some were corporately sponsored while some were private philanthropic endeavors. The corporations were different, ranging from oil and fossil fuel producers to tech companies and major retailers. The private funders were the same. All rich humanitarians that established homeless shelters somewhere. They were from all walks of life and made their fortunes in various ways. The businesses and the wealthy patrons were globally dispersed. There was no distinguishing element that stood out to link any of them together."

Gaelan sounded half excited, half frustrated, "Until?"

"Until I found, through several layers of investments and or borrowing, a capital investment and bank holding company."

"Mr. Rosen, let's just say that I'm not my dad and I don't know what all of that means."

"Well, for one, this organization has the money to invest directly, or indirectly, through a number of sub-organizations, into whatever they want.

And as far as bank holdings, they have controlling shares, or own the companies that have controlling shares, in most of the major investment firms in the world."

"So this business you found, owns a bunch of other businesses and banks, and throws money around like it's candy?"

"Exactly! But they're really slick about it. Some of the transactions are so far removed that I almost didn't find them. You'd have to be actively searching just to have an idea of what's going on. And that's when the weird shit started happening, pardon my language."

"You're okay though, right?"

"Yes, but Gaelan, what is really going on? It's obvious that this organization doesn't want a spotlight on it."

"More like sunlight. Speaking of which, what time is it there?"

"It's seven at night. Why? Where are you? I didn't wake you up, did I?" Rosen was talking incessantly fast.

"Mr. Rosen, you need to stop and listen to me. I want you to call a friend of mine. I'm texting his number to you. His name is Rabbi Saul Feinstein. He's back in New York and he'll come out to meet you. Until he shows up, I want you to head over to the nearest church or synagogue and wait for him. Understand?"

"You want me to go to Temple right now?"

"Do it and don't ask me why, and don't argue. You understand me?"

"Yes. Okay."

"I never should have put you in this position to begin with. I'm sorry."

"Gealan, if I'm helping people, the risk is worth it." Rosen's voice changed, *"But I'm a little frightened."*

"You should be, but keep your head down and do what I say, alright?"

"Yeah. You take care of yourself Gaelan."

"You too."

"Bye."

"MR. ROSEN!"

"WHAT?"

"What's the name of the organization?"

"Oh yeah... It's called Apus De Soare Investiții."
"That's Romanian!"
"Yes! It means Sunset Investments. How did you know?"
"Arrogant Pricks!"
"What's that?"
"Nothing. I'm sending you the Rabbi's contact. Call him, get to the synagogue and stay put."
"Be careful Gaelan. Their reach seems extensive."
"More than you know."

Gaelan was the last to show at breakfast the next morning. He sat down and took a croissant off of Trey's plate.

"Ass munch, it's a buffet. Get your own!"

"Yeah, but it's *all the way* over there." Gaelan motioned to the buffet laid out not three meters away, and ate the croissant. With his mouth half full, he looked around, "Everybody sleep well?" They all looked much better. He fixed his gaze on Natalia. She gave him her normal indifferent look and he smiled warmly in return. He turned back to Trey, "Call Father Denny for me please."

"I'm eating." Trey was dismissive.

"Call Father Denny or I'm going to keep picking off of your plate." Gaelan licked his index finger and motioned toward Trey's food.

"ALRIGHT! GEEZ! Fucking disgusting."

Gaelan smiled in triumph and looked around to see grinning faces, even on Natalia.

"Here, it's ringing. What the hell's so important anyway?" Trey just wanted Gaelan away from his food.

"Trey, everything okay?"

"No, not Trey! It's the younger, funnier, better-looking, more virulent, all around superior one."

Trey slowly lifted his middle finger to Gaelan. Gaelan kept his ear pressed to the phone as he blew into his other thumb and pretended to inflate his own middle finger in reply. They both quickly looked to the sound that came from Natalia, who feigned coughing as she covered her mouth while looking down, obviously giggling. Trey looked back to Gaelan, rolling his eyes and shaking his head in defeat.

"Holy shit kiddo! It's good to hear your voice. How are you?"

"Good. But how fast can you get us fake passports and weapons, heavy caliber again, under the radar?" Everyone at the table was now giving Gaelan inquisitive looks, especially Trey.

"Where?"

"Romania."

"I guess I can have ID's and cover stories in place by tomorrow. I know a girl. I can go through some back channels for the weapons. Kiddo, you know I don't doubt you. God knows we've been through far too much for that—but what's going on?"

"Mr. Rosen, the investor that worked with my dad and oversees my financials—do you remember him?"

"Yeah, from the funeral."

"Yup. Well he put it all together. He found the common thread."

"What common thre... holy shit, are you telling me?"

"Yeah, he found the organization behind it all!" Gaelan could see the eyes of everyone at the table widen, "It's in Romania. So we need ID's and weapons."

"I'll get them even if I have to do it all myself! I'll call back with the details"

"Thanks, Father!" Gaelan hung up the phone and looked around, "He called after we went to bed." Gaelan looked to Trey, "I know it's your team, but I didn't think you'd object." Trey's eyes were as wide as his grin.

Gaelan smiled back, "Let's hit 'em where it hurts."

"Well, I guess you're running the show this time." Trey nodded to Gaelan, "You got a plan?"

"That depends." Gaelan raised his eyebrow, "How do you feel about robbing banks?"

—§—

Natalia and Angel walked arm-in-arm along a brick path in the town of Târgoviște, Romania, enjoying the bright sunlight and cool air. By all appearances, they were young lovers enjoying one another's company while on vacation. They took pictures—lots of pictures—of the town, of the people, of the scenery, of the architecture. What was less obvious was that one small office building, just three stories tall, was in the frame of all their pictures. They took photos of every vantage point, every street, every alley and every piece of terrain that might impede their ingress and, more importantly, their egress.

In a distant hotel room, Trey, Kedar and Gaelan watched the same building through a camera with a super-telephoto lens, set back far enough from the window so as not to reflect light or draw attention.

"I don't see why Angel is out there and I'm not." Gaelan was looking through the lens and taking pictures of the entrance to the building.

"Because we want intel and not close-ups of Natalia's eyes, *dumbass*." Trey sat at a little table cutting an apple.

"What?" Gaelan looked to Kedar to back up his shock, but Kedar only shrugged his shoulders as if to say *Trey has a point*.

It looked as if each of the building's three floors were covered with mirrored windows, but Angel and Natalia reported that while the lobby had glass windows, the glass on the second and third floors concealed solid walls. People came and went during usual working hours, and some would emerge periodically for lunch breaks and smokes. The team recorded every move, taking special notice of the individuals who who came and went in the dark. There appeared to be two shifts.

They sorted the photos into suspected vampires and collaborators. One man came and went at all hours, then suddenly stopped showing up altogether. They dismissed him as a collaborator who displeased his masters. At one point, they noticed two figures come out onto the roof at midday, dressed in full armor and masks.

On day five, Gaelan and Trey went to the port city of Constanța to meet a group of black market arms dealers that Father Denny had set them up with. They couldn't risk involving the Vatican, or having their transactions traced. Trey paid the dealers with money laundered through the Swiss account that Denny had set up for Gaelan. After minimal 'convincing' by Gaelan not to jack up prices, the dealer grudgingly sold them five 9mm Glocks, five .50 caliber Desert Eagles, two thousand rounds of ammunition, 30 meters of climbing rope, fifteen pounds of C-4 explosives and detonators. They parted ways and Trey and Gaelan made their way back to Târgovişte.

On the seventh day, Natalia and Kedar opened a package from Father Denny, discreetly couriered to Târgovişte, to find twin USB drives and twin external hard drives courtesy of a hacker Denny knew 'through a friend of a friend of an old associate.' That same night, Kedar returned to the city, staggering under a duffel full of freshly forged metal stakes.

Timing would be essential—this was no smash and grab job. The plan was for Kedar and Gaelan to enter from the roof and start clearing the building from the top floor down. Trey, Natalia, and Angel, would enter the main entrance exactly ninety seconds later. With the vampires' security team split in two, the hope was for one or the other team to tap into the central database or find a server room, then download whatever data they could access onto the hard drives. The virus Father Denny's 'friend of a friend of an associate' had provided on the memory sticks would reek digital havoc thereafter. The C-4 Kedar had wired for remote detonation would do the rest.

On the eleventh night, a well-dressed woman they had never seen before entered the building, accompanied by two large, shabbily clad figures. They did not re-emerge.

The twelfth morning: go time.

"I still don't know why Natalia can't come with me." Gaelan seemed slighted as they prepped their gear.

"What was it that you would say?" Kedar looked at Gaelan, equally hurt, "I'm standing right here."

"C'mon, you know I love you K."

Kedar smiled, "K?"

"Yeah. Angel, Nat," Natalia raised an eyebrow but didn't rise to the bait, "K and, well, I'm trying to come up with a nickname for Trey that combines douche-nozzle and stick-up-the-ass."

Trey sneered, "If you must know, jackass, Natalia's with me because if we get into trouble downstairs, I know that your hairy ass will come for her."

Natalia opened her mouth to retort, but Gaelan cut her off, "You know, you're right." He looked at Natalia and grinned, "Nat, if things go to shit, you and I are getting out in one piece."

Kedar threw his hands up "Again, standing right here!"

Angel chimed in, "No shit!"

"Oh I'll get you guys too. The four of us are coming out of this alive!" Gaelan turned to Trey, "All I'm saying is that eighty percent is pretty damn good—four out of five. Those statistics are pretty solid."

Trey slowly shook his head, "You know, I didn't think it was possible for me to hate you anymore than I already did, but congrats, you proved me wrong."

They drove to the edge of town and far enough into a wooded area to change into black uniforms with ski masks, check their weaponry and go over their plan one last time. Then they switched into the old sedan they bought with cash, synchronized their watches and drove back into town. Gaelan and Kedar scampered out, several blocks from the back of the building, their ski masks rolled up on their heads to look like winter hats. They were attacking in the middle of the day to use the vampire weakness to their advantage, but couldn't risk drawing attention to themselves before they even got to the building. They pulled their masks down as they got to the alley behind the building. The alleyway was narrower than Gaelan had expected. He hooked the grappling hook they had planned to throw onto the roof to the back of his vest and signaled Kedar to wait. Then Gaelan took a running start and bounded off the opposite building, pushing up and off to leap back and forth until he reached the roof. He grabbed the hook off of his back, dug it into the ledge and signaled Kedar to climb. Then he turned around and froze.

—§—

Trey pulled the car up in front of the building and checked his watch, then pulled the ski mask down over his face. Angel and Natalia followed suit, and darted after Trey towards the building as if their car was on fire.

"EVERYONE GET YOUR HANDS ON YOUR HEADS!" Trey's voice was deliberately raspy. The office was full of nicely furnished cubicles, sixteen of them in two rows of eight, low enough that each worker could see one another. The manager's desk was on the back right, next to the one elevator. The stairs were adjacent to the elevator on the opposite side of the manager's area. Seventeen people, good-looking men and women in their late twenties to early thirties, stared at the three intruders indignantly. "I know you motherfuckers speak English, so EVERYONE GET YOUR FUCKING HANDS ON YOUR HEADS!" Trey, Natalia and Angel walked further in. The employees still appeared stunned, mouths slack as if they beheld the three biggest morons on Earth.

Angel walked up to the first man on the left and, without warning, jabbed him in the throat, grabbed his hair and slammed his face off of his desk, then threw him by his hair into the middle aisle. Natalia shot a second man who ran towards the elevators in the leg. He went down hard and grabbed the wound, moaning and crying in pain.

"Hands—on—your—heads." This time, employees reluctantly complied with Trey's command. Trey motioned his weapon for all of them to come into the main aisle. "I guess we do understand English. On your fucking knees."

"Whose computer is this?" Angel called out from the first desk he went to, "WHOSE FUCKING COMPUTER?"

Trey grabbed the nearest man by the collar and pressed his 9mm into the man's temple. The man winced but said nothing. He then lowered the weapon to the man's knee. Before he could shoot, a young woman spoke up.

"You can shoot out all of our knees," She had a thick Dutch accent and glared at Trey, "but it's clear you don't want to kill us. Otherwise, you would've already made an example or two."

Trey threw the man he was holding to the ground, "Okay sweetheart, you have the big mouth, where's your computer?" He grabbed her firmly by the shoulder of her blouse and pulled her to her feet.

She continued to glare, "You either have no idea who you are trying to steal from, or you are the stupidest people on the face of the planet."

"Where's your computer? NOW!" Trey was angry and could feel Natalia and Angel nervously scanning the perimeter. *This is taking too long.*

The young woman snickered, "If you *did* know who owned this place, then you'd know what would happen if we help you. And if you *don't* know who owns it, you're about to." Steel shutters descended over the windows, keeping the sun out and the occupants in.

"SHIT!" Angel shouted as the last of the sunlight was being cut-off from the bottom floor. Trey had loosened his grip on the young woman and the rest of the hostages began recoiling toward the elevator doors, which then opened.

By the time Kedar reached the roof, Gaelan was fighting three vampires in full body armor. A fourth was convulsing on it's back, its faceplate torn off and its skin boiling in the sunlight. Gaelan was fighting the three ferociously, but couldn't risk changing—that would negate the anonymity their masks provided. One of the vampires moved toward Kedar. Kedar pulled out a stake and readied himself, knowing a gunshot on the open rooftop would attract too much attention. Before it reached him, the creature stopped and cocked its head. The cacophony of the fight behind it had died into near silence. It turned to see what happened only to find Gaelan throwing his one hand around the back of its head and pulling, while punching its lower jaw with the heel of his other hand. The motion snapped the creature's neck and it dropped. It wasn't enough to kill it, but it did give Gaelan a crucial second to rip its faceplate off. Kedar jumped on the limp creature and unstrapped its Kevlar breastplate, driving a stake through its heart. The last two creatures were crawling, severely burned, toward the rooftop entrance. They never made it. Kedar stood after staking the final monster and tapped his wrist. *Time to move!* Gaelan nodded fervently and they opened the rooftop access door.

They went down five stairs and opened a door into a darkened hallway. There were several doors along the corridor. They drew their .50 caliber pistols, but as Kedar was about to kick in the first door, Gaelan raised his hand to stop him. *Me first!* Gaelan motioned. Anfernee had died in just this way—gunned down as he kicked in a door. Gaelan squeezed his fist as if to say please and Kedar acquiesced.

Gaelan splintered the first door, Kedar behind him with his pistol at the ready. A luxurious dining room with a large oak table long enough to seat twenty. The second door: a media room with leather couches and a flat-screen TV big enough to double as a drive-in movie screen. Follow-on doors: opulent suites with expensive looking art on the walls. Kedar set several charges of C-4 each time as they advanced. Again and again, the rooms were deserted. The festivities on the ground floor had drawn the main attention.

Natalia was the first to unholster and shoot her .50 caliber at the vampires pouring out of the elevators. The recoil from the heavy pistol surprised her, but her first shot hit an armored vampire in the chest, sending him sprawling back with a hole through his armor. Shots would slow them down, but not kill them. Several of the armored vampires moved to the left and right, trying to encircle the Venators; *they were armed.* "GET DOWN!" Trey yelled, just as automatic gunfire filled the room.

Trey, Natalia and Angel dove behind furniture to either side. Horrific screams filled the air. Trey peaked around the side of the desk to take a shot and saw the carnage. The unarmored vampires were tearing into the closest human collaborators. The armored creatures shot indiscriminately at everyone. They were cleaning up loose ends. The Dutch woman was just a few feet away from him, leaning against the side of another desk, laboring for breath as blood trickled from the side of her mouth. Her eyes were wide, disbelieving. *Shit!* Trey dove across the aisle as bullets flew past. He pulled her behind the desk and pressed his hands against the entry wound in her stomach, looking into her terrified eyes. With a shaking hand she pointed up at the computer, imploring him silently. He yanked it down before it was hit by gunfire and put the keyboard in her hands.

Natalia and Angel were each taking turns firing and shifting positions. Angel hit one unarmored creature in the face and the top half of its head disappeared in a red mist. Trey quickly fired off several rounds over the top of the desk. The woman keyed in access to the main database with bloody fingers. She grabbed his arm, too weak to speak. He plugged in the external hard drive—the download started automatically.

"Come on. COME ON!" The bar at the bottom of the screen seemed to crawl at glacial speed; the .50 caliber rounds were keeping the vampires at bay for now, but they didn't have long.

"About goddamned time!" Trey ripped out the hard drive connection, then shoved the USB drive into the open port. He took several more shots, reloaded his magazine and took the young woman's hand, "Thank you."

"I've—done –" She coughed and gasped for air, "horrible things."

"Just stay still." She had turned her back on humanity and covered up atrocities that would give nightmares to psychopaths, but Trey felt pity for the dying woman nonetheless. Commotion broke out overhead. Two armored vampires provided cover by the elevator and stairs, while the rest fell back and scurried out of the room.

The two vampires continued to fire at anything that moved. The young woman squeezed Trey's hand with all her might.

Gaelan and Kedar were on the second floor. Two doors sat directly across from each other along a hallway: one open, one shut. Kedar nodded, *my turn, I'll be alright,*

He stopped just before he reached the open door, clinging to the wall while watching the shut door across the way. He spun and pointed his weapon into the room while quickly crossing to the other side of the door. He surveyed everything inside—*clear*! It was full of video monitors, recreational equipment and a kitchenette in one corner. It was some sort of guardroom—*and it was empty*. That left the door across the hallway.

Gaelan and Kedar nodded to one another and slowly drew their weapons down on the shut doorway. Kedar held back, knowing that Gaelan would kick it down. Gaelan motioned his fingers for three…two…before he got to one, the door opened to reveal two armored vampires with automatic weapons. Both sides were surprised, but Gaelan didn't hesitate. He fired .50 caliber rounds point blank into their hearts before the creatures could process the intruders' presence, and shoved his way into the room as they crumpled.

Kedar crouched to shoot the creatures in the face, and watched as Gaelan was slammed against the wall, a wave of bricks and mortar rising up in front of him.

Witch! Kedar opened fire on the female figure with her arms held upright, but with a flick of her wrists, she raised the brick and floor in front of her, blocking his assault. He could hear Gaelan shouting the Hebrew prayer against unclean spirits, still pinned against the wall. The wall seemed to flinch, then crumble. The witch screeched in pain as Kedar's bullet finally found its mark. He kept shooting, hitting the witch once more, then adjusted his aim towards the assailants in the corner of the room. One well-dressed vampire, flanked by two scruffy men, advanced on him.

Gaelan was free of the witch's grip and turned to aid Kedar. His and Kedar's shots hit the vampire simultaneously, and then the filthy dressed men had begun to transform—*WEREWOLVES*! Gaelan thundered with rage through his ski mask and ran to hit the first creature head on. It came down on top of him, but Gaelan had already thrust the pistol into the thing's ribcage and fired into its heart. The monster shrieked and dug its claws into Gaelan. Gaelan bellowed in pain, grabbed his silver blade from his leg strap and buried it into the wolf's temple, pulled it out, stabbed it in the heart and then shot the twitching creature in the head for good measure.

Kedar's shot hit the vampire in the face. The remaining werewolf jumped over the vampire's crumpling form and lunged at Kedar. Kedar fired several rounds, but it was a silver blade to the creature's head that thwarted its advance, not his bullets. Gaelan, still on his back, had thrown his knife into the creature's head. Kedar yanked the blade from the thrashing monster and plunged it into its heart. Then he shot it twice, opening up gaping holes in its head and chest. Gaelan pushed the enormous dead creature off of him and stood.

"Your ribs." Kedar handed the silver blade to Gaelan.

Gaelan winced as he touched the wound, blood dripping over his fingers, "I'm good." He surveyed the room, "What the hell?"

In the melee, neither of them had noticed the small Indian man strapped to a table in the center of the room. As they approached, he spoke in Hindi, his voice weak, "Are you here to kill me?"

Kedar looked to Gaelan and shrugged. Gaelan answered in Hindi, "Uh, who are you?"

"Who are *you*?" The man was weak and seemed confused.

"Do you know English or Latin?"

"Latin?" The man said in Hindi, then switched to English, "You are the hunters? The Blessed Hunters?"

"Yes." Kedar chimed in, "Why do they have you here?"

"You don't know who I am?"

"Are you a monster?" Gaelan asked pointedly and ripped the restraints holding the man by the wrists and ankles.

"I'm no monster." The man shook his head and rubbed his wrists.

Kedar asked, "What is your name?"

"Medhir... Medhir Ramachandran."

"Medhir, we're going to get you out of here." Kedar helped Medhir to his feet and nodded for Gaelan to lead the way.

Gaelan checked the hallway and led them toward the stairs. Footsteps echoed up the stairwell. The elevator door was beginning to open, "UP!" Gaelan shoved Kedar and Medhir into the stairwell, and shuffled up behind them backwards, covering their rear. A fully armored vampire came around the corner, while another vampire, this one unarmored, opened the door to the adjoining floor. Gaelan's shots connected with their neck and chest respectively, but Gaelan knew he couldn't finish them, overpower any other vampires and cover Kedar at the same time. As Kedar pushed the heavy roof access door open, Gaelan heard vampires below him scream something. *What was that?* He burst through the door behind Kedar and Medhir. The sunlight would at least stop the unarmored vampires and even the odds. Kedar was helping Medhir to the rope.

"GO!" He spun and dropped to a knee in front of the roof access door, and emptied a clip as it opened. That slowed them, but a swarm of armored vampires were on him as soon as he stopped to reload. He wasn't going to make it to Kedar.

"I can't climb down. I don't have the stre..." Before the old man could finish, Kedar grabbed Medhir and spun him so they faced each other, put his back to the ledge, took the rope in his right hand and commanded, "Hold me tight around the neck and wrap your legs around my waist, like a baby." Medhir grabbed Kedar. Kedar wrapped his arms around the man and now held the rope with both hands behind the man's back. He lowered himself and began walking backward down the side of the building. His arms and legs were on fire but he knew he could make it down. He looked up several times to see if Gaelan was there, then saw the armored face peer down and begin to pull the rope up.

—§—

"We gotta get outta here somehow!" Angel was yelling to Trey and Natalia between shots. The two vampires were holding their ground, neither advancing nor yielding access to the stairs. The young woman held Trey's hand tight. He looked down "We'll get you out of here."

"NO!" She managed to scream out, "I—will—slow you—down." She was struggling to breathe, "Don't—leave—me—alive." She coughed, "They—will—torture—me." She winced in pain and sobbed a little, "So—sorry. I'm—so—sorry." Trey looked down at her pitifully.

Natalia yelled for Angel and Trey to cover her. She darted and dove over the closest desk to the entry as the vampires shot at her. She reached into her cargo pocket and pulled out one of the blocks of C-4. She tore off a chunk, rolled it in her hands and stuck it to the metal shudders. She thought to herself, *I hope this is small enough.* She stuck the detonator in and dove back toward Angel, "GET DOWN!" She squeezed the trigger and set off the charge.

Trey's ears were ringing as dust filled the air. He had thrown himself on the young woman to shield her body. Sunlight beamed through the blasted shudder, and the damaged shudder to either side. He was momentarily disoriented from the blast, then quickly regained his wits and hearing. He looked down at the young woman. She looked back up at him, her breathing shallow and her eyes tired. She mustered the strength to say, "Go."

"OUT! NOW!" Natalia was yelling to Trey and Angel. Angel had fallen back to the hole the blast had opened, not far from Natalia.

"You're coming with us." Trey was delaying the inevitable.

"Go—now. Won't—live—long." She was resigned to her fate, "Shoot me—and—go." Trey pointed the gun at her head and she closed her eyes. His hand shook for a second and he dropped the pistol. She looked up at him with tears streaming down her face, her voice barely a whisper, "Please."

"NOW! WE HAVE TO GO!" Natalia was screaming at Trey.

Trey reached into his cargo pocket and pulled out the block of C-4. He plunged the detonator into the explosive and put it into her hand, closing her fingers around it. He placed the trigger in her other hand, "Squeeze this to make it blow. Go out in style sweetheart!" Then he leaned in and gently kissed her on the forehead.

She smiled, coughing with the slightest hint of a chuckle. "Go." She whispered. Trey shot at the two armored vampires and noticed that the unarmored vampires were now running out of the stairwell screeching words they didn't understand. Trey dove over several desks and scrambled out the hole, followed by Angel and Natalia. They began sprinting away from the main entrance. The armored vampires emerged to follow.

"HERE THEY COME!" Angel called out as they saw the creatures come into the sunlight.

Inside, the unarmored vampires looked around, and saw the young woman sitting there, struggling to breathe. One of the vampires said to two of the others, "Find out what she knows, quickly."

As they approached her, she looked up at them and smiled. With all the strength she could muster, she said, "I quit!" Then she squeezed the trigger.

Up on the roof, Gaelan was fighting four armored vampires, and losing. They had swarmed him and were overpowering him. His pistol had been knocked away and his knife would have proven useless against the armor. He was bleeding from his ribs where the werewolf had hit him, and now they were capitalizing on his weakness. With every hit he landed, they landed two more. He was furiously fighting but couldn't find an opening. Then they heard and felt the explosion. It wasn't catastrophic, but it was enough to buy Gaelan some time to see the fifth vampire pulling the rope, hand-over-hand, trying to bring Kedar and Medhir back up. He made a mad dash for the creature holding the rope, but he was brought down halfway there. He was fighting once more, trading blows with the other four creatures. He couldn't break free. That's when the second explosion hit. The building shook and car alarms began ringing all over. Gaelan knew he couldn't get to Kedar, so he bellowed at the top of his lungs, "BLOW IT!"

Kedar pulled on the rope as if he could pull the vampire over the edge, but it was no use. The vampire was pulling them up a couple of feet at a time. With each pull, Kedar's legs would buckle and his knees would slam against the side of the building, all the while trying to protect Medhir from harm. The first explosion caught both he and the vampire off-guard, but the creature kept pulling up. The second explosion jolted the building. The vampire had let go of the rope, but Kedar held on. He and Medhir fell backwards over two meters, and his legs and knees bore the brunt of slamming into the wall. Through the chaos above, he heard Gaelan's voice screaming out, "BLOW IT!" Kedar shimmied as fast as he could, burning through the gloves he wore and making his hands bleed. They dropped two meters from the alley floor, landing with a thud. He reached into his cargo pocket and squeezed the first trigger he could pull. He detonated the charges that he and Gaelan had set throughout the upper floors. In a blinding flash, chunks of the roof exploded upward and the vampire that had been pulling on the rope was blown over the side and narrowly missed Medhir and him. He pulled Medhir to his feet and saw that the vampire that fell began to recover.

The roof buckled and rolled under Gaelan's feet, as if the concrete had been liquefied. He lost his footing, but so did his attackers. He spotted his pistol as they all fell to the ground. He dove forward and grabbed it, loading it with a spare magazine from his cargo pocket.

Before the other vampires could advance, Gaelan had already shot one in the chest. It began to hiss and screech, thrashing about violently with its exposed skin underneath the sunlight. He quickly shot it in the head to expose its face.

    Gaelan's targets were close and quick. The next creature thrust itself toward him and he jumped up, kicking his feet out to meet it. He wrapped his legs around its neck and pulled them both to the ground. While the creature thrashed, unable to get a good grip on Gaelan, he pressed the pistol against its faceplate and fired. The creature shrieked in agony as it too was exposed to the sunlight. Gaelan was now down to two adversaries, and he finally felt confident. This time he was the one to advance and attack. Unfortunately, the vampire drew its own weapon and shot Gaelan three times, point blank in the chest. Gaelan flew backwards, landing hard. The vampire approached him as a hunter would approach a kill. When the vampire came up to his body, Gaelan pounced, throwing his body full force into the creature. He slammed the thing's head several times off of the rooftop until its mask began to crack. Gaelan finally pried a crack large enough to let the sunlight in. The vampire went wild with pain. Gaelan recovered his pistol once more, turning and shooting it several times, just before the final vampire hit him full on and the two went over the side of the building.

Just as the armored vampires began to give chase to Trey, Angel and Natalia, the bottom floor of the building blew. The two armored vampires were hit with mortar and shrapnel from the building, which exposed their skin to the sunlight. They began to twist and writhe as if being doused with acid. The three hunters took carful aim, with Trey calling out, "HEART LEFT FIRST."

    Natalia responded with "HEAD LEFT", and Angel with "HEAD RIGHT."

    Trey shot the vampire on the left in the heart, and Natalia squeezed her trigger at the sound of Trey's bullet, blowing a hole in its faceplate. It fell to the ground quaking as it died. Trey shot the creature on the right just seconds later with Angel also firing at the sound of his shot. That creature suffered the same fate.

It was just seconds later that parts of the top two floors of the building blew outward, showering the area with brick and dust. As the streets began crowding with onlookers, Trey and company jumped into the getaway car and drove off. They ripped off their masks and slowly drove several blocks, circling behind the building, right where they dropped Gaelan and Kedar off. No one was there.

Kedar and Medhir had backed away from the vampire in the alley while it was still distracted by the blasts in the building. Before it could fully turn its attention back to them, Gaelan and the vampire he was fighting fell to the ground from the roof above. The original vampire turned to see the other pick up Gaelan's lifeless, bullet-ridden body and throw it forcefully against the alley wall.

The air became thick with dust from the blast as Medhir quickly turned to Kedar and whispered, "Grab me. Quickly. Grab me and hold a gun to my head." Kedar cocked his head in confusion, but Medhir pressed the point, "Use me as a human shield. You have to trust me!" His voice seemed stronger and more determined, "Just put a gun to my head!"

When the vampires spun, Kedar had his pistol pointed at Medhir's temple. He called out in Latin, "Stop or I shoot!" He couldn't think of anything else and he was doubtful as to just how convincing or accurate his Latin sounded. He began wondering why the vampires would care about a human and what his next move would be, when the two creatures stopped advancing.

They called out in Latin, "Let him go and you may go."

Kedar was now astounded. Who was Medhir that the vampires wanted him so badly?

Kedar had barely a second to contemplate when Gaelan pounced upon the nearest creature's back and began slamming its head into the concrete. Kedar could see that Gaelan seemed weaker and sloppier. The other vampire turned to see the commotion and Kedar aimed at the distracted creature and squeezed his trigger. The unnerving click caught everyone off guard. Kedar figured he must have slid the empty chamber forward to holster his weapon and help Medhir. He never reloaded.

The vampire standing heard the click, kicked Gaelan in the ribs and began marching toward Kedar and Medhir. Gaelan was now on his back, bleeding from three bullet wounds, trying to fight an armored vampire and unable to help Kedar. The vampire held Gaelan by the throat and was squeezing. Ordinarily it should've torn a human's head off, but Gaelan was still strong enough to pry its grasp and take a breath.

Kedar shuffled backwards, now pushing Medhir behind him and keeping himself between the other vampire and the old man. He took out a stake and readied himself for a fight he couldn't win, then watched the creature's head snap back while the sound of the bullet reverberated in his ears.

"THERE!" Angel called as they ran into the side alley of the bank. Natalia charged forward and Trey stopped, took aim and put a round into the head of a vampire walking toward Kedar and an old man he had never seen.

Natalia jumped and wrapped her hands and legs around the neck of the creature on top of Gaelan, twisting as she continued her momentum to the ground. The creature was pulled from Gaelan and rolled with Natalia, quickly standing to strike at his attacker when he heard, "Hey asshole." The creature turned in time to see the muzzle flash of Angel's pistol, slightly before it's faceplate broke and its head was torn open. Natalia grabbed her knife and plunged it into the creature's exposed skull. Angel put another bullet in its heart and Natalia staked it for good measure before rushing to Gaelan.

Trey put another round into the other vampire's heart and looked at Kedar, "You ready to get out of here?"

Kedar huffed, "I think so."

"Alright, let's move. Now!"

Trey had no sooner stated the obvious when Natalia and Angel came up to them helping Gaelan walk. Everyone noticed the bullet holes and gashes in his ribs.

"Shit! We really have to move!"

The entire team scrambled through two alleys to find the car, jump in and drive toward the original wooded road at the edge of town. Natalia was holding her hands over Gaelan's wounds and he whispered weakly, "I'll be alright. You know I will."

Angel was trying to mask his disbelief with awkward laughter, "There's no way we made it out of there alive... seriously, how the fuck did we do that?"

Trey shook his head in disbelief, "Like you always say, I'd rather be lucky than good!"

Angel added, "What happened with that collaborator back there?"

Trey was silent for a moment, then spoke up, "She turned in her resignation."

They arrived at the switch point and everyone jumped out of a now blood-soaked car. Trey went to the trunk and pulled out gasoline while Kedar helped Medhir into the other vehicle, then he and Angel pulled off their clothing. Gaelan stumbled several meters away and fell to his hands and knees. The bleeding had subsided a bit, but he was still weakened. Natalia dropped to her knees in front of him and soothingly said, "Do it. I'll be right here with you, so do it." Gaelan shut his eyes and could feel his body heat rise. The fangs in his mouth began to protrude and he opened his inhuman eyes to see Natalia still in front of him. She put her hands on his face and said, "Push." He obliged and flexed the muscles in his body, pushing the bullets through the torn muscle and skin until, one by one, they dropped to the forest floor. He shut his eyes again and concentrated on the vision of her face. His body heat lowered and he could feel his body relaxing into human form.

"Thank you." He mustered through the exhaustion and smiled.

She smiled back and leaned her forehead against his saying, "I thought you were supposed to come save me." Before he could say anymore, she pulled her head back and saw the blood still dripping from his sides. She anxiously inquired, "Your ribs?"

"Werewolves. Claws. I'm gonna need some time for those."

She was motionless for a minute, still holding his face in her hands. He stared into her eyes and then Trey interrupted, "You gonna wait for the local Poliția, or would you like to come with us?"

They quickly averted one another's gaze, then Gaelan sarcastically spoke up over her shoulder, "Don't worry Trey, I'm fine. No, seriously, I'll be okay."

Trey turned back to the getaway car, yelling over his shoulder, "If you want sympathy, you can find it between *shit* and *syphilis* in the dictionary." Then he laughed at his own joke.

Natalia pulled off Gaelan's shirt and wrapped it around his ribs, then helped him to his feet, "Come." They stood to find that Kedar and Angel had already changed into normal clothing and Trey was dousing the getaway car with gasoline. Gaelan finished taking off his clothing and Natalia quickly stripped from her black suit. He stole a glimpse of her body, only in a bra and panties, as she recovered her clothing. He wasn't quick enough to look away before she caught him, "Excuse me?" She wasn't able to fight back the slight smile, "My eyes are up here."

Gaelan winced as he chuckled, "*Ow*, don't make me laugh!" They dressed and got in the vehicle. Just before they drove off, Trey threw a match into the stolen getaway car and they all watched it burst into flames.

They rode in silence for several minutes, all their thoughts wandering, until Trey finally broke the silence, "Is someone going to tell me who the fuck this guys is?" Angel and Natalia also looked curiously at Medhir.

"My name is Medhir—Medhir Ramachandran." His English was impeccable.

Kedar started, "We found him on the second floor, bound to a table surrounded by a witch, vampires and werewolves."

"Werewolves?" Trey was dubious.

"Yup. We killed both of them." Gaelan smiled.

"Gaelan killed both of them." Kedar nodded to Gaelan.

"That brings my total to seven Trey. I'm gainin' on ya!"

"Whatever." Trey was dismissive, "I call performance enhancers. Definitely an asterisks next to your name in the books!"

Natalia tried to tune out the juvenile conversation, "Is there a reason they had so many around you Medhir?"

"Yes, I think you should know..."

Gaelan interrupted Medhir, "That you're a prophet?"

Everyone in the car went wide-eyed, switching glances back and forth between Gaelan and Medhir. Trey was trying to do so through the rearview mirror.

"You said you didn't know who I was. How did you...?" Medhir was unnerved.

"The vampires were screaming in the stairwell, *stop shooting because they may hit the prophet*. It took me back a little too."

"You're a no shit, honest to God *prophet*?" Angel was amazed.

"I think so. That is what they told me based on my occasional visions, but more on the words that I would write. And my friends, I have much to tell you." Medhir sounded relieved.

"Well," Gaelan sounded apprehensive, "in the interest of full disclosure Medhir, I think I have to tell you something first." Everyone in the car turned their eyes to Gaelan, who held out his hand to Medhir to shake it, "I guess I should introduce myself. Apparently, I'm the *sheep in wolf's clothing*."

Medhir's jaw dropped and he seemed to get light-headed, until his eyes finally rolled back and he fainted in the back of the car. Gaelan looked around, "Was it something I said?"

CHAPTER 14
PROPHET

"How? Tell me again how this happened. Tell me what I am supposed to tell the Elders." Gaius stood there in his own nuanced shock, looking at what was left of the Sunset Investment Bank. It was dark now and an armored vampire stood there with his helmet off, his armor heavily damaged from one of the explosions.

"They took us by surprise. Two teams. One from the roof and one from the ground. They had heavy caliber weapons and explosives." The vampire looked at him with scorn, as if he didn't have the right to question him.

"And heavily armored and armed vampires, with a superior numerical advantage I might add, were not enough to beat, what we can assume with some certainty, was a team of Venántium *bank robbers!*" Gaius's voice became increasingly louder, "They hacked our system, downloaded more information than we can accurately ascertain, corrupted our data, and TOOK THE PROPHET FROM US!"

"They made it past the wolves and enchantress as well." The vampire was insolently defensive.

"Well then, I guess that excuses everything. I can just tell the Elders that *they* were the ones that failed and blame it on *them*, can't I?" Gaius turned to stare at the vampire, who in turn averted his gaze.

"Sir," A high-ranking local police officer came over and recognized that there was an awkward conversation ongoing, "I'm sorry to interrupt." He was a collaborator and had been serving the vampires for years.

"It's alright. There wasn't much more to talk about at the moment." Gaius turned his attention to the officer, "What is it?"

"A survivor."

"I thought you were instructed to take the survivors for interrogation." Gaius seemed troubled that no one was able to carry out their assigned task.

"No Sir, not a—*human*—survivor. She is hurt, but alive." The officer gulped.

"Genevieve is alive?" Gaius spun and had the officer lead him.

They entered the structure behind the tape that cordoned it off. The bottom floor was a shell of what it once was. The bodies had been removed, but blood still stained the walls and rubble. They walked up the stairs, now damaged and full of debris. The officer led Gaius and the armored vampire to Medhir's cell. There they found the witch, known as Genevieve, barely alive. She had been shot multiple times and was weak.

"Is everyone here ours?" Gaius looked to the officer.

"Everyone but the two paramedics." The officer motioned over to the two paramedics waiting on the side. They were being held back by several freshly armored vampires now on security detail. There were two other people looking on, a man and a woman, both dressed in well-weathered clothing, mostly leather.

"Alright, make up a story about falling debris and secondary explosions and feed those two to her, then take her out in secret. Bring her to the safe house and begin finding homeless and prostitutes to feed to her until she has her strength back." He looked around at the mess and sighed, then looked back to the armored vampire, "I don't know how you could let this happen."

Before the vampire could defend himself once more, the woman dressed in leather walked up and asked Gaius sneeringly, "How are we supposed to explain this to Lucos?"

"Your people failed as much as the masters!" Gaius was now defensive himself.

"Our people were supposed to escort the witch. They stayed as a courtesy to your inept and incompetent *masters,*" She was now angry and provocative, "and now they're dead."

"Watch how you speak, *beast*!" The armored vampire hissed.

Gaius held up his hand to stop the vampire, then turned back to the wolves, "Go back to Lucos and tell…"

"No!" The man with the woman interjected, "We'll stay and see what the witch has to say. I'm sure Lucos will wonder just how this happened. He'll also wonder how your masters deal with failure."

Gaius exhaled in anxiety. He looked at the witch, then raised two fingers to the new party of armored vampires and nodded. They descended on the paramedics instantly. Their screams and shrieks were short-lived as they were torn apart for their organs and fed to the injured witch. Gaius turned back to the two wolves, "You can tell Lucos that I will be in touch with him soon. Tell him that we apologize for your losses and that we allowed *you* the pleasure of dealing with our failure." Without moving his head, Gaius shifted his eyes to the armored vampire without the helmet, "That is, if you wish?"

The woman smiled, "Oh, we certainly wish."

It took a moment for the vampire to realize what it meant, then he bellowed, "NO!" He exposed his fangs as his face contorted. He took a stance to defend himself, but it mattered little. The two wolves didn't even fully change. Their eyes were inhuman and their fangs and claws were bared. They set upon him and tore him limb from limb, letting him suffer some before finally ending his misery.

Father Denny showed up at his Villa the day after the team had arrived. He met Medhir and they all sat and listened to what he had to say.

"At some point in the Dark Ages, many became aware of the existence of the *others*." Medhir spoke fluent English with only a modest Indian accent.

"You can call them *monsters* Medhir, because that's what they are." Trey sounded like an encouraging sponsor at a rehabilitation center.

"Let him finish!" Denny was more impatient as he had not heard most of what Medhir had already explained to the others.

"As you well know, based on the text of the Hunters, there was an arms race, more or less, amongst ambitious low level creatures and rich land lords of the time. What you don't know is that there have been prophets for every generation since the Prophet Muhammad, and no, Nostradamus was just a parlor trickster." Medhir smiled at his own joke and realized no else did. He continued, "The creatures knew before then that prophets appeared from all parts of the world in succession and knew how to find them. I will come back to that point at the end. They found the prophets across Europe, in China, in India…you get the point. Many had foreseen the conflicts across Europe, the Crusades, the Black Death and then sometime in the early thirteen hundreds, just before the proliferation of the monsters, a new prophecy began. It was revealed piece-by-piece, and foretold of a coming darkness. In fact, it warned of the apocalypse itself. Not the end of the world per say, but the enslavement of mankind as servants or cattle, for the armies of Hell. Not just vampires and their like, but demons—the actual falleN angeLs of Heaven. A five-thousand-year darkness that would allow the night dwellers to walk without fear of the light and turn the hearts of men and women to serve the darkness. Knowing nothing but despair for all of their existence, they will convert, one-by-one, then by the thousands, then by the millions and billions, and they will profess their allegiance to lucifeR himself. Having then stripped the Earth of all faith and harvested a five-thousand-year army of countless despondent souls, the lords of Hell would storm Heaven itself, bringing a second war of the angels and the end of all creation. And it all starts with the opening of the gate to Hell."

"So start checking off your bucket list now!" Angel tried to break the gravity of what had been told to them.

"Where?" Denny asked Medhir with imperative, "Where's the gate located?"

"Oh that's original. As if we didn't already ask that." Trey rolled his eyes at Denny.

"Has he been this much of asshole all along, kiddo?" Father Denny looked to Gaelan.

Gaelan shrugged his shoulders, "Actually, believe it or not, he's warming up." Everyone looked at him in shock, even Trey, "What? I'm just sayin'. He's gotten us this far and even though he's a sarcastic dildo, he's done good."

Trey raised an eyebrow, "Thanks...I think."

"Don't mention it!" Gaelan smiled, "But in all seriousness, let Medhir finish."

"Alright." Father Denny shook his head, "I liked it better when you were a just snot-nosed twerp!"

Gaelan winked, "I love you too!"

Medhir continued, "As I was saying, that Gate to Hell must be opened. I will recite what has been passed down and what has come to me, but to get to the point, in the early thirteen hundreds, part of the prophecy foretold of the warning. The warning to *beware the sheep in wolf's clothing*. The vampires and witches took it to mean that a werewolf would betray them all and prevent the gate of Hell from opening.

Everyone turned to Gaelan, "What? No one knows for sure that it's me."

"You have no idea what your existence means." Medhir's voice seemed strangely ominous, "When that prophecy was told, the creatures had already begun culling those that had been made by the land lords and the ambitious young vampires. But when word of the prophecy spread, the vampires and witches turned on the werewolves in an all out war. All that time, when the Hunters were fighting the remnants of the creatures created without permission, another war raged without their knowledge." Medhir shook his head, "The werewolves finally conceded, subjugating themselves to the rule of the others, albeit a very loose rule. The one rule strictly enforced was that no human could be made a werewolf. The—*monsters*—battled amongst themselves and waited centuries to raise the eternal darkness. But when word spreads that you are finally here, all will rally to find you, destroy you and destroy all who stand by you."

Gaelan let those words sink in. He looked around at the people he loved: Father Denny, Trey, Angel, Kedar and then he stared at Natalia. Before he could say anything, Angel spoke up, "Tell them to fucking bring it!"

"Goddamn right brother!" Trey bumped his fist against Angel's.

Kedar stood and grabbed the back of Gaelan's head and pressed his own forehead against Gaelan's, "We stand with you now, and until the end of days, my brother."

Gaelan felt the squeezing in his hand, and looked to see Natalia now gripping his hand firmly with a faint smile. Gaelan smiled back, then looked around and nodded slightly, "Yeah." His voice was hesitant, "To the end of days."

Father Denny interjected, "Alright, you can all go to the end of days together, but let's try and stop it beforehand, shall we?" He looked around for just a moment and then turned to Medhir, "Medhir, how do we find where this gate to Hell is?"

"*We* don't. Not yet anyway. The final seer will let us know how to find it. It is written that," Medhir began to recite the prophecy, "*If the servants of darkness obtain the keys to the Dark Gate, a five thousand year darkness will be loosed upon the world. The falleN will rise from the pit and the night dwellers will walk without fear of light. The time of man will be stripped of faith and hope and subjugated through despair into damnation and the service of the army of darkness. At the end of the second millennia of the Son of God, the celestial bodies will align. The time of the final seer will come. The pathway to the Gate will be paved and the keys will be revealed. If, in the dark times, the righteous of man stands and fights, the guardians of light may silence the Gate of Hell. Beware the sheep in wolf's clothing.*"

Once more, everyone turned to Gaelan. "Seriously, you all have to stop that shit. Stop lookin' at me like that." He shook his head. They all looked away, knowing how uncomfortable this was making him. This time Gaelan took Natalia's hand and gave it a gentle squeeze and whispered, "*You* can look at me like that." She tried to fight back a giggle, turning her head and pulling her hand away timidly.

Gaelan was trying to hide his anxiety behind humor. A few years before, he was a young high school graduate with a promising future. Now he was a creature who finally overcame the urge to kill himself, only to learn that he may be the only thing that can save humanity and all of existence from the apocalypse. He was twitching nervously, his knee jittering and his fingers rhythmically pulsating. Natalia saw it and took his hand again. He looked over to her, this time with the same look of fear and apprehension she had seen on his face in Germany. She squeezed his hand once more. Trey and Angel noticed their exchange. Father Denny and Kedar were busy talking with Medhir.

"So we're talking about the actual apocalypse, and Gaelan may indeed be this *sheep* that you're talking about." Father Denny's brain was racing.

"I believe so. Yes." Medhir started hesitantly, then ended confidently.

Kedar was trying to remember what was just said, "Medhir, the prophecy says that a final seer, what was it, will come when the stars align?"

"They told me it was planetary alignment. The vampires, well, mostly their messenger, told me that the planets are aligned now, for the next several weeks."

"So all we have to do is wait until they're not aligned and then they'll never know where the final seer is." Trey turned his attention from Gaelan and Natalia back to the conversation.

"Possibly. Maybe. I don't know." Medhir sounded defeated.

"No!" Father Denny was adamant, "Medhir, you said yourself that they found the first prophets without any help." Medhir nodded to him as Father Denny continued, "And even if we keep this one a secret, they will eventually find one in this millennia, when we *don't* have this information. When we're not around. About the only thing that *will* be here is the shee..." Father Denny stopped himself before he finished, "Is Gaelan."

"I won't." Gaelan said.

"No need to beat around the bush *junior*, you know you're immortal." Trey came back.

"I'm not!" Gaelan was adamant.

"Kiddo, from everything you've told me, from everything we've learned, we know that these *things*," Father Denny was confused, "these *monsters*, are immortal."

"Yeah, but *I'm* not." He was still holding Natalia's hand and now squeezing it for support. She looked at him just as curiously.

"Brother, we all heard the vampire we interrogated." Angel was now confused, "The vampire *you* grabbed."

"Yeah, we did. Did you all miss it?" Gaelan looked at them as if the answer was obvious.

Natalia continued holding his hand and finally spoke, "Gaelan, he said he was over thirteen hundred years old."

"Yeah, he said that. But he also said why, plain as day." Gaelan looked around in disbelief, *"Life begets life!"* He scanned the room again, "Don't you get it?"

"Obviously we don't!" Trey was confused.

"I don't *kill* people, therefore I don't live forever. I don't take life, therefore I don't beget life. I'm not immortal."

"But, you're...you know..." Angel didn't want to say the word *werewolf.*

"Yeah, I know, but that's why I eat their hearts. I somehow fought the urge for immortality and decided to hunt them instead." He shook his head, "But like it or not, if some monster doesn't kill me before that, I'm gonna die shitting my pants and gumming my food—just like Trey."

Trey actually chuckled, "Fuck you dicklicker."

"You'll live a normal life?" Natalia's mouth was slightly open in disbelief.

"I wouldn't exactly call it normal, but I know I'm not immortal." He stared into her eyes.

"Ahem!" Father Denny coughed aloud to break up the moment, "So that makes this even more pressing."

"How so?" Angel asked.

"Because right now, we're holding all the cards. If we wait, we're all gone. Gaelan's gone. And then several years or decades or centuries down the line, the planets align again and they find the *final seer* and unleash the apocalypse." Father Denny shook his head slowly, "Or they wind up finding this final prophet without Medhir. Either way, humanity ends—the *world* ends."

"Okay, so all we have to do is figure out how to get Medhir to show us the way to the final prophet, right?" Angel thought it was obvious.

"There is *one* problem." Medhir was hesitant.

"What is it?" Kedar was matter of fact.

"I can not." Medhir said apologetically.

"Why not Medhir?" Father Denny was straight to the point.

"The witch." Medhir said reluctantly.

"What about her?" Trey asked.

"I don't know how," He shrugged, "but the messenger, Gaius—he said that a witch somehow bonds with the seer to show the way to the next seer." Medhir was contrite in his tone, knowing that he was unable to help them.

Trey sarcastically responded, "Oh, so I guess we'll just place an add in the newspaper, *witch wanted, must like long walks on the beach and bonding with prophets.*"

Natalia and Gaelan were staring at each other once again, but this time in disbelief. Gaelan exclaimed, "No way!"

"Yes!" She said with a half smile.

"Holy shit!" He smiled widely back at her.

"Hey!" Trey spoke up, looking at the two of them, then at their hands. Natalia withdrew her hand instinctively. Gaelan took no offense. Trey continued, "You two gonna help save the world, or should the rest of us leave?"

"Well, Captain douche-tastic, it just so happens…" Gaelan stopped talking and looked at Natalia.

Natalia looked at Trey in disbelief, "We just may have the answer to your problem."

"My lords, the seer was taken." Gaius humbly stood in front of the elders. There were ten in all, seven male and three female, dressed in elegantly hand woven suits—all black. They sat in hand carved, throne-like chairs that had been crafted more than a thousand years before. The room had a vaulted ceiling with a candlelit chandelier made of human bones and skulls. The result was a dimly lit chamber with ghostly shadows cast randomly about. To most that were taken there, it usually meant several final minutes of sheer terror. Gaius had been in the chamber too many times for it to affect him. To him, it now seemed a little melodramatic and theatrical. Still, he needed to tread lightly. One of the elders spoke indignantly, "Without the seer, we cannot complete the prophecy."

Gaius closed his eyes and dropped his head while another elder raised his voice, "Tell us, what would you have us do?"

Gaius thought for a moment and spoke cautiously, "All is not lost my lords. We still have our contact in the Vatican. He may be able to give us what we need."

"And yet he hasn't been able to let us know where these hunters are targeting." Another elder scolded.

"There is one other thing my lords." Gaius looked up.

"What is that?" One female elder curiously asked.

Gaius sounded more confident, "The enchantress, Genevieve, survived. She may be able to tell us what we need."

"Why do you believe that?" A dubious Elder questioned.

"She has been mumbling my lords." Gaius smiled, "But the words are not her own."

—§—

"Anything else you want to tell us about Germany?" Trey looked at Natalia half condescendingly, half astonished. She looked back at

Trey with disdain. She had done that only once before, when she and Trey fought over Gaelan. He immediately recoiled, "I'm sorry. You just know…"

"Know what? That everyone of us hates these things! Some more than others? YES! ALRIGHT! I KNOW!" She was uncharacteristically emotional, turning away with her eyes glassed over.

Trey sighed, "I'm sorry. Seriously Natalia, I'm sorry." She held up her hand, refusing to turn around. Trey breathed deeply, "I'll go talk to him."

"No!" Gaelan retorted. Everyone turned to look at him, even Natalia.

"Whatd'ya mean *no*?" Trey was taken back.

"I mean I'm gonna go talk to him. There's no asking permission and no discussion. I got this. And don't give me that stupid-ass look –" Gaelan was referring to Trey's look of disbelief, "I'm goin' to talk to K." Gaelan turned without waiting for a comment or acquiescence. He walked by Natalia, grabbed her hand and squeezed it, then continued after Kedar. Father Denny had already taken Medhir to talk to him about everything else he learned from his time in captivity.

Trey walked over to Natalia and put a hand on her shoulder, "I'm sorry. Natalia, please—I'm really sorry." She stood still. "Besides, I don't think he really went to talk to Kedar." Natalia turned and gave Trey a curious look. He continued, "I mean, look how quickly he left and how adamant he was. I think he just had to fart." She smiled a little, then hugged him.

"Did he take the peanut butter, because if so, he's just licking his own balls again." Angel drank some more of the wine Father Denny had taken out for them and finally got Natalia to laugh, "See!" Angel smiled, "*He's* not the only one that can make you laugh." She squinted her eyes and gave him the finger behind Trey's back.

"He's right you know." Trey looked down at her, "You haven't smiled this much in all the years I've known you." She looked back up at him, her face betraying some semblance of shame and remorse. "Don't look at me like that. Be happy. We're happier when we see you smile." She began to smile up at him, then he added,

"Plus, it keeps me from wanting to drown the little shit." He smiled and she laughed, burying her head in his chest.

Outside, Gaelan found Kedar among the grapevines, still seething. He was pacing back and forth and occasionally swinging at the air.

"K! HEY K!" Gaelan called out as if nothing was wrong.

"Leave me to my own devices right now! *Please*." Kedar didn't want to talk to anyone.

"Fuck that!" Gaelan no sooner said it and Kedar spun with a fiery look in his eyes. He could see Gaelan was holding his katana, "C'mon! I got just what you need." Kedar reluctantly followed him, bustling with anger and feelings of betrayal.

Minutes later, Gaelan was showing him the basics of how to use the sword. Kedar was making two-handed overhead strikes at the wood and straw dummy Gaelan and Father Denny had set up. Then he was taking one-handed upward slices and hacking away in therapeutic violence. He began to go at the dummy in a maddened frenzy.

"Tell me K." Gaelan said nonchalantly.

"Tell you what?" Kedar was breathing heavily, still slicing at the dummy.

"You hate witches as much as Trey and I hate werewolves. So tell me what happened." Gaelan waited patiently while Kedar stopped slashing and stared at the dummy.

Kedar turned, then sat down and leaned against the dummy. He held the katana in his lap and slowly calmed his breathing, "My mother died at an early age. I remember bits and pieces of her, but I was young. My brother was even younger. He could not even remember our mother." Kedar was staring off at the vineyard, "My father sent us abroad to study. He loved us in his own way, but he didn't truly know how to raise us on his own. By now you know I am Saudi, but we studied in England. I did well, but we were always outsiders. We were looked down upon as *bloody wogs*. Eventually I heard the calling to wage war on the West as a terrorist." Kedar looked over to Gaelan, "I'm sorry."

"No apologies K. What happened in the past is just that—the *past*. I mean it. It all seems pretty stupid now, huh?"

"Yes. Yes it does." Kedar looked back to the vineyard, "My brother followed me, though I always tried to get him to leave. I didn't want him with me, but he refused to leave my side. I became quite good at creating and handling explosives, and made a name for myself as a bomb maker. I was good with electronics and was able to make remote detonators that could be powered by cellular phones. I was really quite adept at it, and my brother learned from me. We were prepared to become martyrs for our cause." Kedar's breathing became shallow, "We were supposed to meet our contact outside a village near where American troops were patrolling. My brother came with two others and me. That's when she appeared." Kedar gripped the katana tightly, as if preparing to strike, "Even with her burka, we could tell that she was beautiful and so very alluring." He turned and looked at Gaelan, "Once inside, she removed her head scarf to reveal just how beautiful she was. We were all captivated. Here was one of the most stunning creatures we had ever seen and she was there to help us—to help our cause." He turned back to the vineyard, "She warned us that Americans were in the area, but she was taking us to another safe house until they were gone. So we went with her. She brought us into a small shack on the outskirts of the village. We hadn't seen anyone else." He looked at Gaelan again, his eyes were sad, "It should've made us uneasy, but she was so welcoming. We were so *stupid*." He paused and Gaelan said nothing. He knew where the story was leading.

"She offered us tea and we accepted. We talked about how we would fight the Americans to the death, trying to impress her. After all, she was but a woman," His tone was sarcastic, "and we were freedom fighters." Kedar slowly shook his head, "She had put something in the tea. I don't know why she didn't attack us outright. Maybe she thought we might be hunters, maybe she liked having us wake up as we did." He took a deep breath, "When we did awaken, we were all suspended in the air, seemingly cocooned in dried roots and soil. The roots also gagged us. She giggled, telling us how delicious we looked. She told us that we would give our lives for a cause, just not the one we thought." He leaned his head back and closed his eyes, a small tear rolled from the corner that Gaelan could see.

"The blade she used was sickle shaped. She cut right into the first man's chest. He tried to scream through the roots in his mouth until his eyes rolled back as she sank her hand into his chest cavity. She pulled out his heart and her face contorted into something hideous and unnatural." Gaelan thought about the faces of the witches in Germany while Kedar continued, "She ate his heart in front of us. She rubbed the blood on her face in what I could only imagine was some type of sexual ecstasy. She took out the rest of his organs and began devouring them, leaving his empty body still suspended. The ground seemed to envelope her as daylight approached and she was cradled in an earthen shell to protect her. The next night, the same fate befell the next man we were with. I could see the fear in my brother's eyes as she awoke on the third night." Kedar looked over to Gaelan with his eyes glassed over.

"I made as much noise as I could, trying to get her to take me. When she took the blade to him, he locked eyes with me. He was trying to be brave, but I could see the tears. When she tore..." Kedar became choked up, "When she tore into him, I bit through the roots in my mouth, screaming as loud as I could. I screamed and wailed for my brother, and she didn't put a gag back in. It was as if she took pleasure in my lament. I told her I would kill her, but I never got the chance. By the hand of Allah, there were hunters in the village. Venators heard my screams and made their way to the room. They surprised her with their entrance. She put up a sand wall to protect herself, but didn't see the venator that dove to the side, shooting her. She lost her concentration and the wall fell. They put several dozen bullets into her before decapitating her and stabbing her heart. I finally fell to the ground and crawled over to my brother's body. I held him and cried." Another tear rolled down his cheek, "They didn't try to stop me. Finally, one of them told me it was time to go. I realized then that the wars of men paled in comparison to the war on these creatures." He spoke through gritted teeth, "I vowed to kill every witch on the face of the earth. Now I find out that Natalia let one live."

Gaelan finally spoke, "I let her live too K."

"You didn't know the history!" Kedar snapped.

"Yeah, but she knew Trey's history with werewolves and I'm here." He raised his eyebrows.

"That's…" Kedar stopped himself from saying that it was different.

Gaelan knew Kedar was thinking straight now, "Has there ever been a time that she wasn't there for you?"

"No. Even when I was still so naïve to believe that she was inferior because she was a woman, she was there for me," His voice trailed off, "and saved my life many times despite the fact."

Gaelan snapped back, "Wait! Nat's a *woman*? Jesus, when did this happen?" Kedar smiled. Gaelan continued in a more serious demeanor, "You know that her judgment is right almost all of the time."

"Almost?" Kedar was finally accepting the fact that if Natalia let a witch live, she had good reason.

Gaelan retorted nonchalantly, "Well, she did shoot me in the gut."

"Like I said, *almost*?" Kedar gave him a half-smile.

"That's dicked up K. It hurts me here," Gaelan pointed to his heart, "but even more so, right here." Then he pointed to his gut.

Kedar burst out laughing and after several seconds, his laughter subsided and he asked Gaelan, "How do I make it right?"

"Two simple words."

Everyone was silent when Gaelan came back with Kedar. Kedar walked past them all and embraced Natalia, "I'm sorry." She hugged him tightly, sniffling a little on his shoulder. "I trust you with my very life and everything in between." She said nothing in response, but just gripped him tighter. When they released each other, she looked over to Gaelan with soft eyes of gratitude and he smiled back fondly. Trey walked up to Gaelan and gave him a half nod of approval. Gaelan silently returned the nod.

"Sooooooo, anyone want to tell us how we're going to find this witch of yours?" Angel drank more wine.

"No need." Father Denny came back into the room with Medhir, "She lives about six hours from here, just outside of Paris."

Gaelan looked at his watch, "If we leave now, we can be back before midnight."

Everyone began to move and Father Denny asked, "Are you *all* going?"

Before anyone else could answer, Kedar had grabbed a crossbow and a dagger and exclaimed, "Better safe than sorry." He turned and walked out. Trey shrugged his shoulders and followed him. Angel, Natalia and Gaelan walked out behind them, the latter of whom was shaking his head in disbelief.

Sophie Bertrand had just opened a bottle of wine. She was raised Muslim, but she began drinking at an early age, as well as partaking in other aspects of life that her religion had forbidden. She had just finished watering all of the plants in her small apartment. She loved the plants, and how they took up most of the space. It was a long day of work at the café, followed by volunteering at the women's shelter. After returning from Germany, the only work she could find was waitressing and making coffee at a small café. Every evening she stopped by various community outreach centers to volunteer her time. She had become a regular at seven different places. The guilt of the death of Ilka Müller weighed heavily on her. Maybe, she thought, just maybe a life of service to others would atone for one night of inaction. She took a rather large amount of the wine in her mouth and held it there with her eyes closed, swallowing it slowly, little by little.

But then there were the walks around the city. The walks where she went looking—*hunting*. She couldn't help herself anymore, and she craved the taste of it. She found herself craving it more and more. Her mind was drifting, thinking about the last kill when she heard the knock at the door.

Sophie looked through the peephole and saw a man she didn't recognize, "Yes?"

Everyone on the team spoke fluent French, "Miss Bertrand, Miss Sophie Bertrand?" She was silent and Angel could tell she was uneasy, "Miss Bertrand, I have need to speak with you on an urgent matter. I was wondering if I might come in?" There was still no answer, "Please Miss Bertrand, this is rather important. I need to know something about your time in Germany."

With that, the door unlocked and she called for Angel to come in. He opened the door and walked in, signaling for the others to wait. He was no sooner inside when the door slammed shut and locked by itself. The plants around him burst into flailing limbs and roots, wrapping themselves around him. Some limbs came to a point and held themselves aimed at him, "You shouldn't have come!" Sophie came out of the shadows, her eyes completely black.

Before she could say or do anything else, the lock on the door shattered as it was kicked in. Gaelan walked in and all of the plants went limp. Angel dropped to a knee and Sophie fell down hyperventilating. She shuffled backwards on her rear end into the corner. She was muttering, "Please! *Please!* I didn't mean to do it! I couldn't control myself!"

Natalia rushed past Gaelan and Angel, and went to Sophie's side. Kedar came in, drew a crossbow out of a gym bag and drew down on Sophie. Trey walked up next to Gaelan and asked in English, "You have this effect on everyone?"

Gaelan smirked, "Fuck you." He walked forward.

Natalia was already speaking to her, "What didn't you mean to do? Sophie, look at me! What didn't you mean to do?" Natalia had thought about telling Kedar to drop his weapon, but now she wasn't so sure.

Sophie didn't look at Natalia. Instead, she stared at Gaelan in fear, "He said he'd be back if I did it, but I couldn't help myself. I killed them. I killed them and fed."

Gaelan walked up and squatted down. Something was different about her. She didn't smell right—but she didn't smell wrong either. She wasn't attacking them or trying to defend herself.

"Sophie, calm down." She recoiled when he came closer. He took her hand. She tried to avoid his touch, but he was able to grasp it, "Sophie, what did you do?"

Her eyes were streaming tears and her voice was shaky, "I went for a walk and it was as if I was drawn to them. I saw them in the park after dark. They had a young couple. The first one opened its mouth and tried to bite the girl's neck. I didn't know what else to do and I swore," Her voice had more resolve, more anger in it. She stared at Gaelan intently, "*I swore* I would never stand idly by again. I made the trees spear him, and then the others. I remembered from that night, the hearts were the weak point. I speared all four of them through the heart. I told the couple to run and went over. I don't know what came over me or why, but," She looked at Gaelan with sheer terror and disgust, "but I..." she avoided saying it.

"You ate their hearts, didn't you?" Gaelan said softly. She reluctantly nodded. He asked, "Those weren't the only ones, were they?" She shook her head and shut her eyes, as if waiting for the blow to strike her.

Sophie opened her eyes and saw Gaelan still looking at her, now smiling softly. She looked over to Natalia and saw her smiling as well, "There were three other times. All similar, but different than those things I killed in the park. Each one of them was somewhere secluded and called out for help. Each time I knew something was not right. I was drawn to them and knew that they were the ones being lured. When they exposed their true nature, I skewered them and ate their hearts." She bit her lips having said it aloud herself this time.

"Holy shit, I want to give this girl a medal." Angel smiled and walked over to her kitchen and fumbled around the cabinets. Kedar lowered his crossbow and walked off to the side of the room.

"What does he mean?" Sophie was confused. She was confused by Angel's comments. She was confused as to why Gaelan and Natalia had come back. Most of all, she was baffled as to why they hadn't killed her yet.

"Sophie, I told you that you had a choice." Gaelan could see her face turn to fright again, "But I think I was wrong. I guess once you were exposed, your true nature came out. You feel yourself getting stronger, don't you? You're getting stronger and you crave it—you crave their hearts, don't you." Sophie gave a self-loathing nod. "It's okay Sophie, it's *okay*."

Angel came back after filling a glass of wine for himself and handed her the glass she had poured for herself, "Sophie, I think what Gaelan here is trying to say is that you are truly amazing and we'd like to offer you a job."

She held the glass, again looking around in confusion, "What do you mean?" She looked over to Natalia, "What does he mean?"

Natalia put her hand over Sophie's and Gaelan's grip, "He means, how would you like to have a job where you get to travel the world, help lots of people, kill lots of those things and eat a lot more of their hearts?"

Sophie was now utterly dumbfounded, "It's okay for me to eat their hearts?"

Gaelan smiled, "Only if I get a few of them as well. The other side of me gets cranky when it doesn't eat."

Trey finally spoke up, "That's truly disgusting! Seriously, I just threw up a little in my mouth." He looked over to Sophie, "Pack your bags honey. Before we go serving up any vampire hearta-touille..." Trey looked around, "Get it?" He continued to wait for a response, "Like ratatouille, but with the heart, cause we're in France!"

"Wow, that joke *totally* sucked!" Gaelan looked at him with a raised eyebrow.

"Trey, never again! Seriously, never do that again." Angel seemed utterly disgusted with how bad the joke was.

"You all suck!" Trey retorted, then looked at Sophie, "Anyway, before we go hunting for..."

"Shift kebabs!" Gaelan blurted out.

Angel laughed out loud, "Nice! Now *that's* a good one!" Natalia giggled and Trey heard Kedar off to the side trying to stifle a laugh.

"YOU ALL SUCK!" Trey bellowed, "Sophie, just pack up! We need your help!" Trey flipped his finger to everyone on the team and walked out of the apartment.

"Help with what?" Gaelan and Natalia were helping a bewildered Sophie to her feet.

Kedar had packed his crossbow into the gym bag and hoisted it onto his shoulder, looking back at the young French-Algerian woman, "With trying to stop the apocalypse." He turned and followed Trey, smiling slightly at the dumbfounded look on Sophie's face.

Sophie was wide-eyed, "Is he serious?"

CHAPTER 15
DOWN TIME

"I don't know!" Sophie's English was decent, though heavy with a French accent. She was able to talk to Medhir that way. He was lying on his back and she stood at his head, fingers on his temples.

"How can you not know? You're a witch!" Trey snapped back.

Trey's words hurt her, "And you are..." She waved her hands in anger and frustration, asking in French, "*comment dit-on 'ahs-hole!*'" Sophie's squinted eyes began to well up with tears.

Gaelan chimed in, "Oh, you say *ass*-hole, like this:" He turned to Trey, trying to break the tension, "Trey, you're an *asshole.*"

Trey shot Gaelan an angry look. Before he could speak, Natalia walked over to Sophie and put an arm around her, leading her out. "We're done for now." She spoke over her shoulder and didn't give anyone else a glance.

Trey shot a scowl at Gaelan, "What the fuck?"

"Trey, I was making a joke. A *fucking joke!*" Gaelan was defensive. Angel moved to get in between them as Medhir sat up to observe the commotion.

Before it escalated any further, Father Denny broke his silence, "Gaelan."

He snapped his head over, "Yeah?"

"Your joke sucked." Father Denny's face was kind in his insult.

"Yeah?" Gaelan turned and walked out to follow Natalia and Sophie, muttering, "Well your face sucks."

"What was that? I couldn't hear you." Father Denny taunted him.

"Cause you're old!" Gaelan walked out.

Father Denny looked over to Trey, "Trey, lighten—the fuck—up!"

"It's like he's just trying to get under my skin." Trey was annoyed, "And by the way, you hear confessions with a potty-mouth like that? *Go say ten fuckin' Hail Mary's.*" Father Denny gave Trey the finger and they both looked over when they heard Medhir and Angel laughing. Trey added, "See, Medhir knows a good joke when he hears one."

Medhir was still giggling, "Yes, that was very good, but I'm not one to judge. I was giggling about the asshole comment as well." Medhir started to laugh, "I haven't felt this free and good in many, many years, so I am just happy right now."

Trey looked like he had been betrayed and glanced at Angel, who was laughing now, "What? I'm laughing cause Meddi's laughing!" Angel winced, "Buuuuut, the asshole thing made me giggle."

"You fucking suck!" Trey looked back to Father Denny, then cracked part of a smile, "Was I really being an asshole?"

"Ya know, there's an old saying we have at the Vatican—*does the Pope shit in the woods?*"

Angel and Medhir were cracking up and Trey looked hurt, "Seriously, it was that bad?"

"Trey, let me ask you something." Father Denny spoke softly, like he was teaching high school again, "When you look at Gaelan, what do you see?"

"A cocky, arrogant little pissant."

"And what do you see when he shows his *other side?*"

Trey didn't hesitate, "I see that same arrogant prick with bad hygiene in need of a shave!" Laughter came from the side again.

"So you don't see," Father Denny smiled, "how did you put it? *A goddamned werewolf?*"

"No. Not anymore. He's just Gaelan," Trey spoke with a French accent, "*ahs-hole extraordinaire.*" More laughter erupted from Angel and Medhir.

Father Denny chuckled and then asked, "And what do you see when you look at Sophie?"

And then Trey's smile evaporated, "I said *witch*, but that's not…"

"I know what you meant, but to her," Father Denny sucked air through his teeth, "you probably would've been better off insulting her race, religion and mother all at the same time."

Trey leaned his head back and rubbed his forehead, "I gotta go apologize, don't I?" He snapped his head forward, "But I'm not apologizing to dipshit."

Father Denny chuckled, "You're starting to like him, aren't you?"

"Like a bleeding ulcer. But he does have his moments of usefulness." Trey noticed the shit-eating grin on Father Denny, "And don't give me that look. *Yes,* you were right, so don't fucking gloat! Oh, and I'm still not apologizing to him."

"Fuck'im!" Father Denny smiled, "He called me *old.*" They all laughed, but Trey took note of Father Denny's enjoyment, and how short lived it was.

"NAT, SOPHIE, WAIT UP!" Gaelan called out and trotted along the row of grape vines to catch up to them, "I'M COMING TOO!" When he caught up, he could see the tears still running down Sophie's cheek. He tried to give her a warm smile and spoke in French, "Don't let him get to you."

Sophie sniffed and tried to smile, "Thank you for standing up for me."

"Me? I didn't stand up for you. We've seen you in action," Gaelan pointed between himself and Natalia, "and you don't need anyone to do that for you." Sophie smiled, genuinely this time. Gaelan added, "I just said that because I like to make fun of Trey. It's a hobby of mine." Now Sophie was giggling. "There's the happy Sophie we know."

Sophie's giggling subsided, "How do you know?"

"How do I know what?" Gaelan was confused.

"How do you know what happy me is like?" She raised an eyebrow.

"I...I...*what*?" Gaelan wasn't sure what to say. Natalia enjoyed watching him fumble.

"The only other time we had together, you threatened to tear me apart."

"I didn't say I'd tear you apart." Gaelan was backpedaling.

Sophie tried to imitate his voice in French, *"You know what I am and what I can do. Choose wisely or I'll be back."* She cocked her head triumphantly and raised both eyebrows this time.

"I...wait, why do I sound like a bigger asshole than Trey when you imitate me in French?" Gaelan looked offended. Sophie and Natalia giggled, and Gaelan added victoriously, "Both laughing at the same time. My work here is complete." He looked at Natalia and she continued to smile and turned away.

Sophie noticed, "So how long have you two been together?"

"What?" Gaelan went wide-eyed.

"What do you mean?" Natalia looked at Sophie in disbelief.

"I mean you two. You're lovers, yes?" Sophie looked at them as if it were obvious. Natalia and Gaelan both began denying it immediately—adamantly—they were almost drowning each other out. Sophie nodded slowly, "Hmm. Alright. If you say so." Then she grinned, "But if you don't mind, I'd like to take a walk and clear my head."

Natalia answered with a soft smile, "Go on. Take as long as you'd like."

Sophie walked off and left Natalia and Gaelan standing in awkward silence.

—§—

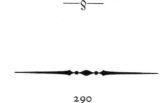

Angel had taken Medhir to town to get some fresh air and go shopping. The idea that he had spent years in captivity was almost too much for everyone to comprehend. That left Trey alone with Denny. Denny sipped on some wine and Trey was enjoying some of Denny's brandy, waiting for Sophie to come back so he could apologize. Trey could see the troubled look on Denny's face, "What is it?"

"What is *what*?" Denny looked at him quizzically.

"I've known you too long Denny, and even while we had our differences, I know when something's bothering you. You used to have that same look on hunts where things went wrong. It's that angsty-guilt thing you do!"

Denny shot him a dismissive look, "You done Dr. Freud?"

"I'm just saying, something's bothering you and I know it—I know *you*."

Denny took a deep breath, and let it out slowly. He closed his eyes and drew several more long, deep breaths, before looking back at Trey and beginning, "We're being eliminated."

"What do you mean?" Trey didn't know if he meant that the church was pulling funding.

"The Venántium, Trey. They're hunting us to extinction." Denny was somber as he shifted his gaze to the wine he now swirled in his glass.

Trey shifted in his seat, "How bad?"

"We're down to sixty percent of our hunters." Denny continued to swirl his wine.

"Sixty percent?" Trey said in disbelief, "How many..."

"We've lost over four-hundred hunters since I began coordinating efforts. And..." Father Denny's glare toward his swirling glass became intense.

"And you think there's a nasty little explanation for it." Trey leaned forward, seeing the look on Denny's face.

"I thought I was picking the wrong hunts—sending people to their deaths, and in essence, I still am." He turned to Trey with glassy eyes, "When I give the order and they don't come home, It's me that sent them to die."

"Denny, you know..."

Before Trey could finish, Father Denny spoke up, "I know Trey, I know. I had originally thought I was making mistakes, and I may still be, but with everything that's going on, I have to think..."

"That someone in the Vatican is selling us out one team at a time." Trey had a suppressed anger in his voice.

"Yes." Denny had the same intonation.

Trey took a drink of brandy while he pondered, then asked, "Why now? Why didn't they do it years, or even centuries ago?"

"I've been giving that a lot of thought too, and it makes sense with everything you've seen and what we've discovered. We're part of a big ecosystem. We've been living in a rainforest and playing our little role to keep things going. We hunted them and kept their dirty little secret while they acted like they were unorganized groups of monsters." Father Denny shook his head in self-disappointment, "And now we find out that they're a powerful, well-funded, intricately-organized entity. That they've been running the rainforest all this time. And now they're getting ready to plow the rainforest down, along with everything that makes up our little ecosystem, and build their dream house."

Trey realized the grim reality, "And we unwittingly stumbled upon their little secret and now we're a real threat." Trey sprang up in his chair, "Jesus Denny, they have to know you're the one pulling our strings!"

Denny continued to look at the wine swirling in his glass, "And that brings us back to the losses. Several weeks ago, after a string of teams disappeared, I stopped sending all the teams on real hunts and started having them go on wild goose chases. The only ones really hunting were you guys, when you were taking down slaughterhouses and then planning the bank robbery." Denny finally turned to Trey, "That worked for a few weeks, then four teams, looking for creatures that shouldn't have been there, just simply vanished. And that's the problem Trey. Someone on my staff, or on the council, is feeding the teams to the creatures—literally."

"Holy shit Denny! Now that we have Meddi, totally by coincidence, they're gonna go apeshit!" Trey was now concerned for all the teams.

"I know. Even before this, I talked to as many of the team leads as possible and told them that I was sending them on bullshit hunts. I told them to go to ground. To barricade themselves somewhere nobody knows about, not even me."

Trey then realized, "Fuck Denny, whoever's selling us out is gonna use you as the perfect scapegoat."

Father Denny nodded with an accepting smile, "I was the one who helped a werewolf escape. I was put in charge of assigning the hunts. Now I'm sitting with blood all over my hands." He finally took a sip of the wine he had been swirling, "They were playing us from the moment they learned of Gaelan's existence. And if this prophecy is true, the only thing keeping them from coming at us in a full-on war is the fact that they may still believe he's dead."

Trey knew the ramifications of their situation, "But now that we have Meddi, they'll know that he told us the prophecy and that we're gonna try and find the last prophet."

"But they don't know we have Sophie, so we may still be just a step ahead of them." Denny sounded cautiously optimistic.

Trey's eyes widened in sarcasm, "Yeah, cause it really sounds like we've been out in front all this time." Denny forced a smile. Trey downed the last of his brandy, "I'm gonna go find Sophie and apologize," He laid his glass down, "cause time definitely isn't on our side."

Sophie walked in silence along the line of grape trees, trying to clear her head. She hated being called a witch, but accepted the reality of her being. She also accepted that the people she now kept company with needed her to be a witch. The entire world needed her in fact. The thought nauseated her. She didn't want this pressure and responsibility. For a fleeting instant, she thought about sneaking off and running. She could change her name and identity. Then she realized that she was now surrounded by people who knew who and *what* she was, and they were not only comfortable with it, they were accepting. Well, mostly accepting, as she thought of Trey's comment. And that very comment brought her back to reality. *You're a witch!* Yes she was, and that was exactly what they needed. She just didn't know how to do what she was brought there to do.

She closed her eyes and began to feel the environment around her. She could feel the ground beneath her and wiggled her fingers, making the solid earth ripple in small waves. She could feel the energy of the roots beneath the soil. She connected with them and the energy pulsed through her body in pleasant currents. She raised her hands and the branches of the grape trees on either side of her responded by moving as she wished. Their branches elongated as she leaned back and opened her mouth. One branch supported her as she reclined and the other fed her a grape from one of the bunches on the branch. She smiled and motioned her hands once more. The branches brought her back upright and pulled back to their original positions. She closed her eyes again and connected with some of the animals. She could feel a squirrel running in the nearby brush. She felt the heartbeat of a rabbit sleeping somewhere near. Circling above the vineyard was a short-toed eagle. She concentrated and connected, feeling as if she were flying and seeing through its amazing eyes. It wasn't long until she spotted Kedar sitting not far from where she was standing. She broke contact with the raptor and walked toward him.

Kedar was sitting in the shade of a tree on part of the undeveloped land, lost in thought. He heard the footsteps approaching.

"You speak French, yes?" Sophie stood behind him, talking in French.

"Yes." He was curt.

"May I sit?" She was very polite.

"I do not own the land. You may sit where you like." He refused to look up at her.

She knelt down about a meter away from him and then adjusted herself, stretching her legs to the side and holding herself with her arms, "The others, they do not mind being around me, or talking to me. You...*you* don't like to be around me."

Kedar slowly turned to look at her, the slightest hint of contempt in his eyes, "I prefer to keep to myself for now."

"Your name is Kedar, right?"

"It is."

"I'm..."

"Sophie, I know." He began to rise, "Feel free to stay as long as you'd like."

"Please don't go." Sophie asked.

The sincerity in her voice gave him pause. He sat back down, "I'm not going to be the best company for you."

"That's just it. You don't really *want* anything from me. You don't even want me around, so it's nice to be around you." Sophie turned and looked out toward the valley's lush greenery in front of her.

Kedar glared at her, "There's a reason I don't want to be around you."

"I know."

"How do you know?" Kedar was indignant.

Sophie recoiled a bit, answering defensively, "Natalia told me how Trey didn't like to be around Gaelan at first. I knew what she was hinting at." Sophie quickly stood, "I'm sorry I bothered you." She turned and scurried off.

Kedar sat for only a moment before sighing and jumping up after her, "Sophie, wait." She didn't stop, "Sophie, please wait." He caught up to her and laid a hand on her arm. She spun and pulled her arm away, scowling. He jerked his hand back, *"Please."*

"WHY?"

"Because I know what you must be..."

"OH YOU KNOW? YOU KNOW WHAT I MUST BE GOING THROUGH?" Sophie was yelling now, "HOW WOULD YOU KNOW ANYTHING?"

Kedar took a deep breath, his voice now calm and steady, "How would I know about being in a strange place and feeling alone? Wondering what everyone was thinking with every cross stare cast your way? How would I know how that type of mental isolation can cause a rational person to do something foolish, like become a jihadist? So as to let one's own brother follow on such a foolish endeavor? Something that would get him killed, not by foreign fighters but by someone like..." Kedar cut himself off.

Sophie looked at him apologetically, "Someone like *me*."

Kedar waited a moment before answering, "No Sophie Bertrand, not like you." She looked at him curiously before he continued, "You're not like the *thing* that took my brother. And if you can, in any way, help us figure out if the apocalypse indeed approaches, and if you can help us stop it, then you are truly special."

"Even if I'm a witch?" Sophie half smiled.

"You're no witch."

"But..."

"You are no witch Sophie Bertrand. Ever since you met Natalia and Gaelan, and now more than ever, you are a hunter. You are one of the Venántium."

Sophie tried to look happy at this sudden acceptance, "I didn't feel much like a hunter when I met them."

"From what I'm told, Natalia owes you her life."

"Well, I'm pretty sure we all owe Gaelan our lives, even if I did think he was going to kill me at first."

"It is nothing to be ashamed of. Loss of bladder control when facing something like that is perfectly normal."

"What? I...he told you that!" Sophie was shocked.

"He...I...he was probably trying to cheer me up when I was not so...*open-minded*." Kedar felt an icy shiver go down his spine with the irate look she was giving him, "I'm in trouble, aren't I?"

"No Mr. Kedar," Her voice was no longer timid, but a mix of confident and indignant, "you are not the one in trouble. As a matter of fact, thank you for the talk. I feel much better now." She spun and walked off with a purpose in her step.

Kedar hung his head and sighed, then followed.

—§—

Gaelan and Natalia walked slowly along the grape trees. The width of the path kept them close together.

Natalia turned suddenly, "Tell me what's really going on with you?"

Gaelan looked over at her curiously, "Nothing. Seriously, I was just fuckin' with Trey to make Sophie feel better. I didn't mean..."

Natalia cut him off with a gentle voice, "That's not it. It's only part of it. You're making a lot of jokes. You're making everyone smile." She gave him a half smile, "You make me smile and I haven't done that in a very long time." They stopped and turned to face one another.

"Is there something wrong with making everyone smile?" He forced a smile himself, then crossed his eyes.

Natalia giggled but quickly composed herself, "That's just it. I know that Father Denny has known you for a long time. He watched you grow and saw you through this. None of us knows you like that." She took his hands in hers, "But I was there when that boy woke up with his world shattered. I saw what you were...what you *are*. I watched you become something more. And I also sat there in a restaurant in Germany and watched how you tried to make jokes to cover your pain and your fears. And finally those jokes stopped and you talked to me. You told me about your pain and fears and self-hate. I saw something in you then, and I see so much more now. So I guess what I'm trying to say is that I know you too, Gaelan Kelly," She squeezed his hands, "and you're making a lot of jokes. And I know that you're trying to hide something. I just want you to know that if you want to talk, I'm here. I'm *always* here." She chuckled, "And I don't want you to have to find a shifter on a Mexican beach just to have a meaningful conversation."

Gaelan forced a laugh and his eyes glassed over. He took several breaths trying to choke back some emotion, then finally began, "We haven't really had this much down time since the night I made dinner for everyone. Ever since then, we've been going and going and it didn't really leave me time to think. When this all began, I threw myself into the hunts to try to take my mind off of every-thing that happened both before and after my parents were...after

I changed. It only delayed what I felt." He looked at her earnestly, "You know better than anyone that I wanted to eat a gun, but you convinced me to fight. Not to let others die because I wanted the easy way out. And I thank you for that." He squeezed her hands back tightly, "And I thought I—*we*—were doing good, but then we really started pulling back the curtain on everything going on. Nat," He looked away and his voice was shaky, "in the last year, I have seen and done things that no one ever should." He laughed awkwardly and turned back to her, "For fuck's sake, I had a demon—a *falleN onE*—inside my body. Inside my goddamned *head*. I have seen death in my life, but that room in New York that Trey and I saw." He gritted his teeth, "I saw that and realized that our little hunts were jokes. We save individuals, and that's important." His face turned grim. He shook his head and looked away in disgust, "But hundreds, maybe thousands, are being slaughtered like cattle everyday and we're just finding out about it. And it's probably been going on for centuries. Now, when we thought we were hurting their pockets, we find out that this is all a means to an end. That this eternal darkness prophecy is basically the apocalypse. And everyone thinks that I'm this *sheep in wolf's clothing*. And I'm scared Nat!" He turned and looked back into her eyes with a despondent look, "I'm scared that I'm not this *sheep* that everyone is talking about. But I'm even more terrified," He took a deep breath, "that I *am*."

Natalia's mouth was slightly open as she realized how he felt, and that he may actually have the weight of the world on his shoulders. She didn't know what else to do, so she leaned in and hugged him tight. He squeezed her back and laid his head on top of hers. She could feel his deep breaths and the raw emotion behind each one. She relaxed her embrace on him and looked up into his eyes. She placed a hand on his cheek, "Prophecy or not, we'll all be with you. *I'll* be here with you."

They stared at one another for several seconds before Gaelan leaned in. Natalia closed her eyes and could feel the heat from his face as it approached hers. Gaelan's heart was beating rapidly as their lips began to meet.

"NAT? SOPHIE? WHERE ARE YOU GUYS?" Trey was calling out.

Gaelan tilted his head forward and leaned it against hers, "How do you say, *ahs-hole*?"

Natalia giggled and chided him, "Be nice." She turned and called, "WE'RE HERE!" She then turned back to Gaelan, "Anytime you want to—*need to* talk—I'm here. I'm always here." She squeezed his hand then walked to Trey. Gaelan followed a step behind.

"Where did Sophie go? I need to talk to her." Trey was looking around.

"You need to back off a little." Natalia reprimanded.

"I know, I just came to…"

"AHHH, FUCK!" Gaelan yelled out as something struck his leg. He no sooner turned to see what it was and another lash caught him across the ass, "OOOOW, WHAT THE FUCK?" He began spinning and seeing the thinner branches of the grape trees growing out and whipping at his legs and rear end. He grabbed one and another wrapped him along the knuckles leaving a red welt, "GODDAMMIT!" He shook his hand and looked to the end of the row of trees. There was Sophie, her eyes pitch black, and a dumbfounded Kedar passively standing next to her. "SOPHIE, *CE QUI LA BAISE?*"

Sophie walked toward him and responded indignantly in English, "You tell him? You tell him about my pee?"

Gaelan went wide-eyed and looked at Kedar, "You told her I told…OWWWW!" Another branch thwaped him across the thigh, "JESUS SOPHIE, CUT THE SHIT!"

"OR MAYBE I CUT THE PEE!" She yelled indignantly and waved her hand again, lashing his ass.

"KEDAR?" Gaelan looked for help. Sophie turned and her black eyes scowled at Kedar. She saw the look in his face and could tell that it brought back a dark memory. Her eyes immediately went normal and the branches receded.

"Je suis désolé…I am sorry." Her eyes began to well up again and she turned to walk off, but Kedar stopped her.

"Sophie?"

She turned with a tear on her cheek, "Yes?"

Kedar smiled, "You should've used larger branches."

She smiled and wiped her face. She turned to see Natalia slap Gaelan in the back of the head as they walked back toward the house. Then Trey marched up to her.

He stopped just inches from her, looking down imposingly, "I was going to say I'm sorry, but," She recoiled slightly as he leaned in and embraced her tightly, lifting her off the ground, "I think I'll just say that I totally *love* you right now." He planted a sloppy wet kiss on her teary cheek, then pretended to spit, "Ugh, salty!" Sophie began to giggle uncontrollably as Trey set her back down, "Seriously, you can do that as much as you want!" He raised an eyebrow, "As a matter of fact, you should do it quick before he's too far from the trees."

Gaelan called out "I CAN STILL HEAR EVERYTHING YOU'RE SAYI...OWWW, MOTHERFUCKBALLS!" One final branch leapt out and caught him on the ass, and he took off running past Natalia into the house.

Trey hugged her again; "You are my favorite person in the world right now! And I am truly, truly sorry for what I said in there."

She looked at Trey and smiled widely, "Please, I am the one who is sorry that I could not help."

"You can try again when you feel up to it, but for now..." Trey held up his elbow and grinned.

Sophie took his arm and began to walk, but then stopped and turned toward Kedar. When he offered his elbow she gladly wrapped her free arm in his. They walked three abreast toward the house. For the first time in as long as she could remember, Sophie didn't feel like an outsider.

—§—

Father Denny returned to the Vatican after just a few days to avoid suspicion. He hadn't heard anything from the other Venators that he had ordered to lay low. Before he left, he made several calls about the slaughterhouses they had identified. Local authorities had found sites full of horrific evidence but abandoned—maybe, just *maybe*, the team thought, the carnage was slowing...for now.

"It's all your's kiddo." Father Denny pulled Gaelan aside the morning before he left. Gaelan wrinkled his brow at the neatly typed list of offshore bank accounts and access codes. "What's all mine? You giving away your stuff? Should I be worried about you?"

Father Denny laughed, "I'm fine. And let's just say you're fine too, for life."

"What are you talking about?"

"What do you think the USB drives were for?"

"I thought it was to get information and place a virus on their network."

"It did that, for sure, and a Trojan horse, designed to attack their holdings. It started to skim tiny sums of money into phantom accounts, and gradually got bigger and bolder until it was discovered and they shut it down. But by the time that happened, those phantom accounts had re-invested the money through legitimate accounts and business ventures, reinvested revenues into government bonds..."

Gaelan interrupted, "You *laundered* the vampire money?"

"Clean as a whistle, and now you know how to find it."

Gaelan looked at Father Denny in amazement, "Are you telling me..."

"Yeah kiddo, you guys really *robbed a bank*. Before all was said and done, we took over $60 billion and spread it out among anonymous offshore accounts. That's one fat checkbook we got."

"Why not give it back to the Vatican?"

"First off, I'm not letting the Vatican get their greasy little paws on it. The way I see it, you can put it to good use. That, and at the time, I thought you were immortal and might need enough to last you forever. Just in case you're wrong about not living forever, there's your nest egg."

"Holy shit!" The reality was starting to sink in, "Holy shitcakes!"

"Don't spend it all in one place."

Once Denny was gone, the team took some time to relax. Natalia bought a stuffed animal wolf for Gaelan to send to Becca Guerin. Gaelan showed her how to make his vegetable lasagna. While she minced broccoli florets, he explained, "Mince the heads fine and mix them into the ricotta. One important thing is we gotta make sure the noodles don't overcook like this..." Gaelan took an over-cooked lasagna noodle and gently slapped Natalia across the face with it. It stuck to her cheek and she stared at him with a look of utter disbelief. Gaelan started to giggle uncontrollably, held up his hands and backed away, "I'm gonna pay for that one, huh?" An evil grin crossed her face and she picked up a handful of ricotta cheese. Before he could duck or get his hands in front of his face, she hit him square between the eyes at point blank range, causing Cheese to explode all over his face. She cackled.

"That's it!" He grabbed two noodles and twirled them like nunchucks. Natalia grabbed another handful of cheese, ready to let it fly. It was only the appearance of Trey, with an utter look of disbelief on his face, standing in the doorway, that brought them up short.

Natalia pointed at Gaelan, "He started it!"

"Good thing you're holding cheese, RAT!" Gaelan twirled noodles faster than ever.

Trey blinked several times, then turned and walked out without saying a word. They both erupted in laughter.

Over the next few days, Gaelan showed Natalia how to fight with the katana and throw knives more accurately. They grew closer each day, but didn't share any more 'moments' together. Trey and Angel decided they wouldn't be outdone by Gaelan, and cooked several meals for the group. Sophie spent most of her days talking with Medhir and trying to 'bond' with him, or getting to know Kedar. Everyone spent the evenings together eating, enjoying Denny's wine and brandy, laughing and trying to forget the horrors of the outside world.

One evening, they gathered in the family room, bellies full of Angel's cheese croquettes, pisto and baked fish. Medhir told them about his years as a prisoner and what he tried to do to keep his mind clear. Trey brought out the pictures of the surveillance on the bank and Medhir was able to point out the man who talked to him most of the time.

"This one here." Medhir tapped the figure in the picture, "His name is Gaius. He serves the vampires."

Trey shrugged, "We figured he was a blood-cocktail when we stopped seeing him there those last few days."

"He would go off for a few days at a time and then always stop back in to make my dinner and discuss events. He was always very polite, but I did not trust him." Medhir took a sip of brandy—his third of the night. He hadn't let himself drink much but he was enjoying his freedom, as well as talking to anybody other than Gaius, "Hopefully I will not ever see him again." He laid his head back and closed his eyes.

Natalia was sitting in an upholstered chair and Gaelan was sitting on the floor leaning against the arm of the chair, near her leg. She refilled his wine glass with a nearby bottle. Sophie sat on the sofa between Medhir and Trey. Medhir dozed.

"Gaelan, what is it like?" Sophie broke the companionable silence.

Gaelan shifted uneasily.

"I am sorry. I didn't mean to…"

"No, it's okay." He eased his weight into Natalia's leg a little, "When it first happened, it was excruciating. My body temperature would soar and I could feel every bone break as I transformed. I thought I was dying."

Angel interjected, "I know, I heard your screams."

Kedar laughed, "And then he threw you into a tree." The rest of the group giggled.

"K, you are such a shit-stirrer." Gaelan then looked to Angel with a grimace, "For the thousandth time, I'm sorry."

"Water under the bridge. Besides, I heard you had your own dealings with trees as of late." He raised his eyebrows in Sophie's direction.

Before she could apologize again, Trey grabbed Sophie's hand and kissed it, "Like I said, my favorite person right now." Angel

Gaelan's Destiny

then jumped up and kissed her other hand in an accentuated gentlemanly manner. Medhir stirred at their laughter and settled back to sleep.

"Whatever. I earned my ass whipping—seriously, I did." They all chuckled and he continued, "Anyway, I eventually learned to hold it in. I figured out how to recognize the signs and concentrated on something peaceful and beautiful to choke it back." Gaelan nudged Natalia's leg. She took a sip of wine to hide her smile. He continued, "In the beginning, my memories of when I was...you know...they were sporadic and I wasn't even sure what I had done as a monster. But now I remember everything, and the change is now more or less painless. I guess I've adapted."

Trey leaned forward, "Okay, I can swallow all that, but what's the deal with the full moon? We know now that the transformation can happen anytime. So why did we always find wolves around the moon cycle?"

Gaelan thought for a moment, "Ya know, I'm not really sure. I know I get hungrier and more agitated around the full moon, so there's gotta be something there, but I don't know what it is." The memory of his parent's deaths came flooding back to him. The creature's silhouette against the full moon, "Not yet anyway."

"What about silver?" Angel was puzzled.

"No clue." Gaelan shrugged, "They're immortal, so the one thing we know is that we're missing out on at least a thousand years of knowledge that can answer all of this."

"You will live forever?" Sophie was shocked.

"No. That's just it. When they attack humans, they feed not only on the flesh and blood, but also on the the *life* itself. That's why the other girl changed during your initiation ritual. She fed on a human." Sophie's face tightened momentarily at the memory.

Medhir stirred. His neck was tilted back with his eyes closed, and he slowly turned his head to the side. Sophie got up and grabbed a blanket from the back of Kedar's chair and carefully placed it over Medhir, tucking in the sides. She smoothed his hair, and whether out of maternal instinct or pity for his years of imprisonment, she leaned in and kissed him on the forehead. She instantly shot straight up and her eyes rolled back, revealing just the lower whites. Medhir's eyes were similarly rolled back.

"Don't touch them!" Trey snapped. He recognized that it was finally happening.

They stood silent for an excruciating minute. Finally, Sophie's hand dropped from Medhir's head. Kedar shot forward and grabbed her as she crumbled, gently setting her down on the couch next to Medhir.

"Did you see it?" Medhir's voice was barely audible, his eyes half closed. Sophie nodded.

Trey dropped to a knee in front of Sophie, "Sophie sweetie? Can you tell us where to find the prophet?"

Sophie shook her head, "I don't know *where,* but I can see her. *Paper*! I need paper!"

Natalia was already grabbing paper and a pencil. Trey continued, "You said 'she.' Did you see her?"

Sophie nodded, "Yes. She is young. Scared." She began scribbling and then turned the paper toward Trey, "She is…" she snapped her fingers looking for the English word, "*Asian*." The paper read: 银川老女孩孤儿院

"We need to get on a plane right now!" Gaelan was the only one that could read the writing.

"What's it say?" Angel asked the obvious.

"Yinchuan Elder Girls Orphanage."

They all began scrambling to get their items as Trey got in touch with Father Denny, "The prophet—she's in China!"

Fifteen hundred kilometers away, Genevieve bolted upright in bed. Her eyes rolled back and her spine arched in a trance that lasted almost a full minute. Finally released from its grip, she flopped back, weak, and opened her eyes, focusing on the familiar figure at her side.

"Gaius?"

"Yes m'lady?" Gaius took a knee next to her.

"What happened? Where is the prophet?" Genevieve winced.

"He was taken from us, don't you remember?"

Images flashed through her head: masked intruders... bullets... She touched her hand to her wounds, "They took him?"

"Yes. We have brought you here to tend to you."

He did not have to point to the body hanging in the corner; Genevieve could smell it. It's rib cage was splayed and its organs missing. She could taste the iron from the blood still fresh in her moth. She licked her dry lips. "I'm feeling better. I think that..."

"What did the witch see?" Genevieve, Gaius and two vampires turned towards the interruption.

"My name is Genevieve. I am mistress of the coven..."

The female wolf cut her off, her arms crossed in irritation, "I don't care who you are and where you're from, *witch*. What—did—you—see?"

Genevieve was about to retort, but bit her wrath back when she saw the look of expectation on Gaius' face, "A young girl...Chinese. I saw a sign—Yinchuan Elder Girls Orphanage."

"How can you be sure? There's no fortune-teller here." The leather-clad wolf asked.

"I had already begun a bond with him before I was attacked. The bond persists—I see what the other one sees."

"Then your *masters* have what you needed and we're through." The leather-clad woman turned on her heels.

Genevieve hissed after her retreating back, "Animals."

"They lost the pack members assigned to protect you." Gaius explained. "Can you travel m'lady?"

She shook her head.

"Then you'll have to identify the seer here." He turned to other vampires in the room, "The Elders would have us act quickly. Call and organize a group to travel to the Yinchuan Elder Girls Orphanage and bring the girls here. Once we identify the seer, the rest will be a gift for her." He bowed neatly to the enchantress while the vampires grumbled at the order.

Genevieve caressed his cheek and lifted his chin with her hand, "Oh Gaius, I could just eat you up."

As the two werewolves walked away from the building, the woman took out a phone, "It's Nessa. Alfarr and I just left the witch and the vampires' errand boy…" The she-wolf stopped, hand on her hip. "Yes…yes, they know where she is…China. Yinchuan…I understand." Nessa hung up and looked to Alfarr with a smug smile, "A very big country is about to get very crowded."

CHAPTER 16
ADOPTIONS

Gaelan booked a charter flight out of Montpellier, France. By the time that they arrived at the airport, the pilots were waiting, one engine turning, and they were headed for Yinchuan Hedong International Airport. Angel had insisted that they bring Medhir along: Only Medhir and Sophie knew what she looked like, he argued, and Medhir was the only one who could relate to what she was going through. Of course, Sophie refused to be left behind.

Gaelan was able to call Father Denny from inside the chartered jet, "Yeah...just don't tell him about me...NO! I'll take care of it when I land. And tell him not to use Venántium resources for the weaponry...We will...We'll call you later."

"You're sure we can trust this guy you know?" Trey sounded dubious.

"Yeah. He'll come through." Gaelan sounded as if he was trying to convince himself as well.

Trey nodded, "Okay. If he can get us the hardware, we may be in business. Of course, we're going in totally blind. We have no idea what he'll actually be able to arm us with."

"Well, if all else fails, I got the old pig-sticker." Gaelan patted the bag holding his katana.

Trey huffed, "Great, and the rest of us can use sticks and foul language."

"He'll come through. What's the plan?"

Trey shrugged, "We try not to draw attention to ourselves, but I figure we all go in together...well, everyone but Meddi. He's still not a hundred percent, so we stash him at the safe house first. Sophie IDs the girl, we bring her with us, then grab Meddi on the way out."

"Okay, then what?"

"I don't fucking know!" He turned to Medhir, "Meddi, what happens from there?"

Medhir shrugged, "How did you put it? *I don't fucking know*. It will depend on if she has started to have visions or predictions."

Trey continued, "Okay, so then we find a place to lay low until we can make our way back to Denny's place with the prophet."

"My contact should be able to help us with that too. I told Father Denny to make sure he got us a safe house off the grid and without..."

Angel interrupted, "...The Venántium knowing, we get it! Who is this guy anyway?"

"I met him on a hunt while I was here. He's good people."

"Wait. Didn't you only do one hunt here?" Natalia was the first to catch on.

Gaelan chagrinned. "Uhhhhh, yeah."

"The one where you faked your death?" Trey looked at him wide-eyed.

Gaelan whispered through closed teeth, "Yeeeeeeeeeah."

"THIS GUY THINKS YOU'RE FUCKING DEAD?!"

"Well, I'm about to go Lazarus on his ass. Besides, does anyone else know anybody in China that's not Venántium?" No one spoke up, "Exactly! So we stick to the plan, get in, get out. No complications!"

They passed through customs with relative ease and made it out to the waiting area. A man, clearly waiting for them, eyed them suspiciously, "The weather in the province is quite unexpected." His hands were stuffed deep in his pockets.

"It is, but we were hoping you could help us with whatever weather we encounter."

"Ahhhhh, Father Denny told me you were coming. My name is Zhang. Zhang Jie." Zhang held out his hand.

"Trey Marshall. It's great to meet you. This here is Angel, Kedar, Sophie, Medhir, Natalia and you already know..."

"Hello Zhang." Gaelan walked up from the back.

Angel whispered, "Oh shit, here we go."

Zhang's mouth fell open. "You're dead."

"How's the old saying go? The report of my demise may have been slightly exaggerated." Gaelan replied in Mandarin.

"You're alive because you're a..." Zhang stopped short of saying it.

"Yeah...Yeah I am. I went down after the cobalus to kill the rest of them, and to fake my own death."

"Why?" a mixture of confusion and anger tainted Zhang's voice.

"To protect those I care for. My family. Father Denny. These dumbasses behind me. Binh and Binji...and *you*. As long as you believed I was dead, you would be safe and I could do what I do best."

"That is?" Zhang shoved his hands back into his pockets.

"Kill every monster I can." Gaelan raised his eyebrows.

"They're all human?" Zhang nodded at the team.

"Yes." Gaelan said with certainty, then blanched. "Shit...no. Not everyone."

"What?" Zhang was taken aback.

"One of the women, she's French-Algerian, and she's a witch. And I hate to say this, but we really need to get moving."

Zhang furrowed his brow, "And why am I supposed to trust you? Supposed to trust any of you?"

"Because I'm the same guy that you met at that gas station. I'm the same guy that fought by your side in Pingluo. I'm the same guy that watched you mow down dozens of those fuckin' things. I'm the same guy that still counts my lucky stars that you were there to save our team and those townspeople. And I'm the guy that's going to go on this mission, with or without you...But I'd rather it be *with*."

Zhang sighed in frustration, "And what am I supposed to call you?"

"I told you going into that hole that my name was actually Gaelan Kelly. But you can call me Dumbass. Jackass. Asshole. Any variation on "ass" that you want actually. It's what these guys do."

Zhang's face remained stony.

"Gaelan, what's up?" Angel was getting impatient.

"Zhang, we really need your help." Gaelan implored.

Zhang took a step back and then in a sudden motion, whipped something towards Gaelan.

Gaelan caught the projectile before it struck him, rounding on Zhang with a mixture of shock and anger. The others dropped their bags, about to jump in, when Gaelan looked down at the object. Zhang's barely suppressed laughter brought them up short. Gaelan held up the lollipop for them to see. Zhang began to laugh in earnest as he unwrapped his own lollipop and stuck it in his mouth, "You should see your face!"

"You were fucking with me?"

Zhang was trying to talk through his laughter, "You had Father Denny call me to set this up, but you didn't want him to tell me about you. He ignored you and told me that you were still alive and wanted to avoid some type of scene here."

As Zhang kept talking, he turned and looked at the group, still holding up the lollipop. They looked at him in bewilderment as he handed the candy to Natalia. She held her baffled look, subconsciously unwrapping the candy and putting it in her mouth while Zhang continued, "He said you'd probably be all melodramatic and walk out last to surprise me. I can't wait to tell him." He was now laughing loudly, deepening his voice to imitate Gaelan, "*Hello Zhang. You're so flamboyant!*"

"This whole time you were fucking with me? Seriously?" Gaelan sounded hurt.

Zhang walked up to him, choking back his laughter, "It's good to see you … *Gaelan Kelly.*" He embraced Gaelan.

Gaelan smiled and lifted Zhang in the air, "Stop making fun of me dickhead."

Trey coughed, "Can we go back to English so we know what's going on?"

Zhang abruptly apologized, "I'm sorry. I couldn't resist playing a joke on him. My apologies to you all. Welcome to China."

Trey cocked his head, "So you were just messing with him?" Zhang nodded and Trey smiled toward the rest of the group, "Oh, I like him!"

Sophie ran up, hugged Zhang and kissed him on each cheek. "You make me happy."

"Seriously?" Gaelan gaped at Sophie. She smirked and picked up her bags to walk out. "Do you have anymore lollipops?" Angel asked as they made their way after her.

There was a bag of them waiting in the SUV parked outside.

"A prophecy? Really?" Zhang shook his head as he drove towards the safe house. Zhang was in just as much disbelief as everyone else that heard it, yet he was all in on the plan to basically kidnap an orphan girl, "I'm sure she's not going to take this well."

"Well then," Trey put his hands on Zhang's shoulders from the back seat, "you're gonna have your work cut out for you Doc!"

"I'm a trauma surgeon, not a psychiatrist, you know that, right?" Zhang glanced at Gaelan with a worried look, then asked, "What?"

Gaelan shook his head with shit-eating grin on his face, "Nothing. That's the face I remember. I barely recognized you with all this confidence. What's been going on with you?"

"Yeah?" Angel chimed in, "Aren't you freaked out by the prospect of monsters and Armageddon?"

"Not after the cobalus at Pingluo. I went back to the training compound with the survivors and became a de facto Venator. I even taught first aid classes there. I go back once a month to repeat the class. I join teams on hunts whenever I can…"

"YOU'RE HUNTING?" Gaelan was shocked.

"Yes. Only in China. It's always shifters."

Angel leaned forward, "So you've never seen a vampire or a werewolf?"

"No, neither." Zhang then eyed Gaelan, "Well, not a *real* werewolf anyway."

Gaelan made a face. "How much longer to the safe house? We spent over 20 hours on the plane and I don't need to remind you that we are literally burning daylight here."

The ride to the safe house took another 30 minutes. It was a series of apartments, taking up the entire bottom floor of an inconspicuous corner building away from the heart of the city. It had a good view of every avenue of approach and would be easy to defend in a siege. There was a garage with quick access to the street if need be. They walked inside and all squeezed into the apartment Zhang was staying in.

Trey asked, "Were you able to get us weapons on short notice?"

"No."

"NO?" Trey sounded concerned until he saw Zhang turn and pull out a rifle case.

"I brought my own." Zhang grinned and opened the case revealing twin QBZ-95's.

"Your own?" Gaelan sounded like a concerned parent.

"Yes. After Pingluo, I started investing in weapons and ammunition like the Venántium have. Here, there's two more of those, two SKS rifles and six QSZ-92 pistols...9mm variant. All the weapons have UV lights attached and I have hundreds of rounds for each of them, all with silver points on the heads of the rounds, dipped in holy water and blessed in all major religions."

Angel walked up to Zhang, "Brother, you need a different hobby, but I gotta say, I totally love you right now!" He then turned. "Dibs on one of the SKS's!"

"Okay, Medhir, stay here and watch for us. This girl is going to need you." Trey turned to the others, "The rest of you, saddle up. The sun's already set and we're a day behind."

They walked into the garage and loaded into the SUV they arrived in, along with a larger, armored looking SUV.

"I bought this and made some upgrades. We should take both vehicles, just in case we need to split up. There's a quick reference map in both vehicles with obvious landmarks to get to the orphanage and get back to the safe-house, in case we get separated." Zhang had thoroughly prepared.

Angel raised an eyebrow, "You have months of canned goods at home, don't you?"

"Maybe." Zhang chagrined.

"Dude, you really need a new hobby." Angel shook his head and got in.

"Zhang, where did you get the money for this?" Gaelan had that overprotective tone again.

"I'm a surgeon. I also had money from my wife dying."

Gaelan felt like an ass, "Zhang, I'm sorry. I didn't..."

Zhang laughed it off, "It was a car accident, years ago, and she'd be glad I was spending it and keeping busy."

"Keeping busy? That's one way to put it. I'm buying you replacements though!" Gaelan smiled, thinking about the billions they had stolen. They loaded up and began the trek.

It was dark by the time they arrived at the orphanage. The two-story building was set apart from encroaching urban squalor by its extensive grass field. The main part of the building was brick, dotted by a few windows. The building itself was not quite centered on the property, with the large field next to it, undoubtedly for any athletic activities they may have had. The main entrance opened into a well-lit lobby.

Gaelan, Sophie and Zhang headed to the front door. Zhang had come up with an impromptu plan: Sophie and Gaelan would act like a couple on a tight travel schedule looking to adopt, which would explain the after hours visit. "I will be your local *fixer*" he grinned. Zhang figured that the cover story might buy them extra time before the authorities were alerted to the 'kidnaping'. Gaelan marveled at how Zhang had evolved from the timid doctor he knew to the quick-thinking agent of the Venántium.

The door to the lobby was unlocked, and the reception and security desks were unmanned. Zhang was about to call out when Gaelan grabbed his arm.

Sophie's voice was shaky, "I smell it."

Gaelan nodded, "Blood... *death*." He scanned the hall for possible ambush sites. Sophie walked forward, her senses heightened. When she reached the reception counter, she froze in horror. Gaelan and Zhang ran forward. The congealing blood was visible before the two bodies. An older man in a security guard uniform and a middle-aged woman in a black suit were lying on top of one another, their throats torn wide open. There should've been more blood... *vampires*!

"They're gone." Gaelan shook his head before Zhang could render aid, "We can't help them. Get back to the vehicles and tell them we're not alone. Sophie..." She was still staring at the bodies, "Sophie!" His voice was a harsh whisper. He grabbed her by the upper arms and turned her to face him, "Use it! Feel their pain. Feel your rage! Feel the desire to kill whatever did this and *use it*! You with me?" She nodded, her face morphing from shock to focused anger. "Good girl! Go with Zhang and protect the others while I look around." Gaelan hadn't even finished the sentence when he heard screams from the floor above. He took off running, yelling back over his shoulder, "DON'T LET THEM LEAVE WITH THE PROPHET!"

Niu Dang was reading a book in bed, waiting to be called to dinner. Visitation hours at the orphanage were over, not that there were many visitors anyway. Many of the girls sat in groups in the long hallway full of beds and side tables, but Niu sat by herself. Most of the girls thought her odd because of the night terrors and the multiple foster families that had taken her in, just to return her to the institution. They called her bad luck. Niu "Chēlún" Guo wheeled her chair over and smiled.

"Don't get too close, the others might smell my scent on you." Niu smiled at Chēlún.

"Naaah, too much grease. Masks the smell." Chēlún patted her wheelchair and they both laughed. "You know they don't dislike you. They just don't know how to take you."

"I know. Months of the bad-luck-boogeygirl must be rubbing off on everyone. Seriously though, I'm going to keep reading. Go talk with everyone and then we'll hang out after dinner." Niu went back to her book.

"Okay nerd girl. Don't doze off and start screaming on me. You'll ruin my reputation." Chēlún joked.

"As what, an Olympic sprinter?" Niu poked fun right back.

"That's harsh nerd girl!" Chēlún smiled and wheeled back to the group of girls sitting at the end of the long room.

The girls looked up as one when the doors swung upon, and six casually dressed adults walked in. Five of them were men. Only adult females were allowed in the sleeping area. Only one of those men looked Asian. *What was going on?* The girls all went silent. A blond man strode to the nearest group of girls, eyeing them intently, but silent. Chēlún was among them.

"May I help you?" One of the older girls stood, and bowed politely.

His voice was cool, and barely loud enough for everyone to hear.

"You can all line up and follow us downstairs. We'll be taking a trip." His smile added no warmth.

"A trip? Should we pack?" The girl had no sooner asked the question when the man backhanded her to the ground. A collective gasp erupted as the girl held the side of her face and sobbed.

"WHY DID YOU DO THAT? SHE JUST ASKED A QUESTION!" Chēlún wheeled forward trying to put her chair between the man and her friend. Surely he wouldn't strike a girl in a wheelchair. She was partially right. Instead, the man seized her by the hair and lifted her into the air. Chēlún yelped in pain and shock as she felt her hair pulling away from her scalp.

Through the terrified screams Niu yelled for her best friend—her *only* friend—by the name they shared, "NIU!" She ran forward, unthinking, straight into the man holding her friend's limp form. It was like hitting a wall. Before she could recover, his open palm smacked her to the ground, and she saw stars. As her vision came back, she saw Chēlún whimpering on the ground, holding the back of her head. The dull pain in her cheek gave way to a stinging, throbbing feeling, and tears filled her eyes. Her focus on the pain was broken when one of the men that was standing by the door came sliding across the floor down the center aisle. She turned back to the doorway to see the commotion and saw the face from her dreams... *his* face! She could feel her blood run cold and her stomach turned into a knot. The day of the nightmare had finally come: The monsters were here.

Trey recognized the horror on Sophie and Zhang's flush faces as soon as they burst out of the building.

"What is it?" Trey handed Zhang a rifle.

Zhang nodded in gratitude as he took the weapon, "The security guard and the receptionist are dead. We were looking around when we heard screams."

"Where's Gaelan?" Natalia asked.

"He ran upstairs. He told us to get all of you and surround this place. He said not to let them leave with the prophet!"

Natalia's eyes went wide and she darted back to the SUV, then bolted past everyone toward the orphanage.

"NATALIA, WHERE THE HELL ARE YOU GOING?"

"HE'S UNARMED!" Natalia didn't break stride. They could see that she carried Gaelan's katana as she disappeared through the entrance.

Trey surveyed the area. His mind was racing a mile a minute. He saw a bus that belonged to the orphanage in a side driveway adjacent to the main building, "K, can you hotwire that thing?"

Kedar took off running without bothering to answer.

Trey was talking as fast as he could, "Angel, you and Zhang cover the main entrance. Get everyone you can into the bus; we don't have time to sort out who the prophet is they'll kill anyone left behind."

"Where are you going?"

"I'm going around back to clear the building from behind and find another entrance!"

"We're on it!" Angel nodded and slapped Zhang on the chest as they scrambled into position.

"Sophie, you ready for a fight?" She nodded silently at Trey. He grabbed her hand and squeezed, "Watch over all these guys. Let the witch out and make these fuckers pay." Sophie's face went cold at Trey's words, her eyes fully black by the time she nodded slowly in response.

Trey got to the far corner of the orphanage and spun around, clearing the way with his rifle. There was no one there, but he could see a back entrance with a dumpster next to it. He ran up to the door and turned the handle—it was unlocked. He pulled it open quickly and brought his weapon to bear. In the hallway were four men and three women. The women screamed and one of the men, dressed in white kitchen garbs, jumped in between Trey and the others while wielding a large kitchen knife. Trey's index finger was tickling the trigger but his experience told him that creatures don't attack with kitchen utensils. Plus, none of them reacted to the UV light hitting them. Two of the women were in casual attire and the other woman and all the men were in white kitchen uniforms. He knew this was the staff. The vampires didn't even bother clearing the building—*they were brazen.*

Trey partially lowered the barrel of the rifle and put his finger on his lips to shush them, then tapped his ear and pointed up, trying to ask them if they heard commotion upstairs. They all emphatically nodded in unison. Trey waved for them all to run out the back entrance and get to safety. Even with the language barrier, six of them didn't need to be told twice. The cook with the knife stood his ground and shook his head. Trey gave him a wide-eyed look and half shrugged his shoulders. The man tapped his own chest and pointed up. Apparently he was very protective of the occupants and wasn't going anywhere. *He's got balls,* Trey thought, *I'll give him that*. Trey sighed and nodded in agreement, then took out the pistol Zhang had given him and handed it over to the stranger, now his wingman. Trey used his index finger and thumb to make a shooting motion and then forcefully tapped his own head and heart. The man nodded again with a curious look as to why that was so important. As they pressed forward and up to the second floor, he actually chuckled about the exchange and thought to himself, *Gaelan and his language skills can suck it!*

Gaelan had run up the stairs when he heard the screams rise then fade in the distance. Several men and women amassed outside the doorway to what appeared to be sleeping quarters. The smell of death emanated from them. Gaelan broke into a trot, accelerating and picking up momentum as they turned. His eyes were changing and he could feel his fangs extend. One of the women hissed at him in Latin, "What are you doing here, *animal*?"

Gaelan slowed his stride and took several deep breaths. His mind raced. There were werewolves with the witch and vampires in Romania—*they don't know who I am*! He knew he had to spin it, "After Romania, we're not taking any chances. We'll make sure you don't fail again!" *Shit*, he thought, *even I'd buy that*. He heard a voice coming from the inner room.

"I'll inspect."

"You'll do nothing of the sort, *beast*!" One of the men stood next to the woman. The other vampires closed ranks behind them.

"I wasn't asking and I'm not going to repeat myself." He never broke stride as he pushed them to the side. He entered the room in time to see a vampire smack a girl across the face and knock her to the ground. There was another girl crying at his feet and five other vampires just inside the doorway. It was going to be a tough fight. One of the creatures grabbed his shoulder and Gaelan spun, throwing the vampire over his shoulder and into the room, watching it slide past the girl on the floor. He scanned and saw the rest of the girls several meters back, huddling and whimpering. The girl on the floor looked up at him. Whatever color she had left drained from her face when she saw him. It wasn't just a look of horror, but of *recognition*. The vampires must have found her already.

The vampire that had hit her rounded on him. "Who is that?"

One of the vampires from the hallway announced over Gaelan's shoulder, "Wolf!"

"I wasn't told that you would be here." This was apparently the one in command.

"There's a lot that you're not told. We don't ask for permission to make sure you don't fail!" Gaelan retorted. *That's it*, he told himself, *sound confident and arrogant*, "Have you found her?"

"Not yet. We'll be taking them all back to the enchantress. She will identify the seer."

They don't know yet! He strode further into the room, walked up to the group of girls, and looked them over as if perusing a menu, then strolled over to Niu. "Pity you can't identify her here. They look so... *tasty*." Gaelan licked his lips, deliberately lascivious.

The head vampire seemed amused at the idea of eating them, "Oh, none of them will go to waste. Once we have the seer, the rest will make for a tasty meal."

Gaelan reached down and forcibly lifted Niu to her feet. "This one here looks especially delicious. I love to taunt them." He circled around her and could smell the fear coming from her. Tears streamed down her cheeks, and he could hear her heart racing. He stopped directly in front of her and leaned in, taking a long, exaggerated inhale. He whispered Chinese ever so softly in her ear, "When I draw them in, grab the other girls and run. The people with the guns downstairs are good guys."

Niu looked up at him in confusion and then turned towards Chēlún's whimpers. Gaelan followed her gaze, noticing Chēlún's overturned wheelchair for the first time. He taunted aloud, looking around at the vampires, "Don't worry, I'll see to your friend *personally*." One of the vampires gave a half-laugh.

Niu's legs felt like jelly. This was her dream! Her lip started to quiver as she looked back up to Gaelan's eyes. All sense of time stopped as she waited for him to turn back to her. She felt as if it took forever, and when he did, his eyes were no longer human. He spoke the words that made her dread going to sleep every night for over a year. He laughed, fangs now visible in his mouth, and snarled, "You should be running." This was the moment she jolted awake each night from her nightmare, but this time the man with the inhuman eyes… *winked*.

Gaelan spun hard, jutting out his arm and striking the lead vampire with the heel of his fist directly in the cheekbone. He felt bone crack and the creature careened to the side of the room. He yelled out, "No one tells me when I can and can't eat," as he grabbed the next vampire, picked him up and swung him into the rest of creatures. He turned to make eye contact with Niu and motioned his head for her to alert the rest of the girls. "I DON'T CARE! I WANT TO FEED!" The rest of the vampires ran in to subdue him, diving on top of him and trying to pin him down.

Niu ran to the other orphans and motioned for them to run past the melee. She then ran back to pull Chēlún into the hallway. One of the vampires turned, its face now contorted, to see the last of the girls running into the hallway. It jumped up and ran after them with a snarl, two more creatures following suit. Gaelan no longer had all the creatures' attention. One of the female vampires chided him, "Fool, they're running. Now we…" Before she could finish, she heard the screams and then the gunshots began.

Natalia had sprinted up the stairs but stopped short of the second floor when she heard Gaelan speaking to someone in Latin. She laid down on the stairs, pressing her body as close to the steps as possible and listened. She could hear Gaelan playing into it. They thought he was just another werewolf. She waited for whatever he was going to do. She held her rifle in one hand and his sword in the other.

Minutes later, she heard the commotion. She peeked her head up enough to see the individuals in the hallway scurry inside the room. She popped up and began walking down the hall with the rifle trained on the doorway. The first girls emerged, terrified to find Natalia with a raised weapon. She raised her index finger to her lips and motioned for them to run past her and down the stairs.

Natalia could hear gasps and whimpers from the girls as they made it downstairs—they had caught sight of the bodies behind the reception desk. They continued to pour out of the doorway. Just as the last girl was running from the room, a vampire rose up behind her and grabbed her by the hair. Natalia instantly fired into the creature's chest. It reeled backward in pain, pulling the girl down with it. Two more vampires jumped into the hallway. The first vampire got back to its feet and thrust the girl in front of it as a shield. All three of them slowly marched toward Natalia. She had no shot around the girl.

Natalia had backed up almost to the top of the stairs when more gunshots rang out and the two trailing vampires dropped. She whipped her head to the side—Trey and an Asian man were firing on the vampires. When the vampire with the girl spun towards the disturbance Natalia dropped her rifle and charged, drawing the sword. Just as she had practiced with Gaelan, she swung out and through, driving the blade across the middle of the creature's face and severing the top of its head like a melon. She pulled the girl free as she drove the tip of the blade into its heart.

Trey ran up and put several bullets into the heads and hearts of the creatures on the ground. Then he put a hand on the Chinese man's shoulder and then pointed to his head and heart as a reminder. The man nodded frantically, eyes wide with horror and disbelief. Natalia retrieved her rifle and motioned for the girl to run and join the others, then dove back into the room.

Inside, Gaelan was furiously battling seven vampires, his body slashed, bitten and bleeding. Two more vampires had been thrown to the side, reeling from their wounds, while in the middle of the room two girls were huddled together on the floor. As Trey took aim, Natalia called out.

—§—

When the gunshots started, Gaelan snarled, "Guess that's my cue." With a burst of energy, he rolled onto his chest and pushed himself up, sending the vampires on top of him in all directions. He was no longer providing a distraction, and he didn't have to worry about the girls. He turned and looked at Niu, eyes still inhuman, screaming in Chinese, "GET OUT OF HERE!"

"I'M NOT LEAVING HER!" She screamed in panic.

The vampires charged at him from all sides. He grabbed the closest creature by the arm and spun, using the vampire as a weapon and battering the onslaught back. He turned and pulled the next closest in and, fangs bared, bit into the side of its neck while pulling on the top of its head. The creature shrieked in agony for only a second before its head ripped off.

Gaelan let out a vicious roar, now teetering on a full-fledged change. His mouth was frothing and his hands were sharpened claws. The other creatures continued their assault, slashing and biting while he dove onto and clawed at the chest of another vampire. Her sternum let out a crack as he ripped her chest open. He quickly tore out the heart and devoured it. He was ready to fully change when he heard Natalia's voice, "GAELAN!" Almost simultaneously, gunfire tore into the furthest vampire. The creatures spun and hissed at the intruders, which gave Gaelan enough of an opening to break free.

Natalia charged forward, tossed Gaelan the katana and slid down next to the two girls, shooting to keep any vampires from them. The interruption bought Gaelan several seconds of respite. He gripped his sword, closed his eyes and took several breaths to fight back the change, then targeted the opponents Natalia chose to shoot and carefully went to work. Each time she hit a vampire, he gutted it, beheaded it and impaled its heart.

To the side of the room, Trey had shot the final two vampires several times. Without a second thought, the Chinese cook bounded forward, kicking into the chest of the first vampire and using that momentum to push off, spin around and kick across the jaw of the second. His moves were quick as he landed on his feet and punched his kitchen knife into the heart of the nearest creature, then spun and roundhouse kicked the second, before thrusting the knife into its heart as well. He then plunged the blade through the second vampire's eye socket, pulled it and threw it directly between the eyes of the first.

"Holy shit!" Trey gaped for a second, then walked forward and shot both creatures in the head for good measure.

In less than a minute the room was full of dismembered and decaying vampire bodies. The cook ran over to check that the two girls on the floor were safe as Gaelan helped Natalia to her feet. Gaelan looked at the cook and then to Trey, "Who's your friend?"

"I think he's Bruce fuckin' Lee. I have no clue what his name is, but the guy's a natural."

Gaelan squatted down and scooped up Chēlún.

"Are you going to eat me?" Her voice quivered.

Gaelan shook his head, "No sweetheart, we're taking you to safety." He then looked to Niu and scolded her, "I told you I would take care of her. Next time, get moving when you're told!"

Niu was filled with a mixture of fear, excitement, confusion and anger, "I wasn't leaving her! Who are you? What do you mean next time?"

"Don't worry about that right now, but that look you gave me—this wasn't the first time you saw me, was it?" Gaelan raised an eyebrow, hoping his hunch was right. Niu shook her head and looked away. His voice softened, "Don't worry honey, this will all make sense in a little while. It's not going to get any easier, but it'll all make sense."

Gaelan turned to the cook, "What's your name?"

"My name is Junjie...Junjie Wén." Junjie grabbed Chēlún's wheelchair, still partially shocked at what he saw and what he did.

"And what about you two?" Gaelan looked down at the girls as he led everyone into the hallway and toward the stairs.

"I'm Niu Guo," Chēlún sniffled, "but you can call me *Wheels*."

"I'm Niu also. Niu Dang."

"Okay. My name is Gaelan and we're going to get you all out of here." He looked over his shoulder to Natalia and Trey, "Your buddy here is Junjie, the girl in my arms you can call Chēlún and this little firecracker right here is Niu—and I'm about ninety-nine percent sure she's the prophet." Natalia and Trey didn't know what to say.

Gaelan looked to Junjie and the girls, "That's Natalia and Trey. In English, Trey means grumpy old troll that smells of dung." Junjie, Niu and Chēlún began to giggle.

Trey walked behind them, "I heard my name. You just made fun of me, didn't you?" He looked to Natalia, his voice now a whine, "He just made fun of me!" He raised his voice, "I swear, I'm gonna shoot you in the fucking back. It won't be silver, but it'll hurt like a bitch. I swear to God, I'm gonna do it!" Natalia shot him a reproaching look, "What? He totally started it!"

Chēlún looked up to Gaelan, "What is he saying?"

"I really don't know. He's speaking in his grumpy-old-dung-troll-language." The girls giggled again. They approached the bottom of the staircase.

"Chēlún, shut your eyes honey." Gaelan pressed her head into his chest. "Nat, the bodies. Don't let her see." But it was too late. Niu had caught a glimpse of the two bodies behind the reception desk and her breath shallowed. Natalia turned Niu's head and pressed it into her shoulder, leading her down the stairs and out. Junjie stopped and looked at his two co-workers with a heavy heart, bowing his head for a moment. Trey sympathetically squeezed his shoulder, then led him outside.

Kedar had jumpstarted the bus and pulled it onto the street in front of the entrance. To their surprise, it was a stream of orphan girls, not their friends or the vampires, that emerged from the doorway. Zhang ran forward, corralling them onto the bus. What seemed like an eternity later, their team finally emerged, accompanied by two more girls and a Chinese man no one had seen before.

Angel jogged out to meet them in the courtyard. "What the hell happened? We good?"

Trey answered, "As good as can be, but we have to beat feet. They're not even trying to cover their tracks anymore."

Gaelan nodded, "Trey's right. There's bound to be more."

Sophie and Kedar loaded Niu and Chēlún on the bus with the other girls, then Junjie jumped aboard as well.

Zhang and Angel boarded the heavy SUV and Trey, Natalia and Gaelan ran back towards the smaller SUV.

"Let's get—out—of..." Gaelan threw his sword in the backseat, and was about to climb aboard, when he suddenly straightened and sniffed the air. Coming out of the shadows from between the buildings behind the orphanage—WEREWOLVES! He didn't even have time to think before he saw *it*! He bellowed in rage and took off in a full sprint toward *it*! This time he didn't try to choke it back. He welcomed the change and within several strides, his body was fully transformed.

"GAELAN!" Natalia's scream fell on deaf ears.

Trey yelled to the convoy. "GO!" Kedar gunned the bus and Zhang sped off behind it to cover their exit. By the time Trey turned back around, Natalia was sprinting after Gaelan with her rifle in hand. At least six werewolves were converging on Gaelan at full speed.

"NATALIA NO!"

She didn't even turn or break stride, "I'M NOT LEAVING HIM!"

"Goddammit!" Trey took off running after her.

Gaelan ran across the lawn adjacent to the orphanage, crashing straight through the first two creatures and sending them careening in separate directions. He dove on the next one, rolling forward and coming upright to throw the creature to the side. *It* was next and *it* was coming straight at him. As Gaelan lunged, *it* spun and slashed him deep across the chest. Gaelan rolled and popped to his feet but *it* was on him before he even got upright, tackling him back to the ground and driving both sets of *its* claws through Gaelan's thickened hide. *It* stood up, lifted Gaelan over *its* head and slammed him to the ground, tearing his skin painfully in the process. *It* bent over and sank *its* massive jaws into Gaelan's shoulder. Gaelan roared in pain and tucked and rolled forward, bringing his adversary with him and freeing himself from the bite.

Before Gaelan could capitalize, two more wolves tore into him. He tore and slashed and broke free in time to lunge at *it* once more. *It* rolled underneath Gaelan's attack and came up slashing into his ribs, spinning to tear into the back of his shoulder. Gaelan spun and ripped his claws across *its* chest, finally drawing blood. The other wolves circled the two of them and tore into Gaelan's back with each pass. Gaelan, in his bestial form, focused on the one in front of him and pounced. *It* blocked Gaelan's slash and thrust *its* claw in an uppercut into Gaelan's abdomen, tearing through his flesh and into his organs. *It* lifted him off the ground, staring straight into his eyes.

Gaelan was running on pure instinct and rage—unbridled hatred for *it*. But somewhere inside the primitive wolf he also knew he couldn't beat *it*—that *it* was too strong. The other werewolves snarled as *it* raised *its* claw to finish Gaelan. The first gunshot caught them all off guard, hitting *it* in the shoulder. *It* roared and dropped Gaelan, hunching down over him, still intent on finishing the kill.

The rest of the wolves that had been circling the two spun and went for Natalia. The closest one to her dropped at a second rifle crack. She didn't even need to look over her shoulder to see that Trey had taken the shot. He hit the monster in the chest and it screeched and gurgled, the silver-tipped and blessed bullet doing what it was suppose to. With five other werewolves to worry about, they couldn't stop to finish that one off.

Natalia sprinted past the writhing monster and tried to fire on the run. The bullets tore up dirt around the other wolves as they scattered, but *it* was too close to Gaelan for her to take a less than well-aimed shot. Instead, she sprinted straight toward the monster. Another rifle crack rang out and another wolf roared in pain. Trey had hit another, then sprinted to try to catch up to Natalia. The wolves weren't just spreading in different directions. They were forming a circle around their prey.

Seemingly unconcerned by the onslaught, *it* dug *its* massive claw on Gaelan's damaged chest while he receded to human form, sinking *its* nails deep into his flesh. *It* thought about charging the woman for a moment, but instead, stood and spun, using *its* momentum to throw Gaelan toward her. He fell at her feet and before she could get a shot off, *it* bounded backwards and joined the circle of wolves moving in and out of the shadows on the lawn. Natalia dropped to her knee, still grasping the rifle trigger with one hand and placing the other on Gaelan's damaged and bleeding chest.

Trey reached them several seconds later, sliding next to her and placing his back against hers, with Gaelan to their side, "The two I hit are still too slow to attack and we have open ground to help us, but those others are gonna move fast. We can't let one through or it'll run us over and the rest will tear us to pieces. Don't try to target or shoot until one of them is coming directly at us. If we get distracted by aiming, it'll leave us with a blind side."

"And when they all decide to attack at once?" She said, voice seething.

"Then we hope we can shoot faster and better." Trey figured they had a minute or less to live, and his stomach tightened as he saw the monsters converge on them from all directions. That's when the field illuminated and the thunderous noise erupted.

"Are we going to go back and help them?" Sophie was standing next to Kedar in the front of the bus as they sped through the streets of Yinchuan.

"No! We can't! One of these girls is the prophet and we can't risk it!"

Gaelan hadn't had the chance to tell him and the others who Niu was, and Sophie hadn't examined any of the girls' faces. "It's why Trey told us to go."

"I can protect us!" Kedar glanced up at Sophie's words. She met his gaze, eyes black. "I can protect us!" she repeated.

He was convinced, "Here, take the wheel!" They switched spots and he ran to the back of the bus to frantically wave at Zhang.

"Should we turn back?" Zhang was asking Angel.

"We can't. We have to get the prophet to safety! It's the reason for all of this." There was nervousness is both of their voices. They hadn't seen what spooked Gaelan, but they knew it wasn't good.

Zhang caught the movement from the back of the bus and asked, "What's he doing?"

Angel spotted what Zhang was looking at, "TURN AROUND!"

Zhang slammed on the brakes and took the next turn without question, but then he pulled over, "Can you find your way back there?" He said as he unstrapped his seatbelt and jumped out of the car.

"Yeah, but where are you going?" Angel hadn't even finished the sentence when Zhang had opened the back door and jumped back in. Angel climbed over into the driver's seat and slammed on the gas, "What the hell are you doing back there?"

"I'm making sure we're ready for whatever it is that's back there. Hit that button for me." Zhang motioned to a button on the console for the moon roof. Angel pressed it and the bulky roof over Zhang's head opened, while simultaneously opening compartments all over the back of the vehicle.

Angel glanced over his shoulder to see what Zhang was fidgeting with, then caught a glimpse, "Holy shit!" He went back to watching the road and saw the turn for the orphanage, "GET READY!" Angel gunned it, jumping the curb and driving up and onto the lawn. His headlights illuminated a strange tableau—Trey and Natalia crouched over a naked body, and werewolves converging from all directions.

"NOW!"

Zhang, standing in the back with half of his body out of the top of the vehicle, saw and processed the same scene. He didn't hesitate as he squeezed down on the pistol grips of the Minigun he had attached to the turret, installed on the SUV moon roof. In a blinding flash, 7.62 mm silver-tipped, blessed bullets streamed downrange at 2500 rounds per minute. The rounds tore up the grassy field before finding the first werewolf. It was nearly cut in half, flesh and innards flying from its body. Zhang turned to his next target. The wolves were fast, but not fast enough. Zhang howled in satisfaction as most of another wolf's leg turned into a red mist. The creature shrieked in pain and slid face first through the grass. Zhang finished it with another burst.

Angel drove a tight circle around Trey and Natalia and what they could only assume was Gaelan. Zhang spotted one of the injured werewolves that either Trey or Natalia had shot, lurking in shadows. He fired and hit the thing mid-section, tracking upward until the creature's head blew clean off. Once the creatures saw their third pack member fall, they fell back. Even *it* disappeared into the shadows with a final, defiant, roar. Angel stopped the vehicle and he and Zhang jumped out, ran around and opened the doors to the back.

It took all four of them to lift Gaelan into the back of the SUV. Natalia jumped in with him, holding his head on her lap. Zhang jumped in the driver's seat while Trey and Angel ran to the other SUV. They sped off into the night and toward the safe house.

What they hadn't seen were the two collaborators that stood and watched from a distance. They had been summoned to transport the orphans for their masters. What they couldn't know was that the collaborators had turned to each other when they saw one werewolf fighting several others. What they hadn't realized was that the collaborators heard Natalia yell the name, *Gaelan*.

It was a beautiful afternoon in Romania, but Gaius wasn't able to enjoy it. He sat in the darkened room with Genevieve as she healed.

"Yes?" He stood after several seconds of someone speaking on the phone and trying to keep his voice collected, "How? Are you sure?" His voice was becoming slightly frantic, "And you saw this with your own eyes?" Now he was angered, "NO! GET TO RO-MANANIA!" He took a deep breath and calmed his voice, "We need to brief the elders." He hung up the phone and lifted it to slam it against the ground before stopping himself. He brought his hand down smoothly and turned to see Genevieve looking at him with the slightest hint of fear, "I'm sorry m'lady. Forgive my momentary loss of composure. There have been … *complications.*"

"The final seer?" Genevieve stood and walked to him.

"Yes m'lady." He gritted his teeth as he spoke, "The Venántium took her."

"What will you do?" She took his free hand.

"I have to inform the elders." He clenched his fists.

Genevieve wrapped her arms around his waist, kissing his neck, "Sweet, sweet Gaius. You've watched over me all this time. I am going to stay and do whatever I can to help you." She took his face in her hands, "We may not have her, but I was shown where she was for a reason. It just hasn't become obvious yet." She pulled his face to hers.

Gaius leaned into the kiss of the witch, letting a calmness wash over him. When their lips parted, he smiled softly, "I just hope it becomes obvious soon m'lady."

CHAPTER 17
ALIVE

It crept out of the tree line and darted toward the cabin. The woman who came around the side of the cabin was caught off guard. She screamed in terror as it grabbed her and tore into her throat. The taste of blood—*sweet human blood*! The other human screamed and charged. It grabbed him and lifted him off the ground...

Gaelan woke up struggling for air. His body felt as if it was on fire and the memories of the night before hit him. He was fighting *it,* and *it* was beating him—*to death*. He was gripping the sides of the bed when he felt a hand grasp his. He looked over saw the face of his angel.

"Nat..." His voice was raspy and weak.

"Shhh. I'm here." She squeezed his hand tighter.

Gaelan wasn't awake for more than a minute when all sorts of voices began whispering. Zhang had secured a safe house with a number of rooms, but hadn't anticipated bringing home dozens of orphans. There were people sleeping everywhere in every room. Two of the girls heard him wake up and the news spread up and down the hallway in seconds. Shortly thereafter, heavy footsteps approached.

"He's awake?" Trey came thundering into the room, looking at Natalia and then to Gaelan. The question was answered when he saw the latter's eyes open, "*What the fuck,* Gaelan?"

"Trey!" Natalia tried to calm him down, but it was no use.

"WHAT THE FUCK GAELAN? WHAT THE FUCK WERE YOU THINKING?" Trey bellowed. By now, Kedar, Angel and Sophie had come running into the room. Zhang and Junjie stood in the doorway to the bedroom watching the exchange while more girls squeezed in behind them trying to see what was going on, "YOU ALMOST GOT EVERYONE FUCKING KILLED GAELAN! YOU ALMOST GOT THE PROPHET KILLED! YOU ALMOST GOT NATALIA FUCKING KILLED!"

"TREY!" Natalia snapped back.

He lowered his voice to a growl, "No Natalia, he's a big boy. He can answer for himself. He can tell us just whAT THE FUCK HE WAS THINKING!"

Gaelan's bottom lip was quivering and his breath was shallow. Natalia put her second hand around his and squeezed harder. The first teardrop formed at the corner of his eye. His voice was shaky and barely audible, "I couldn't beat him." Natalia rubbed a comforting hand on his forehead and through his hair.

"Well no shit Captain Obvious! You GOT YOUR ASS KICKED!" Trey took several deep breaths through his nose before continuing, "You got the ever-living piss beat out of you and the only reason why you're alive—that Natalia and I are still alive, because yes, we were stupid enough to go after you—the only reason any of us are still here is because of Zhang's gun fetish! And in case you didn't hear it Gaelan, you neaRLY GOT EVERYONE FUCKING KILLED!" Trey was squeezing his fists trying to restrain himself.

"GODDAMMIT TREY, KNOCK IT OFF!" Natalia was ready to fight.

"No. He's gonna hear this!"

The first lone tear trickled from of the outer corner of his eye and down his upper cheek as Trey continued. Barely anything that

Trey had said registered. *It* had beaten him handily. *It* had nearly killed him...*again*. "I couldn't beat him. After all this time."

"We already established that Gaelan!" Trey hissed.

Gaelan was hardly listening to Trey. He muttered again, "After all this time, I finally found him." Tears now streamed down his cheek, "After what he took from me..."

Gaelan may have hardly heard Trey, but Trey was close enough to hear everything that he was mumbling. His shoulders dropped as his gut flipped on itself in shame. He walked over to the opposite side of the bed from Natalia and dropped to a knee. Gaelan continued, weeping, "After everything he did. I found him. I found him and I couldn't stop him."

Natalia realized what he was saying, covering her mouth with her free hand to mask a pitying sob.

Angel put his hands to his forehead and huffed with an open jaw.

Kedar stood there with clenched fists as Sophie walked up just behind him.

They all finally understood why Gaelan had done what he had done. They all realized that he had finally found the werewolf that attacked him. The werewolf that killed his parents in front of him. The monster that made him what he was. He found *it*...and he couldn't beat *it*.

Trey looked from Gaelan to Natalia and then back to Gaelan, "I wasn't much older than you were when I did a tour in the Canadian army." His voice was calm, "After I got out, I became a cop in Vancouver. One day I answered a call about a break in at an art gallery. One of the gallery assistant directors was the most beautiful creature I had ever seen. Her name was..." Trey was lost in thought for a minute and his eyes glassed over. He took a deep breath and continued, "Her name was Laura. Laura Burdick." Trey had a small smile when he said her name, "I tried to look authoritative. I walked around slowly with my chest puffed out, trying to impress her. She wasn't having any of it until I turned and walked into an open door." He chuckled at himself, "She was shocked to see that I had cut my head open. But I refused be the fool, so I said '*Obviously the burglar placed this door here to throw us off his tracks. Cunning one he is*' and kept going about my business. The other officers laughed their asses off at me, but it didn't matter. Somehow, she saw something in me. We were married a year later. Life was good. We were in love. I made detective and she became gallery director. On our third anniversary, I took her camping." Trey shook his head looking away, "With all my military and police training, what could go wrong, *right*? It was cold, clear and dry. And that moon." He gritted his teeth, "That *full* fucking moon. We were in the tent. We had just gone to sleep when it tore through and grabbed Laura. She screamed and I darted out after her with the pistol I had under my pillow. I couldn't even process what I was seeing. It was," His voice was raspy and tears began to trickle from his eyes, "tearing into her. I just went after it. I jumped on its back and shot into its rib cage. It just made it angry and it threw me off. It pounced toward me and that's when the shot hit it. It fell just a couple of meters away and tried to crawl at me when two or three more shots hit it. This guy came over and placed a foot on its neck, then put a round through its back and into its heart, and then one more into the back of its skull. I was already running to Laura." Trey's voice cracked a little, "She was…" Trey tried to compose himself, "Her legs, abdomen and arms. Her throat. Her scalp. She looked at me with wide eyes. She…she died in my arms." Trey sniffed and wiped his eyes on his free forearm and squeezed Gaelan's hand with the other, "Denny was the one that saved me. It's the reason I hate them so much. I hated you once—you know that. And it's the reason I understand. I get it now. Don't worry, I get it." More tears trickled down Trey's face as he squeezed Gaelan's hand even harder.

Gaelan turned away, whimpering, "I couldn't beat him. He took everything from me and I couldn't beat him Trey." Gaelan sobbed.

Trey tried to shush him, "Stop! Fuck that! We all got out in one piece and that's what counts, right?" He turned to Angel, "Lucky rather than good, right?"

Angel walked over and took a position by the end of the bed, laying a hand over the blanket on Gaelan's shin, "Damn right. Besides, the Zhang-inator got us out of there, so no worries."

Gaelan turned back to Trey, "I'm sorry Trey. I'm so sorry. I almost got everyone killed and I couldn't even hurt him."

"Gaelan, *you're* not supposed to hurt him." Trey reached out and put his free hand on Gaelan's cheek, "*We're* supposed to hurt him. You're not supposed to do it by yourself! Let me tell you something. Nobody fucks with my family and gets away with it, and you're family Gaelan, whether you like it or not, you're my little brother now! My *family*!" Kedar was at the bedside next to Natalia. Sophie stood at the foot of the bed with tears in her eyes. Trey went on, "And family sticks together and fights together. So all you need to know now is that you don't get to do this alone. We'll do it together! And now we know he's out there, so we're gonna hunt that motherfucker down and tear him limb from limb! *Together*! Okay?" Trey gave Gaelan's hand one last squeeze, "Get some rest brother. We'll talk more later." He stood up and looked over to Natalia. She mouthed the words *thank you* through silent tears. Trey forced a smile and squeezed through everyone standing in the doorway. He went out into the hallway, leaned his head against the wall and cried. He cried and began punching the wall in anger. It wasn't until Kedar, Angel and Sophie came out and stopped him that he calmed down.

Inside the room, Niu had squeezed her way through the crowd and made her way to the sobbing Gaelan. She walked over to him and kissed him on the cheek, "Thank you."

He looked at her through watery, burning eyes and she smiled. She turned and walked back out.

Natalia remained by his side as Gaelan sobbed anew. She leaned over and kissed his forehead, whispering, "I'm not going anywhere this time."

Gaius had waited for the two men to arrive and took them straight to the Elders. They entered the darkened, vaulted chamber and stood in front of the ten thrones, "Tell them what you told me."

Gaius could see the hesitation in their faces and restated impatiently, "*Tell them.*"

Both men spoke in their native Chinese. The first one began, "My lords, we waited for the other masters to come back with the orphans. We watched the orphanage from several streets away. We saw others go in and figured the masters would…*dispatch*…them. Then we saw the same strangers come out with the orphans. The masters were nowhere to be seen."

The second man started, "Just when they were about to drive away, one of them ran into the field next to the orphanage. As he ran, he…" The man nervously looked around.

Gaius said in a more soothing voice, "You can tell them."

"He became a—a *werewolf.*"

One of the elders interrupted, "The wolves stole the prophet from us? They wish another war and eradication?"

"My lords, he hasn't finished." Gaius looked to the second man and nodded.

"He ran across the field and began fighting with *other* werewolves. And the others with him ran to help him, but they were human."

Several of the elders stood anxiously and one of the females thundered, "ARE YOU SURE?"

Both men dropped to their knees in terror, "YES MY LORDS! YES!"

The elders began speaking in Latin to one another, "It can't be." One of them turned to Gaius, "Gaius, you're aware of what this means?"

"I am my lords. The sheep in wolf's clothing has come."

One of the men on the floor quivered, "My lords, there was one more thing."

One of the male elders growled, "SPEAK!"

"The female human. She…she yelled a name to the werewolf."

"What was it?" Another female elder asked.

"It was Guy-ling…Gah-lon…"

"Gaelan?" Gaius' felt the knot in his stomach.

The elders glared at Gaius. The male in the middle leaned forward and hissed, "What do you have to say for yourself Gaius?"

He struggled for a moment, then grumbled, "If my lords will permit me, I'd like to go to Italy...for an espresso." The screams of the two witnesses followed Gaius out of the chamber.

Gaelan slept most of the next day. He finally awoke when Zhang came in to change his bandages.

"How are you feeling?" Zhang began unwrapping the bandages around his ribs.

"Weak. Sore. Like a failure." Gaelan clenched his fists. Natalia was asleep in the chair next to his bed. Angel had come in behind Zhang and walked over to lay a blanket over her.

"She's been there since we dragged you in here." Angel spoke while Zhang pulled back the bandage from Gaelan's chest. The wounds were deep, but he was beginning to heal, "Glad you changed back to human form before we had to get you in the back of the truck, cause I wasn't lifting your *hairy* fat ass."

Gaelan chuckled then winced, "Ahhh, don't make me laugh dickhead. By the way, how *did* we?..."

"I wasn't kidding. Zhang lit those things up with a Gatling!" Angel turned to Zhang, "And it was awesome and all, but I'm serious, we need to get you a different hobby!"

Zhang smiled, "I like my guns. And my trucks. And my trucks with guns on them. *Really* big guns!"

Gaelan sat up painfully and swung his legs over the side of the bed to face Zhang while he changed the bandages, "I seem to remember you shooting dozens of Cobalus from the top of a truck. Now your gunning down werewolves like you're on safari. What's gotten into you?"

Zhang smirked, "I just follow the old Chinese proverb."

"Which one's that?"

"Never bring fangs and claws to a minigun fight."

"*Fuuuuck*! Stop making me laugh." Gaelan grimaced and Angel snorted.

Zhang laughed and finished wrapping Gaelan, "What now? Is this thing about a prophecy real?"

"Far as we can tell." Angel chimed in.

"And that girl. She's…"

Zhang didn't even finish and Gaelan nodded, then asked, "Where is she?"

Angel walked around next to Zhang, "Resting right now. Zhang here translated when she was learning about her *destiny*."

"And how did that go over?"

"Like another old Chinese proverb." Zhang raised his eyebrows, "Like a fart in church."

"I'm gonna stretch my legs." Gaelan stood unsteadily and Zhang and Angel grabbed a hold of him.

Trey sat with Medhir, Sophie and Kedar in another room. Niu and Chēlún slept on the bed several meters away. He asked, "How's she doing?"

Medhir shrugged his shoulders, "About as well as can be expected. She laughed, then she cried, and she became serious and then she cried again."

"Poor girl. She has much to deal with." Sophie sympathetically gazed at her.

"It could be worse you know." Medhir was matter-of-fact and before anyone could ask how, he stated, "The vampires could have her."

Trey nodded, "That's a good point. And we still don't know how they knew where Niu was."

Gaelan walked in, supported by Angel and Zhang. Angel announced, "Look who decided to get out of bed."

Trey jumped up to help him over to a chair, "Here. Take it easy, okay?"

Gaelan sat down and looked at Trey, "I'm sorry. Really."

"I told you it's not important. Can I get you anything?" Gaelan shot him a bizarre and suspicious look. Trey was taken back, "What?"

"Stop being nice to me. It's weird."

"It's not weird." Trey snapped.

Gaelan looked around the room and everyone nodded.

"Totally weird, brother." Angel added.

"Told ya."

Trey shook his head, "Fine then, *dickwad*."

Gaelan shot back, "Fuck you, anal wart."

"Dude? Seriously?" Trey had a disgusted look on his face

"Too far?" Gaelan shrugged.

"Yeah, way too far." Trey grimaced.

"Is smegma-breath too far?" With that, Trey rolled his eyes. "Okay then. We'll stop just short of scrotum-zit."

Trey leaned forward with a scowl and said in a weary sarcastic tone, "I so totally hate you right now, so how's about I go get you a nice tall glass of shut-the-fuck-up and a plate full of your-welcome-for-saving-your-little-candy-ass!"

Gaelan smiled, "Awwww, you really *do* like me." He then looked around, "How are the rest of the girls doing?"

Zhang answered, "Confused, tired and scared. Junjie and I got them settled as best as we could. I had a guy I know make papers for those two so you can get them out of the country."

Kedar chimed in again, "We have our jet ready to leave within an hour of notification provided you are well enough to travel. Zhang and Junjie are going to take the other orphans someplace for their safety, until they can be taken out of the country."

Gaelan looked back to Zhang, "You've come a long way since we first met."

"Well, I needed something to do in between saving your life." Zhang teased, "It's getting to be a habit you know."

"Don't get cocky! But, seriously, don't ever quit either!" Gaelan grinned.

"It's not like I have better things to do or anything." Zhang continued to joke.

Gaelan felt a hand on his shoulder and looked up to see Natalia. He gazed at her fondly and laid his hand on hers.

Angel broke the momentary silence, "Meddi, how long do you think before she actually sees something?"

Medhir pondered for a moment, "I was much older than she was, but I also never had such potent visions as the ones she described. Most times I awoke not remembering much of what I had seen, but writing the same words down over and over. If she truly is the last prophet in this line, it may manifest itself in a different way. I would imagine that since her last vision has come to pass, she is ready for another."

"Do we need to put an antenna on her head or something?" Angel joked and Natalia whacked him in the arm with the back of her hand, "Owww, I was just kidding!"

Trey stood up and looked at Gaelan, "You think you can travel?"

"Yeah. I'm good."

"Alright then, let's get moving. Kedar, can you wake Niu?"

Zhang walked to Trey while calling to Kedar, "Wake Chēlún as well." He handed trey two sets of forged passports, "Good luck trying to separate the two of them." Everyone grabbed their gear and made their way to the vehicle. Trey and Junjie exchanged silent nods—*Welcome to the fight and I'll keep them all safe.*

At the airport, Gaelan waited for everyone to say their goodbyes to Zhang, then he embraced him, "Thank you! For everything!"

"By everything, you mean saving your life a second time?"

"You're not gonna let that one go, are you?"

"Never." Zhang smiled.

"You be careful and help out Junjie and the others."

"You be careful as well. And if you get a chance, figure out how to save the world." Zhang gave him a smile then left. Just a short time later, Gaelan, Natalia, Trey, Angel, Kedar, Sophie, Medhir, Niu and Chēlún were all on a charter jet back to France.

Lucos walked through the streets of Rome toward the coliseum. Something had been different in Gaius' voice this time. He could've refused the meeting, but he didn't. The ignorant bliss of the human herds both amused and disgusted him. He turned down a darkened alley that cut toward the café where they normally met. The smells of food and drink that inundated his senses faded, replaced by something familiar. He spotted Gaius standing at the far end of the alley and braced for the attack.

The first two vampires landed on him from the rooftops above. Two more landed behind him and another two rushed past Gaius. By the time Gaius reached what he thought was the vampires subduing Lucos, four of them were dead. The fifth vampire flew past him and splattered on the walls—half to his right and half to his left. Gaius watched as Lucos pinned the last vampire against the ground and punched right through its head, then tore a hole in its chest to crush its heart.

Gaius barely had time to breathe before Lucos pounced on him, grabbing him by the throat and slamming him into the alley wall. Gaius stared into Lucos' inhuman eyes. He could feel the claws around his neck. He went limp, fully submissive.

"YOU DARE LET THEM TOUCH ME?" Lucos growled, still contemplating a full change, "YOU LURED ME HERE GAIUS! YOU LURED ME INTO A TRAP!" He slammed Gaius against the wall.

Gaius gurgled a response, "You—left—me—no—choice."

Lucos spun and threw Gaius to the ground. Gaius rolled several times, then scurried backwards a little, waiting for the attack.

"No choice?" Lucos eyes and claws had receded, "NO CHOICE? I COME WHEN YOU CALL GAIUS! I SENT MY WOLVES WHEN YOU ASKED!" He took several breaths and calmed himself. His voice was full of disgust and betrayal, "You! You were the last one I thought would do this! And you tell me *I* left *you* no choice?"

"Gaelan Kelly." Gaius stood up, then bellowed, "GAELAN KELLY!" Now he stamped forward toward the man—the *thing*—that just tore six vampires apart, "You said he was dead. You told me that you looked for him. And now we know, for sure, that he is *alive*. He is alive and HE TOOK THE FINAL PROPHET!" Gaius was now screaming in Lucos face.

"I took the information your spies in the Vatican gave us. That was it."

"I asked you..."

"WHAT DID YOU WANT ME TO DO GAIUS?" Lucos bellowed, then lowered his voice, "What did you want me to do? You have all of the technology and networks at your disposal. Maybe you thought that I would have smelled his clothing and sniffed him out like the dog I am, eh?"

"He's a *werewolf*!" Gaius thought it was obvious.

Lucos began to laugh facetiously, "Is he? Really?"

"*Yes*!" Gaius huffed in frustration, "And I thought you would know how to find him." Lucos continued to laugh at him. Gaius looked at him and pleaded, "Please. The elders! They will..." He struggled to find the words, "I needed your help and now I have nothing."

Lucos' laughter trailed off and he stared at Gaius in pity and disgust "You lead this life of servitude, yet you could be so much more."

"Please Lucos."

"You never needed a werewolf to track him Gaius."

"I don't understand?" Gaius was even more confused.

"How do those elders you've decided to serve put so much faith in you?" Lucos shook his head in bewilderment, "Let me ask you this? If you needed to find a human, how would you do it?"

Gaius sounded frustrated, "I don't know? Track his bank accounts..."

"No, not like that. I mean a human in hiding. How do you do it?"

Gaius' eyes lit up, "Target his loved ones. Friends, family!"

"He's no werewolf Gaius. He's a Venator! If he still thinks he can be human, than you should treat him like one." Lucos turned to walk back up the alley.

Gaius called out, "Do you think he still has anyone he cares for?"

Lucos stopped and turned back to look at Gaius, "We all have somebody we still care about Gaius." He stared at Gaius intently, "All of us."

Gaius watched as Lucos turned and walked out of sight, then dropped his head and sighed.

Father Denny sat in his office drinking wine and thinking. He had finally heard from Trey that Gaelan was awake. Hearing Trey get choked up recounting Gaelan's confession had brought tears to Denny's eyes. He should be there for Gaelan—and for Trey. He should meet the young lady named Niu that might hold the key to the fate of the world! At least he had heard from all of the remaining Venántium teams that he had ordered to ground. For now, no more casualties or disappearances weighed on him. He was pouring himself a second glass when the door was kicked in. Several men rushed in followed by a smug-looking Cardinal Klug. Two men pinned Denny by the arms, shattering both the wine glass and bottle as they pulled him to his feet. Two other men stood by. Behind the Cardinal, Denny could see members of staff and other Council members, including Father Francesco Librizzi.

"Dieter, what's going on?" Denny bit back his anger.

Denny wanted to beat the smirk of Klug's face, "Well, well, well, Father Beaudreau. I finally get to tell you that you will pay for being a collaborator. We will finally prosecute you the way we should have when they first brought you here."

"What are you talking about?"

"One name Dennis—*Gaelan Kelly.*" Klug had a sinister grin across his face, "He was spotted in China."

"Who gave you the information Dieter?" Denny didn't try to deny it.

Cardinal Klug struck Denny across the cheek with the back of his hand, "SILENCE TRAITOR!"

"Deiter, you have to listen to me. Something is coming and neither the Venántium nor the Vatican will be able to stop it. Gaelan is our only hope."

"Remove this piece of filth." Cardinal Klug ordered.

As the men pulled him out in front of the onlookers, Denny looked to Father Librizzi, "FRANK! DON'T TRUST ANYONE HERE! TAKE CARE OF THE TEAMS!" He looked to the members of his staff, "PROTECT THE TEAMS!" He pulled against his captors as they dragged him away, "PROTECT THE TEAMS!"

The four men walked Denny down the corridors toward the holding cells. He waited until they came to a ninety degree turn in the hallway and made sure he got as close to the facing wall as he could. Just before the two men holding his arms guided him to the right, Denny kicked his foot out and pushed off the facing wall. He knocked himself and the two men holding him backward and to the ground. He rolled backwards and turned to punch the third man behind in the kneecap and the fourth in the groin. He came up with a knee to one's head and an elbow downward into the other's face. He turned and kicked one of the original guards in the face and grabbed the other and slammed his head into the wall. In seconds, four men were unconscious and Denny was standing face to face with Cardinal Dieter Klug. He stuck his hand out and grabbed Klug by the throat, "You're a *fucking traitor,* Dieter." The Cardinal stared at him with wide, fearful eyes. Denny threw him to the ground and ran.

He knew the alarm would be sounded and that the outer walls and exits would be guarded. Instead of heading straight out, he made a beeline toward St. Peter's Basilica. He wound his way through the grounds of the Vatican avoiding the security personnel looking for him. Once inside the Basilica, he immediately wove his way into a large group of tourists. He remained with the group, but watched the men waiting for him at the main gates to the city. Dennis looked around and noticed a young couple with a crying child within the group, then made his way toward them. He motioned toward the child with open arms, signaling he would like to help. The couple smiled at the priest and handed the child over. Denny smiled at the infant, rocked her up and down and blessed her on the forehead, ending in a kiss. The entire time, the group made it's way out of the city. The security personnel finally spotted him, but kept their distance while he held the child. Denny handed the baby back to the adoring couple and eyed the security personnel, now numbering at least a dozen, closing in on him.

As the tourist group waited to cross the road outside the city, Denny took off, dodging cars and narrowly escaping an oncoming bus. By the time the personnel were able to follow, Denny was winding his way through side streets and alleys to a parking garage not far from the city. He made his way to an old silver sedan, removed a lockbox from the undercarriage, and retrieved a large bag from the trunk. Inside were several changes of clothes, a burner phone, passports with aliases he could use, and over fifty thousand dollars in cash. He switched his clothes, grabbed a new phone and began driving toward France, dialing the phone as he sped away.

Gaelan took it easy in France, trying to heal his still fresh wounds. He sat in with Medhir and Niu, trying to translate and explain what he was and what she was. She was still trying to comprehend it all, but she at least felt there was some greater sense and purpose to her visions and nightmares. Knowing that monsters really existed was disconcerting, but knowing she may be able to help stop them motivated her to try to learn what she could from Medhir. Chēlún stayed by her side the entire time and was improving her novice understanding of English by listening intently as Gaelan translated.

Kedar and Sophie had retrieved some supplies from town. Trey, Angel and Natalia were discussing what their next move should be while they waited for Niu to complete the prophecy. Trey's phone rang while they talked, "Denny, we're drinking your wine. What's…" His smile fell, "What?" Then his face went taut, "Jesus Christ! Alright, we'll meet you there! Be careful!" Trey hung up the phone and darted toward the room where Gaelan was sitting with the others, Angel and Natalia following close behind.

Kedar and Sophie were sitting with Gaelan and the orphan girls when Trey walked in with an alarmed look on his face.

"What is troubling you?" Kedar asked.

"Denny was arrested by the Council."

"Arrested?" Almost everyone gasped in unison.

"He's on the run. He said he'll meet us in the States."

"Not here?" Angel asked.

Trey looked at Gaelan, "Gaelan, they know you're alive."

"Aunt Sarah!" Gaelan stood up.

"We know! You get in touch with her and have her hold tight. We'll charter the jet."

Angel shot up, "I'm on it. I'll let the pilots know to have the engines running."

The ride to the airport was quick and the jet was waiting for them. Gaelan called his Aunt twice before she finally picked up the phone.

"Hello?"

"Aunt Sarah, it's Gaelan!"

"Gaelan? It's four in the morning. Are you okay sweetie?" Her voice was tired.

Gaelan hadn't even thought about the time difference, "Aunt Sarah, I'm in France. I need you to listen to me and listen to me very carefully..."

"France? Gaelan, why... "

"AUNT SARAH, LISTEN TO ME! You're in danger. I can't explain it all right now, but I'll be there in a day. I just need you to get the family together and stay inside—*especially at night*. Just stay there and wait for me. Please Aunt Sarah, promise me you'll do this." Gaelan sounded frantic.

Sarah was now awake, "Danger? Gaelan honey, you're scaring me."

"Just please do it. I promise I'll explain when I see you, but lock yourself in and don't invite or let anyone in. Please Aunt Sarah!"

"Okay honey. Okay."

"Okay. Remember, don't *invite* or *let* anyone in. I'll see you in a day. I love you." Gaelan abruptly hung up and the group was looking at him, "I etched blessings in their foundation. If they stay inside, they should be okay." He sounded like he was trying to convince himself."

A young man walked down the aisle of the private jet, "Here's more of what you asked for, Sir."

Gaius looked up from the paperwork he was studying to take the documents the man offered, "All this time he was right under our noses. No one even thought to look into the disappearance of one of our elders on a feeding expedition."

"No one was looking for the name because they thought he was dead and…" The man hesitated.

"I know." Gaius sounded rueful, "I said I had *someone* looking into it." He then perused the other new documents, "Interesting. *Very interesting.*"

"What do you find so interesting?" Genevieve stirred and laid a hand on Gaius' shoulder stroking it seductively with her fingertips.

"The officer involved in detaining Mr. Gaelan Kelly was later taken by our missing elder, Jonas, but managed to survive the ordeal. Jonas was never seen again. I'm beginning to think that maybe we should have a conversation with the young lady."

Genevieve smiled, "Mmmmm, sounds delicious."

The flight to Columbus, Ohio took nearly ten hours. Gaelan didn't try to rest. They would be arriving at his aunt's house after dark it was only a matter of time before the wealthy, connected creatures managed to track down his only remaining family. He fidgeted for a little while, then took out his sword and knife and sharpened the blades. He put away the weapons and fidgeted more. Natalia came over, sat in the seat next to him, wrapped a blanket around her self and put her head on his shoulder. There were no words spoken, but the simple act calmed him down and got him to sit still. He finally nodded off, only to be awoken by the sound of the landing gear dropping. Natalia looked at him, squeezed his hand and nodded. He nodded back. By the time the jet was taxiing clear of the runway, they were itching to go.

Trey had decided that Kedar and Sophie would stay with Medhir, Niu and Chēlún at the airport and await Father Denny's arrival. Trey, Angel, Natalia and Gaelan grabbed the awaiting car and drove to Gaelan's Aunt's house.

"They're fine junior, I know they are." Trey said confidently. Gaelan's leg twitched as he silently nodded to Trey. Natalia put her hand on his leg to try to calm his nerves once more. It was early evening and the lights in the house were on when they pulled up. Gaelan led them up to the front door and looked at the foundation to either side. The blessings that he etched into the foundation were still intact and the door was locked, not kicked in. He held his breath as he rang the doorbell. When his Aunt Sarah opened the door, she didn't even have time to say anything before he wrapped his arms around her and picked her up in a huge embrace, breathing a sigh of relief.

She wrapped her arms around him, feeling his katana inside the saya strapped to his back, "Gaelan sweetie, what's wrong? You sounded panicked on the phone."

He didn't let her go, "I was worried. I can't let anything happen to you guys because of me."

He finally let her down, "Sweetie, we have to talk about this. You scared me on the phone. I feel like you're becoming delusiona..." She stopped herself before saying it as she noticed his friends, "Who is this?"

"Aunt Sarah, this is Trey, Angelo and Natalia. They're here to help me out."

Sarah eyed them suspiciously, "Why are they with you? What's going on?"

"Long story short, I've been helping people out and I've made a lot of enemies with the wrong kind of individuals. You're in danger and we need to get you out of here."

"Gaelan stop this." Her eyes glassed over, "We're not your parents and nothing is going to happen to us. We're not running off because you have some kind of notion that you're the target of the mafia or whatever you've imagined. And all of you…"

Before she could continue, Gaelan heard laughter from within the house, "Is everyone here?" He pushed in and went to the dining room.

"Gaelan!" Sarah called after him. Trey, Angel and Natalia walked in and followed Sarah toward the voices.

Gaelan walked around the corner, smiling as he saw his Uncle Bob with his cousins BJ and Linda. As Bob bellowed a happy welcome to him, the sound was muted by the beating of his own heart in his ears. A young man sat next to Linda on the far side of the table. They locked eyes, even as he returned Uncle Bob and BJ's embraces weakly. Linda was still sitting next to the man with a wide grin on her face saying something that Gaelan didn't even register. His blood ran cold

"GAELAN? Are you hearing us?" And Sarah followed him into the room—he hadn't heard a word she said. Gaelan kept his eyes on the man.

"Yeah, I hear you Aunt Sarah."

The man broke eye contact momentarily to observe Trey, Angel and Natalia behind Gaelan, while his cousin Linda called out, "Gaelan, this is Anthony."

The man's smile grew and seemed slightly sinister, "It's a pleasure to meet you." He held his seat next to Linda, his hand over her arm.

"I'm sure it is."

"GAELAN! What's wrong with you?" Aunt Sarah tried to scold Gaelan but he held out his arm and forced her behind him. He moved closer to the table and put Bob and BJ behind him as well. Trey, Angel and Natalia came up alongside his family members, giving Sarah an uncomfortable feeling, but now she was quiet, remembering his frantic phone call.

Gaelan's voice was calm but held a serious tone, "Linda, have you two known each other long?"

Linda was still all smiles, "Actually we met earlier this evening. A colleague of mine asked if I could give him a ride home. He doesn't live far from here and I..."

"Invited him in. You invited him into the house to meet everyone, right?" Gaelan knew the answer before it was said.

"Yeah, of course. Anthony lives right near here and I thought I would introduce him to everyone since he said he would love to meet them."

"Uh-huh," Gaelan spoke to Linda with his eyes still on Anthony, "and I'm sure you met him after sunset."

"Yeah, we met in the lobby of my building at the end of the day. It was..."

Gaelan cut her off and addressed Anthony, his voice now menacing, "You dare come near my family? My only remaining family?"

"They were just going to be a means to an end, just to bring you out. But now..." Anthony seemed at a loss for words, "I can't tell you what an honor it is." Linda winced at the vice-like grip on her arm.

"Gaelan, Linda!" Aunt Sarah cried out, sensing her daughter's fear. Bob went to take a step forward but Trey pulled him back.

"Anthony!" She struggled, "You're hurting me!"

Gaelan's voice was now menacing, "You shouldn't have come alone."

Anthony now smiled widely. Sarah and Bob could swear they saw points at the end of his teeth. He coldly responded, "I didn't."

BJ called out, "MOM, DAD, THE WINDOWS!"

Sarah, Bob, Trey, Angel and Natalia looked at the inhuman faces in all of the surrounding windows. Gaelan didn't move his head, but simply shifted his eyes right and left. Rage built inside him. His eyes came back to Anthony and he coldly rasped, "That's better."

The power to the house suddenly cut out and Trey pulled Bob and BJ back. Angel grabbed Sarah and Natalia rushed forward as a thunderous crash shook the house accompanied by an agonizing shriek and a window shattering. Natalia grabbed Linda in the dark, who screamed when she realized that Anthony was no longer beside her, despite his hand still gripping her forearm.

"GET TO THE CAR!"

Trey pulled out a pistol and Angel and Natalia had stakes. Linda yelled out, "WHAT ABOUT GAELAN?" Everyone could hear the yelling and screaming from the side of the house. When they burst out of the front door, two vampires were on the front lawn waiting for them, their faces inhuman. They had time only to take one step toward Gaelan's family and friends when two more came flying out from the side of the house, hitting the lawn and rolling several feet. Gaelan crashed after them with his sword in hand. He landed on the closest prone vampire, stabbing it through the heart. The other two vampires pounced.

Sarah, Bob, BJ and Linda were being dragged towards the car as they watched Gaelan behead a man, then run him through with the sword. He grabbed the next man by the throat with his free hand, lifted him up and slammed him, back first, into the lawn. From the car, they watched as Gaelan used both hands to press his katana through the figure's neck, then turn the sword vertical and easily push it into the man's chest cavity. Sarah gasped, while Linda began to mutter, "Oh God, oh God...", BJ and Bob stared, the latter, mumbling, "What in God's name?"

"HANG ON!" Trey tossed his pistol to Natalia in the passenger seat, then slammed the vehicle in reverse. Sarah and her family turned and watched as the other prone figure, with one limb severed midway up the forearm, tried crawling from Gaelan. He grabbed Anthony by his ankle, yanked him up and swung him like a ragdoll over his head, slamming him into the ground on his other side. They could hear through closed windows as Gaelan bellowed, "YOU SHOULD'VE LEFT MY FAMILY ALONE!" As they pulled away, they watched him jump on Anthony and begin to flail at his chest with his bare hands. They were too far to see Gaelan finally get to Anthony's heart and devour it.

Trey made it to the end of the block when another vampire jumped on the hood of the SUV, it's fanged face grinning ear to ear. Sarah and her whole family screamed as Natalia shot it through the windshield and watched as it rolled off onto the hard street below. They all turned to see the figure push itself up and begin running after the car, "JESUS CHRIST!" BJ screamed. As Trey made another turn they continued to watch the figure running after them, only to catch a quick glimpse of another figure barreling into him from the side, sending him flying. Bob questioned it aloud, "Gaelan?" Trey drove aggressively back to the airport as Natalia and Angel kept watch for more vampires.

It took Gaelan just over an hour to find his way back to the airport. His clothes were dirty with several tears from claws, and he carried his katana in his saya over his back. Father Denny had arrived, and he and Trey were waiting for him. Gaelan gave Father Denny a bear hug. Trey handed him clean clothing, "You good?"

Gaelan asked, "You get them out okay?"

"Yup."

"Then I'm good."

"What now?" Trey shifted his look between the two of them.

"We gotta get somewhere safe." Denny said.

"France?" Gaelan asked.

"Did you grab their passports while you were back there?" Trey asked in reply.

Gaelan winced, "FUCK!"

Denny interjected, "It doesn't matter. They can't travel under those names anyway. It'll give us all away. We have to stay in the States until I get them new papers."

"How about New York...Tom?" Gaelan asked.

"He and Carly helped us out before." Trey agreed.

Father Denny's eyes went wide, "Shit kiddo—Carly!" Gaelan didn't understand at first, *Your arrest!*

"I was never processed!" Gaelan's heart skipped a beat.

"But you were brought in. If they know you're alive and have the resources…"

"They'll put two and two together!"

Trey spoke up, "We gotta warn Tom, but we can't bring Niu there! We need a safer place to go!"

Trey was right, "Okay, I'll take one jet and go to New York. You guys take my family, Niu, Chēlún and Meddi in the other jet, but where?"

Trey looked at Gaelan, knowing the idea wouldn't go over well, "Michigan."

Gaelan paused for a moment, then protested, "No!"

Denny asked, "Michigan?"

Trey looked to Denny, "The mom and daughter from the werewolves in Canada!"

Gaelan corrected him, "Their names are Jennifer and Becca Guerin and they've been through enough."

Trey made his argument, "They're off the Venántium radar and they at least know me."

Father Denny added, "He's right kiddo. If they're trustworthy and off the grid, we need to take a chance."

Gaelan reluctantly nodded, "Just be careful."

"We will. I'm going to talk to our pilots." Trey turned and hurried inside.

Gaelan looked to Father Denny, "I have to go talk to my Aunt." Father Denny nodded and Gaelan added, "I'm glad you're here and you're alright." They walked through the terminal building and into the hangar. Kedar and Sophie had gathered Gaelan's relatives, Niu, Chēlún and Medhir near the chartered jets.

Aunt Sarah, Bob, BJ and Linda all stood and walked toward Gaelan. Bob had a look of apprehension, BJ of awe, and Linda was smiling with tears still in her eyes. But Aunt Sarah had no emotion on her face as she walked towards him. The rest of her family stopped several feet away while she went up to him. She made no effort to embrace him. She just stood and looked at him.

Gaelan broke the silence, "Are you all okay?"

"Okay Gaelan? You called and said people after you may target us, then you turn our house into a warzone and then you ask..." the volume of her voice gradually escalated, "iF WE'RE OKAY? WE'RE NOT FUCKING OKAY GAELAN!" He wasn't used to his aunt cursing at him, "Some weirdo used Linda to get to you, SO NO, SHE'S NOT FUCKING OKAY!" She was breathing hard, "I think we all watched you decapitate a man, SO NO, NONE OF US IS *FUCKING OKAY* GAELAN!" Tears formed in her eyes, "We want to go home and your friends won't take us."

Gaelan shut his eyes and grimaced, knowing the news wasn't going to be taken well, "You can't go home." He opened his eyes to meet her glare, "It's not safe."

"Safe from *who*, Gaelan?"

"Not *who. What.*" He sighed, "Those weren't people I killed back there..."

"STOP IT! JUST STOP IT!" By this time, Trey and Angel had come back and walked over near Denny. The entire group was listening, "I'M NOT BUYING INTO YOUR DELUSIONS!" The tears began streaming down her face as she lowered her voice, "I'm sorry that my sister—that your parents—died the way they did. But you don't get to bring turmoil into our lives and then have your friends tell me some story about monsters trying to end the world, SO JUST STOP!" The tears rolling down her cheeks did little to hide her contempt.

Gaelan didn't have time to sugar coat it and his tone was a bit curt, "Aunt Sarah, the fact of the matter is whatever you want to believe, those *things*, now know that they can use you to get to me. And whether you want to believe us or not, you can't go home because it's not safe!"

Sarah glared at him for several seconds before suddenly slapping him across the face, "GODDAMN YOU GAELAN! YOU BROUGHT THIS ON US!" She began to weep as Bob rushed forward to both restrain and comfort her. He wrapped his arms around her and pulled her back as she screamed once more, "GODDAMN YOU TO HELL!" Then she broke down sobbing.

Gaelan felt flush from embarrassment and anger. His eyes welled up and he looked at the ground in humiliation, then turned to go talk to the aircrew of the other plane. He walked slowly, with his shoulders hunched in shame. His aunt's words resonated in his head. *God—damn—me.* He made it several steps with everyone watching before he stopped and defiantly stood upright. His body seemed to twitch a little before he turned to look back at his aunt. His eyes were an unearthly glow of yellow and red. His jaw looked swollen with sharpened teeth and prominent fangs. His voice was inhuman as he scowled at her, "HE ALREADY HAS!" Sarah's jaw dropped in fear and disbelief. Bob and BJ stared in horror and amazement, and Linda gasped and covered her mouth in an attempt to stifle a scream.

Gaelan closed his eyes and concentrated, feeling his teeth recede. When he reopened his eyes, they were back to their normal blue. His nostrils flared as he repeated. *"He already has!"* He turned abruptly and stormed out of the hangar.

Father Denny walked over to Sarah and her family, holding his arm out and pointing at the chartered jet, "Get on the plane! Now!"

Natalia caught Gaelan in the hallway that connected the hangar and the lobby, "Hey!" She grabbed his arm and, unable to turn him, pulled herself in his path. She could see in his face that he was struggling to choke back his emotions. She said nothing more, but pulled him in and hugged him tightly. He rested his head on top of hers and trembled. He trembled in anger, frustration, sadness and fear. His body slowly settled and he held her, squeezing her tight.

Angel walked in, "Natalia?" She looked around Gaelan and gave him a gentle headshake. Angel gave her a half smile and nod in return and walked back out, letting the others know that she was going with Gaelan.

Both jets were airborne within thirty minutes.

CHAPTER 18
CONSEQUENCES

Gaius stepped off of the plane into the crisp Long Island night. He sniffed the fresh air then turned and offered a hand to Genevieve, "M'lady."

"Gaius, you're such a gentleman." She took his hand and held it as she descended the stairs.

"Talk, *errand-boy*!" A tall and good-looking man in a long black leather coat commanded.

"Watch your tongue..." Genevieve stepped forward to defend Gaius but Gaius stopped her.

"M'lady, it's alright." Gaius turned and bowed his head to the vampires awaiting his arrival, "My lords, time is of the essence."

"You don't know the half of it, *boy*. We received word that the *sheep*—the target's family—escaped. We can only assume that *he* is the reason. We are no better off than when we started." The head vampire didn't try to hide his distain for the elders' emissary.

"My lords, allow me a few minutes. Please." Gaius walked back to the jet. The vampires leered at Genevieve condescendingly. Finally, one took a step toward her, and she flicked her hand as if swatting a fly. The ground beneath the vampire seemed to liquefy and move like a large wave beneath him, throwing him back several yards. No other vampire approached her.

Several minutes later, Gaius emerged from the jet. He acknowledged Genevieve first, with a warm smile, "M'lady." Then he turned to the vampires, "My lords, shortly after the target escaped with the others, five different chartered jets took off from the nearby airport. One to Spain, one to Atlanta, one to Aspen, one to Muskegon, Michigan, and one to LaGuardia Airport here in New York."

"Stop boring me mortal. What are your intentions?" The head vampire snarled.

Genevieve looked to Gaius in an affectionate awe. He turned back to the vampire, "My personnel will send a dispatch to all loyalists in those areas. I'll also have them look into buses and trains that left that area. In the meantime, we'll stay here and continue looking into what we came for." Gaius turned to Genevieve and, in an action uncharacteristic of his normal protocol, he extended his hand. She took it with grin and held it while they walked to the nearest car. The head vampire let out a low growl and followed them.

Gaelan sat facing Natalia in the back of the jet. She looked at her watch, "Rabbi Feinstein will meet us when we land. Any word from the others?"

Gaelan looked out the window when he responded, his voice apathetic, "Father Denny was trying Tom but there wasn't any pickup. I tried Carly and it went to voicemail. I left a message right before we took off." He continued to stare out the window and gave a pathetic little laugh, "I did get in touch with Mr. Rosen, but he told me that both Rabbi Saul and I are delusional, and that I need help. That's the second time tonight I've been called crazy."

Natalia leaned forward and took his hands in hers, "She shouldn't have said those things to you."

He turned his head abruptly to look at her, "Shouldn't she? I *did* bring this on them. Their lives as they know them are over and that's on me." He looked away again, adding in disgust, "She was right."

Natalia lifted one hand, gently laid it on his cheek and turned his head back to her, "And would you have changed what we did? Would you have sacrificed everything we've learned? Would you rather their lives as they know it be over when a—what was it? An *eternal darkness*, is unleashed upon the world? No Gaelan," She caressed his cheek with her thumb, "she was *wrong*. You didn't bring this upon them and she shouldn't have said those things. They are alive because of you and life as we all know it is over regardless." Gaelan forced a smile and Natalia crossed over to sit next to him. Once more, she leaned her head on his shoulder and closed her eyes.

The knock at the door caught Jennifer Guerin off guard. A single nod sent Becca into the coat closet with a double-barrel shotgun, waiting to hear her Mom's all clear. Jennifer looked through the peephole and then swung the door open, "Trey, right?"

Trey answered, "Yes Ms. Guerin."

"I told you, it's Jennifer! And," She smiled widely with an ironically welcoming voice, "you're *not* welcome in my house."

"And I'd never ask to be let in." He smiled and walked through the threshold. He was taken back when she threw her arms around him and hugged him. He added, "I was expecting to be told to piss off."

"I told you, any and all hunters are always welcome here!" She squeezed him tight. He squeezed her back before being forcefully pushed away, "Wait! Is this about Gaelan?"

"Uhhhh, yes and no."

"Did you hurt him? Is he okay?"

Becca came running out of the closet, "DID YOU HURT GAELAN?" Trey backed off, "Okay, first off, we have a lot of catching up to do. Second," He looked at Becca, older than he remembered, "you are horrible at staying hidden. We have to work on that. Third, he's fine, but he's not happy that I'm here getting you two involved."

"You two are working together now?" Jennifer gave Trey a suspicious look.

"It's like a wise and beautiful woman once told me," He gave her a mischievous grin, "he's no more a werewolf than she or I."

"Well," Jennifer subconsciously played with her hair, "she sounds like a fantastic lady. Now what's this you mean about Gaelan not wanting you to come."

"Were you serious about all hunters being welcome?"

"Yeah, why?"

Trey stepped to the doorway and waved, then a large van pulled up into her driveway and eleven other people piled out as if from a clown car, including two young Asian girls, one in a wheelchair. When they were all inside, Trey looked at her again, "Like I said, we have a lot of catching up to do."

Jennifer looked everyone up and down and turned to Becca, "Sweetie, call for pizza cause I sure as hell ain't cooking."

A Michigan state trooper drove up to the private aviation fuel and services business at the Muskegon airport. He casually walked in and tipped his hat to the man behind the counter, "Evening."

"Evening officer, what can I do you for?"

"Oh, I'm just checking in on a tip about possible human smuggling on a chartered jet. You wouldn't happen to have seen a group traveling with a young Chinese girl, would you?" He could tell from the rapid change in the man's facial expression what the answer was.

"Yes sir!" The service attendant said excitedly, "Matter of fact, there was a group of maybe twelve or so that flew in on a Gulfstream not much more than an hour ago. They had two Asian girls with them! Don't know for sure that they were Chinese, but they seemed very out of it. Kinda twitchy if you ask me."

"You don't say! You know which way they went?"

"No sir. They had a rented van delivered. One of those big ole' fifteen passenger jobbies. They crammed in and left in a hurry."

"Thanks. You've been a big help." The trooper nodded his hat again and walked out.

Once he was in his car, he dialed his phone, "I think I have them landing here at Muskegon and leaving in a fifteen pax van. I'll check the security footage and get a plate number, then you can try and track which way they went."

Rabbi Saul Feinstein met Gaelan and Natalia as soon as they debarked their jet. He gave them both a big hug and then shot Gaelan a fearful look.

"What?"

"I haven't heard from Carly or Tom. I tried reaching out to Seth Rosen and he shut me down."

"Me too. Let me see something." Gaelan checked his phone and there was no message from Carly. He sent her another one:

Hey! It's Gaelan.
In New York now.
Need to see you—IMPORTANT!

He looked back up to Natalia and Saul, "Alright, let's get Rosen and get out of the city."

They had taken only a few steps when the response to his text came.

On my way to Murphy's Law.
Can you come?
Something not right—worried!

Gaelan showed the text to the others. Natalia started, "Go. Take the train and get out there. We'll get Rosen and meet you there."

"Keep my sword and knife and bring them with you." Gaelan knew that carrying such things would make him conspicuous on the train.

Natalia protested, "What if there are more?"

He forced a smile, "You know me. I'll improvise!"

She nodded tensely.

"You heard the lady—Go!" Saul shooed him on his way. Gaelan turned to walk away, then stopped abruptly. He turned back to look at Natalia with a scared expression on his face. Without a word, he walked back to her, took her face in his hands and pressed his lips to hers. She closed her eyes and kissed him back for what seemed like an eternity. Their tongues and lips parted as they leaned their foreheads together, eyes still shut, breathing heavily.

She whispered passionately, "Come back to me."

"I will." He lifted his head, kissed her on the forehead and left.

Natalia looked at the huge grin on Saul's face and asked defensively, "What?"

"I called it! I totally called it." He walked toward their vehicle singing the tune from the musical, Fiddler on the Roof, "*Matchmaker, matchmaker, make me a match…*"

"Just get in the damn car!"

Jennifer Guerin had Trey move the van into her garage and made room for everyone to sit down in her living room. No one had realized just how hungry they were, but eight pizzas and multiple bags of chips and cans of soda and beer later, they were finally ready to talk. Jennifer and Becca wanted to hear everything.

After a jumbled retelling, Jennifer motioned to Medhir and started to sum things up. "So he is a prophet that you found on a hunt when you were trying to rob a bank to get back at a 'syndicate' led by vampires that is a lot more organized than you ever thought?"

Trey replied through another bite of pizza "Yup!"

She looked over at Niu and Chēlún giggling with Becca. Though neither could speak much English, Becca had made them feel at home by painting their nails and putting temporary tattoos of flowers and hearts on their cheeks. Jennifer motioned to them, "And

Niu over there is the last prophet who will predict how the world is going to end?"

Father Denny took a gulp of a beer, "More about how they will try to end the world, which will give us the chance to stop them."

Jennifer looked around to Angel, Kedar and Sophie, "And you're all working with Gaelan on this?"

Angel cocked his head. "I'm going to have to correct you. *He* is working with *us* on this." Trey laughed bumped fists with Angel.

Jennifer asked Sophie, "And Sophie, you're a..." She was looking for the right word.

"She's gifted in elemental powers." Trey raised his eyebrows towards Sophie, quite impressed with himself.

She stood up, walked over and kissed him on the cheek with a smile, then sat back down next to Kedar, "I am a *witch*."

"Hey, language missy!" Angel joked.

Jennifer then asked Father Denny, "And you..."

Before she could finish, Trey answered, "Are Yoda." He mocked the character's voice, "*When bright the full moon is, hero Gaelan will become. Truuuuuust in him you must.*"

Father Denny made sure the girls weren't looking and gave Trey the finger. They all laughed.

Sarah interjected from the corner of the couch, "Have you all lost your minds?"

Angel didn't miss a beat, "Yeah, but I found mine. These guys, though..."

"I'M SERIOUS!" Sarah scolded him.

Jennifer's voice was calm, "I take it you're just learning about this?"

"About *this*?" She motioned her hands to everyone in the room, "What is *this*? Everything you're talking about is nonsense!"

"Sweetheart, we all saw..." Bob tried to calm her down.

"WE DON'T KNOW WHAT WE SAW?"

Niu and Chēlún looked at Becca to try to ascertain what was going on. Becca motioned to the adults, made a face while rolling her eyes, and continued to paint the toenails of her giggling guests.

BJ chimed in, "Mom, we saw those things."

"We don't know what we saw!" Sarah cut him off again. Sophie stood up and went to the kitchen.

"MOM! Gaelan saved my life. We saw him—*change*!" Linda was less mindful of her mom's feelings.

"You saw Gaelan change?" Jennifer looked at her wide-eyed, and Becca spun to see Sarah's face as well. Then they saw Trey, Angel, Kedar, Sophie and Father Denny all shaking their heads in unison. Jennifer looked back to Sarah, "Oh. You saw something, but *you'll know* when Gaelan changes." Sophie came back with the potted fichus from the kitchen and set it down in the living room.

"You mean there's more?" Linda was shocked.

"This is ridiculous. We were in shock and our eyes were playing tricks on us!" Sarah turned her head in disgust and buried her brow in her hand.

"Mom!" She ignored BJ's cry.

"Sweetheart!" Bob called this time, but she waved him off with her other hand.

"MOM!" The sound of Linda's voice finally caught her attention and she spun to see what was the matter. What she saw was a long thin branch of the fichus unnaturally extended, moving like a snake in her face. It reached out and tenderly caressed her cheek, then slithered its way back to the pot, receding to its normal length. Sarah turned her stunned gaze to Sophie, whose pitch black eyes slowly were just turning back to normal.

Sophie gave a little smile and shrug, "*Witch*."

Sarah broke down and began to sob in her hands. Bob rubbed her back to comfort her. The room was silent as she looked up with tears streaming down her face. She gazed from Jennifer to Sophie to Trey, and finally to Father Denny. Her voice cracked in fear and despair, "What really killed my sister?"

As her family huddled around her, Father Denny told them the story of what happened to Gaelan and his parents. He was telling them about Gaelan transforming in front of him in the high school chapel when they were interrupted by a knock at the door.

Seth Rosen sat in his office in Downtown Manhattan. He had watched the sun set above the cityscape hours before, and was working late to catch up on the backlog of client investment portfolios he'd neglected while he was helping Gaelan. *A wild damned goose chase* he thought to himself. *And that crackpot rabbi—monsters?* He felt anger and then the pangs of pity stir inside him. *With all the traumatic events Gaelan had experienced in his young life, it's no wonder he's having delusions. God only knows if he's buying into the mad ravings of some other lunatics.* He was lost in thought when a voice behind him brought him back to his office.

"Night Seth." Rosen turned to see his colleague, thirty-six-year-old Michael Lipinski, waving to him as he headed to the elevator.

"Working late too Mike?" Rosen answered.

"Yup. Never ends, does it?" Lipinski added.

"Never does. Have a good night." Time to head out. Rosen pulled on his cashmere overcoat, threw a scarf over his shoulders and headed to the elevator.

Most people had gone home already so no one disrupted the ride down seventeen floors. Rosen had begun whistling along with the acoustical version of *Wind Beneath My Wings* playing over the speaker. He was looking down, examining a smudge on his wingtip, when the elevator doors opened at the garage level. His whistle continued for a microsecond even as he raised his head and caught sight of the unthinkable—Just across the lane that separated the elevator doors from the first row of cars, Michael Lipinski was hanging limp in the arms of another man, his briefcase on the ground. The man's face was leaning into the side of Lipinski's neck, and his head seemed to be twitching rhythmically. Dark fluid soaked through the collar and shoulder of Michael's jacket—*blood.* Rosen thought about a number of things: yelling, reaching for his phone to call 911, running, getting back in the elevator. But the man—the *thing*—dropped the now lifeless body of his throat-torn colleague. He could see at least three other bodies littering the empty parking spaces. The thing took a step toward him. Behind it were more just like it. They looked at him with those inhuman faces. The eyes, the distended jaw, the fangs—*They weren't crazy!*

Jennifer looked through the peephole at the state trooper standing impatiently outside. She tucked her pistol into the back of her pants. Trey came up beside the doorframe next to her with his weapon drawn, looking at her apologetically. She opened the door cautiously, "Yes officer. Is something wrong?" She had put on her best innocent-girl voice.

"Ma'am, there's an Amber Alert on a van carrying an abducted Chinese girl. Video footage shows the vehicle passing through here and not leaving. We're doing a house-to-house canvas to look for the two young ladies."

When the officer said "we", Jennifer looked over his shoulder to see two men in business suits standing with their arms folded.

"Would you mine if we came in to have a look?" The trooper was courteous.

Jennifer could sense Trey's tension through the doorframe, "It's a free country, right?" She took a step back and turned sideways, as if to invite him in without saying it.

"Ma'am, I need you to invite me in officially. You know, for legal reasons." He smiled graciously.

"Oh, I understand." Jennifer said. She looked to the side of the door and could see Trey's anxious face as he shook his head emphatically. She reached over by him, "Here, let me turn on the lights." With that, Jennifer flipped the switch next to Trey's shoulder and the screeching and shrieking began. She went to slam the door, but the trooper thrust his foot forward and blocked it from closing. Trey didn't miss a beat, shooting the trooper through his instep to make him withdraw. Kedar ran forward and slid next to Jennifer, kicking the door closed and covering it with his sidearm. Angel and Sophie kept watch on the others.

Trey looked to Jennifer, "What the fuck was that?"

"Last time you visited," She was speaking as she secured the several bolts on the door, "you saw the UV spotlight outside the door, *remember?*"

Trey heard the man scream and the remnants of the other shrieking subside. He looked at her despondently, "I'm so sorry we brought this on you."

"Sweetheart, just keep my baby safe and all is forgiven."

Trey looked to Kedar, "K, find some stuff we can use, and fast!" Kedar nodded and took off toward the kitchen. Trey called out, "Angel!" But Angel was already taking Kedar's place. Trey looked at him, "We gotta get outta here. See what we're up against."

"On it!" Angel said as he began scurrying to the windows to peer outside.

Trey looked back to Jennifer, "You got anything else in here we can use?"

"Holy water and a UV lantern with a few more pistols. Gaelan insisted." Her voice was scared but collected.

Father Denny was already by them, "Where?"

"In the closet, top shelf. Becca's double barrel is in the back right corner with a box of shells, all blessed." Father Denny took off toward the closet.

"God I love that kid sometimes!" Trey turned to Jennifer, "Don't ever tell him I said that!"

This time Jennifer had more fear in her voice, "Just get my baby out of here alive, okay?"

Trey knew Gaelan was right. They never should've come. He looked at Jennifer, "I'm getting you both out of here, along with everyone else."

Jennifer forced a smile at him as they barricaded the door.

Outside the house, the two vampires standing behind the trooper sizzled in the UV light. The trooper had tried to force his way in, but yelped in pain as he fell back with a bullet hole in his foot. He quickly hobbled back toward the two creatures he served, only to be pounced on by one. It tore into his throat and insatiably fed. The other vampire bellowed, "NO!"

The feeding vampire looked up, dropping the twitching trooper to the ground, "What?"

"He was the only one that could cross the threshold. Now we need to get them out."

"So we burn them out!" The vampire's grin dripped with the blood of the trooper.

"We need the prophet you fool."

"Then don't make it too hot! Slow smoke and heat. That'll bring them out."

The first vampire nodded and turned to the others, more than a dozen, ordering them to make torches.

Gaelan ran from the train station to *Murphy's Law*. The lights in the bar were on and there were a few vehicles in the lot. He breathed a sigh of relief until he opened the door. The smell hit him immediately—*Death*! He walked in, leaving the door open behind him. Once inside, time seemed unnaturally slow as he took in the carnage all around. He could see five bar patrons, a middle-aged couple at a table, and two men and one woman at the bar, all dead. Most of the bodies had their throats torn open, skin peeled back in places, some dismembered, but with little blood around them. The woman at the bar had been torn open at the midsection and many of her organs were missing.

Gaelan's heart was racing. *Tom?* He placed both hands on the bar and swung his legs to the side, up and over. He landed in a pool of blood. *Tom!* Gaelan stood motionless, looking down at the decapitated corpse of Tom Murphy. He knelt down and gripped Tom's hand, bile rising to the back of his throat. He leaned forward and gently closed the eyelids on the head, *torn*, not severed, from the body. Gaelan's eyes watered over, knowing that he had somehow brought this on everyone. He held the hand of a man who celebrated his return from combat when he came home a broken veteran. A man who knew Gaelan before he was attacked by a werewolf. A man who, in a show of sheer blind faith, had helped Father

Denny stop Trey and his team from killing him. A man who had helped them discover the slaughterhouse, and who had helped Carly through the rough times. *CARLY!*

Gaelan solemnly placed a hand on Tom's chest, then called Carly's number. He was still crouched behind the bar when he heard her phone trill somewhere in the bar. From his crouch, Gaelan bounded up and cleared the bar with little effort. He thought he was going to be searching for Carly's phone, or worse yet, her corpse. Instead, he now looked her in the eyes. A firm hand gripped the back of her hair and another pinned her arm behind her back. Tears streamed down her cheeks. Seven men and three women, stood between him and the wide-open entrance to the bar. Two of the women were dressed in black suits, while the other was dressed in lace, and stood just behind the man in front.

Carly whimpered, "Tom?" Gaelan shook his head, a world of sadness in his eyes. Then he shifted his gaze to the well-dressed man standing in front of the group. It was a face he recognized. Any remnants of sadness turned to rage as he growled, "Let—her—go!"

"Gaelan. Gaelan Kelly." The man's voice was cordial, even inviting. He turned to the others with him and smiled, "I feel like we're meeting a legend." He turned back to Gaelan, "I'm sorry, you'll have to forgive me, but I am a big fan." He clasped his hands together in praise. "Oh, where are my manners, my name is Gaius and…"

"I know who you are." Gaelan glared, once more shifting his gaze to Carly, then back to Gaius, "Medhir told us about you. You're a fucking leech!" Gaelan glared at him.

"Ahhhh, Medhir. How is he? I do miss our conversations." Once again Gaius sounded as if he were chatting over dinner "And he did love my bread and soup recipes. I actually miss cooking for him, but alas, you seemed to have taken him along with something else that belongs to us." The smile faded from his face as he raised his eyebrows.

Gaelan was holding back as much as he could, "You're not going to lay a finger on Niu! You're never going to see Medhir again! And you have three seconds to let her go!" Gaelan motioned to Carly, but before he could continue, she called out.

"Gaelan, RUN!" More tears streamed down her cheek as the vampire holding her, the same one that had insulted Gaius at the airport, squeezed the back of her neck to silence her.

Gaelan barked in return, "LET HER GO!"

"Gaelan, *my friend,* you know I can't do that. As good as you are, and we do know you're good," He looked around with a smile and nod, "I mean, all of the processing facilities, the bank, the orphanage. My goodness Gaelan, you're amazing! But as luck, or *fate,* would have it, all good things must come to an end." Gaius' smile was cold. "You see, right now we have some of our, uhhh, *people,* up at that little house in Michigan."

"I will tear every one of you apart if anything…"

"IT'S ALREADY HAPPENING GAELAN!" Gaius' tone was curt. "Forgive me please, but I need you to know now, that it's over. Your offensive, the small victories, the luck—it's all *over.*" Gaius looked at him with contempt. "You were never going to win my friend. Surrender now, accept your fate, and one phone call will ensure quick deaths for your comrades—your friends—your family. Resist, and…" Gaius winced at the prospect. The other vampires began to move in.

Gaelan looked to Carly again and her eyes said everything—*run while you can.* She knew something. Then she broke her gaze and looked at the floor to the side where the vampire restrained her, mumbling, "Finally a vampire gets to be a human's bitch!"

The vampire holding Carly turned her and bared his fangs to her face. She had seen the vampires chagrin at Gaius' commands.

Gaelan took a step forward, "DON'T YOU FUCKING TOUCH HER!"

Gaius spun and hissed at the vampire restraining Carly, "Control yourself!"

Carly whispered more taunts through gritted teeth, "That's right *fido.* Be a good boy and listen!"

The vampire pulled Carly to the side and barked at Gaius, "DO NOT PRESUME TO ORDER ME, BOY!"

Carly seized the opportunity, clasping her hands together and swinging her arms around into the monster's forearm. It was enough to knock its grip free and let her fall to the floor. She reached down to the ankle holster that they didn't even bother to check her for. Before they could pounce, she had drawn her weapon. She rolled and fired three shots before the gun was knocked to the ground and she was pulled to her feet by her hair. Genevieve screamed, "NO!"

Gaius stumbled one step backward and looked down at the three holes in his chest and stomach.

Angel slid up next to Trey and Jennifer, "I count at least eight, probably more, surrounding the house."

"Okay, but they can't come in." Trey chambered a round.

"That's not all." Angel added. "Torches. They're going to burn us out."

Father Denny scurried up alongside them and handed Angel a pistol, "They don't want to hurt Niu. They need her."

"Then they'll smoke us out. Wait til it gets bad." Angel surmised.

Trey nodded, "Then tell us we can go if we surrender Niu." He saw the look on Jennifer's face, thinking of her daughter, and added, "And as soon as they had her, they'd burn us all or tear us to shreds as we tried to flee."

Jennifer ran her hand threw her hair, "Oh God!"

Trey put a hand on her shoulder then looked to Angel and Denny, "What about the van? It's in the garage. We pack in and make a break for it!"

Angel shook his head, "They positioned their cars on the driveway to block our access to the road."

"Sophie can take care of that. I know she can." Trey insisted.

Denny knew the odds, "I'm sure she can, but we'll still be too slow. We only have one UV lantern and it won't last long. If there's eight or more, they'll swarm us from all directions. They'll get the tires, then the windows. Even with the pistols, they'll start picking us off before we could get clear. We either have to whittle down their numbers or…"

Trey interjected, "We'll need a distraction that will let the van get clear!"

Smoke began to enter under the front door. Jennifer whimpered, "Shit!"

Kedar came back in with several beer bottles. Angel sarcastically observed, "Yeah K, good time to take up drinking."

Kedar dismissed the comment as he took a pistol offered by Denny, "It's all I could come up with from the items in the kitchen. They'll blow when ignited. It won't be big, but it'll stop any creature close to it."

They had fallen back by everyone else to get away from the smoke, which was making its way through the wet towel Becca had run over to her mother. Sarah and her family huddled tight. Medhir had his arms around Niu and Chēlún, who were gripping one another and whimpering in their own language.

Trey thought for a moment and took several short, deep breaths, "That's it then. I'm the distraction!"

"Bullshit Trey, I'll go. You can get them out of here." Denny objected.

Jennifer muttered, "I'll go."

"You ain't fast enough anymore old man." Trey wasn't kidding.

Jennifer said it a little louder this time, "I'll go."

"Neither are you brother. I'm faster than everyone here, now get your asses to the van." Angel went to reach for the bottles.

"I'LL GO!" Jennifer shouted at them all.

"Don't be ridiculous! Get Becca and get ready for the van!" Trey barked back at her.

She put a hand on his face, "We don't have time for this, so listen to me and listen to me carefully. The reason I took Becca on those trips..."

"Mom, don't!" Becca came over to hug her mother.

Jennifer kept talking with her other arm around her daughter, "The reason I'm always here is because I'm *dying*." She could see the immediate heartbreak in Trey's eyes, "Breast cancer. We thought it was in full remission, then we found out it spread. My lymph nodes and now into my lungs. It's inoperable." The tears were forming in her eyes as she talked, "Doctors gave me less than a year. All this time I've been thinking about Gaelan, knowing he wouldn't let anything happen to my baby." She looked down at Becca and choked back a sob, "But I know that I've found the person that will look after my little angel until the end of time." She caressed Trey's cheek while tears streamed down her face. "You take care of my baby Trey Marshall! You promise me, the way Gaelan does. You promise me that you'll take care of my little Rebecca forever!" Becca was crying hysterically into her mom's side while she listened.

Trey's eyes welled up, along with most everyone around them. He nodded adamantly.

"Say it!" She wept.

"I promise. I promise you that I will watch Becca, protect her with my life from now until the end of time, and never, *never,* let anything happen to her. I *promise!*"

She hugged him tight, then kissed his cheek gently, then dropped down to her knees and sobbed with her daughter.

Seth Rosen turned and frantically pressed the button to the elevator doors, which had closed behind him. He spun to see the nearest vampire calmly stroll toward him, seven more closing in all around. Rosen pressed his back up against the elevator doors, as if pressing himself flat against the wall could protect him. The vampire was halfway across the thoroughfare between the parking spaces and the elevator when the headlights hit him. He turned and hissed, distending his mouth and baring his full array of razor-sharp fangs. The lights turned brighter and his skin started to sizzle. He turned away screeching.

Inside the car, Natalia looked at Rabbi Feinstein, who had just pushed a large purple button on his dash marked 'UV'.

"Better than your standard high-beams, huh?"

"DRIVE!" She bellowed at him and he responded by slamming on the gas and driving full on into the creature, sending him flying several yards back.

Rabbi Feinstein slammed on the brakes, pulled his parking brake and turned the wheel hard, spinning the UV beams toward the rest of the creatures, who dove behind pillars and parked cars. He saw the bodies lying on the ground, "My God!"

Natalia jumped out with a shotgun adorned with a UV light, pointed it at the first creature and put several rounds into it. She didn't know if she hit its heart and head, nor did she have time to care. She turned to Seth Rosen, "GET IN!" He stood there, frozen with fear and shock, "NOW GODDAMMIT!" She ran to him, grabbed him by the shirt and swung him toward the car. Rosen felt his legs work without truly having command over his own senses, then dove into the backseat of the sedan. Natalia jumped into the passenger seat and yelled at the Rabbi, "DRIVE!"

"WHY ARE YOU ALWAYS YELLING?" He bellowed back at her and spun the tires, turning the wheel hard back in the direction they came from. Natalia rolled down the window and turned to see all the creatures scrambling after them, unnaturally fast. Just before the quickest was almost to the rear bumper, she ignited a UV lantern and dropped it out the window. The creature stumbled over it and screeched in pain as its skin burned. The others stayed beyond the edge of the blinding light as they sped off.

Natalia turned to Rosen, huddled in a ball on the backseat, mumbling repeatedly, "They're not crazy. They're not crazy."

"*Now* you wanna believe us?" Feinstein looked through the rearview mirror.

Natalia bit back at the Rabbi. "How were you when you first found out?"

"Better than Mr.-doesn't-want-to-listen in the backseat here!"

Natalia shook her head, "Are we going to get Gaelan?"

"First we gotta switch vehicles. They'll be looking for this one. Then yes!"

Angel and Kedar had brought Father Denny boxes of nails, screws, staples and pushpins. Father Denny prayed over the items and blessed them, and Kedar taped the projectiles to the bottle-bombs. Angel went over to Sarah and her family. "BJ, when we go to the van, there won't be much time. Get that wheelchair in the back and jump in." BJ nodded frantically. "Bob, you're a big dude. You get to carry Chēlún. Her life is in your hands, so don't let her down." Bob gave a single serious nod of consent. "Sarah, you and Linda get Niu in right behind Bob. She is everything we have right now. You can't let anything happen to her or this is all for nothing. Do you understand?" They too nodded. None of them spoke as they held hands, Linda crying. Angel looked to Medhir, "Meddi, you stay behind Bob and BJ and don't leave Niu's side!" Medhir silently nodded.

Father Denny talked to Kedar and Sophie, "Will it work?"

"It will. I promise." Kedar knew his explosive expertise wouldn't fail them.

"Okay, then Sophie sweetheart, you have to clear the way so the van can get through. Can you do it?"

Sophie looked to the side and saw Trey standing over Jenifer and Becca as they sobbed on one another's shoulders, then turned back to Father Denny with a determined look, "I can do it."

Father Denny gave her a reassuring smile, and then joined Trey by Jennifer's side.

"Please mommy! *Please* don't do this." Becca could barely breathe.

Jennifer was trying to calm herself while talking to her daughter, "Sweetheart, this is my chance to let my death mean something. I'm going to leave you soon anyway, and now I know you're going to be taken care of. I can help save those people over there. I may even help save the world. The only way mommy could live forever is to become one of those monsters outside, and that's not what you want, is it sweetie?" Jennifer tried wiping Becca's eyes. Becca shook her head, "Me either. Tonight, I'm going to help save the *world!* And goddammit Rebecca Marie Guerin, you are going to live to tell everyone how your mom did so, do you understand me?" Rebecca nodded emphatically and buried her head in her mother's shoulder.

Jennifer looked up at Trey, "She's your daughter now Trey Marshall. Don't you dare let me down!" She sniffed and wiped her eyes.

"No ma'am!" Trey's voice was raspy, broken, eyes watered over.

Jennifer saw Father Denny and Kedar, the latter holding the explosives. She gave Becca a kiss and hug and made Trey take her child from her, still screaming hysterically. She called out as Trey took her away, "I LOVE YOU BECCA. MOMMY WILL ALWAYS LOVE HER LITTLE ANGEL AND I'LL ALWAYS BE WATCHING OVER YOU! I LOVE YOU BABY GIRL!" She could barely catch her breath as Kedar strapped the explosives to her and explained the pull-cord.

Father Denny blessed her with her last rites, made the sign of the cross on her forehead and then kissed it. "God be with you Jennifer."

"No! You damn well better make sure He's with my baby!" She was now determined and angry.

Father Denny nodded, "Don't go until I signal you."

Jennifer turned, crouched down and scurried to the window on the side of the house opposite the garage. Angel got everyone to the door entering the garage. When he pulled the wet towel from under the door, thick smoke started to billow in instantly. Everyone put wet rags over their mouths and he counted, "One—Two—Three!" He opened the door to a veritable wall of smoke. The wall on the far side of the garage and the garage door were warping from the heat of the flames outside and on the roof. Kedar and Sophie rushed to the driver and passenger seats, while Sarah, Linda, Bob and BJ did as they were assigned and got Niu and Chēlún into the van. Trey buried Becca's face into his shoulder, her sobs still filling the air, and ran in. Medhir followed close behind.

Angel opened the garage door and paused it after several inches, bellowing a very audible "GET READY!" Kedar had already started the van and revved the engine loudly.

Even through the commotion, they could hear the heavy scrambling footsteps on the roof. Slashes tore into the garage door. Something screeched, "HERE!" from outside. The vampires were ready for their escape.

As soon as they heard the footsteps on the roof, Father Denny kissed his hand and held it out to Jennifer, giving her the signal and saying farewell. Without hesitation, Jennifer opened the window and clambered out. She dropped several feet and took off running, her only thought being the safety of her daughter. She had a large piece of property and her nearest neighbor was over a quarter mile away. She sprinted as hard as she could, and finally looked back to see the horror behind her. Her house was on fire. She could see one lifeless body toward the front of her property and several figures scurrying around, at least two dashing between the flames on the roof. She tripped and fell as she looked. She let out a painful bellow and the vampires turned their attention to her direction. She turned forward and yelled to the phantom people who weren't there, "GO! HURRY!" She scrambled to her feet and began limping forward, once again waving frantically toward people in front of her that didn't exist, "RUN!"

Behind Jennifer, the vampires hissed, one shouting, "IT'S A TRICK! THIS WAY!" One by one they followed, but four remained behind by the garage. Eight creatures in all dashed toward Jennifer. The first ran past her and slashed her calf. She crumpled and screamed in pain. Several vampires ran past while three descended on her. She curled up on the ground, shielding her face and stomach. The other vampires circled back unable to see anyone else. They surrounded her, hissing, "Where are they?"

Jennifer mumbled something inaudible in response. The creature had no sooner rolled her over, when Jennifer relaxed her body, revealing the improvised explosive devices on her chest. Tears ran down her face as she screamed aloud, "BECCA!" pulling the cord. Shrapnel soaked in holy water and blessed by Father Denny tore through the vampires as they were propelled several yards away by the blast.

Inside the garage, the entire group huddled in the van and choked on smoke. The sound of the distant explosion was unmistakable.

"MOMMY!" Becca screamed as Kedar floored the accelerator. The van smashed through the garage door, sending shards of fiberglass and metal in all directions. The occupants gagged and gulped at the fresh air that finally replaced the strangling smoke inside the vehicle. The four remaining vampires descended, one on top, one on either side, and one on the back of the vehicle. Sarah's family and the orphan girls screamed as Father Denny shone the UV light into the face of the creature on his side, watching its skin sizzle as it smashed through the window. Angel went to shoot but spun toward the back of the van just as one of the rear doors was wrenched from its hinges.

On the other side of the vehicle, a creature smashed through the window and grabbed Becca with one hand, holding the vehicle with its other. Trey held Becca tight with both arms, worrying that trying to take a shot would allow the vampire to pull Becca from him. Medhir grabbed a capsule of holy water from his pocket and burst it over the vampire's hand. Its flesh sizzled and it released Becca with a howl. With a surge of anger and adrenaline, Trey pounced forward with a pistol and punched the weapon directly into the creature's mouth, blowing the top of its head off. It fell to the ground rolling, but with its heart intact.

The vampire on Father Denny's side succumbed to the UV rays, and Angel hit his mark on the creature to the rear. As they raced down the driveway, they could see the three vehicles blocking their path. The creature on the roof began slashing through the metal when Trey, Angel and Father Denny all shot upwards simultaneously. They felt the creature roll along the roof until a large mass tumbled off over the back of the car. It hit the ground hard, but quickly pushed itself to its feet.

Becca screamed again, "MOMMY!" and they all turned to see several of the figures that had gone after Jennifer were already up and closing on the vehicle fast. Sophie raised her hands and her eyes turned black. The ground beneath the vehicle blockade seemed to liquefy and rumble, but the vehicles just rolled too and fro several feet. Kedar kept accelerating toward them as Father Denny calmly said, "Sophie, you can do it!"

Sophie's skin became pale and her veins were now very visible. Her nose began to bleed as she screamed in pain. The ground beneath the vehicles shot up like pillars, sending the automobiles flipping through the air like leaves blowing in the wind. Father Denny, Trey and Angel focused their fire on the group of vampires closing from the side and Bob grabbed the UV and shone it in their direction. Kedar hit the main road and sped off while the monstrous figures behind grew more distant. He looked to the side and could see that Sophie lost consciousness. He grabbed her hand and felt a pulse, then continued to grip her hand as they raced toward the hope of safety. Becca collapsed, sobbing into Trey's arms. He held her tight, kissing her head and rocking her.

Two of the vampires had seized Carly and pulled her to her feet. Three tried to grab Gaelan, who swung his arms and swatted them back several yards. He turned to advance as Genevieve held Gaius. She swung her arm up and earth broke through the floor to create a barrier between them. Gaelan bellowed in anger and punched the obstruction. It lost its form and fell into a pile of dirt as Genevieve screamed in pain and fell backwards. Instead of falling on her, Gaius spun and caught her, pulling her upright. She and the rest of the vampires froze and Gaelan stopped his advance. Carly spoke again, "You've seen how they view us Gaelan. They'd never let a human have this much power! Never!"

Gaelan watched as Gaius made sure Genevieve was alright and turned with a smile toward him, and then to Carly, "Clever girl." He looked down at the holes in his suit and flexed. Three bullets fell into his hand. He held them straight out toward Carly and dropped them one by one on the floor, "That suit was Italian. Handmade in Florence in 1876. One of my favorites, and I've kept it pristine for so, so long." His voice was eerily calm.

Genevieve muttered, "Gaius?" He turned and caressed her cheek, then kissed her gently on the lips and smiled. He made sure she could stand, then spun and walked over to the insolent vampire that had lost his grip on Carly, "Was the human girl too much for you to hold…*boy*?"

"I am over seven-hundred years guuhh..." The creature's sentence abruptly stopped with a gurgle as Gaius punched his hand directly into the vampire's chest. He ripped out the heart, then slashed across the vampire's throat, opening up a gaping wound. Gaius dropped the heart, grabbed the top and bottom of the injury on the creature's throat and tore its head clean off. Gaius dropped both parts of the carcass and wiped his hands as if he just got a bit of oil or dirt on them, "I apologize for the unpleasantness, but I abhor such discourtesy." He snatched Carly by the back of her neck and the other vampires backed away in fear and confusion.

"Get your hands off of her!" Gaelan stood his ground, knowing he could not cover the distance in time.

"Ah ah ah." Gaius held a now clawed finger without looking at him, "Remember what I said about such impoliteness."

"I...I saw you! I watched you walk in the daylight. In Romania. In the bank."

Gaius turned and smiled impishly, "My dear young Gaelan, I perfectly detest the sunlight for reasons I'll not explain now, but suffice it to say that while most vampires cannot suffer it without dire consequences, the very first—the *original vampire*—can." He rolled his free arm and dropped his head as if introducing himself and taking a bow, "Now, Gaelan Kelly, you have my complete and utter attention. And thanks to this brave and cunning young lass, I am known to the world once more." Gaius turned to Carly and gave a sympathetic half-smile, "Such a pity."

Gaelan's heart raced as he looked from Gaius to Carly. She was resigned to her fate. She calmy mouthed the word, *RUN!* Gaelan snarled to Gaius, "I swear to you, I don't care how powerful you are, if you fucking touch her, I will tear off your goddammed head and shit down your neck! You will never see your FUCKING ETERNAL DARKNESS COME TO PASS!"

The mention of the latter caught Gaius' attention. He laughed condescendingly, "Perhaps you wanted to wait until my dying breath to threaten that." His face changed instantly, his eyes a vile black with a glowing red sliver, his facial structure more jagged and his fangs longer than the other vampires. His teeth were in Carly's neck before she had time to gasp.

"NOOOOOOOOOOOO!" Gaius fangs tore through her neck muscles and carotid artery. Gaelan charged and barreled through the other vampires into Gaius, who allowed himself to be knocked backwards. Gaelan caught Carly and put his hand over the gaping hole in her neck, trying to stem the overwhelming flow of blood. He was just in time to lock eyes with her, the fear and uncertainty in them made his stomach turn and his limbs feel like jelly. Within seconds, there was no life in her eyes and her tensed body fell limp. "Carly? Sweetie, please! CARLY!" Gaelan knew she was gone but refused to believe it. He turned to see he was surrounded but all of the creatures held their ground. He then looked to Gaius, who was holding a hand up to restrain them all.

"I haven't been hit like that in a very, very long time. It's refreshing actually. You have power Gaelan. *Such power.* And such a pity."

Gaelan gently lowered Carly to the ground, closed her eyelids, kissed his hand and touched her cheek. His friend—his first love—was gone. He stood and clenched his fists, then turned toward Gaius without saying a word while his eyes changed, fangs growing in his mouth.

"That's it Gaelan, show me what you have." Gaius readied himself this time. Gaelan charged furiously at Gaius and hit him head on. Gaius protected himself by catching and holding back Gaelan's claws at the wrists, raising both their arms up to block Gaelan's advancing jaws. Gaelan managed to slam Gaius into the wall again and again, unable to free his hands, until he let the change take him. In seconds, he was the werewolf. Gaius' grip on him was broken and he slashed the vampire once across the chest, but Gaius was able to block the second assault across his forearms. Gaelan grabbed him and flipped him up and over his head, slamming him to the floor. He lunged down with his jaws wide open and that's when Gaius caught him by the throat.

Gaius was breathing heavy, "Good. Very good." His muscles also swelled, unlike any of the other vampires Gaelan had fought. The suit he wore tore open and his skin turned scaly and grey. His face was harder and his brow and cheeks formed small horns. His voice was deep and wicked, "But now it's my turn." He stood and was every bit as large as Gaelan. He slashed three times, tearing Gaelan's midsection and chest before Gaelan absorbed the third slash on his forearms. Gaius struck his massive foot forward and sent Gaelan flying back, then lunged forward to continue his assault.

They stood trading blocks and slashes until Gaelan swung up and sliced Gaius from his torso to his neck, doing more damage to his hardened skin than the vampire expected. Gaius, now enraged, grabbed Gaelan and spun, throwing him over the bar and through the back wall, into the kitchen area. Gaelan crashed hard, tearing the range top from the wall as he came down. Even as he stood, Gaius was already there, slashing him, striking him and lifting him up and throwing him to the ground. Gaius turned and held out his hand. One of the female vampires timidly rushed to him and handed him a knife. Gaelan tried to stand and Gaius buried the silver blade though his ribcage and into his heart, dropping him to the ground.

Gaelan was bloodied, exhausted and beaten. A silver blade protruded from his heart and he could barely breath. His wolf mind was working on pure instinct. Gaius went to lift him again, but this time Gaelan struck out with his claw and stabbed Gaius in his knee, raking downward along his shin and ripping back toward his calf. While Gaius roared in pain, Gaelan spun and swept the legs out from beneath him. With both of them on the ground, Gaelan kicked forward and into the reeling monster, putting space between them. Gaius slid back and hit the far wall of the kitchen hard while Gaelan slid and slammed back into space that the range top once occupied.

Gaelan's enormous chest was heaving but it was useless. The blade in his heart felt like a hot iron and the tears in his hide were excruciating. He could barely move as he watched Gaius stand and limp toward him, now joined by the other vampires. Genevieve came to the entryway leading to the kitchen.

Gaius spoke in a deep growl, "You fought well Gaelan—honorably. That is not a trait found often. Unfortunately, the *sheep in wolf's clothing* cannot be allowed to live." He turned and looked at the other vampires, who cowered under his gaze, "Fear not my children. Tonight we ensure our destiny." He turned back to Gaelan and said aloud coldly, "Tear him apart."

Gaelan's wolf mind knew he couldn't win. Death was imminent. He had been listening to the words the creature in front of him spoke, not fully comprehending what was happening, but smelling the gas that was filling the room around them. The gas line leading to the range top stove had been severed in the fight and sat just over Gaelan's shoulder, continuing to stream gas into the room. His wolf mind and his human mind were communicating—melding—*LIGHT IT*! Gaelan's snout turned to the line and sniffed hard. He turned back toward the vampires with a growl, raising his claw and sliding it across a piece of metal where the broken stove once stood.

"OUT!" Gaius turned and ran straight at Genevieve, grabbing her in his arms and diving through a window as the building around them erupted. The explosion engulfed several of the vampires in flames, with some that survived dragging themselves out to the pavement. Gaius, naked in his human form, helped Genevieve to her feet.

"You saved me!" She began to take a knee, "My lord."

He stopped her, his voice once again pleasant and unassuming, "No m'lady. You do not bow to me. You stand *with* me."

"*With you,* my lord?"

"Of course. Why rule the world if you have no one to stand and rule by your side?" She smiled and kissed him deeply, until he broke her embrace, "And please, go back to calling me *your dear Gaius* again. It's so much more intimate."

One of the better faring vampires timidly interrupted, "My lord…and lady. We have to go."

Gaius offered Genevieve his arm and led her to the lead car.

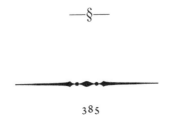

Rabbi Feinstein was driving along the town's main thoroughfare when they saw the explosion about a mile away. The sound and shock wave hit a moment later.

"What the hell?"

"Gaelan!" The concern in Natalia's voice was unnerving.

The smoldering remnants of *Murphy's Law* came into view a minute later. A naked man kissed a beautiful woman, then led her to the first of three shining cars that drove away. There was no other sign of life.

Rabbi Feinstein grabbed Natalia's arm, "We have to go. If he's alive, he'll find us."

She fell back into the seat, a feeling of emptiness overtaking her and tears began to stream from her eyes, "Gaelan."

CHAPTER 19
SHATTERED

Angel let the hand holding his phone drop to his side. He closed his eyes and hung his head against the blaring headlines: *Ailing Mother Linked to Domestic Terrorism... Mother and one police officer dead, daughter missing.* Natalia had just told him about the news from New York: *Terror at the Workplace... four investment bankers murdered and dismembered in parking lot, fifth missing and wanted for questioning.*

Seth Rosen was their only suspect. And another: *Gas Explosion Kills Seven at Long Island Pub... Seven bodies were found badly burned at Long Island's Murphy's Law Pub and Grill; Police searching for owner in questions relating to insurance fraud.* How many 'accidents' like these had been staged throughout the years?

They had found new vehicles and driven the van into a canal.

"Kedar and Sophie, you two are staying with Niu and Medhir." Father Denny ordered. "You're their best chance of survival. Zhang is flying over to meet you with the adoption cover story. He'll have fake papers." He turned to Trey, "You..."

"I'm taking Becca!"

Denny didn't even try to argue, "Yeah, I know. They're looking for two Chinese girls and one in a wheelchair, so you need to take Chēlún. She won't be happy splitting from Niu, but having Becca there will soften the blow." Trey nodded apathetically and rubbed Becca's back.

Denny looked at Sarah, "You have to split up. They'll be looking for your family."

"We're not splitting up!" Bob stepped forward.

Linda spoke up, "Dad, he's right. We need to split up to get out of here."

BJ looked at his dad, trying to sound confident to mask his fear, "I'll stay with Mr. Marshall and help out with Becca and Chēlún."

Linda spoke next, her voice tired and scared, "I'll go with Mr. Silva."

Father Denny nodded and looked at Sarah and Bob, "Then we'll make our way to meet Gaelan and the others, and split from there."

"Gaelan's not coming." Angel's voice trembled. Everyone stared at him as he continued to look at the ground, "That was Natalia. They got to Rosen in time, but by the time they got to *Murphy's Law*, it was gone."

Father Denny retorted, "What do you mean, *gone?*"

"The press is reporting it as a gas explosion, or maybe arson. They saw vampires leave but no sign of Gaelan. He's not picking up his phone. The fire department removed at least seven bodies."

Father Denny's heart sank, but he had no time to show it. He looked around, "Fine, then Sarah, Bob and I wait for Natalia and Saul. We split from there. We all know where to get passports and tickets. You check in with me every twelve hours, no exceptions. Set a fucking alarm if you have to! We need to get Niu out of here and figure out what this FUCKING PROPHECY IS!" Denny clenched his fists.

Angel came forward, "We got it. Niu is the priority. Once you have your passports, we'll coordinate where we'll meet. Don't forget to check in. Got it?" Silent, teary-eyed nods were the only answer he received.

"Good. Let's get the fuck out of here."

—§—

Gaius entered the chamber of the elders once more.

"Where is Gaelan Kelly?" The male elder had no sooner finished the question when he turned to Genevieve, "And what is *she* doing in here?"

"*She* is here at my behest." Gaius replied haughtily. "As for Gaelan Kelly, I won't say he's dead for sure without a body, but he had a silver dagger through the heart and he was beaten handily."

"And yet, there is no body Gaius." Another elder interjected, "Perhaps your affinity for a werewolf has clouded your judgment yet again."

"He ignited the building around us. If he survived, then I trust his death will be slow and excruciating. And if he does survive, I will handle it."

"Like you handled it this time?" One of the female elders queried, "And what of the prophet?"

"It seems that she and the group she was with slipped through our grasp."

"Your grasp!"

"I believe I was taking care of Gaelan Kelly when your chosen elite let mere mortals slip through their fingertips."

"Or *failing* to take care of him, from your own account!" Another female elders hissed.

"Perhaps one of you would prefer to go in my stead."

"*My lords?*" The original elder male spoke directly to Gaius.

"Pardon?" Gaius asked ever so politely.

"To go in my stead, *my lords*. Or have you forgotten your place?"

Gaius smiled and stepped forward, remembering Lucos' words about choosing a life of servitude, "My apologies." He continued to saunter toward them, "It seems that I *have forgotten* my place, Alek." He spoke the elder's name, "I have forgotten my place as the original. As *your* creator. The one who turned each and every one of *you*." He leered at each of them individually, "I've forgotten my place as the one true ruler of our kind."

Alek stood, "You forsook that claim after the peace with the wolves! After you failed to eradicate their kind! When we realized you were no longer fit to lead!"

Gaius continued to stroll toward them, "I forsook nothing Alek. My leadership was usurped."

"Usurped? You were weak of will and resolve. We only called upon you to deal with the sheep in wolf's clothing because you'RE INACTION ALLOWED HIM TO EXIST!" Alek stood defiantly.

"Is this how you all feel?" Gaius locked eyes with each of them as he spoke their names, "Aldred? Aurelia? Heimirich? Quintus? Dougal? Cassia? Marco? Emmerich? Moira?" Each one avoided his gaze or looked to the others, but none echoed Alek's sentiment. They knew something was off.

Alek continued, "You went into exile after the peace! A PEACE THAT NEVER SHOULD HAVE EXISTED! YOU SHOULD HAVE ALLOWED THE WAR TO CONTINUE! YOU SHOULD HAVE ERADICATED THEIR KIND!"

Gaius stopped and turned back to Genevieve, "Forgive me m'lady, I apologize." She smiled and tipped her head as he spun and flew threw the air, covering the remaining ground between he and Alek. He landed just in front of Alek, his tone soft, like a father taking blame for his child's wrongdoings, "Alek. Dear Alek. Your lust for power was what drew me to you—and now it is your undoing."

Alek swung his claw, but Gaius caught it midair and backhanded him to the ground. Two of the other elders leaned forward as if to help Alek, "STAY WHERE YOU ARE!" Gaius barked and turned back to Alek, "I made you Alek. And now I have to rectify that mistake." Alek bared his fangs, his face fully transformed, and lunged for Gaius. Gaius transformed into his true form for the second time in as many days, caught Alek by the throat and in one swift motion, tore into his neck. He brought his knee into Alek's gut then slammed him to the ground. The body of the elder was strong, but Gaius was stronger. He slashed and tore at Alek's spine until the bone was exposed, then thrust his claws deep between it and the ribs. He pushed further in and ripped out Alek's heart and discarded it. He then went back to Alek's throat and tore into it with his massive jaw until Alek's head was severed.

Gaius, massive, horned and scaled, stood over Alek's carcass, blood dripping from his claws and mouth. He returned to his human-looking form, naked once more after tearing though his clothing, "Hmmm. So many centuries have passed since I've taken that form." He looked at the other elders in turn, "And two of my favorite suits ruined on top of it." He turned to Genevieve and extended a hand, "M'lady."

Genevieve walked through the expansive chamber, her eyes glowing with pride and affection for Gaius. She made her way to him and took his hand, still full of blood, and smiled warmly. Gaius asked, "Which of these seats do you wish m'lady?"

"The one closest to you of course my lord." She smiled coyly, "I'm sorry, *my dear Gaius.*" He pulled her close and kissed her passionately. She could still taste the blood of an elder vampire on his lips and in his mouth. She pressed herself against his naked body and whispered, "Always closest to you my dear Gaius."

He smiled and whispered, "Always." He looked around at the other elders, "Are there any objections to your queen taking her seat at my side?" The elders looked at each other with uncertainty, until Moira, the first female elder to question Gaius dropped to a knee, "My seat is hers my lord!" Gaius looked around and one by one, the elders dropped to their knees echoing her sentiment, "My lord…my lord…my lord…" Gaius looked around at the vampires at his feet. "Arise my children! Your father has been away too long! The Eternal Darkness is within our grasp and soon you will walk the earth without fear of sunlight, bathing in the blood of humanity. Our time is now. Arise!"

The vampires rose and chanted his name, "GAIUS! GAIUS! GAIUS!" Soon the elders joined them. He raised his hand and they fell silent, "Go and send word to Lucos and his wolves. Tell him I request a council at his choosing and venue. Now leave us. Your queen and I," He looked into Genevieve's eyes lustfully, "have to discuss matters at hand." The vampires hurried from the chamber as Gaius tore off Genevieve's clothes in the middle of the elder's chamber.

—§—

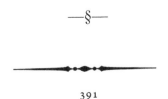

Saul, Natalia and Seth Rosen arrived in Western Pennsylvania to meet Denny, Sarah and Bob. Natalia buried her head in Father Denny's shoulder, concealing her tears.

Father Denny whispered in her ears, "It's not over. I know, in my heart, he's not gone!" She looked up at him and sniffed, nodding at his sentiment. She took Gaelan's katana off of her back and handed it to him. He shook his head, "No, you're gonna give that to him." A tear formed in his eye, "You are gonna give it to him when he comes back to us."

Natalia tearfully looked down at the katana and whispered, "Come back to me Gaelan. Come back to me."

Kedar drove down a crowded suburban highway in broad daylight. Sophie refused to sleep but they didn't talk. They drove the most populous routes to meet Zhang in San Francisco. They had little to say with Niu sleeping in the backseat. The events of the previous night had taken their toll on everyone, but Niu had no one to translate for her until they met Zhang.

Niu dreamt. People were dying, slaughtered by fellow men. They were starving. They were dying of illness and disease. Some were just dying for no reason. She saw a body being stabbed in the side. She watched as the face of a man she knew met her eye and then threw himself into a hole. She saw the sun turn dark and monsters rise to attack urban areas. She saw the world encased in darkness. She woke up with a start and tears in her eyes. The words of the prophecy were in her head but Kedar and Sophie couldn't understand her. She could hear them in her thoughts, over and over. In her mind, part of it echoed continuously, *beware the sheep in wolf's clothing. For he and the Light piercer are the keys to the dark gates.* The face of the man throwing himself into the hole—the face of the man opening the gates of Hell—was Gaelan Kelly.

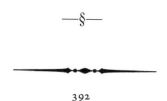

Miles from *Murphy's Law*, in a sewer drain, Gaelan's skin sloughed in horrid chunks from where it was charred. He was crumpled. Broken. Torn. Yet, on the cold and the wet ground, Gaelan Kelly let out a gasp, and awoke!

ACKNOWLEDGMENTS

I initially completed all three books of the Gaelan Kelly trilogy at the same time. I self-published Gaelan's War in December of 2017, and went through an steep learning curve on just how the whole process works. I have taken the past two-plus years to refine my second and third books so that readers could enjoy the entirety of the story all at once. With that being said, I could not have done it without the support of some incredible people.

First and foremost, my mother Ellen, an avid reader who proofread books two and three several times for her window-licking son. To all my beta readers: my sisters, Chrisy and Meg. My godson James Anthony and niece Shannon. My friend and fellow Strong-Islander, Christina, who helped me catch a bunch of mistakes. To Romey and Kristine, for all the love and support in this undertaking. To my reserve/part time squadron-mates who, truthfully, I didn't think could read, much less walk and chew bubblegum at the same time. Nonetheless, Mikey the J, Boudreaux, Spit, Piper, Boss, Mouth, Gator, Grail, Rabbi, Tuck, Zach and KenDoll all read my crazy story and gave me great feedback. My old F/A-18 family, Farva, and Monkey and Jen (who no longer want to camp in the Shenandoah), and Juice and Amy, all kept on me to get books two and three out there. Of course, my Basic Officers Course lifelong friends, Joe, Gary and Captain Dan, who all kept wanting to know what happens to Gaelan.

My incredible kids, Keegan and Fiona, who actually asked me to read the drafts (edited for content) and gave me wonderful insight into how I conveyed a lot of the emotion and action. I love you guys. And of course, my beautiful wife Katie, who edited my overly-verbose drafts and made sure the book sounded like it was written by an adult – I couldn't have done it without you sweetie!

I'd also like to give a shout out to all those readers I haven't met, but who read and reviewed my first book. The fact that you liked it, and your kind words, inspired me to re-write and refine books two and three and get them out there. I apologize for the wait, but I hope you like the full story arc.

Finally, I once again applaud my awesome interior layout designer Phillip Gessert, and incredibly talented cover artist Stewart Williams, for their impeccable craftsmanship. Both can be reached at Reedsy.com.